Bloodletting & Germs

A Doctor in Nineteenth Century Rural New York

THOMAS C. ROSENTHAL, M.D.

Professor Emeritus, Family Medicine and Geriatrics
Jacobs School of Medicine and Biomedical Science
University at Buffalo

Bloodletting and Germs:
A Doctor in Nineteenth Century Rural New York
© 2020 by Thomas C. Rosenthal M.D.

All rights reserved. This book or any portion thereof may not be reproduced or used in any manner whatsoever without the express written permission of the publisher except for the use of brief quotations in a book review.

ISBN (Print): 978-1-09831-538-2
ISBN (eBook): 978-1-09831-539-9

A historical novel set at medicine's enlightenment, giving voice to the personal and professional tribulations of a country doctor adjusting to science, pandemics and social transformation.

Key Words

Pandemic, Aurora, Apothecary, Underground Railroad, Licensing, Melancholia, Contagion

Dedicated to my wife and anchor, Georgia.

Contents

Preface 1
Definitions 3
The Allen Family 6

Part One: Seasoning

1. Discovering Aurora, 1834 9
2. Promoting the Villages of Aurora, 1834 19
3. A Dinner Party, 1834 27
4. Becoming a Graduate Doctor, 1832-1833 30
5. Closing the Deal, 1834 35
6. A Business Launch, 1834 40
7. Mixing Physic and Pharmacy, 1834 45
8. Open for Business, 1834 51
9. Getting Organized, 1834 54
10. An Evening with the Underground, 1834 61

Part Two: Rational Medicine

11. Licensing and Medical Societies, 1834 69
12. A Case of Melancholia, 1834 75
13. The Physic Art, 1834 84
14. Drugs, 1834 90
15. Copaiba Oil, 1834 99
16. Walking and Listening, 1834 108
17. Lectures, Sectarians and Quacks, 1834 114
18. Snake Oil, 1834 123
19. Courtship and the Mansion of Happiness, 1834 128
20. Making a Home, 1835 136
21. Consequences of Impulse, 1835 141

22. Comments on Midwifery 144

23. A Delivery to the Family of Allen, 1835 156

24. Doctor, Employer or Father, 1835 161

25. Complexities, 1835 165

26. Welcoming My Brother, 1836-37 172

27. Allen Family Grows, 1836 176

Part Three: Science

28. Life, Smallpox, Typhoid and Miasma, 1836-1850 183

29. Medicine and Science Grapple, 1836-1850 192

30. Measles and Scarlatina, 1836-1850 197

31. Family Life, 1845-1854 202

32. The Spirits Rap, 1850s 207

33. The Fugitive Slave Act, 1850-1860 214

34. Cholera, 1850s 218

35. Breakthroughs, Cancer and an Ovarian Cyst, 1851-1860 229

36. The War, 1860-1870 239

37. Post War Health in the Home and School, 1866-1876 251

38. Tonsillitis, Diphtheria and Emerging Contagions, 1870-1876 262

39. What Meaning Has Death, 1876 270

40. Comforting the Mind, 1850 to 1884 280

41. Germs, 1878 295

Part Four: Apoplexy

42. Apoplexy at the Ebb of Life, 1884-1885 311

Postscript 320

Photos and Illustrations 324

Selected Sources 328

Acknowledgements 335

Preface

I practiced Family Medicine and Geriatrics in western New York State for forty years. As I retired my wife and I visited the one room East Aurora historical museum where the town historian, Robert Goller, displayed artifacts once belonging to Dr. Jabez Allen. Included, without explanation, was a nearly two-hundred-year-old hand written copy of Dr. Allen's medical diploma alongside the original. Five years of painstaking research has revealed the impact that simple copy had on a doctor, and a village.

Dr. Allen's story is much like that of many physicians, who in the nineteenth century tried to reason with the contradictions between emerging science and the bloodletting and the purging of bowels they had been taught. Dr. Allen practiced in the village now known as East Aurora from 1834 to 1884 and that hand copied diploma nearly cost him his license, but never stymied his devotion to his adopted community. For fifty years, Dr. Allen raised a family, befriended some of the most famous medical men of the nineteenth century and a U.S. President. He struggled to understand germs, and according to his obituary, "Dr. Allen was highly respected by his medical brethren in both city and country" while practicing according to his motto: "No cure, No pay."

This is not a word for word account of Dr. Allen's medical practice. The text captures the challenges facing pioneering doctors practicing in communities buffeted by quacks, epidemics, and Civil War. The nineteenth century was an exciting time to practice medical science, but discoveries arrived fragment by fragment, journal article by journal article, and misconception by genuine breakthrough. The reader will become familiar with the medical treatments and theories referenced in nineteenth century medical sources as Galen's Four Humors were relegated to history and experiments replaced rationalizations. Most importantly, the concept of germs emerged.

I have anchored the story on the known events of Dr. Allen's life drawn from a family bible, property deeds, medical society minutes, diaries of contemporaries, newspapers, and the oral history passed down to a great-great-granddaughter. The patients, events and motives I have attributed to Dr. Allen are based on over four hundred nineteenth century textbooks and journal articles. Actual events and probable reactions are merged into a first-person memoir as might have been told to his niece, an aspiring writer, and his nephew, a Cornell professor who authored several regional history books.

The characters Abiatha, Dr. Phineas J. McCarthy, Margaret Fairling, Allie Johnson, Civia Morgan and her husband Elmas have been created from several of Allen's contemporaries. Patient names have been altered. All others are real people serving in roles consistent with what is known about their lives. Narratives are modernized and abridged in the interest of clarity, but preserve the biases and prejudices of the extant nineteenth century literature referenced in the bibliography.

Physicians of all eras are haunted by episodes in which a preconceived opinion or an overwhelming desire to be useful compromised their intent. Health professionals of the twenty-first century will be surprised by the relevance of many nineteenth century concepts, even as they are struck by the scientific naivety. Readers will ponder, what of today's beliefs will seem naive to tomorrow's practitioners as they experience the challenges of caring for neighbors, making a living and doing the best you can do when what is possible is often not enough.

The Author
www.thomasrosenthalmd.com

Definitions

Animalcule: Obsolete general term for microscopic organisms.

Antiphlogistic: Any substance or treatment that reduces swelling or inflammation.

Apoplexy: A sudden fit of paralysis and dizziness that causes an unconscious state.

Apothecary: One who dispenses and compounds of drugs.

Bacterium: A single celled spherical, spiral, or rod shaped organism lacking chlorophyll and capable of reproducing by fission. Often considered to have both plant and animal like properties. Plural: Bacteria.

Carbolic Acid: A toxic white soluble crystalline acidic derivative of Benzene used as a disinfectant and antiseptic. Poisonous if taken internally. Also, known as Phenol.

Catarrh: Increased production of mucous from the nose and throat associated with inflammation.

Cazenove Creek: Today known as Cazenovia Creek.

Contagion: The agent of a communicable disease. The term originated long before development of modern ideas of infectious disease.

Consumption: The most common term used to describe Tuberculosis in the nineteenth century. It is derived from the Latin root "con" meaning completely and "sumere" meaning to take over.

Dropsy: Swelling from accumulation of fluid, edema.

Gangrene: Death of tissue from infection or the interruption of blood supply.

Germ: A minute life form capable of causing disease. The term is not in technical use.

Intussusception: The in folding of one segment of the intestine within another. Usually leads to decreased blood supply and gangrene of the bowel segment.

Lithotritist: A person skilled in cutting to remove a stone from the bladder.

Lyceum: A public hall for lectures and concerts. The lyceum movement in the United States sponsored a variety of public adult education programs and entertainments and flourished from the middle of the nineteenth century to the early twentieth century.

Physic: The study and practice of medicine, particularly illnesses of the interior of the body that required an understanding of systems. Initially surgeons dealt with the exterior of the body such as surface tumors and wounds.

Phthisis: Derived from a Greek word for consumption, it was commonly used to describe the pulmonary complications of Tuberculosis.

Quinsy: Complicated, severe, painful tonsillitis, often complicated by a peritonsillar abscess.

Salicylate: The salt of salicin that is obtained from the bark of several species of willow used to treat fever and arthritis. Native Americans used an infusion of the bark of the willow for fever and other illnesses. Salicin was isolated from willow bark by German scientists in 1828 and marketed as Aspirin by the Bayer company.

Saltpeter: Nitrate of potash often used as a diuretic.

Scarified: To make superficial incisions, or deep scratches, in the skin.

Scarlatina: Also, known as scarlet fever. Today we know it is caused by a streptococcus infection of the throat or skin.

Scrofula: Glandular swelling. Most often used to refer to lymphadenitis found in consumption or Tuberculosis.

Sinapism: A plaster containing powdered black mustard that is applied to the skin as a counterirritant, generally producing redness of the skin.

Tanno-gallic acid: A phenol compound found in grape seeds and stems. Can also be leached from oak barrels. It is often used to make antioxidant teas, as a gargle to stop bleeding tonsils, and to tan leather.

Undulant fever: In 1887 David Bruce found that undulant fever, Malta fever, Mediterranean fever and Crimean fever were caused by a bacteria species he named Brucella. The disease came to be called Brucellosis.

Vesicles: Small blister like sacs filled with fluid that form on the skin.

Virus: An agent or venomous substance that causes infectious disease. First known use in 1728 and later applied to contagions that passed through filters. Directly observed by electron microscope in the 1930s.

The Allen Family

Obadiah Allen – b. December 10, 1778 – d. Feb 10, 1860 marries Phoebe Fargo – 1803

    James – b. June 16, 1804 – d. Oct. 4, 1852. m. Rebecca

    Jabez – b. July 16, 1808 Dorset Bennington VT – d. July 14, 1885 – East Aurora, NY (1808 is year indicated on Tombstone).

    Phoebe – b. Aug. 19, 1810 – d. 1842

Dr. Jabez Allen Sr. (above) Marries Millicent Dec 22, 1834

Millicent Susan Johnson b. Sept 7, 1813 – Delhi, NY – d. 1899 East Aurora, NY.

    Parents: Samuel Johnson & Millicent Crisfield Johnson (b. May 26, 1781, d. October 21, 1864). Brother: William Johnson, father of Crisfield Johnson who became professor at Cornell and author of "History of Erie County."

Children of Jabez and Millicent:

    James – b. Oct. 15, 1836 – d. 1849

    Deloran – b. Sept 16, 1847 – d.? - migrated to Kansas

    Orange Fargo – b. Oct. 14, 1849 – d. July 2, 1915 m. Sept. 7, 1875 Emma Hannah Griffin b. Jan 21, 1858 – d. Oct. 23, 1943 East Aurora, NY.

    Jabez Jr. – b. Jan. 22, 1854 - d. June 25, 1876 (druggist)

    Note: Lucas– b. 1834 is listed without further reference.

Source: A family Bible, in possession of Michalann Hobson, Dr. Allen's great-great granddaughter.

Part One: Seasoning

1. Discovering Aurora, 1834

Accident plays a role in deciding our path.

Vermont had an early spring in 1834 allowing a timely start for America's frontier, which I determined to be Cincinnati, Ohio. On my horse Parsley, I traveled the Mohawk Valley, crossed the northern limits of the Finger Lakes, and near the Genesee River headed southwest on Big Tree Road. With only Parsley to listen, I planned my new life as a graduate medical doctor.

In many places our route was little more than a cleared path, easy for a horse, but many days I helped some family push their overloaded ox cart out of the mud that lingered in the valleys. Occasional clusters of cabins interrupted the mostly mature forest, and, often as not, at least one cabin declared itself a tavern. Mercifully, good weather allowed me to take comfort in a bedroll under the stars.

My first day on Big Tree Road I took a noon meal at an establishment calling itself the National Hotel. The proprietor was an older gentleman who served a hearty meal with generous helpings of conversation. When I introduced myself as Dr. Jabez Allen, he told me the only other Jabez he knew was Jabez Warren who surveyed and clear-cut Big Tree Road. "It goes back a way, 1803 I believe, Warren farmed land not far from here. He was an ambitious fellow. Took on the Holland Company's contract to survey and clear a one-rod wide road along an old Indian foot path past a huge ceremonial tree all the way to Lake Erie. At the time, some called it the Middle Road because the idea was to open up settlement through the middle of land the company had purchased from Indian tribes. The twelve dollars a mile Warren was paid secured him a damn comfortable future."

Two hours at the National was a welcomed respite. I'm not saying that two weeks traveling with only a horse to talk to didn't encourage many a witty thought, but Parsley was no great conversationalist. I already missed Vermont, especially my father Obadiah, my older brother James and his wife Rebecca, and my younger sister Phoebe. My mother, also named Phoebe, passed away in a typhoid outbreak last summer, and I missed her the most. The family farm was now in the capable hands of Phoebe's husband who reckoned the farm could support but one family.

I returned to Big Tree Road recharged by the notion that another Jabez had blazed my trail. Parsley, also fed and watered, seemed happy to resume our travel. She was a good, healthy mare who had weaned her second filly a couple months before our departure. I had come across the word parsley in a book, liked it, and gave it to my horse.

In my saddle bags, I carried a clean suit and enough medical supplies to assure a modest start in my profession. My father and mother, the former Phoebe Fargo, had done well in East Dorset, Vermont. Dad was a farmer and a merchant who knew how to manage a dollar. He acquired land, and with my mother's help, they made Vermont's hard scratch productive. He also cultivated connections, becoming what might be called a mercantile trader. He made most of his money brokering, selling, and trading farm equipment, like horse drawn rakes and mowers. Father also knew a good horse when he saw one. His honesty gained the trust of farmers throughout Vermont and for each transaction he took only a fair share.

Every summer typhoid menaced our Vermont neighbors and last summer it took my mother. After her death, father lost his ambition for the farm, but fortunately Phoebe's husband, a natural born farmer, took over. Father now holds the mortgage for Phoebe and her husband.

James, four years my elder and always more determined and adventuresome, had decided to try his hand at physic. After graduating from Castleton

Medical College in 1828, James returned to East Dorset and became the first doctor with a medical degree to practice in Bennington County.

Being the middle child, I suppose I never was as adventuresome as James, nor as settled as Phoebe. I did like to read and Castleton was a short day's ride from East Dorset. With my brother's encouragement, I became his apprentice and attended the required two terms of lectures at Castleton. I enjoyed the book study and took naturally to seeing patients. After graduation James allowed me to retain half of all the income I generated, but competition with Thomsonian herbalists and Homeopathic dilutions meant there wasn't enough paying work to support both James and me in East Dorset, or anywhere in New England. So, my late blooming, twenty-six-year-old energies pushed me west. I figured a growing city like Cincinnati needed doctors and sister Phoebe thought the move would cure what she called my "shiftless determination." I had just enough confidence, and naivety, to strike out for the great State of Ohio.

Two days from the National Hotel, the Big Tree Road entered the upper village of Aurora. After passing a few cabins and a couple of sturdy plank houses, I came upon the first three-story building since Syracuse. It was the Globe Hotel where I purchased a bath, a meal, and a soft bed for the night. The Globe proprietor, Mr. Charles P. Persons, greeted me with a generous handshake, a smile and led Parsley off to his stables. A cold bath and clean towel were soon delivered to my room. In medical college, they said a cold-water bath relieves nervous afflictions and reduces flatulency. Besides, the Globe charged 25 cents for a cold bath, half that of a hot bath. I then downed my one clean suit and collar for dinner. With so many irregular, poorly trained men calling themselves doctors, Castleton professors said it was important for a graduate physician to appear the part of a gentleman.

I found myself dinning with two other westward travelers and a local gentleman who was boarding at the Globe. One traveler was also heading to Cincinnati where his brother-in-law's harness business was buried in work. The other was on his way to Indiana where he had secured a section of federal land on which he had to establish a farm within the year, then send for his wife and child. The boarder, a Mr. Hiram Barney, had arrived from Springville that winter to teach Greek philosophy and Latin as the live-in assistant to Mr. Daniel Howard, principal of the Aurora Academy. The Academy attracted eighty students from prominent families in Buffalo and Aurora, half of whom boarded with village families. Mr. Barney, Hiram, was waiting for his rooms to be prepared in the Academy's newest expansion. Besides lecturing, his responsibilities included discipline and student refinement. Being the bookish sort, I asked about the Academy's library, which Hiram bragged was the most extensive collection outside of Buffalo or New York City. It had recently acquired an anthology of Waldo Emerson's essays.

Our after-dinner brandy was interrupted by Colonel Calvin Fillmore. Col. Fillmore ran another tavern less than a mile further west on Big Tree Road, but was clearly on good terms with Mr. Persons. The Colonel was inquiring after Dr. Johnathan Hoyt who commonly left word at the Globe when he was out on a house call. That night Hoyt was attending the confinement of a woman in Wales Center, about six miles distant.

Sensing some urgency in Col. Fillmore's inquiry, I introduced myself as a graduate physician and asked the nature of the problem. His eighteen-month-old grandson had been ill for several days with recurrent, painful episodes of diarrhea. They had tried everything in their medical book, but tonight the child had grown weaker.

It is a poor habit to attend to a patient of another doctor, none-the-less, I offered my services until Dr. Hoyt could return. In short order, I was following the Colonel further west along Big Tree road. The night was cold, clear and the stars shone brightly. Daytime muddy wagon ruts now sparkled in a frozen moonlight. The Colonel ushered me to his tavern's second floor where his daughter-in-law, the young Abiatha Fillmore, sat at the bedside of her pale listless son.

I immediately commenced my examination. The child scarcely responded to my touch. His tongue was parched and his skin easily tented. He was warm but did not feel feverish. His pulse was hard, and during bouts of pain it quickened, though he barely woke. The child's abdomen was tender and the stool I examined seemed a mixture of blood and mucous that appeared like jam made of currants. As I took out my stethoscope the child's mother gasped. I encouraged her to hold it and see that it was simply a wooden tube with a flange on one end. Her fears abated. I found the child's breaths to be shallow but clear. Abiatha showed me her copy of Gunn's *Domestic Medicine* saying that she tried every remedy listed.

These many years later it seems easy to confess that I was perplexed. The child's condition was extreme and the presentation did not match anything I had seen. After nearly three years working with my brother and two semesters of lectures at Castleton, I was embarrassed and uncertain. My mind raced as I considered how seriously ill the child appeared. I was compelled to act, to do something that would afford comfort, and bring some hope to his mother.

The child had red, sore gums and was at the typical age for molars to emerge. Lacking any strategy for dealing with the child's real problem, I absurdly lanced the child's swollen gums hoping to ease any systemic symptoms teething is known to ignite. Then, to hide my ignorance, I explained that I needed to prepare a prescription. With that I retired to my room at the Globe to consult the few books I had with me. Books have always comforted me, but this was a race against my own ineptitude.

I trusted Eberle's *Practice of Medicine* for details about symptoms and remedies. I searched his chapters on Cholera Infantum, Enteritis and

Dysentery but did not find anything to match my patient's symptoms. Eberle's recommendation, common to all diarrheal conditions, was bloodletting followed by spirits of turpentine in castor oil or calomel.

Within the hour, I returned to the child's bed to relieve the child of six ounces of blood. The procedure soothed the child's pain. Next, I administered half of the castor oil/turpentine compound I had mixed precisely according to Eberle's directions and left specific instructions for the remainder of the compound to be administered in two hours if the child had not yet improved. Being unable to sleep, I returned to the child in two hours. The boy clung to life with the quiet poise of a youth unfamiliar with death. I moved on to Eberle's next steps and administered a tobacco enema with little result. Still frustrated, I began alternating the castor oil and turpentine with calomel and senna in the hope of purging the poisons attacking the child.

I dosed in a chair and awoke just after daybreak to find a woman clearly experienced in nursing attending to the child. After brief introductions, she took me aside and inquired if I was of the opinion that the child was destined to pass. Though I tried to act profoundly confident, I was comforted by the nurse's presence and confessed my fear that the child would not recover.

Later that morning Dr. Hoyt, having completed his delivery, visited the child. It was Dr. Hoyt who had recommended the nurse. He inquired as to why I had not bled the child a second or third time and asked if I thought the application of a blister to the abdomen might help. Dr. Hoyt also asked if he might inspect my stethoscope. He had seen one demonstrated at a medical society meeting and had considered its purchase. Dr. Hoyt concurred that the unfortunate child was dying. I do not want to appear unfair to Dr. Hoyt, but I have always suspected the poor prognosis was the reason he asked me to continue working on the case.

I came to learn the child's mother, Abiatha Fillmore, was a widow. Her husband, the Colonel's son, had died from the Cholera while she was pregnant with the child who now lay so ill in her father-in-law's home. Abiatha was a plain woman but brave, reserved and composed. She suffered her anxiety and exhaustion with a solemn dignity.

The next morning the child was called to his eternal life. As I closed the child's eyelids Abiatha whispered, "God's will." Our throats tight with the effort of holding back tears, the Colonel wanted to know what killed his grandson, and I worried that whatever it was might affect others in the community. With Abiatha's consent, I arranged with Dr. Hoyt for an autopsy.

After moving the body to Dr. Hoyt's office, we limited the autopsy to the abdomen and the organs most likely responsible for the child's death. Opening the cavity released a foul odor and copious amounts of serous pus. I was impressed with Dr. Hoyt's skill at separating and displacing the intestines to preserve the hepatoduodenal ligament. Dr. Hoyt followed the course of the small intestine to a gangrenous area of obstruction where the jejunum seemed to engulf itself. Neither Dr. Hoyt nor I could find reference to this type of intussusception in our textbooks but this area of bowel clearly exhibited a burden of inflammation and explained the child's demise.

The grandson of Col. Fillmore had been the first patient of my independent practice, and he was dead. My one night in Aurora had turned into four. I had slept but a few hours, read and re-read my medical books, and spent countless hours at the child's bedside. Still, I had failed. It was either exhaustion or my regards for the family that compelled me to stay for the funeral. I ordered another bath and packed my saddle bags for departure after the next morning's service.

There was a light rain falling as the family left the cemetery and Dr. Hoyt approached me to say Col. Fillmore and Mr. Persons asked if they might have a word. We retired to a corner in Col. Fillmore's tavern where I was introduced to General William Warren and Dr. John Watson. A William Johnson was to join us. While waiting General Warren told me that his father was the Jabez Warren who surveyed Big Tree Road. Along the way his father had found the broad Aurora valley inviting, purchased six hundred and forty acres, and moved here in 1804. Dr. Hoyt was the current town supervisor and with some pride guessed there might be 2,400 people living in Aurora township.

Col. Fillmore found Aurora when leading his Vermont troops along the Big Tree Road to join the battles against the British in the 1812 War. He used his Army payout to buy several tracks of land around Aurora, eventually buying the home on Main Street. He expanded his land holdings by buying the property of those who failed the rigors of homesteading. In 1819, he convinced his brother Nathaniel to buy one of those farms a mile south of the village. Dr. Hoyt and Dr. John Watson both attended lectures at Fairfield Medical College near Utica. In 1824, Charles Persons had purchased a general store started by his brother Robert and added the hotel that he now called the Globe. At that point, William Johnson joined us. Though new to Aurora, he was an enthusiastic promoter and represented Millard Fillmore's law practice where he was serving as a clerk.

Col. Fillmore started the formal conversation, "Dr. Allen, where is your bill? You have spent the best part of four days attending to my grandson and comforting my daughter-in-law. Here you are about to leave town and I have yet to receive your bill. I fear that you may fail at this physic business, if you are not prompt with your charges."

"Col. Fillmore, I am most honored to have been called to care for your grandson and most grieved for his death. Your daughter-in-law is a fine woman and has suffered much in her short life. I apprenticed with my brother who never sent a bill for services that failed to enact a cure. I have determined to adopt the same policy. I shall not add to your burden with a bill. My motto sir, 'No Cure, No Pay.'"

With a mischievous grin Dr. Hoyt responded, "Dr. Allen, you are unlikely to be a financial success and likely be the ruin of the rest of us if you don't send a bill for services. I must reassure the businessmen at this table that most of us do not press charges when there has been a death. And, while we may decline to bill poor families, we always bill the well to do. To this latter point, Col. Fillmore is unfamiliar with not receiving a bill."

Dr. Hoyt went on, "Son, Dr. Watson and I have practiced in the upper village of Aurora for twenty years. Dr. Hasack also had a large practice, but suffered a sudden death and his loss has placed quite a burden on us. The British haven't threatened us in twenty years, and with the opening of the Canal our farmers are quite prosperous and able to pay on their accounts. We fear that if we do not attract another regular doctor, the quacks and sectarians will overtake our town. The nurse we employed to assist you is a gentle, capable woman and very smart. She says the same about you."

Now Col. Fillmore made his offer, "Dr. Allen, consider staying right here in Aurora and leasing a room in my tavern to start your doctoring business. The first three month's rent will be considered payment for your services to my grandson and his mother. By that time, we may find you better space, but for now, that will get you established."

A good-natured Mr. Persons added, "Though your late-night strolling has proven a bit of a nuisance, you are welcomed to stay at the Globe until you get settled. Be warned that I do expect payment for room and board whether you sleep well or not."

To my surprise, these town fathers were asking me to stay on the very day they buried my first patient.

Dr. Watson, who had been quiet, spoke next, "Dr. Allen, I have spent hours in my carriage attending to the fine citizens of this township. They are good, hard working folks. They pay what they can and I make a reasonable living. I don't take kindly to those who call themselves doctors but never saw the inside of a lecture hall. We have been successful in shielding our community from most quacks and sectarians. Unfortunately, when a regular doctor is not available it opens the door for the quack to enter and the quacks get paid before we do. There is room for you in our town."

At this point the Colonel's wife Jerusha came in to retrieve Col. Fillmore who had a funeral breakfast to attend in the adjoining room. In closing General Warren offered a tour of Aurora the next morning to introduce me to the village.

I accepted.

2. Promoting the Villages of Aurora, 1834

Home is where a heart finds comfort.

The next morning, I joined my Globe colleague, Hiram Barney, for flapjacks, maple syrup and coffee. Several days of sharing meals had kindled a friendship, and Hiram was excited about my possibly staying in Aurora and offered a tour of the Aurora Academy after my village excursion.

General William Warren arrived at 9:00 a.m. sharp. In short order, we mounted his carriage and before his horse gained full stride General Warren launched his story like a salesman to his wares, "Like you and the Fillmores, my family hails from Vermont. I was married before my father got in his head to leave Vermont. He rented a farm east of here in Wyoming County, but being the entrepreneurial type, father took the Holland Company contract to survey and clear cut the Big Tree Road."

The General continued, "Of course, dad recruited me to the effort. Before he died in 1810, he told many a traveler how the mile-wide Aurora valley felt like home on his first pass through. The Holland Company, pleased with the timely completion of the road, and desperate for pioneers to encourage others to buy land, offered my father six hundred and forty acres at $2 an acre on generous credit terms. In 1804, he moved my mother and younger siblings to Aurora and in 1805 Florence and I became the seventh family to settle in Aurora."

Doctoring stimulates a fascination for the way people join gestures with words. General Warren's clean shaven face showed years of rugged outdoor exposure and a determined visage. His self-confidence, common to experienced leaders, was lit with an enthusiasm that stirred my interest. I hardly allowed him a breath before asking, "This fine carriage and harness give evidence to your success and your introduction as General Warren suggests you have led men in battle."

As I hoped, my words invited a comprehensive history of the General's adopted community.

"With the Seneca Indians just to our north and perennial rumors of a British invasion from Canada the New York legislature decreed that all communities organize a militia in 1810. Having been an ensign in the Vermont militia, it fell upon me to organize and drill the sixty Aurora men who volunteered. When the fighting started in 1812, our men were joined into a regiment that saw battle at Black Rock, Buffalo, and an excursion into Canada organized by Dr. Cyrenius Chapin. It was Winfred Scott himself who promoted me to the rank of General. We haven't fought a battle since 1815, but our militia drills every month and we march in every July fourth parade."

"When the British burned Buffalo, ox carts loaded with household goods carrying fleeing families, wounded soldiers and the occasional Indian hightailed it to Aurora. A good many moved into cabins deserted by failed homesteaders and, often as not, temporary shelter turned into permanent housekeeping. When the war ended and the troops got paid, men were hankering to buy land and find wives."

"It was then I tried my hand at milling lumber to supply those moving up from log cabins to frame houses. In fact, the first house my wife, Florence, and I built is the two-story home that Colonel Calvin Fillmore bought from us in 1822 and turned into a tavern. The war gave me an itch to make a living doing whatever Aurora needed. Besides the lumber business, I bought and sold several buildings and homes along Big Tree Road while continuing to farm and sell lumber."

"Florence, also embraced life in Aurora. She started the first school in our home and had me teaching figuring a couple of semesters. We have helped several newcomers get started. One of them is Colonel Fillmore's nephew, Millard Fillmore, now a congressman. Millard rented a room from us and I set him up in his first office on Main Street. Right from the start it was clear the lad knew how to spin a tale."

General Warren then told me how his father, Jabez Warren, and his uncle, Henry Godfrey, ended up with over fourteen-hundred acres on which the upper and lower villages took root. By the end of 1807 there was a tavern, saw mill and grist mill and by 1811 Dr. John Watson set up as the first physician. The Globe Hotel is the largest structure of the upper village and a little over a mile west is the lower village called Willink or just the 'lower village.'

From there the General moved onto a geography lesson, "Sixteen miles east of Lake Erie, Aurora, is where the lake plane rises to meet the hills, a lift that guarantees a good supply of snow, which melts off the hilltop clay soil onto the valley's fertile dark loam to nurture our winter wheat. Towering pines cover the hills and hemlock; beech and maple trees fill the valleys. Just northwest of the village, the Cazenove Creek joins the Buffalo Creek on its way to Lake Erie. Like so many things in western New York, the Cazenove Creek was named after an agent for the Holland Company, Theophilus Cazenove.

"Black bears feast on the nuts of the beech trees. Gray wolves and panthers thrive on the plentiful deer. The woods are full of raccoons, squirrels, wild turkey, partridge, and the occasional rattlesnake writhes among the rocks. Trees along creek beds might hold 50-60 passenger pigeon nests. Auroreans have been known to cut down a tree full of plump chicks, then dress, salt and dry them for winter consumption."

"French trappers once claimed there were 12,000 Indians in Western New York. The more peaceful Kahquah Indians that populated the uplands of Lake Erie were decimated by Smallpox and Measles opening settlements to raids by the Iroquois, particularly the Seneca. Chief Red Jacket, who favored a coat given to him by the U.S. Secretary of War, assembled hundreds of braves, squaws and children to a peace council with the Federal Army in 1794. Negotiations fell apart until the army's cannon forced the Seneca to accept $10,000 worth of goods and an annual stipend of $4,000. That's when the agents of the Holland Company convinced the Iroquois to sell virtually all the land west of the Genesee River and moved the Indians to reservations along Buffalo Creek, Tonawanda Creek and Cattaraugus Creek."

"Most of our settlers have been poor New England farmers and European immigrants attracted by the Holland Company's deal of one hundred acres for five dollars down. Those favored by God and unafraid of hard work did well, eventually expanding their holdings by assuming the mortgages of the less fortunate. Those who fell on hard luck have become our wage labor force."

"Most settlers started like Florence and me, with a sixteen-foot square log cabin with a puncheon, split log floor, a wood shingle roof and one glass window. Water came from a nearby spring until we hand dug a well. You could get almost anything done, digging a well, clearing a field, or raising a barn, if you let the neighbors know you have a jug of whisky to open at the end of the day. Three men and an ox can clear an acre of land in a day with the brush stacked as a makeshift fence until replaced by a split rail fence. If successful, most settlers build a barn out of planed lumber in their third year and later build a house to show everyone they had made it."

"I can assure you, Aurora still welcomes newcomers. Unmarried men arrive on foot with only a bedroll, a Bible and an axe. Families come by ox cart and all but the poorest bring a cow, a couple of pigs, and maybe a few sheep. The first year they have to focus on food, wearing their clothes so thin that they're nothing but patches. They clear a field, plant winter wheat, depend on wild game through the winter, and plant field corn in the spring."

"Today the successful farms are getting larger and gaining from the new ideas, like rotating wheat and corn with peas and beans. The legumes feed bigger pigs, making for greater profit from salt pork shipped to New York City by the canal. With a bushel of corn fetching 25 cents, more if you could store it for a few months, farmers are doing pretty good. Some have even branched out to collecting wood ash to make potash and shipping that at a profit. Commerce makes for lots of traveling, so many households with an extra bed and a little liquor are hanging a "Tavern" sign for extra cash. You likely noticed the Fillmores hired a fiddler to compete with the neighborhoods."

The General's enthusiasm peaked as he described how cash paid as wages stimulate the expansion of Aurora's commercial district. Tea and coffee are now available year around, and though Auroreans like their maple syrup, sugar has become cheap and plentiful. "Wages change the nature of a town. Wage laborers rent housing and buy food, clothes and services that define an economy. Immigrants have this figured out. That's why they settle in the North where they are not competing with slaves. All those barges we send down the canal return with goods to be sold in our stores. America is changing, Jabez, and Aurora is a great town to take advantage of it all. Wages are good for a doctor's business."

The next few hours bore out the General's promotion. He had me visit the Aurora Boot and Shoe Manufactory; the Aurora Hat Factory; the Norton and Williams store with a 'complete assortment of broad cloths;' Joseph Riley's store promoting a 'large assortment of cashmere and satin fresh from New York City.' There was the Iron Foundry and Plough Factory competing with the J. Adams Carriage and Manufactory, both offering carts, wagons and sleighs of all sizes. At the Athearn and Sheldon Store the proprietor bragged of his West India goods and Pipes and half Pipes of cognac, brandy, gin, St. Croix rum, wines, sugars, teas, coffee, tobacco and spices. J. Howard Jr. sold hardware and dry goods. Of the two bookstores, one had a sign declaring, "More new books received weekly."

There was the Blacksmithing Establishment for shoeing horses and oxen, the W. Smith Saddle, Trunk and Harness Maker newly relocated from New York City, and the S. B. Briggs Farm Supply. We walked through the Village Plant Nursery's selection of apple, pear, peach, cherry and grape seedlings. They had ornamental trees, flowering shrubs, roses, strawberries, raspberries, gooseberries, and currants ready for spring planting and a catalog with more. The stationary store sold all kinds of forms for writing your own summons, confessions, and affidavits. There was even a portrait painter, Mr. Waldo, who I thought displayed a really fine talent.

We passed the Aurora Academy, several farms and proceeded west to the lower village of Willink. Along the way, I learned that a Buffalo-Aurora railroad had been incorporated and surveyed in 1832, with construction to start soon. As a non-investor, General Warren worried he was missing an opportunity, but he thought steam locomotives were dirty and prone to starting fires.

General Warren's sister Anna and her husband, Phineas Stephens, owned the two hundred acres where the Big Tree Road crossed several Indian trails, themselves now becoming highways. Wilhelm Willink had been a collection agent for the Holland Company who became quite unpopular so most people called the area the 'lower village.' We turned north towards Buffalo on Seneca Street until we reached the eighteen-cent toll over the Buffalo Creek bridge.

Returning to the lower village, there was a post office, another harness shop and a large general store that stocked everything from dry goods, to hair pins. to horse blankets. Several men sat around a wood stove drinking coffee, chewing tobacco and generally getting in the way according to store owner Stephen Holmes. They seemed glad to see anyone, asked several questions, and were generous with laughter. One stove watcher claimed, "You'll like it here; old doc Hoyt made enough money to buy him one of those Caribbean islands." The town constable strolled in as we were leaving and joked that if it wasn't for public intoxication and the occasional lost horse, he would have to find a real job.

Over mid-day dinner at the Eagle Tavern we met the General's sister, Anna Stephens. She told me about the Aurora Union Library founded by Colonel Calvin Fillmore and the Aurora Union Debating Society in which Congressman Millard Fillmore regularly participated. Also, Almon Clapp, who married General Warren's daughter, was about to start a newspaper he was calling the *Aurora Standard*. The afternoon included a tour of the General's milling operations in Griffins Mill, a couple of miles further west. Water flowing over a sixteen-foot-high dam across Cazenove Creek provided power to grind flour in season and plane lumber year around. The area had a pungent odor from two nearby tanneries that depended on waste bark.

By mid-afternoon the General, still indulging me like a favorite nephew, let me off at the Aurora Academy. Classes were just being let out and Hiram Barney informed that he had accepted an invitation for both of us to attend an evening diner party at the home of the attorney, William Johnson.

I met the Academy's preceptress, Miss Mary Hartwell, and the principal, Daniel Howard, who said the Academy was one of the few secondary schools to accept girls because Colonel Fillmore had made it a condition of donating the land on which the Academy was built. A school year consisted of two twenty-three-week terms with tuition determined by the courses taken. Common English was $3.00; Mathematics, Latin and Greek Languages was $4.00; French and Hebrew Languages was $5.00. New classrooms, dormitories, library and apartments for Hiram and Miss Hartwell were under construction to accommodate prominent Buffalo families willing to pay $1.50 a week to board their children. The new library would be absorbing Colonel Calvin Fillmore's Aurora Union Library and charge $2.00 per annum for access to a collection that included works by Voltaire, Adam Smith and Emerson.

As Hiram and I walked back to the Globe Hotel I prattled on about my tour of Aurora. In his few months of residence in the township, Hiram had come to appreciate how prominent families nurtured their village and shared their affections. We stopped at the Fillmore tavern for a whisky where the widow Abiatha was already back at work. She delivered our drinks just as Colonel Fillmore returned from the day's chores. Joining us, the Colonel added a new enticement. If I were agreeable, for a reasonable wage, Abiatha would serve as my assistant. She was smart with figures and he bargained that she could help with billing records and collections, welcoming patients, tracking orders of service and collecting messages when I was out on calls. Abiatha did not say a word.

It was all a bit overwhelming – New friends, thriving village, welcoming physicians. My father, whose entrepreneurial skills I failed to inherit, would advise me to avail myself of the Fillmore and Warren aptitude for business. After one drink and a promise to decide by morning, Hiram and I continued to the Globe to change for the evening's dinner party.

3. A Dinner Party, 1834

New friends unlock new lives

In Vermont celebrations were held midday on holidays or Sundays after church so leftovers could be eaten in the evening before they spoiled. Only the wealthy could afford the whale oil for multiple lamps required to hold fancy evening dinner parties. One Castleton classmate, who hailed from the upper crust of Boston society, said his family ate breakfast at 9:00 a.m., luncheon at 2:00 p.m., and dinner at 8:00 p.m., like well-to-do Londoners. An invitation to a dinner party provoked my apprehensions.

My attire, for better or worse, was preordained as I owned but one clean suit. Hiram, thinking we should observe the strange custom of being a little late, met me in the Globe's lobby at 7:00 p.m. to walk the quarter mile to the Johnson home. I wore no coat because mud from my journey still clung to the only one I owned.

By the standards of East Dorset, the Johnson home was stately. Even in the fading light of the evening one could appreciate the pointed external window framework and matching double hung front door accentuated by scalloped shingles and intricate eave supports. The whale oil lamps burning inside gave the windows a festive glow.

Hiram and I were greeted at the front door by Miss Millicent Susan Johnson who offered a bright smile and an unexpectedly confident handshake. Expressive brown eyes lent sincerity to her sophistication. She moved gracefully in a modest blue hooped dress, with a flexibility that suggested she either required no corset, or refused to be bound by one.

Displaying proper decorum without a hint of shyness, Millicent took my arm to greet the other guests. Of course, I knew General Warren who, with his wife Florence, lived just across the street. They both joked that they were always available for a Johnson dinner party. Next, we greeted Colonel Calvin Fillmore and his wife Jerusha. Jerusha's hands confirmed that she was no stranger to hard work, though she looked very handsome in her evening attire. Lastly, we were introduced to Millicent's brother, William Johnson, and his fiancée Rebecca Brigham.

Just then a maid approached us with a tray. To my surprise it was Abiatha, dressed formally in a black uniform with a white apron and holding a tray of crystal goblets filled with white wine. With self-possessed assurance, William informed the group that he had selected a French wine he imported by the case. We soon retired to the dining room where a floral wallpaper seemed to bounce color off the glassware. Little name cards seated Hiram and I on either side of Miss Millicent.

I found myself strangely jealous of Millicent's attention, asking endless questions and learning that she and her brother had been born near Delhi, NY. The family had moved to Aurora two years ago when Millicent was nineteen. Their father, Capt. Samuel Johnson, had distinguished himself in a Revolutionary war battle at Ticonderoga. For his service, he received a land grant in Delaware County with virgin hardwood that he cut and transported down the Delaware River to Philadelphia. Until her father's recent death, Millicent had been "as busy as a soul needed to be" caring for her father who took ill shortly after arriving in Aurora. The home would be transferred to William upon his marriage. Millicent was named after her mother. The elder Millicent had withdrawn after Samuel's death, preferring the solitude of her upstairs' bedroom to a dinner party.

Abiatha served dinner with a style and grace that belied her difficult circumstances. The first course was a mutton broth with vegetables accompanied by potato bread. This was followed by another French wine, this time a Bordeaux that, like so much else, was well beyond the experience of a farmer's son. The main course was wild turkey served with a vegetable stew and a side of squash. Dessert was a British plum pudding followed by a cordial of blackberry brandy.

After dinner, it seemed everyone had a story to augment General Warren's tour. When the Aurora Union Debating Society came up, consensus was that the debates were an entertainment high point, particularly when the ever-eloquent Congressman Millard Fillmore attended. Every month the men decide on an issue and draw lots to determine teams. Recent topics included, "Have women more influence over men than brandy?" and "Is the drunkard a greater nuisance to society than the profane swearer?" The group really became energized recalling one titled, "Is it right to take life for any crime?" Each month the losing side is fined 30 cents and the money is used to provide refreshments at the next debate.

Millicent impressed me as a serious woman, intent on her church work and widely read. She was very capable of an opinion and clever in the polite conversation of a dinner party. There was a brief moment of discomfort when William, perhaps under the wine's influence, teased Millicent that at age twenty-one she risked being an old maid. Millicent's retort was that she had yet to find a man equal to her intellect.

As we bid our goodnights Millicent and William invited both Hiram and I to join their regular Friday evening salon. Admission required a contribution to good conversation with extra credit given for ideas that agitate a good argument.

As we walked back to the Globe Hiram said, "That is what I've come to like about the people of Aurora: They seem quite content with who they are and where they are. It's almost as if they feel entitled to be themselves. It lends a quiet sort of confidence. They enjoy nice things with no reason for pretense."

It had been a very busy day prefacing what would be a long night of decision making.

4. Becoming a Graduate Doctor, 1832-1833

All knowledge is about the past. All decisions are about the future.

Fewer than three weeks had passed since I left Vermont. My father had been encouraging and a little envious. My sister and brother-in-law were pleased to discharge my claim to the family farm and my brother was relieved that I would not be competing for patient fees. None of them thought that, at age twenty-six, it was premature to strike out on my own.

What would they think now if I gave up on Cincinnati? Though becoming mercantile, Aurora is far from urbane and still quite rural. Reliable access to books and supplies and the village's diverse social order was appealing. Dependable mail service was also an advantage.

Establishing my worth in a village with other doctors would seem a challenge equal to practicing on the frontier. Competition can goad physicians to treat just to prove their worth above that of the competition and Dr. Hoyt already questioned my reluctance to repeatedly bleed the Fillmore child. I worry that my inclination to retreat to books for advice and avoid heroics or excessive treatment may open me to further criticism. After all, the relationship with a patient is so personal, and the remedies selected are so individualistic, that two doctors seldom agree. Finances were another consideration. An 1831 article in the *Boston Medical and Surgical Journal* argued that the medical profession is an unlikely path to wealth. Medicine is crowded with competitors and offers little chance for bold speculations that make men like Colonel Fillmore, General Warren or Millicent's father affluent. Botanical doctors, homeopaths, or remedies lifted from home medical books often drain a patient's purse before a regular doctor is called. Even well-established regular doctors might struggle to generate an income of $800 a year. The whole reason for leaving Vermont was my concern about making a living. But perhaps, just like the General said, "A growing mercantile economy like Aurora's would mean more cash and fewer barter transactions than in a frontier economy."

Then, I wondered, should I start my practice in a tavern? Though located in a gentile neighborhood and modestly distant from established physicians, locating my office in a tavern might suggest I encouraged intemperance. Also, it seemed disrespectful to hang the handsome name plate my brother gave me below a tavern sign. Worse yet, taverns attract the loitering class who could obstruct and even harangue patients.

I needed an office with space to keep repulsive objects as catheters, specula, forceps, splints, trusses, and amputating knives out of sight. Yet, precision instruments like my microscope should be on display. Also, there needs to be one wall available for my diploma, license, and a certificate of medical society membership.

It is important that patients know I am a graduate of Castleton Medical Academy, the tenth medical college to be established in America. Harvard was the first in 1783, and now the list includes: University of Pennsylvania, Dartmouth, Transylvania, College of Physicians and Surgeons of New York City, University of Maryland, Brown University, Yale Medical Institution, and the College of Physicians and Surgeons of the Western District of New York in Fairfield, New York.

The sixteen-hundred residents of Castleton in Rutland County already supported a secondary school based on an economy secured by the slate and marble quarries. Their doctor, Selah Gridley, was the Founding President of the Vermont Medical Society, village postmaster and general store owner. He had no formal medical degree, but had been licensed by the Connecticut State Medical Society. After hosting a steady procession of medical apprentices, Gridley decided Castleton needed a medical college in 1818.

Admission required reading the first six books of Virgil's Aeneid and the first four orations of Cicero. Students served a two-year apprenticeship and attended two fifteen-week lecture terms, which were of identical content. The college charged $40 for each of the two lecture terms and $10 for each of the apprentice years. At a cost of $35 each, a textbook was required for each of the four courses: 1. Anatomy and Physiology; 2. Chemistry; 3. Materia Medica and Medical Therapeutics; 4. Surgery and Obstetrics. Lectures were supplemented with daily recitations based on the textbook assignments.

Materia Medica lectures covered the plants, minerals and inorganic salts from which medicines are derived and practical instruction on compounding prescriptions. Chemistry lectures focused largely on the examination of urine. Anatomy included exhibits of pathological specimens and dissections when available. Surgeries were demonstrated in the amphitheater and deliveries were practiced on a manikin. Among the highly-qualified faculty were: Professor William Tully who taught Materia Medica and Therapeutics at both Castleton and Yale Medical College; Dr. Alden March, a graduate of Brown, who introduced us to the newest of Laennec's techniques for listening to the chest and lungs.

Curriculum was based on the modern theories of miasma. Miasma arose from fetid ground or stagnant water to cause an inflamed circulatory congestion in susceptible patients. The great thinkers of medicine, Broussias, Clarke and Rush, agreed that this congestion caused weak capillary circulation, pooling in the vena cava, a diminished pulse and a buildup of byproducts in the liver. Bleeding relieved the circulatory congestion, and mercury, usually in the form of calomel, stimulated bile secretion from the liver and prevented accumulation of noisome feces in the intestines.

Castleton required a dissertation and periodically quizzed students on readings assigned during apprentice months. They also required students to pass oral final exams in each subject.

Dissections supervised by a skilled surgeon or anatomist are essential to medical training. However, neither Castleton's catalogue, nor any other medical college catalog, makes mention of cadavers or dissections. The bylaws for Castleton clearly state, "No body for the use of this institution shall be taken from any burying ground in this County. But bodies, such as may be necessary, shall be procured from the great seaports of the neighboring states." Reality was that even the customary $15 fee was inadequate to assure a suitable supply of cadavers.

Cadavers required immediate dissection, arriving fresh or partially embalmed in a barrel of brine. Students were expected to respect the body and cautioned to avoid injury during dissection. A plaque in the surgical/anatomy hall reminded us that forty students attending England's St. Bartholomew's medical college had died from minor cuts sustained during dissections.

All admonitions failed to prevent three of my classmates from procuring a body in an episode called the "Hubbardton Raid." A woman in Hubbardton, Vermont, seven miles from Castleton, was buried on a Saturday. Monday morning grave markings intended to detect any alterations to the burial site were notably disturbed and the coffin was empty. The Hubbardton Sheriff led a posse of three hundred men to Castleton, surrounded the main college building and demanded the body be returned. Dr. March was appointed to mediate and immediately dispatched a messenger to fetch his keys, inexplicably left at home that morning. The tactic provided time for the offending students to hide the already dissected body below the floor boards. However, limited space required removal of the head, which one student carried under his coat and deposited it in the haymow of a neighboring barn. Once Dr. March's keys were retrieved, the Sheriff and a small committee searched the lecture hall, discovered the lose floor board, and found the headless body. At this point, Professor March expressed bewilderment and negotiated an arrangement whereby a return of both body and head would lead to no arrests. The offending students were disciplined, but not discharged. Since then, at the start of each term, a Rutland newspaper publishes a story about the 'Hubbardton Raid' to discourage any further grave robbing.

All told, my education at Castleton cost nearly $700. Though tightfisted in most matters, my brother James waved the usual preceptor fee of $100 per year and charged me only half the allowable apprentice room and board of $250. During much of my second-year James allowed me to retain half of the patient charges I generated. This income and my share of the family farm subsidized my journey to the frontier.

Fairfield Medical College in Herkimer County outside of Utica, New York, was another highly respected rural medical college. It was chartered to grant the M.D. degree in 1812 as the 'The College of Physicians and Surgeons of the Western District of New York,' but was more commonly known as Fairfield. Drs. Hoyt and Watson were both graduates of Fairfield.

Eventually Fairfield was absorbed into Geneva Medical College, which later moved to Syracuse. Homeopaths formed their own institutions and produced men calling themselves 'doctor.' We call them 'irregulars' or 'sectarians.'

Rural practice can be demanding. I saw how East Dorset demanded my brother be available, caring, and authoritative. In exchange, he held the community's confidence and respect. His attendance at the bedside fostered close relationships and kinships that might be unique to rural practice. Observations which worked on my mind as I contemplated whether Aurora township was to be my home.

5. Closing the Deal, 1834

Friendship is constant in all things save business.

It's hard to say I awoke the next morning as I am not sure I slept. As we sat down to Mrs. Person's breakfast of coffee, fresh eggs, and corn bread Hiram hardly said, 'Good morning,' before inquiring about my deliberations.

"Hiram, sometime in the wee hours of the night I realized that I could not make a decision about the rest of my life, so I chose to focus on the next five years. In that context, the opportunities in Aurora are too good to ignore. My relief at this decision was immediately disturbed by the idea of opening physic practice in a tavern."

Genuinely pleased, Hiram welcomed me as fellow inductee to Aurora citizenship. He also agreed that a tavern location might burden my launch asking how I was going to negotiate the location with the Colonel. We pondered that question as I accompanied Hiram on his walk to the Academy bidding him a good day at the Fillmore tavern. Colonel Fillmore was finishing his breakfast and Abiatha was refilling his coffee cup.

He greeted me with an enthusiastic, "Good day Dr. Allen. I trust you have good news?"

"Colonel, I cannot imagine any doctor receiving a better offer from a finer gentleman. Your hospitality has caused me to acquire an honest affection for Aurora. If the fine folks of Aurora will have me, I will stay."

Then, turning to Abiatha, I added, "And, Abiatha, it would please me greatly if we can agree on terms that result in my being advantaged by your service."

My declaration having produced no change in the Colonel's smile, I continued, "However Colonel Fillmore, there is one part of our arrangement that will require adjustment. Your tavern is a handsome building in a very good location. Please take no offense, but I think it unwise to introduce my practice to Aurora from a tavern, no matter how fashionable an establishment it is. I must seek an office where my shingle can hang independently."

"Son, perhaps I underestimate your business acumen. I am pleased to welcome you as a neighbor and I am forced to agree with you."

Then, turning to his daughter-in-law, "Abiatha, would you kindly show Dr. Allen two buildings I own that may be options for his practice. Both will need some modification, which will be done at the good doctor's expense but my offer for waving the first three months' rent shall apply to either. I shall meet you both back here at noon to negotiate specifics." With that, the Colonel handed Abiatha two keys and departed for his morning errands.

Abiatha removed herself to wash the morning dishes during which time I was joined by Jerusha who told me of her initial fear and present joy with the move to Aurora she and the Colonel made all those years ago. She assured me I would find life in Aurora agreeable and she thought Abiatha was sharp as a tack, adding, "She will profit from finding herself new opportunities and situations."

Both potential office sites were uptown, near the Globe Hotel. Abiatha and I walked the quarter mile to the first store front, a former general store and larger than I could afford. The second was almost across from the Globe at the corner of Big Tree Road and Church Square. The shop's specialty had been custom leather working for saddles and harnesses with the scent of new leather still lingering. There was a front room, a back room and a storage area behind that on the first floor. The proprietor had lived in an upstairs room where he had installed an oversized stove with a side arm for cooking and a reservoir for heating water. It had good exposure on Big

Tree Road, provided a place to live, and I could continue to keep Parsley at the Globe's stables across the street. But insecurities naturally haunt me, causing Abiatha to point out that the Colonel wouldn't last long in a small village if he were not fair at business and a good landlord.

Her reassurance prompted me to ask, "How do you feel about the Colonel offering your employment as my assistant?"

Abiatha replied, "Mrs. Fillmore has shared in my grief and has been a great comfort, but the ties that bound us are broken and I fear my presence reminds her of loss. I doubt she will hurry me but I must agree, it is appropriate that I make my own situation."

After some measurements and discussion about placement of furniture and fixtures, there was still time for a walk around town and a casual job interview. Abiatha told me how her mother had died from consumption when she was seven and how she has been cooking and cleaning ever since.

"My father insisted I continue my schooling and most evenings I read aloud from the Bible just as Mama had done. On nights when the candle held out, he would ask me to finish with a few pages from Robinson Crusoe. We owned only one other book, a tattered Buchan's *Domestic Medicine*, to which we faithfully turned in times of illness. I loved solving Arithmetic problems on my chalk board and Papa put a penny in a jar whenever I earned extra credit. Then, when I was fourteen, father died in a lumbering accident working for General Warren. I had to quit school and earn my bed and board as a Nanny for a family with seven children. That family was as poor as any, but they were fair and the lady of the house taught me domestic particulars that I could not have learned on my own. I shared a bed with their two oldest daughters and being trusted with cleaning, cooking, gardening and mending made me feel safe. In spare hours, I worked problems in an Arithmetic book a teacher gave me my last day in school. Those Math skills secured a bookkeeping position at the Warren lumber mill where the Fillmores were frequent customers. It is there that I met the Fillmore boy I married, and despite my humble background, Jerusha warmed to me. After the birth of my son, we became quite close. But here I am, twenty-two years of age and on my own again, seeing opportunity in becoming a doctor's assistant. Dr. Allen, I assure you, I know business and figuring."

I realized we had stopped walking. On a day filled with decisions, the easiest was going to be hiring Abiatha.

Back at the Fillmore tavern Abiatha took directly to assisting Mrs. Fillmore in preparing the noon meal while the Colonel and I discussed business. He acknowledged my choice of office by saying, "How do you expect to pay for a fine facility like that on a doctor's income? A store front like that, in a good location, should net a landlord $20 a month based on a rent of $12 a month and three percent of the sales. In a doctor's case, I should think a similar arrangement would be fair."

Abiatha was making numerous trips through the dining room discreetly tracking our conversation and coaching my negotiations with a frown or a slight shake of her head. I countered at $8 a month and no payment on margin telling the Colonel that margin payments would limit my mission to treat all patients and accept barter as good as cash for those unable to pay.

Not to belabor our negotiation, nor recount the number of times Abiatha adjusted place settings in the dining room, I agreed to pay $12 a month rent, guaranteed for two years, payments to start immediately, and no margin on receipts.

We celebrated our arrangement over the noon meal graciously provided by the Fillmores. Then, it was time to negotiate with Abiatha. She started with a gentle rebuke for having agreed to $12 a month, convinced that the Colonel would have accepted $11 a month. Abiatha agreed to keep my accounts, greet patients, keep my office and quarters clean and perform other chores appropriate and necessary to serve patients for $4 a week. The only condition was her desire to assist Mrs. Fillmore at the tavern temporarily, if there were hours I did not need her.

Before I left Abiatha teased that she had been prepared to accept three seventy-five a week.

6. A Business Launch, 1834

You get into a fix and you get yourself out of a fix.

Early the next morning I took an accounting of my new office. Entering from the puncheon sidewalk, the front room and all rooms in the building were sixteen feet wide. The front room was eighteen feet deep. The room behind that was sixteen feet deep with a staircase against the back wall. The third room, which had been used for storage, had dozens of pegs and hardware for working leather. The apartment upstairs was all one room, sixteen feet wide and thirty-four feet deep. There were windows front and back and that large wood stove. About then Abiatha arrived with the broom, mop, pail, vinegar and lemon oil that she put to good use while I removed most of the hardware and fixtures in the back room.

Later, at Abiatha's suggestion, we visited the furniture maker, Arthur Fox, who by chance had a desk that proved too large for the man that ordered it and a table too small for another customer. He offered the desk, table and four matching chairs to me for immediate acquisition. While Abiatha negotiated a price on the available furniture, I made a sketch of a patient exam table with horse hair padding under a leather cover and hinged straps hidden off the backside to restrain patients undergoing procedures. I also ordered a four-poster bed, two three-legged stools, and four cupboards, one for personal use and three for office use. Before leaving I added a wooden chest to be placed at the foot of the bed. Again, Abiatha haggled a fair price with Mr. Fox and encouraged the earliest possible delivery. The ninety-six dollars of banknotes I transferred to Mr. Fox represented nearly one-sixth of my share of the Vermont family farm.

Next, Abiatha borrowed the Fillmore buckboard and we visited several stores to select cooking and cleaning supplies, bed linen, dry goods and a ledger. I also bought a night pot to save unlit trips to the community latrine and a wooden pail for fetching water from the main street pump. At each store, Abiatha introduced me as the new Doctor in town and crowed about how I was a graduate of Castleton, 'The best medical college outside of New York or Philadelphia.' If Abiatha were as good at Bookkeeping as she was at Marketing, I was destined for overnight success.

The last business for the day was hanging that shingle James had given me.

The next morning, I visited Almon Clapp's print shop and ordered a supply of business cards, invoices, envelopes and paper all printed with my name, address and office hours and my motto, 'No Cure, No Pay.'

Then I called on Dr. Hoyt for advice on obtaining medical supplies and to request his support for my application for a New York State license. Pragmatic as always he responded, "I hear you selected that store front at Main and Church Square for your office. Good location, if you can afford it. Medical supplies and drugs are the easy part. I will give you a list of mail order venders I have found reliable. Medical books I order from Cushing and Bailey in Baltimore, Maryland. They keep a good stock at good prices. Mail in an order today and the book is here by the next month. Same with drugs."

"And, as you likely know, New York passed one of the first Medical Practices Acts in 1806, but the legislators have been messing with it every year. The damn fools keep getting swayed by the Homeopaths wanting to sell their dilutions, and the Thomsonians wanting to sell their herbs. They think they deserve as much recognition as a Graduate Doctor, dismiss licensing as regular graduate doctors trying to monopolize medical practice, then buy what votes they need to get themselves included. Now the law is as irregular as a quack's practice. I tell you, quacks and sectarians are all the same, they read one book and think they're doctors."

Dr. Hoyt continued, "I suppose you should get a license, though the only advantage is that you can sue a patient for unpaid fees. You'll soon find out that the Homeopaths and Thomsonians demand their fees upfront, making us regulars the last to be paid. There is supposed to be a $25 fine if you practice medicine without a license, but no one's ever been fined. I guess there isn't any law to keep people from believing a quack.

"You got to apply to the Erie County Medical Society to get a license. John Watson and I are charter members and with our support I would expect smooth sailing. But you being a graduate of an out of state medical school means you'll need to pass an oral exam given by our Board of Censors. Buffalo is having a hell of a problem because the canal attracts all types of irregulars, so Watson and I need to convince the Board of Censors to schedule a hearing, get you examined, and get you a license by January 1835. In the meantime, just go ahead and practice. We need you to keep the quacks out of our town."

Dr. Hoyt went on to say the next semiannual Erie County Medical Society meeting would be in the first week of June. He generally boarded the stage coach for the three-hour ride to Buffalo the day before so he could attend all of the day long society meetings. Society business was conducted in the morning with lectures in the afternoon. He then caught the last afternoon stage out of Buffalo. There is a $1 fine for missing a Society meeting but usually he or Watson stay in Aurora and split the fine. With me in town they will both attend the June meeting.

I walked back to my office repeating "January, January, January!" Here I had nearly exhausted my resources signing a lease and ordering supplies and the earliest I could be licensed was January 1835!

I needed to pay rent. I needed to pay Abiatha. I needed to eat. The more circular my reasoning, the more alarmed and lonesome I felt. I had to keep walking to shake the image of firing my only employee, being evicted by Colonel Fillmore, or working in a lumber yard to stay out of pauper's prison. General Warren said there were Indian trails around the sinking ponds, so I headed there.

It took about two miles to find more rational thinking. Keeping abreast of new drugs challenged many physicians. The 1831 revision of the *United States Pharmacopoeia* resulted in three versions, one by a New York group, another by a Washington group, and a third when the Washington group revised their revision. All contained substantive changes from the first *Pharmacopoeia* of 1820.

More importantly, there were no regulations covering pharmacy or apothecary practice in 1834, so the sale and distribution of anything in the *Pharmacopoeia* required no license. Dr. Hoyt had grumbled about the burden of all these new formulas as much as he had about quacks and sectarians. Most remedies contained several ingredients and stocking them was both expensive and time consuming.

By the time I returned to my office Abiatha's cleaning efforts had replaced leather smells with that of soap and lemons. Abiatha liked my idea, "I've seen advertisements for drug stores in a Buffalo newspaper and think doctors and patients would welcome a reliable source for medicine, particularly if a little credible advice was included. You don't get advice in the general store."

That evening and much of the night I thought through a medical business aimed at protecting the citizens of Aurora from the uncontrolled and disorganized hawking of medicinal remedies. Put that way Drs. Hoyt and Watson might just go along with the idea. And, if they were sincere about wanting to add a graduate doctor to Aurora, this would accomplish their goal and relieve them of the time-consuming task of compounding drugs.

In the process, it may allow them to see more patients and actually enhance their own incomes.

As Abiatha said, the cities were already seeing stand-alone pharmacy practices. There were two pharmacy colleges in 1834, one in Philadelphia and a second in New York City. Most importantly, without requirements for a license I could start as soon as I could stock supplies.

We could market the business on assuring quality and protecting patients. The sectarians, irregulars, and outright frauds could hawk fantastic panaceas, but the public could be confident that only quality medicines listed in the *Pharmacopoeia* could be purchased in my store. Besides, my brother always said patients were more willing to pay for potions than they were for brains.

I wanted to be a regular doctor, but a drugstore could support my 'No Cure, No Pay' medical practice.

7. Mixing Physic and Pharmacy, 1834

The roots of medicine are deeply cultural and humanistic.

I paid another visit to Dr. Hoyt to describe my apothecary model, hoping he would see its potential and offer some advice. He wasn't happy. "Young man, what this village needs is a regular medical doctor to take care of them. That means going to their homes, getting to know their families, and applying the doctor's skills to their ailments. How are you going to do that from a store?"

I countered, "Serving the community is my intent. Your service to Aurora has blessed you with the affection of many patients and it seems Physic has provided you with an honest income and a warm coat. Waiting for a license challenges my ability to follow your worthy example. The current *United States Pharmacopoeia* lists 620 drugs. I'm sure you have little problem stocking your favorite compounds, but stocking seldom used agents eats into your income. If I can gain your trust and maintain a stock of active, high quality drugs, you will be relieved of this burden. I do not propose to be a dry goods grocer, but rather an assistant to good doctors like yourself and their patients. A drugstore will broaden your treatment options and lower your costs."

My logic apparently softened Dr. Hoyt's position. "Jabez, you sound more like Dr. Cyrenius Chapin than I would have thought on first impression. Chapin is a first-class businessman, physician and a former prisoner of the English during the War of 1812. Hell, the man invaded Canada! He practices in the heart of Buffalo, out of an office above the drugstore he owns. Chapin regularly takes on apprentices, some of whom find Chapin's various businesses more interesting than Physic. As a result, the man has quite a network of enterprises that will interest you. His drugstore is managed by Mr. George Keese, one of those former apprentices. Chapin is also a charter member of the Erie County Medical Society and a man of character with engaging stories easily told after a little whiskey. His acquaintance will advantage your Society application and I'm sure he can teach you something about the drugstore business."

Dr. Hoyt wrote a letter of introduction to Dr. Chapin and the next day I saddled Parsley for the 18-mile ride to Buffalo. Dr. Watson had been out on house calls so my drugstore conversation with him would have to wait.

Apothecaries were quite a mixed breed. Some druggists sold mostly patent medicines, of which there were thousands. Some maintained more of a laboratory where they experimented with European innovations, native medicines, and botanicals. Without apothecaries we wouldn't have guaiacum, sassafras, copaiba, Peru balsam or quinine. They often perform procedures and practiced much like regular doctors.

A good horse might cover forty miles a day, if given ample rest stops. Parsley quickly assumed a comfortable trot getting me into Buffalo in a little under three hours. It took another hour to find the Swan and Pearl Street office of Dr. Cyrenius Chapin. After reading Dr. Hoyt's letter of introduction, Dr. Chapin's wife was very welcoming. She expected the doctor home from house calls for the evening meal. In the meantime, she directed me to a nearby hotel and invited my return for dinner that evening.

After securing a room for the night and stabling Parsley, I visited the newly opened Commercial Bank of Buffalo and deposited $200 in bank notes drawn on the Bank of Vermont. It would take several weeks to clear the deposit but the clerk assured me I could begin drawing on my account within the month. I spent the afternoon visiting the terminus of the Erie Canal. In a penny pamphlet, I learned that Buffalo had been chosen over Black Rock for the canal's terminus because Lake Erie was slightly higher than the Niagara River and the amount of excavation was less. The population of Buffalo had more than doubled in the nearly ten years since the Canal opened and now exceeded 10,000 people. Late afternoon I spent an hour ambling through the drugstore below Dr. Chapin's office where I introduced myself to the very professional appearing Mr. Keese.

Mrs. Chapin had invited Orlando Allen to join us at dinner thinking we might find some kinship. We failed in that effort, but I was fascinated by the breadth of responsibility Mr. Allen had for the Chapin enterprises. Also, a former Chapin apprentice, Allen now managed Dr. Chapin's five farms, boasting hundreds of first class cattle and horses. Allen also directed the Erie County Agricultural Society that Dr. Chapin had started with several prominent men from Aurora.

When Dr. Chapin joined us, I found him much like Dr. Hoyt described, a man in his early sixties with contagious energy, broad shoulders and a robust personality. Upon Dr. Chapin's arrival his footman, a free black named James, served us each a glass of bourbon. Taking Dr. Hoyt at his word, I tried to get Chapin talking by asking how he came to Buffalo and was amply rewarded, "Hoyt probably told you, in 1803 I was Buffalo's first regular physician. It was nothing but a small village at the time and doctors on the frontier were few and far between. After years of being pushed around by those self-absorbed doctors in Niagara County, we finally managed to organize Erie County's own Medical Society in 1821 and I was damn proud to be elected its Founding President. Things needed shaking up so my first speech went right to the heart of troubles we had collecting on doctoring services in Buffalo. I sure got criticized for that one, but it had to be said. Why should a regular doctor live in poverty when these damn itinerate quacks get paid upfront for tonics and potions that contain nothing but cheap whiskey and sugar."

"But you want to know about getting a license. Well, the first thing the Society needed to do was to get Erie County into compliance with New

York's Medical Practice Act requiring county medical societies to regulate the practice of physic and surgery within the county. Back then we mostly needed to keep those damn sectarians from steeling our patient's money. Since the canal opened things are totally different. Now, like Boston, there's one hell of a lot of doctors in Buffalo. You know, we're in greater need of horses than doctors."

"Every little burg along this damn ditch they call a canal has got some smart aleck doctor who wants to start his own medical school. The New York State Medical Society claims there are now almost 4,000 physicians in New York. Communities like Aurora may still be looking for doctors but there sure are plenty of us in Buffalo. I stay in business only because I'm faithful to my patients, and they to me."

"Then too, there are plenty of idiots who say New York's licensing laws are just a way for our buddies in Albany to grant regular doctors a monopoly. Now Washington's got that damn fool President, Andrew Jackson, saying all men have equal potential, like it doesn't take effort to learn physic. Instead of realizing how easily a quack can kill you, Jackson wants to repeal all license laws. They want every blasted Homeopath, Hydropath and Thomsonian to have the same rights as trained, licensed regular doctors."

"We already have several fine Castleton graduates practicing in Buffalo. Your problem is that State law says being a graduate of a medical college outside of New York requires you to pass an oral exam given by the Erie County Medical Society's Board of Censors. Some of our younger members are using the law to keep out new doctors. The Board of Censors has declined to schedule a meeting for the past two years, effectively keeping any outsider from getting a license. Mostly everyone thinks highly of Dr. Hoyt and old man Watson, but I warn you, it may be an uphill battle getting you a license."

Either the whiskey or vexation put an edge to my response, "With all due respect to the Medical Society, I will practice physic in Aurora. I am a qualified medical college graduate recruited by Colonel Fillmore and General Warren, who know you from the war. I have the support of Dr. Hoyt and Dr. Watson, the men most affected by my presence. I have already signed a lease for an office and I need to make a living. Like you, I plan to open a drugstore capable of meeting the needs of the medical profession and citizens of the town of Aurora. I will not have doctors practicing a half-day's ride away keep me from practicing Physic."

"Calm down my boy. Dr. Hoyt's letter asks me to support your application and I will," Dr. Chapin said with a grin. "I like the way you define our profession. It's true, I have served Buffalo as a doctor, soldier, educator, farmer and businessman. It is a mission, I tell you, and I have done well by keeping to a solid code of conduct. Keep your spirit, boy. I'll ask Mr. Keese to spend some time with you in the morning and give you a few hints about the druggist business. If you have time you might also visit Ebenezer Johnson. He is another doctor who has combined Pharmacy with Physic practice in Black Rock."

Once the business of the evening was complete, Dr. Chapin told stories until the whale oil lamps began to dim and the whiskey jug went dry. I confess to no recollection which occurred first. I retired to my hotel realizing I had just learned a great deal about being a community's doctor, being successful, and enjoying life.

The next morning, I spent a couple of hours with Mr. Keese in the Chapin Drug Store. I should not have been surprised, but Dr. Chapin had already been to the store and asked him to accommodate my needs. Mr. Keese provided me with the store's inventory list, a gift of enormous value. He also wrote letters of introduction to several suppliers he recommended. Finally, he would not let me depart without a letter of introduction to Dr. Ebenezer Johnson.

I made the six-mile ride to Black Rock, now merged with Buffalo, and visited Dr. Johnson's store. Dr. Johnson was also the Mayor of Buffalo and rumors claimed he was the wealthiest man in Buffalo. After a couple of hours waiting in his store taking notes on his inventory and observing customer transactions, I left my letter of introduction and a thank-you note with the store manager. Johnson's store was more like a general store than I had in mind but I learned some things about how general merchandise can support drug sales. With Parsley fed and watered, we took off for the long ride to Aurora.

Three-quarters of the way home I stopped at the North Star tavern where Parsley could rest, water and finish the oats I carried. I celebrated a productive day with a good meal and a private whiskey. I had a good location, a capable assistant in Abiatha, the confidence of a man like Dr. Chapin, and a genuine excitement about my predicament.

It was dark by the time I reached the Globe. I stabled Parsley and welcomed a peaceful night's rest.

8. Open for Business, 1834

Start where you are.

The next morning, Abiatha encouraged me to sit at my new desk and write a business plan for a combined Physic and Pharmacy practice. It's more accurate to say that Abiatha mandated a process she observed General Warren update annually. Abiatha said budget projections would focus my attention, making it more likely expenses and income would balance. A couple of patients drifted in and I treated them with the compounds I could prepare from my saddle bags. Both promised to return within the week to pay my fee.

After church that week, I saddled Parsley for a casual ride around my new town. Once off of Big Tree Road there was a frame house every two or three rods and still the occasional log cabin. I passed several small milling operations and a tannery on a creek just a block north of Big Tree Road. I rode old Indian trails around the sinking ponds noting how on such a sunny spring day the ponds' reputation for miasma and malarial afflictions seemed unwarranted.

After a pleasant meal, I retired to my room at the Globe to reconcile the inventory Mr. Keese had provided with the budget Abiatha and I had established. In the office, the next morning, it became obvious that even a limited order for drugs and supplies was consuming a huge portion of my new bank account and all options beyond Aurora would be eliminated. In the few weeks since leaving Vermont I no longer suffered what my sister called "shiftless determination." I was now a fretful businessman.

Several attempts to visit Dr. Watson found him either out on a call or busy with patients. His wife served as his assistant and declined to make any arrangements for Dr. Watson after hours. I had only one brief, but polite, encounter in his waiting room and had to assume his comment, "Fine location young man," was the most advice I would garner from Dr. Watson.

There were few patients those first few weeks, so I spent much of my time constructing benches in the hope that soon there would be patients to wait on them. I also built a long, chest high counter along the right side of the front room that transitioned along the back to a desk level work area facing the street. Finally, I built shelves along the right side and back wall of the front room for display and storage of drugs.

I engaged Mr. Waldo, the painter, to letter the front window and was quite pleased with the result. He painted my name in eight-inch letters curved above smaller letters declaring 'Physician and Surgeon.' Below that he arranged 'Quality Drugs and Medical Advice.' And finally, concave to my name he painted the moto adopted from one of my brother's maxims, 'No Cure, No Pay.'

For the few patients who drifted in we charged 50 cents if they wanted a private consultation. I found that I enjoyed these consultations and learned a great deal about the view people take toward medicines, about what they understand, and what they misunderstand about physician prescribed compounds and patent tonics. Slowly my patient base grew.

An expectant intonation supported by a pleasant smile made Abiatha adept at collecting. She made simple direct statements about charges that sounded like persuasive invitations. I sounded apologetic. I made several home visits but only once was I paid before leaving.

At the end of the fourth week Abiatha aimed her direct, pleasant but persuasive voice on me. "Dr. Allen, I regret to say that I will be seeking a different employment situation. I am obliged to alter my circumstances with the Fillmores, though they carefully avoid the subject. To be independent I require a financially stable situation. You are a kind man with high ideals, but I fear your venture will fail. You have paid me every Friday, and I appreciate that. But no business can survive without collecting fees. I do wish you good fortune, and promise to give you adequate notice before leaving."

I was thunderstruck. Without effort or forethought, I had allowed myself to depend on Abiatha. I genuinely liked her and felt secure in her ability and judgement. Perhaps my sister was right, I find dependency easy.

"Abiatha, my practice needs you. No, that is only partly true, I need you. In these few weeks, I have admired your strength and taken advantage of your courage. Establishing a practice may be my test, but you are my instructor. Truth is, I cannot conceive of making it without you."

There followed several moments of silence. Abiatha's brown eyes naturally show an empathic expression, but at this moment they indicated resolve.

Finally, Abiatha responded, "Dear Dr. Allen, I will begin a casual search for another situation, but you must start thinking in business terms. You cannot do good, if you cannot sustain your business. I have known General Warren to forgive debts for families falling on hard times, but he knows what his costs are and how to accommodate his goodwill. You must learn the same skills. If you are willing, I will rejoin your efforts to establish a budget, even one that incorporates your 'No cure, No pay' idealism. Perhaps we can make it work. For now, I pledge to return tomorrow for our usual Saturday morning hours. If you are serious, and willing, after hours we can revisit a plan for success."

With this, we shook hands, as would any two partners facing a crossroads.

9. Getting Organized, 1834

Begin where you are; accomplish what you can.

Abiatha's proposed resignation got my attention. That Saturday afternoon and evening Abiatha and I reexamined expenses and revenues based on four weeks' experience. Using the ledger that we purchased, Abiatha listed building overhead, merchandise, drugs, equipment and supplies like she had done for the lumber yard. On another page, we calculated the number of patients I needed to see and the number of drugs I needed to compound in order to cover my expenses. Abiatha suggested pricing all compounds at twice the supplier charge and add a preparation fee based on 50 cents an hour.

Abiatha assured me, "At General Warren's lumber mill they taught me to calculate the cost of obtaining and milling lumber, then charge the customer double that amount. Everything, including the tools they sell, are priced at twice what it cost to get the tool into the store and ready for sale. That's called a fifty-percent markup." The rigor of her calculations was a whole lot more formal than the way my brother did business. While it was clear I was going broke, having an Abiatha calculated target for profitability lessened my apprehension.

Monday morning our first customer was Mrs. Murray who wanted to buy a fifty-cent bottle of Anderson's Pills on credit. Edinburgh's Dr. Patrick Anderson markets these pills worldwide to clean the bowels after over-indulgence. They contain Aloe and the two purgatives Colocynth and Gamboge.

Abiatha motioned me aside to whisper, "Are these pills vital to a person's health?"

I assured her that they were not considered important enough to be listed in the *United States Pharmacopeia*. Abiatha politely informed Mrs. Murray that, because the pills were imported, we could only accept cash payment. Just as politely Mrs. Murray said she would return the next day to pay. Abiatha assured her that the pills would be ready for her when she returned.

As the door closed on Mrs. Murray, Abiatha explained, "I know the Murray family well. You might have noticed her fine clothes and nice new hat. Mr. Murray keeps his wife on short tether that simply does not match her aspirations. She is known to owe money to every business in town. If you gave her credit she would become a frequent customer, until you ask for payment."

Our second patient was accustomed to a routine spring bleeding to maintain what appeared to be excellent health. I obliged him by removing sixteen ounces of blood in my surgery. He was quite pleased and as he paid my fee he told Abiatha that we seemed organized and competent.

By the end of the week Abiatha listed our charges on poster paper that we hung behind the counter.

Dr. Jabez Allen: Table of charges (1834)
Drug Management Advice: 50 ₵
Ordinary Home Visit under one mile: $1
Each additional mile: 25 ₵ (Reduced if feed provided to doctor's horse)
Obstetrics, ordinary, not over six hours: $5; complicated: $20
Catheter, single introduction: $2
Venesection (Including: Bloodletting, cupping, blistering.) office: 50 ₵; in home: 75₵

Application of Leeches: $2 per application (may vary with market and availability)
Vaccination, single patient: $5
Pulling a tooth: 50¢
Extirpation of tonsils: $10
Cutting for bladder stones: $50
Removal of fingers or toes: $1
Removal of testicle: $25
Amputation (Leg, Arm): $30
Reduction of thigh fracture: $10
Other fractures: $5
Dislocation Reduction: $10 (fingers $5)
Pumping stomach: $5
Most Pharmacy items: Priced individually.
Minimum Charge: 50¢, $1 with advice.

That week I made a house call to a farm four miles out of town. The calculated visit charge was $1.75. I also left four doses of medicine with the family. Before leaving the home, I tallied my total charges at $2.25 and, using my best imitation of Abiatha, I was paid on the spot. I planned to crow a bit upon my return, but Mr. Fox was unloading my newly built furniture and the second wave of my medicine order had been delivered.

Drugs ship as powders or bricks. To compound a medication, I shave off what is needed, weigh it and mixed it in a mortar and pestle with other components as called for in the prescription. Often as not, I mixed in a little jam, maple sugar or cherry juice to ease its reception.

By the second shipment the store was stocked with senna, sugar, the red dye cochineal, rhubarb, Epsom salts, cinchona bark, incense, cream of tartar, American ipecac, opium, borax, tartar emetic, medicinal wine, olive oil, calomel, divine cordial, bougies, rubber catheters, various surgical instruments, lances, carbolic acid infused catgut sutures, syringes, white arsenic, black bromide, cupping glasses, and a barrel of sauerkraut for treating the Scurvy. The store was now a place of wooden boxes, drawers, jars, carboys and medicinal odors.

Each day we greeted a few new patients. Some wanted remedies suggested by their home medical books and were pleased to receive a little inexpensive practical advice. Everyone was invited to return for a doctor visit should further attention be needed. Gradually patients appeared with written prescriptions from Drs. Hoyt and Watson. Then a few from Dr. Wallis who practiced in the lower village and treated a lot of eye conditions requiring medicines applied by a dropper. Those I compounded using distilled water and a careful measure of salt with the active ingredients as ordered.

Abiatha's curiosity was boundless. She learned to dispense a few common medicines, carefully following every detail of my instructions and began to serve customers with routine needs. Customers also brought in empty bottles asking if we could provide a refill. The labels on patent medicines usually boasted a "secret" ingredient and tasted like alcohol and a bitter hint of dissolved opium. I enquire as to the nature of the problem and recommend either an alternative or a medical evaluation. Only about one in four wanted an evaluation, but slowly my medical practice grew.

Opium was shipped as a sticky, yellowish brick, which I compounded into Laudanum, a bitter tasting one-to-ten mixture of opium dissolved in brandy. I used it to treat pain, cough, anxiety, dysentery, menstrual troubles, or simply to improve mood. Four drops of Laudanum also relieve the many symptoms of teething.

Professors at Castleton warned that the occasional patient will experience a rapid return of symptoms when stopping medicines containing opium. Those predisposed to morally intemperate behaviors may even develop a craving for opium tonics. Patrons of "red door" opium establishments in

New York City, Philadelphia and Buffalo are thought to be victims of this latter effect. Those of decent and honorable habits have little to fear but sometimes a slow taper is desired until all signs of the patient's infirmity are resolved.

Shortly after opening my store a Pharmacist in New York City, Ewen McIntyre, reported that a shipment of calcium carbonate from England actually contained calcium sulfate. This is exactly the type of fraud from which I intended to protect my patients. Soon newspapers carried reports of other druggists finding adulterated shipments. Reputable suppliers began enclosing an analysis of their drug lots and I refused orders from those who did not, testing what I could in my store and including a printed guarantee with my preparations. Most doctors did not have capacity for such testing, so my note of guarantee attracted their attention.

I also took to requiring all prescriptions to be written in Latin to weed out those written by non-graduate doctors and quacks. A few complained that Latin simply concealed the ingredients, but the truth is that Latin gives every article a specific title and reduces errors. I would then write clear directions on how patients should take their medications. I believe my quality guarantee and clear directions established my willingness to take responsibility for my work and reassured patients and doctors alike.

Graduate doctors can be more critical of each other than they are of quacks. Serving doctors, as well as their patients, made my business vulnerable to pejorative comments. I took care to speak no ill will of any graduate physician because the truth is that the prescribing physician had examined the patient and I had not. Once a physician selected a remedy, it was my obligation to compound the medicine correctly using pure and unadulterated drugs. If one of my own house calls took me near the practice of a referring physician, I stopped by and thanked them. Soon I knew all the graduate doctors within ten miles of Aurora, and liked the lot of them.

When a physician or their immediate family needed a medicine from my store for personal use I supplied it at no charge. However, I never paid a kick-back fee for a referral and if a customer asked for a recommendation, Abiatha allowed them to look at an alphabetical list of doctors in their area and offered no particular endorsement.

Soon I had regularly scheduled home visits. Parsley and I carried what supplies I could pack into two leather saddlebags connected to each other by a thick, broad two-foot-long leather strap with a hole that fit over the saddle horn. I carried powders, liquids, and hand rolled pills as well as my lance, cutting knife, forceps, lint, ligatures, sponge, bandages, plasters, catheters, stomach pump, syringe, splints, caustics, heating iron, sutures, and a tourniquet. I carried a bit of opium but whiskey was the most common anesthetic and was provided by the patient. When treating the lady of the house I politely referred to whiskey as brandy, spirits or tonic.

When I arrived at a home I carried my saddlebags to the bedside. I started all exams by placing my hand on the forehead, a habit I continued long after obtaining a portable thermometer in 1850. Next, I would characterize the pulse, look at the tongue and the skin, and consider the patient's general appearance. Only then did I ask about symptoms, where it hurt, and question their appetite and bowel movements. I ended every exam by applying my stethoscope to the patient's chest, back and stomach. The stethoscope was my image maker. Not only was the information it obtained a mystery to the patient, but few doctors used one in the 1830s.

Soon I was doing well enough to engage Mr. Fox in the construction of an operating chair for my surgery. He built an excellent adjustable chair of wood and leather with a matching cabinet and wheeled stool. The chair became my favorite way to see patients and I think patients enjoyed the sense of ascending to a throne for their consultation.

Abiatha proved to be genuinely clever, with an instinct for business. Every payday I thanked her for some clever thing she had done and she would laugh, "Clever be daft, it's pure ambition, aggressive honesty and hard work that's paying the bills." I never did understand what "aggressive honesty" meant but I was glad it was on our side. Abiatha freed me to enjoy the intellectual challenge of medicine and contemplate the passions that governed our patients.

The modest upstairs living quarters proved a comfortable situation supplemented by the occasional meal at the Globe or the Fillmore tavern, or a whiskey with Hiram Barney. Routines were settling in when young Millicent Johnson delivered a hand-written invitation to join her and her brother for a lecture by abolitionist George Washington Jonson with a reception to follow at their home.

10. An Evening with the Underground, 1834

Lives well lived are filled with complexities.

The lingering June sun and a gentle breeze made for a pleasant carriage ride to the Congregationalist Church with William Johnson and his fiancé Rebecca Brigham as Millicent schooled me about George Washington Jonson.

"We would be proud to claim Mr. Jonson, who likes to be called GWJ, as a relative but his last name suffers the loss of an "h". GWJ taught school in Aurora and wrote law with William under Millard Fillmore before he became an agent for the Holland Company. He then acquired ten acres of downtown Buffalo property that he divided and resold a profit sufficient to support his current life as a gentleman scholar. GWJ is now known as an anti-slavery activist with a knack for charming newspaper headlines."

Hiram Barney was just entering the church when we arrived and Millicent seemed to gush over the happenstance encounter. My annoyance surprised me when she asked him to join us.

GWJ began his lecture by declaring that, "Many free Negros have worked hard, purchased their own land, and now pay taxes just like the white man. Like all taxes, their taxes support the courts, the roads, and the schools. It is not kindness to provide the Negro access to public services, it is justice."

Jonson described the 1834 National Convention of the Free People of Color held at the Asbury Church in New York City. And, he spoke of the encouragement his friend Millard Fillmore provided to Gerrit Smith, Frederick Douglass and William Lloyd Garrison in organizing the Liberty Party. He followed with several inspiring stories, including, "Sunday past the citizens of Buffalo assisted a fugitive slave who had been seized by two agents of a Kentucky slave owner. It was no less than the hand of God that moved the mingling crowd, separated the agents from their prey, and concealed the Negro in the city's embrace. Witnesses declared the event as astonishing as parting of the Red Sea."

He implored the audience, "Pity unaccompanied by resolve is of little consequence. You must to do more than pity the plight of the Negro. Each of us, and all of us in an immoral society will find misery on our day of judgement." Exciting rhetoric filled with urgency that gave me pause to reflect on how dim the flame of political activism burned within me.

After the lecture, GWJ and Hiram joined us for brandy at the Johnson home. In the safe confines of their sitting room I learned that Millicent and William championed the Fugitive Slave Movement. With New York making slavery illegal in 1827 and England's King William doing the same for Canada in 1833, Western New York was becoming a gateway to safe harbor for the runaway.

Millicent described the structure, "Jabez, after the King's proclamation, the first Anti-Slavery Society in Erie County was organized at the Griffins Mills Presbyterian Church. Judge Phelps of Aurora, Daniel Bowen of Buffalo, and our friend GWJ were among the founding activists. Most of us work in the shadows because moving slaves requires self-directed actions by invisible activists. By contrast, GWJ works in the open to make slavery an issue of human rights instead of property rights. His task is to remove the blemish of slavery from the United States Constitution."

GWJ put the movement this way, "Dr. Allen, let me paraphrase William Lloyd Garrison. Contrary to all American values, slave owners buy and sell humans. If these are not acts of monsters, I should like to know by what name they shall be called?"

The Johnsons were taking a risk in revealing their secrets to Hiram and me. "I am humbled by your activism, and the confidence you show in me by revealing secrets hidden within Aurora's homes. There are those in Vermont that shelter and transport fugitive slaves, but until tonight I gave only passing thought about their plight. My father hired men when he needed them. He thought it foolish to own slaves and be obligated to feed them year-round when hired labor demanded less responsibility and less expense. I never understood the rationale for slavery."

With a hint of scold, Millicent responded, "You sound like a typical northern businessman. If you think Southerners are willing to consider any system different from their granddaddy's, just read George Fitzhugh. He fancies slaves to be better off than wage labor, and that cotton grows only because slaves get whipped if it doesn't. Oratory like you heard tonight is essential, if slavery is to be abolished. In the meantime, we must assist every human soul willing to run. I cannot be passive!"

William picked up my theme, "Don't be too hard on Jabez. Andrew Jackson and his Democrats would have us believe that every American should be sovereign unto himself. But I see political power shifting from rural America to the cities. Eventually that will redefine America. The Whigs' Henry Clay has promised to protect the rights of all citizens and end slavery. The problem is that slaves are the most unrepresented minority group in America. I just don't see a political solution for slavery's curse. Slavery will end only when slave owners realize its economic burden. The cotton gin is the first step in changing the economics of cotton. Just as Jabez suggests, a mechanized south will sour on the economics of slavery. Until that day comes, no political party that acts on the abolition of slavery will prosper. One reason to assist the fugitive slave is to increase the cost of slave ownership."

GWJ picked up on William's theme, "Ah, if only we could force slave owners to pay the costs of sheltering penniless runaways. It is not easy to raise funds for ventures performed in shadows. We call our collections North Star Funds, leaving only the informed to understand our need."

The Johnsons described a secret highway of homes, barns, cellars, and taverns called 'stations' that provide safety for the runaway while 'conductors' arrange and organize transports of slaves who are called 'freight.' I learned that Dr. John Watson and his brother, Dr. Ira Watson in a village four miles east of Aurora, are station masters but nothing is written down because written records facilitate prosecution. Runaways are generally ferried across the Niagara River to the Elgin Settlement in Buxton, Ontario, where the Mission Committee of the Presbyterian Church and the Quakers of Orchard Park support simple accommodations and job training.

Millicent believed we all should be humbled by the fugitive's courage. One couple escaped with only their nursing infant child. Once established in Elgin, the wife, disguised as a man, slipped back to the Kentucky plantation. Hiding near a spring, she conspired with her oldest boy to flee with the remaining children in the dead of night. Without food, they traveled continuously for three nights to a station in Ripley, New York, then to Fredonia, Arcade and Aurora. Having assisted this woman on all three passages through Aurora, Millicent said, "I was filled with joy at seeing that woman and her children on their last leg to freedom, like the rapture at the gates of heaven. The Underground Railroad is an adventure of piracy, secrecy, and daring seldom available to women."

GWJ provided a broader context, "The stories generated by fugitives and shared in the parlors of American homes are the most effective way to bring attention to abolitionist principles. Most northerners don't give slavery much thought until they hear a story like Millicent's. What Millicent calls an Underground Railroad is an act of mass civil disobedience in the tradition of the American Revolution. William and Millicent, by the luxury their father's success made possible, have turned his revolutionary idealism into activism."

I couldn't leave the subject without asking GWJ what he thought of New Orleans Dr. Samuel Cartwright. Cartwright claims his many autopsies confirm the Negro is strong, less susceptible to malarial illness, and has a brain that is eleven percent smaller. The slave owner who ministers to the Negro's physical needs and protects him from abuse easily renders his inferior intellect spell-bound. According to Cartwright, slavery is not only God's intent, it is the Negro's salvation. Cartwright also describes 'mental alienation' as a disease specific to the Negro that provokes him to run away from responsibilities. Once affected, only a whipping will keep him from absconding.

Cartwright's rationalizations were well known to GWJ and he returned the question, asking me what influence Cartwright held over the medical profession.

I continued, "Journals are filled with essays both condemning and supporting Cartwright. If I had to render an opinion, I would say that the regular medical profession suffers the same prejudices as the rest of America. Southern doctors, like Cartwright, see slaves only in the context of slavery. As a Northerner, I have only treated the occasional free Negro and given little consideration to their situation. There is one thing I am certain of: I cannot think of myself being owned, whipped or sold."

GWJ responded, "I assume then that you would oppose conducting medical experiments on slaves? I speak of Alabama's Dr. Sims who writes of a technique for repairing vaginal fistulas he perfected on Negro women strapped to a table. Or, Dr. Thomas Hamilton's experiments to determine the maximum heat a Negro can tolerate before dying. While claiming the Negro is different from the Caucasian, these monsters apparently think them similar enough for experimentation?"

I responded, "Yes, and autopsies conducted at Bellevue Hospital in New York refute Cartwright's findings, but get little attention compared to the agitations of Sims, Hamilton and Cartwright. I can only conclude that the culture of slavery requires a belief that the enslaved person is inferior."

Hiram rose to provide the evening's closure by quoting Thoreau, "Being free is all about being your own man. If people around you are doing wrong, you must leave them and do right. You fight them by not being part of them. Only then will they realize the burden of their evil."

We were just a few steps out of the Johnson home when a grinning Hiram poked me in the ribs, "You and Millicent appeared quite impressed with each other tonight. I thought maybe the rest of us were invisible. She is a handsome lady and you are an eligible bachelor. It will not be long before honor will demand that you declare your intentions, Dr. Allen!"

All I would confess was this had been the first evening since arriving in Aurora that my attentions were distracted from a total absorption with myself and my practice. It was a welcomed respite.

Part Two: Rational Medicine

11. Licensing and Medical Societies, 1834

There may be no natural way to organize medicine.

In preparation for the Erie County Medical Society biannual meeting on 4 June 1834 I copied every word from my Castleton diploma onto poster paper. My drugstore was now the stagecoach stop for several coach lines that crisscross Aurora, so I handed Dr. Hoyt the envelope with the completed application and the copied diploma as he boarded the Buffalo bound stagecoach to meet with Dr. Chapin and present my request for membership.

Six graduate doctors applied for licensure at that meeting. The others were Drs. Francis L. Harris, James P. White, H.N. Munson, L.B. Benedict and Silas Smith. Dr. White grew up in Livingston County, New York, graduated from Jefferson Medical College in Philadelphia but had apprenticed with the prominent Dr. Trowbridge of Buffalo. Training in New York meant an automatic approval for all of them.

Immediately upon his return to Aurora Dr. Hoyt assailed me, "Jabez, what possessed you to give me a hand-written copy of your diploma? Cyrenius and I presented your documents and vigorously defended your professional ethics and abilities. But, the opposition mounted a vigorous challenge and claimed inadequate proof of medical college graduation. I had no option but to ask your application be tabled."

Anticipation melted into defeat. Frustration forced me to leave the office and walk out a rage that corkscrewed around Dr. Hoyt's anger, my own foolishness, and the society's games.

I thought I might find Hiram for a couple of whiskeys, but my legs took me to the Johnson home. Without hesitation, Millicent grabbed a sweater and walked me back out into the cool June evening. A few steps later I was spilling my troubles and condemning myself.

Millicent's effort to calm me, "Jabez, you just gave the scoundrels a pretext" was enough to send me into a full-scale harangue, ripping both the Medical Society and my impetuous nature. Millicent held my arm, listened and walked.

The worries, frustrations, and fears of a young man in a new town spilled out in a self-absorbed rant. I described a life of procrastination, my mother's death, my brother James' reluctance to take me on as a partner and my brother-in-law's acquisition of our family farm. Vermont was happy to see me go and it was now clear that Aurora was foolish to take me in. I had just about exhausted my self-pity when Millicent kissed my cheek. It was just a peck really. Defeatism crumbled.

Perhaps all events, when examined, turn on simple acts. At our first meeting I found Millicent attractive, fascinating and well informed. After GWJ's lecture I found her adventuresome and filled with political idealism. The evening of my rant, I realized her compassion. Fifty-years later, my cheek flushes with recollection.

We walked a while longer and eventually found ourselves back at the Johnson home. I thanked Millicent. Before I left, I kissed her.

The next week I received a letter from Dr. Gorham F. Pratt, Secretary of the Erie County Medical Society, confirming Dr. Hoyt's account. My application would be eligible for reconsideration at the January 1835 meeting. No Board of Censors exam would be scheduled. I needed to learn everything possible about licensing in New York and what it meant to my practice. Dr. Hoyt, General Warren and Dr. Chapin all suggested I write to the State Medical Society. They responded with several pamphlets written by the Albany County Medical Society.

Licensing in New York was a mess.

During this time young Chad Haven ran into my store shouting, "My dad's powerful sick and his doctor refuses to do anything. Mom says you got to come quick!"

I saddled Parsley and followed the boy ten miles to the village of Boston. Chad's mother, Millie Haven, had been told that her husband Jasper had "inflamed paralysis of the bowels caused by obstinate constipation." Bragging that he was not a homeopath who dabbled in infinitesimals, that doctor administered 33 grains of mercury calomel, half an ounce of oil of turpentine, and 28 drops of croton oil, all listed on the bill he insisted be paid before he left. This was five times the usual dose of calomel and the croton oil is such a powerful purgative that a few drops will burn the skin. Turpentine oil is usually reserved for eliminating intestinal worms. The man clearly belonged on the list Dr. Hoyt kept of unlicensed quacks.

Thirty-eight-year-old Jasper Haven was in a dreadful state. He writhed with intense abdominal pain and showed evidence of calomel overdose with salivation, loose teeth, and grey pallor. All I could offer was several doses of opium and hope that he would live long enough to recover. Eight hours after my arrival, Jasper Haven died. Murdered by an ignorant quack. I left no bill for Millie Haven.

Quacks with no education and no license give doctoring a bad name. The Medical Society might deny a qualified doctor his license, but it has no power to remove a dangerous quack from practice. And, murder by quack goes unpunished if the quack calls himself a doctor.

I poured over the pamphlets from the Albany County Medical Society. They thought graduate doctors acted like a trade and should reorganize as a profession. Licensing will never do more than establish minimum standards, but a self-governing profession could enforce higher standards including: Rigorous medical training, continuous learning, peer interaction, and scientific publication. A profession could enforce the Society's 1823 Code of Ethical Conduct that included obtaining consultation in difficult cases. Only those practicing by these standards could call themselves a member of the profession.

The Thomsonians, Homeopaths and Hydropaths argued that graduate doctors were nothing special, often diluting drugs and using botanicals. Testifying before the New York Legislature, Thomsonians claimed it was the inalienable right of a patient to request care from any practitioner. The Society pamphlets dismissed these claims as the culture of Jacksonian populism and claimed that Physic was a science backed by two-thousand years of rational examination of internal balances defined by Galen's humors. When blood, phlegm, black bile or yellow bile became unbalanced the organs produce byproducts that overtax the liver and congest the vasculature and cause illness. Bleeding and forced bowel activity are, "Established medical practices. They are rational and have stood the test of time and should not be abandoned on a sectarian whim."

There were also forces challenging Physic from within. Large hospitals in Europe were admitting large numbers of patients with similar ailments, exposing patterns of disease previously unrecognized. Physicians based in those hospitals were keeping patient registries, comparing treatment outcomes, and even experimenting with remedies. New findings were being published, and republished in a rapidly expanding medical literature supplemented by regional medical journals. Single case reports analyzed by nothing more than the author's opinion and rationalizations were giving way to large, multiple case series from Paris, Berlin, Edinburgh, and more recently from Philadelphia and New York. Recently some reported mysterious microscopic animalcules in the phlegm, pus, urine and blood of fever patients.

The Albany pamphlets conceded that county medical societies had become little more than trade guilds, protecting the local interests of doctors. Rules were so arbitrary that some medical societies admitted homeopaths. Massachusetts passed its first licensing law in 1819, but annually debated its repeal. Illinois passed their first law in 1819, repealed it in 1821, reinstated it in 1825, finally abolishing the law in 1826. Ohio, my intended destination, once had a strict licensing law that was repealed in 1825 and Georgia licensed Thomsonians herbalists. Now only thirty percent of those calling themselves 'doctor' in New York had attended a medical college.

New York's original 1806 Bill included a $25 fine for practicing medicine without a license but that was rescinded in 1807. The only remaining legal advantage to being licensed was the right to recover unpaid fees in Court. In a practical sense, a license meant nothing.

Adding to the problem, medical colleges were popping up in small towns all along the canal and producing more than 100 New York State graduate doctors each year. Competition for students was so high that admission standards were dropped and exams were eliminated. Dr. John Watson would soon quit the Erie County Medical Society over what he called the Society's 'political shenanigans.'

Dr. Erastus Wallis of Aurora's lower village was a member of Erie County's Board of Censors and in line to be its President. He explained it this way, "The Censors are only paid if their deliberations result in an applicant's approval, so once convened applicants are seldom rejected. Societies face a conundrum, standards need to be high enough to make membership valuable, but more members generate more dues and greater political influence. Also, failing a candidate attracts adverse newspaper stories and lawsuits. Like Erie County, most counties simply refuse to convene their Board Censors."

There being no licensing laws covering apothecaries, I resolved to practice good medicine and good pharmacy without a license. But, my resolve did not stop me from coveting the peer recognition and prestige I associated with a license. Also, I supported Erie County Medical Society's efforts to promote community wide Smallpox vaccination and improve birth and death records.

So, I continued to write letters and in the process secured the friendship of Dr. Horace Camp who represented the Erie County Medical Society in Albany. He kept me informed of the statewide entanglements, including news that New York's Thomsonians had collected 50,000 signatures on a petition that demanded full licensure. The Legislature's response was to do nothing.

So, as the summer of 1834 progressed, I determined that with Abiatha's business acumen, my good intentions, and a kiss from Millicent, I was going to make my Aurora venture a success.

12. A Case of Melancholia, 1834

Caring for patients affords a window to the human soul, theirs and mine.

I was on house calls when Millicent Johnson left a neatly printed note reminding me of her invitation to the Johnson's regular Friday evening salon. The topic for discussion next Friday was a proposal before the Village Council to erect a monument of Commodore Oliver Hazard Perry, the Hero of Lake Erie.

Two villages in Western New York were named in honor of Commodore Perry, who in 1813, lead his ships in nine decisive victories over the British navy in the Battle of Lake Erie. His battle flag proclaimed, 'Don't give up the ship!' but he is best known for a report to his Commander and future United States President, William Henry Harrison, that read, 'We have met the enemy and they are ours.' Now a local citizen's group wanted Aurora to erect a statue honoring Perry. Controversy arose because since the war Perry was court martialed for engaging a fellow officer in a duel.

Friday evening the assembled guests yielded to a conclusion that Commodore Perry's memory would not benefit appreciably by another statue. The food and wine were exceptional and two guests who had served with Perry kept the conversation spirited. As the guests were leaving William Johnson asked if I might stay for a brandy nightcap and ushered me into the library where Millicent and William's fiancée Rebecca were waiting. The hour was late, so William got right to the point, "Jabez, we would like your opinion, and perhaps your assistance. Millicent and I are deeply concerned about our mother and hope that you might help."

In the year since the death of Captain Samuel Johnson, their mother, the elder Millicent Johnson, had become a recluse who seldom left her rooms on the second floor. William and Rebecca were engaged to be married shortly before Mr. Johnson's death but had postponed the wedding date out of fear the festivities might prove too taxing for mother Millicent's frail condition.

Taking William's hand, Rebecca added, "Jabez, I fear further delay might put a strain on our engagement. We are very much in love and eager for marriage but my father questions William's commitment with every delay. At present, we have plans, but no date."

William continued, "Mother did allow Dr. Hasack to visit once, but as you know, Dr. Hasack suffered an unexpected death and Mother has refused any other medical attention. In the last several months she admits only one lady friend who brings mother a bottle of Dover's powder each week. Mother dissolves the Dover's powder in brandy and takes several doses a day. Jabez, I fear our mother's health is deteriorating and hope you might consent to see her."

Straightaway I switched on the professional persona that cohabitates with the social me, "Dover's powder is a very popular combination of ipecacuanha and opium. In moderate doses, it stimulates the bowels and soothes the nervous system. Forgive my implication, but does your mother have a history of melancholia?"

Now Millicent spoke, "At the risk of upsetting William, who resolutely protects mother, I have always thought our mother possesses a weak nature. I may be struck by the hand of God for saying this, but mother was seventeen years younger than our father and I have always thought he addressed her as one would a child. That he loved her I am certain, but he was often brusque and his tone more of a disciplinarian than an adoring husband. Even as a child I would recoil at her tolerance of his patronizing ways."

With unflinching resolution, Millicent continued, "I loved my father but will never tolerate such treatment from a man. Mother coped by silent withdrawal. I believe she suffers an unremitting guilt that she could not be the wife he seemed to desire, though in fact I think she was. Unfortunately, that guilt now seems to consume her and I worry she may now be insane."

Friendship complicates delivering medical advice. Though most of my patients become friends, it is different when the sequence of acquaintance is reversed. When friends ask for medical advice I wonder if they seek the simple support of a friend or if they want the objective evaluation of a Physician. I deferred once again to a 'Dr. Allen' response, likely coming across as a lecture.

"Philadelphia's Benjamin Rush wrote that melancholia, depression and insanity are a spectrum of diseases associated with exhaustion of the mind. I favor the view taken by Professor Griesinger, Director of the German school of medical psychology. Griesinger writes that melancholia is a disease of the brain characterized by delusions fixated on a specific topic. The patient suffers a debilitating sadness, not uncommonly associated with hypochondriasis and vague feelings of oppression, anxiety, dejection and gloom. The disposition is one of pain and indifference. My words are impersonal, but do they describe your mother's situation?"

William spoke next, "Our mother is only 59 years old and widowed now for nearly a year. Father dominated all of us, including our mother. Though welcoming and attentive to us children, I recall mother spending long hours alone in her bedroom complaining of 'a little headache, nothing serious.' Millicent and I spent a great deal of time reading books and being quiet to avoid upsetting mother or father. Mother rose to every occasion that demanded she appear gay and cheerful, but always seemed exhausted afterwards."

Millicent now picked up the story. "Mother endured seven pregnancies, five of which resulted in miscarriage. William and I are her only children. Her exhaustion has been chronic and Father's death added further burden. She has long-standing constipation for which she takes regular doses of senna. She blames a painful right hip on events surrounding her last pregnancy and she leaves her rooms only for Sunday church. Would you agree to take mother on as a patient?"

I was both flattered and unsettled by Millicent's request. "I would be honored. To proceed we must accept that treatment may be prolonged and carries no guarantee. These matters can prove very resistant. Our opening may be your mother's hip complaint. May I suggest that you tell her you have asked me to examine her hip, in the hope that I might suggest something to relieve her pain? If you allow me that opening, I will take it from there."

The next week Millicent informed me by messenger that her mother had agreed to see me. Assuming the agreement had taken some effort on Millicent's part, and some courage on her mother's part, I made my first call the very same day.

Though Mrs. Johnson remained dressed, I conducted a thorough exam of the right hip and abdomen. She localized her discomfort to the anterior right hip, which showed limited range of motion and discomfort with rotation. Flexion was normal. Heberden's nodes, indicative of chronic arthritis, dominated the knuckles of her fingers. Based on this, I informed Mrs. Johnson that her symptoms were most likely due to a chronic arthritis of the right hip for which the letting of blood provides temporary relief. With Mrs. Johnson's consent, I applied a tourniquet to her right thigh, located a vein in the back of her knee, and withdrew twelve ounces of blood. Mrs. Johnson reported improvement just as the procedure achieved the desired impression on her pulse. I asked if I might help her take a few steps, and placing my arm around her waist we walked the circumference of the room. It was then that I noticed Mrs. Johnson was crying, which she dismissed as tears of joy over her relief. Her face, however, did not message joy and I hugged her a little closer.

At this point Eberle's text on arthritis suggests the application of purgatives or emetics but I felt Mrs. Johnson too frail for aggressive measures. I also noticed that her jar of Dover powder was nowhere in sight, which I took to mean that she had no desire to be challenged about its use. I prescribed tincture of the colchicum seed, twenty drops to be taken every four hours with a scruple of calcined magnesia until slight nausea or stooling occurred. She accepted my promise to return the next day.

The next day a half empty bottle of Dover's powder sat on the table next to Mrs. Johnson's chair. When I sprung to suggest she stop using Dover's, my folly awoke a stinging response, "Are you incapable or incompetent? You are the second doctor to examine me and you appear to be no better at remedy than the other. My pain returned during the night, worse than ever. Dover's provides my only relief."

My thoughtless remark threatened to derail the relationship I was attempting to establish. I made a quick retreat by refocusing on her right hip pain. "Mrs. Johnson, can you estimate what time your hip pain returned?" I asked, while noting that in her angry scold she had stood to confront me. The day before she had risen only for our little walk around the room.

"It was in the early hours of the morning, if you must know," she replied.

"Please advise me if you were awake prior to the pain returning or if you think the pain woke you up from a sound sleep?" I asked.

"I find your question impertinent but will humor you only because my daughter has begged me to do so. I arose to use the night pot and the pain recurred while returning to my bed."

"I assume the pain was quite intense yesterday. How would you judge its intensity today?" I continued.

At that moment, Mrs. Johnson seemed to realize she was standing, forcing a more nuanced assessment of her pain, "I will confess to moving better, but young man, it comes at the cost of excruciating pain."

"Then, Mrs. Johnson, if you will humor me I would like to offer a repeat letting of blood, a change in medication and another twenty-four hours of observation."

"If you must. But, only to appease my children. I fail to appreciate what Millicent sees in you other than persistence. I insist that this time you release the blood from my arm."

There was a hint of incongruence between her words and her expression. She was acting dismissive, but unwilling to discharge me. Bleeding's effect is systemic, though most effective when performed at the source of pain. The real issue was Mrs. Johnson's desire for control so I subtracted six ounces of blood from her arm. During the procedure, I said that I had treated her blood from yesterday with citric acid and allowed it to stand undisturbed. As blood settles a white band, called the buffy coat, forms between the red blood and yellow plasma. A wide buffy coat indicates aggressive antiphlogistic treatments are required. Then I hesitated, hoping I could draw on Mrs. Johnson's curiosity for a response.

"Come, come young man. What did your buffy coat reveal?" Mrs. Johnson inquired. My trap was sprung.

"I am relieved to report that your buffy coat was narrow. And now, seeing that you have had little response to the colchicum, I am confident we can focus our treatments, achieve considerable relief and that you will soon resume the activities you find enjoyable. The wisdom of your own instincts has seen you through the first and most critical phase of treatment, the phase when strict rest is essential. If you are willing, I shall apply myself to your continued recovery."

I did not push Mrs. Johnson to agree. She had invested her energies on a reclusive state, I would not resolve it by a few simple words. I contented myself with the permission implied by her silence.

According to Eberle's textbook, Heberden's nodes on the fingers are consistent with the chronic rheumatism that visits the weight bearing joints and hands of older persons. I prescribed a compound of gum guaiacum and cinnamon to be taken three times a day and a preparation of camphor dissolved in ether to be massaged onto her hip three times a day. I told Mrs. Johnson about Dr. Eberle being a respected Philadelphia professor who held guaiacum in high opinion. I also recommended that she allow her daughter to apply hot compresses to her hip before each application, thinking that would increase the interaction between mother and daughter.

I found Millicent in her mother's room several times over the next few visits. Though she obtained transient relief from bleeding, I bled Mrs. Johnson only once more based on Eberle's suggestion that repeated venesection had limited use in rheumatism without obvious inflammation. After two weeks of almost daily visits, I encountered Mrs. Johnson in a pensive mood. I took a position sitting on her foot stool, leaned forward, took her hand, and waited for her to speak. Her words are stamped in my memory. "Since Mr. Johnson's death it appears that everything around me is precisely as it used to be. But that's impossible. His death changed everything. All that is around me wears aspects of the old, as if denying his death."

Allowing the silence to settle again, I moved to hold both her hands. She then resumed, "Will this gloom ever lift? It's either a nightmare or a devils' torment. I seem unable to cross over to widowhood. How does one settle into a life that one does not want? Enjoyment of any kind seems a sin, all associations with friends exposes me to that sin. Even attending church, I feel overcome with fear that I might experience pleasure. I am both grateful and angry that you have reduced the pain in my hip. If I must go out into the world, I am frightened because I do not know who I am to be."

Mrs. Johnson's description of survivorship is not taught in medical lectures. Her words unwrapped my own wounds over my mother's death and the Vermont life that could no longer be. It is the meek who offer the most startling wisdom. A few more moments passed before I became aware of how firmly I held Mrs. Johnson's hands. We had both shed a few tears, for ourselves, and for each other.

Hippocrates believed melancholia was caused by excessive black bile, combining the ancient Greek word *melas* meaning black and *khole* meaning bile. Eberle classifies it as an emotional insanity characterized by depression and occasionally mania, often following a sudden reversal of fortune. Courage and initiative are exhausted and replaced by a feeling of illness that dominates the patient's attention. Recovery requires gently forced activity that refocuses the patient's attention from herself to others.

Mrs. Johnson had not abandoned logic but I was struck by the contrasting ways we confronted our demons. After my mother's death, I slipped into near manic behavior that included giving up all rights to the Vermont farm and throwing myself onto the frontier. Mrs. Johnson had slipped into depression. Yet, we shared much in common, and she had many things to teach me.

That night I obsessed over my books, reading about melancholia and depression in Berrios, Eberle, Griesinger, Minor, and Roberton texts. Most agreed with Rush's contention that bleeding relieves the cerebral congestion, but done too frequently bleeding may lead to mania. Griesinger advocated for applying leeches behind the ears and plasters of tartar emetic to the neck. Opium, in doses higher than Dover's, produces the most immediate results and alcohol is uniformly condemned.

According to Griesinger, activity of the body works on the mind. Idle lounging becomes a habit and leads to considerable enfeeblement. Religious instruction may be allowed, but total reliance on its potential is to be discouraged. The wealthy may indulge in prolonged travel, but for most relief lies in early rising, a nutritious diet, and finding simple activities that can be repeated under agreeable conditions.

Fortified by my reading, I bargained a temporary substitution and taper of Laudanum for Dover's powder in the doses recommended by Griesinger. More importantly, we agreed that each morning, unless I was otherwise distracted by work, we would take a walk together.

It would be foolish to deny the walks were an excuse to see Mrs. Johnson's daughter regularly. But I was also driven by a genuine curiosity about melancholia and its remedy and determined to keep notes for an empirical analysis of her recovery. English suffers an inadequate selection of words for fondness and devotion, but I fell in love with both the senior Millicent Johnson and her daughter Millicent that summer.

A few families invited me to meet their daughters, nieces or cousins, but eventually I realized that most encounters left me thinking of Millicent. I joined Millicent, her brother William, his fiancé Rebecca and Hiram to attend every lecture, concert, debate or event that summer. Soon the nuances of courtship gained purchase on my attention.

13. The Physic Art, 1834

Any literate person can read a textbook. The art in Physic is knowing when to apply the remedy.

The idea that disease is a punishment from God is widespread, but my observations favor the greater influence on health to be proper water, eating, evacuation, and constraint of passions. I will agree that an immoral life invites disease or impedes the body's response to remedy.

Benjamin Rush's belief in aggressive bleeding and purging emerged during his experience in the 1793 Yellow Fever Epidemic in Philadelphia. Rush claimed that every patient submitting to his aggressive remedies survived. The principle is captured by the parable, 'Don't stand on the dock.'

> If you are standing on a dock and see a man in the water struggling and crying for help, you could encourage him by pointing out how strong and well-nourished he appears by yelling: "Many men faced with drowning have saved themselves by their own exertions." If, in spite of your good cheer, the man keeps crying for help you might prepare a little beef tea to refresh him so he might continue his struggle. You may even point out that the cold water has positive effects on his constitution. Alternatively, you could grab the man by the collar and yank him out of the water. Of course, having done so, there will be bystanders who describe your methods as violent. Procrastination protects you from error, but allowing nature its opportunity may leave the patient beyond cure. Your task is to cure, not stand on the dock.

Dr. Rush, one of four doctors who signed the Declaration of Independence, was a prolific and charismatic writer and teacher at the University of Pennsylvania medical college. He rationalized that Americans, being more robust than Europeans, required a greater intensity of purging and bleeding to eliminate disease. And, he warned that disease gives no warning before turning deadly.

Rush died in 1813, at the age of sixty-seven, but not before a former student applied the techniques of bleeding and purging Rush had taught him. By the time I entered Castleton, the occasional medical student found sport in mocking Rush but few professors questioned his heroic remedies. No better theory rose to challenge the logic of purging disease from the body, and doing something seemed better than doing nothing.

By 1834 there were three times as many medical journals in print than during Rush's career. Many included summaries and comments about articles published in other journals allowing village doctors to follow international developments for the price of a few subscriptions. Reprinted lectures by Harvard professors Drs. Jacob Bigelow and James Jackson Jr. suggested even deadly illnesses like Smallpox, Measles or Cholera are self-limited and resolve without treatment in many patients. In fact, those most likely to survive received only modest bleeding or purging. They could not endorse Homeopathic dilutions but conceded that dilutions may have done less harm. To Bigelow bleeding and purging remained important remedies but suggested greater nuance in their application.

Challengers countered that treatments become established because they work, therefore they should not be abandoned recklessly. Furthermore, only an incompetent doctor would 'stand on the deck' while a disease progressed beyond all hope. Since Hippocrates and Galen, the very identity of medicine had been based on bleeding and purging.

John E. Cooke proposed that Rush's disease model simply needed refinement. According to Rush, miasmas weakened the heart and diminished the pulse. The enfeebled circulation caused blood to accumulate in the capillaries resulting in the heat and redness of inflammation. In Cooke's model, congestion of the vena cava, the large vein returning blood to the heart, resulted in capillary stress and organ damage. Cooke's remedies were little different from Rush. He promoted bleeding to relieve congestion and purging to stimulate the secretion of bile and accumulated waste. Cooke recommended doses of calomel that produced a profound intestinal cleansing.

In Paris, Dr. Broussias offered his own refinements. In the Broussias model it is the overstimulation of one or more body organs that produces excessive byproducts. There may be many reasons why such overstimulation occurs, but the result is inflammation observed as swelling, heat and erythema. Broussias favored antiphlogistic remedies, particularly leeches, to release accumulated fluid, blood and heat.

Another Parisian, Pierre Charles Alexander Louis, published an 1836 treatise based on 77 patients with Pneumonia who were bled before or after the fourth day of their illness. Those bled early recovered three days faster than those bled later. Though forty-four percent of patients bled early died and twenty-five percent of those bled late died, Louis' recommendation was to perform venesection early.

My colleague, Buffalo's Austin Flint, published a treatise agreeing that ailing organs produce byproducts that strain the liver and it is the buildup of these byproducts that define the patient's symptoms. The theory logically explains the predisposition women have for nervous ailments as the uterus is known to be highly innervated.

But a group of 'contagionists' was emerging. They proposed that some diseases, particularly fevers, are communicated from person to person by agents carried in air, water or on fomites like blankets and rugs. Within the contagion camp were subgroups who argued that the agents spreading fever were chemical in nature. Others suggested that Leeuwenhoek's microscopic animalcules discovered in the seventeenth century might be the culprit. Still others postulated the existence of small invisible bullets. Their unifying observation was that quarantine seemed to prevent the spread of fevers.

But 'anti-contagionists,' clung to the belief that bad air miasmas arising from filth and decaying matter caused disease. One only had to look at the squalid and diseased conditions of an overcrowded city to be convinced.

My brother discouraged overconfidence in any single theory. To him it was dangerous to blindly adhere to Rush's aggressive venesection, Cooke's large doses of calomel, Broussias leeches, Homeopathic dilutions, or Thomsonian botanicals. I bled, purged, supported, and comforted patients according to my perception of their immediate needs. Without such nuance, the practice of medicine devolves into rote application of habitual remedies. I select remedies that deplete overexcited processes, or stimulate depleted processes.

In 1834, I brought my experience and my stethoscope to the bedside. The stethoscope was the first step in collecting information independent of the patient's perception. The 1850s saw the development of a bedside thermometer and urinometers to determine specific gravity of urine. I used a drop of Fehling's solution to detect urine sugar, and I used my microscope to look at urine sediment. With these tools, it started to become obvious that the observed measurements returned to normal before the patient began to feel better. Still, I like to lay my hand on the forehead while asking how the patient feels.

In recent years, I am definitely releasing blood less frequently but bloodletting remains an important part of Physic. The venesection technique involves tying a cloth ribbon snuggly around the arm about two inches above the elbow. As a vein becomes visible it is cut with a lancet in a lengthwise fashion. The blood then runs down the arm into a pewter bleeding bowl with markings to measure the amount of blood released. Patients report alleviation of pain and a feeling of giddiness just as the pulse begins to rise, usually after six to sixteen ounces have been removed. The cut is then covered with a square compress of soft linen and firm pressure is applied for several minutes. If bleeding continues, cold water or astringent vinegar is applied.

Leeches provide for a slow, steady localized bleed and are preferred for letting of blood from the scalp, chest or abdomen. A freshwater specie of leech, *Hirudo medicinalis,* first used by Linnaeus in 1758, has a resting length of just over one inch and extends to five inches after feeding. It has a small anterior sucker with three jaws that leave a Y shaped mark. Leech saliva prevents clotting and renders the bite painless. In about thirty minutes, the satiated leech loosens its grip, and falls off having removed about an eighth cup of blood. The site continues to bleed for another twenty-four hours and cupping can be employed to increase the amount of blood released.

Leeches are shipped in a jar partly filled with pond water. Upon receipt, I replace the lid with a sheer cloth to allow air. Though leeches can breathe in water, they prefer air and tend to attach themselves to the sides of the container, just above the water. They are very elastic and can constrict their bodies to escape through very narrow holes, so the cloth must be well secured. The leech is attached by rubbing the patient's skin until red then holding the leech against the skin until peristaltic motions indicate attachment. A sprinkle of salt will detach the leech if need be.

Cupping, blistering or scarifying at the site of the affliction, or at the soles of the feet for a systemic effect, is sometimes employed. These measures, like lancing an abscess, release poisons directly from a site of inflammation.

Once bled, patients report a fullness over the liver that should be relieved by cathartics. The Physician must judge whether the patient is best served by a cathartic that will cause a thin watery discharge, one that will stimulate vomiting as well as defecation, or one that is slow in its action.

In as little as two-days, faster in extreme illness, blood may accumulate and liver congestion may return demanding retreatment. None-the-less, the experience of competent physicians over two thousand years attests to the effectiveness of bleeding and purging.

14. Drugs, 1834

The best Physician knows the worth and perils of medicines.

Two books, the second edition of the *United States Pharmacopoeia* published in 1830 with the English and Latin names of 620 drugs and Dunglison's *New Remedies,* defined my stock and trade as I began practice. The pharmacy schools in Philadelphia and New York City organized what became known as the American Pharmacy Association and formed an inspection committee to verify the purity of drugs. The groups first code of ethics called for the expulsion of anyone who knowingly sold adulterated medications. The notes in my prescriptions guaranteeing quality were only slightly ahead of the field.

Since the days of Columbus, the Americas had been explored for new compounds to supplement those imported from Europe. Discoveries included guaiacum from the West Indies, sassafras from Florida, and copaiba from Brazil. Peru gave us the expectorant balsam and cinchona, also called quinine, for intermittent malarial fevers. Constantine Rafinesque documented the dramatic increase in available compounds in his *Medical Flora of the United States* published in 1830.

For generations doctors had been limited to a few compounds chosen out of habit, experience, and available resources. A widely-held principle of geographic specificity credited the local doctor with knowing his patients and community diseases better than anyone. However, national drug lists like the *Pharmacopoeia* joined new medical journal reporting in challenging the limits of parochial medical practice. As the choice of remedies expanded, Physician owned dispensaries, like Chapin's drugstore, served patients of doctors choosing not to maintain and compound a large stock of drugs, and competed favorably with non-physician drug merchants called chemists, apothecaries or pharmacists who also saw patients and prescribed drugs.

Fundamentally, there are three classes of drugs: Depletives, stimulants, and alternatives. Bleeding and purging are depletive tactics, meant to rid the body of accumulated organ waste. The stimulants, including alcohol, cantharides (Spanish fly), arsenic, opium and quinine, are used when the patient is run down. Alternatives like strychnine, foxglove and antimony were intended to shock the body and reset internal rhythms.

A word on placebos, which are very effective in distracting patients who are morbid about health. My preferred formula starts with a pound box of No. 35 un-medicated homeopathic globules, which cost me 35 cents. I immerse one half in extract of belladonna, and the other half in tincture of iodine for twenty minutes. Following this I roll the compounds on a newspaper then spread them out to dry. I mix the powders with either powdered cinnamon or licorice root and bottle them. When prescribed I give very specific instructions for mixing with either beef tea or sassafras tea. The more gravitas, the better.

Certainly, the majority of people are sensible enough to take medicine only when sickness demands it. However, for those convinced of the need for a daily bowel movement, I prescribe daily doses of senna. That said, I do not minimize the importance of healthy defecation. Every patient is asked about the character of their stool so that I might assure that all organ wastes are properly eliminated. I compound senna by boiling half an ounce of leaves from the senna legume in a pint of water, adding four ounces of sulfate of soda and mixing it with four ounces of antimonial wine. A draught is taken at night or mixed with another cathartic for an enhanced effect. It also works well to relieve infant colic.

More potent cathartics include the root of a Mexican plant called Jalap, and Glauber's Powder, a sodium-sulfate compound developed by the

German physician John Glauber. But Calomel, a tasteless mercury chloride salt usually mixed with rhubarb, is a cathartic that is central to the remedy of many ailments. Calomel acts on the liver and intestines to reliably release bile and produce a profound defecation. Maximum tolerated dose is signaled by copious salivation and overdosing results in loosened teeth, an ashen gray discoloration of the throat, and sedation, as I described in Jasper Haven. The customary dose of Calomel is 3-6 grains and I am of the opinion that prescribing a dose greater than 10 grains should open one to criticism. Islamic merchants brought Calomel from China and called it *calos* (good) and *melas* (black) because of the expulsive dark stools it caused. Calomel's affect is so profound that it has attracted the witticism, 'Within the last few days I have passed everything except my hat.'

In its sublimate form mercury prevents the secondary afflictions of Syphilis. At the first sign of the painless nodule known as a chancre I apply a poultice of mercury in lard to the chancre itself. Then the patient is instructed to take one twelve grain mercury sublimate pill on day one, none on the second day, two on the third, none on the fourth, three on the fifth and so on, until one hundred and twenty pills are consumed. A daily dose of senna will maintain a regular action of the bowels.

Another cathartic, Podophyllum, comes from the Mayapple or American Mandrake plant that grows in the Eastern United States. Natives boiled the roots of the woody plant and used the water to cure stomach problems. It is both an emetic and cathartic with actions on the liver similar to Calomel, for which it may be substituted. Podophyllum also eliminates most intestinal worms and topically it cures Warts.

Castor oil is obtained by pressing the beans of the *Ricinus communis* plant. Since ancient times it has been used as a laxative and to induce labor. Castor oil's unpleasant taste has led to its use in disciplining children, or to speed the passage of swallowed objects. The latter is to be discouraged because castor oil may prevent fecal encapsulation, increasing the potential of injury from sharp edges.

Emetics such as antimony and potassium tartrate or "tartar" emetic have been used to reset the intestinal system and induce vomiting since the Middle Ages. Antimony is compounded by filling a cup made of pure antimony with wine and letting it sit for 24 hours. Sips of the wine are taken until vomiting occurs. Antimony is also the main ingredient in Mrs. Moffat's Shoo-Fly Powder, a patent medicine commonly used to counter drunkenness. Another emetic, ipecacuanha or ipecac, induces vomiting in high doses and relieves cough in small doses. The dried rhizomes of *Carapichea ipecacuanha* are soaked in alcohol and the solution is then dried into a powder. A pugil, the amount you can grasp between the thumb and fore-finger, is dissolved in water and given every ten minutes until vomiting occurs.

Dysentery, acute and chronic, is a universal malady. When acute the remedy is complete cleansing of the intestines to eliminate the offending irritation. When chronic, the sub-nitrate of bismuth will slow evacuations. Compounding bismuth is complicated, so it quickly became a common prescription doctors sent to my store. First bismuth must be ground to a powder in an iron mortar then dissolved in a mixture of nitric acid and distilled water, shaken vigorously, and allowed to sit until a white precipitate, sub-nitrate of bismuth, forms. This is dried and stored in a dark bottle. Some prescriptions called for mixing bismuth with ginseng for an enhanced effect.

Several medicines were borrowed from the Seneca Indians, including one derived from the bark and leaves of the willow, osier or Salix plant to treat headaches and joint pain. The active ingredient became available in a crystalline form called salicin and later, in the 1870s, an acetylated form came as a tablet called Aspirin by the Bayer Company of Germany. At doses that are high enough to cause ringing in the ears it was very effective for treating rheumatism associated with warm, red and swollen joints.

The stimulant quinine has proven effective to remedy fevers, particularly the ague and intermittent or malarial fevers associated with exposure to swamp miasma. Quinine works in both the milder form of malaria seen in New York and the severe forms common to the southern states. The bark of the Peruvian cinchona tree, also called Jesuit bark, is stripped, dried, ground into powder, and then dissolved in brandy to make it palatable. When treating chronic intermittent fever, a five-grain dose is repeated every four hours until flushed skin, headache, tinnitus, and nausea develop, a condition called Cinchonism, then continued at a slightly reduced amount. In 1831 Thomas Bearn, a Huntsville, Alabama doctor, published a case report in which heroic doses of quinine cured a young woman with a high fever, then Bearn went on a lecture tour that made quinine so popular it was added to many patent medicines.

A tea brewed from the dried bark of the North American sassafras tree remedies chronic fevers and the secondary symptoms of Syphilis, though heavy use imparts a body odor and even Jaundice. Indians use sassafras tea for urinary problems, or rub the leaves directly onto wounds to promote healing and cure acne. It's also used in curing meat. My store sells toothbrushes made from sassafras twigs to impart a pleasant breath, though the smell may cause suspicion of Syphilis treatment.

Laudanum, the ten percent tincture of opium previously described, is used to relieve pain and to treat hypochondriasis, hysteria, menstrual cramping, nervous irritability, and cough. A bedtime dose assures a good night's sleep, which alone cures many nervous conditions. Cheaper than whiskey, Laudanum is a bitter reddish-brown liquid that also curbs diarrhea. It is sold in most general stores, but some choose to purchase it from my drugstore because of my standardized preparation. I put it up in brown glass bottles and do little to mask its bitter taste to limit overuse.

Morphine gradually replaced Laudanum. It is derived from the opium poppy, more consistent in its action and promoted to be less habit forming. As the hypodermic needle and syringe became available in the 1860s, an injectable form of morphine profoundly improved our ability to counteract the pain of acute injury, subdue patients in extreme turmoil, and relieve breathlessness. Unfortunately, those of compromised moral energies have found need for continuous use.

The alternative class of drugs includes foxglove, which James Meade first described in his 1797 Medical Repository paper titled *On the Digitalis Purpurea*. The British Physician, William Withering, then published a book in 1785 further illustrating its remarkable ability to reverse breathing difficulties caused by the accumulations of fluid. There are several forms of Dropsy, one seen in advanced cases of consumption and another associated with Bright's disease. The third, and least common form, is associated with a rapid pulse and a clear sputum. In the latter form, Foxglove calms the pulse and reduces symptoms. The dried leaves of purple foxglove are ground and exposed to warm distilled water, the decoction of which must be consumed fresh as its potency lessens in a matter of days.

During acute episodes of asthma and chest congestion I instruct patients to lean over a bowl, head covered with a towel, and breath in the vapors created by placing a tablespoon of the oil of turpentine in hot water. Oil of turpentine can also be mixed with egg yolk and oil of roses to form a paste that heals burns, or relieves painful joints and muscles.

Taken orally, oil of turpentine cures Tapeworm. I recall one severely malnourished fourteen-year-old boy who upon exam was discharging fragments of tapeworm from his anus. I administered an ounce of oil of turpentine at my first visit and left instructions to take doses at 9:00 a.m. and 3:00 p.m. the following day. Though he vomited a portion of each dose, thirty minutes after the third dose he commenced to discharging segments of the worm per rectum. In the evening of the second day the boy passed twenty feet of the worm *Taenia lata,* his only complaint being a throbbing warmth in his stomach, diarrhea and transient dizziness.

Aconitum has analgesic, sedative, and anti-inflammatory properties that can reduce fever, slow the pulse and bring on sweating and diuresis. It is used to remedy cough, pneumonia, laryngitis, croup and asthma. Aconitum is also called aconite tuber, monkshood, friar's cap, soldier's cap, wolfs bane and ranunculin. The fingers can become numb when handling the plant's flowers as can the lips and mouth. If concentrated on an arrowhead it will cause paralysis and death, so it must be carefully dosed one grain at a time and repeated with caution. Used topically, a tincture of aconite can relieve neuralgia, rheumatism, and sciatica. In highly diluted forms the homeopaths use aconite to treat anxiety and headache.

The root of North American *Veratrum viride* induces a pleasant delirium, arterial sedation and slows the pulse. Also, known as Indian poke, Indian hellebore, corn lily, and itch-weed, it can be deadly to livestock. Various doses were tested on dogs in an 1857 issue of the *Boston Medical and Surgical Journal.* I prepare Veratrum by digesting eight ounces of the bruised root in one pint of brandy. The initial dose is ten drops, increased by one to five drops every two or three hours until the pulse slows or the patient becomes nauseous. One of my patients, a woman with Pneumonia, suffered a pulse of one-hundred-thirty. I was urgently called away and had to leave specific instructions for dosing Veratrum. A few hours later she was pale, vomiting, sweating profusely and her pulse was under sixty. I had to discontinue the Veratrum, but everyone was pleased with her rapid recovery from the Pneumonia.

Strychnine, from the Asian plant *Strychnos nux-vomica*, like Veratrum, slows the heart while strengthening the fullness and intensity of the pulse. Patients experience a heightened sense of touch, hearing and vision, but even slight overuse will cause convulsions.

Ergot, in Latin *pulvis-ad-partum* (the powder of birth), scientific name *Secale cornutum*, is made from the mold that grows on rye. After observing its use by native midwives, John Stearns of Saratoga County, New York, published a letter about Ergot's ability to stimulate labor in an 1808 issue of the Medical Repository. In 1813, Oliver Prescott confirmed Dr. Stearns' findings recommending that a half drachm of the rye mold powder be dissolved in half a pint of sugar water, one third given every ten minutes until contractions intensify. Ergot's action is variable and it should not be used as long as the natural pains are efficient and labor is progressing. Besides augmenting labor, Ergot can reverse obstructed menses, induce abortion, and has saved the lives of many women by arresting hemorrhage following delivery.

Lobelia and capsicum, made popular by Samuel Thomson's botanical theories, cleanse the stomach and promote sweating. I sell dried, powdered *lobelia inflata* twigs, also called Indian tobacco or puke weed, in my Pharmacy to be made into a tea. It is good for clearing mucus from the throat, lungs, and bronchial tubes or as a paste to treat bites, bruises, poison ivy, and ringworm. Like tobacco, Lobelia has a pleasant effect on the senses and the Seneca smoke it as a remedy for cough. The Lobelia plant has a hairy stem, pale green or yellowish leaves and violet flowers, growing to a height of three feet in both Vermont and New York.

Alleviating surgical pain ranks as the single most rapidly accepted advance in medicine during my lifetime. The gas, nitrous oxide, was discovered in the late 1700s but real change did not occur until the more easily managed liquid Chloroform, compounded by mixing chlorinated lime with Ethanol, became available in the 1830s. Ether, also a liquid at room temperature is slightly less predictable, but causes fewer irregularities in pulse than Chloroform. By the 1850s medical journals were filled with reports about the use of Chloroform and Ether for dental extractions, amputations and parturition.

Whenever possible, anesthesia is applied with the help of an experienced assistant who soaks a sponge or cloth with Ether or Chloroform, covers the patient's nose and mouth, then reapplies the cloth as needed to assure complete somnolence. In the absence of an assistant a short procedure can be performed by instructing the patient to hold the cloth themselves. As they achieve a light anesthesia the patient's hand, and the cloth, drop away allowing about ten minutes to complete the procedure.

Topical antiseptics inched their way into surgical management during the Civil War in the form of bromine, iodine, carbolic acid (phenol) and nitric acid. Records detailing large numbers of injuries and amputations revealed that antiseptics slowed the onset of gangrene. Lister would later champion dilute carbolic acid as his disinfectant of choice.

During my first year in Aurora, I was very careful about my finances, reinvesting all I could in the store, books and practice. Abiatha was ever the observer, the organizer, and the business brain of my enterprise. Just as importantly, she knew everyone in Aurora and everyone seemed to respect her. We often laughed when, after consulting me, a patient would catch Abiatha's eye for a reassuring node of approval.

One day in the late summer of 1834, I returned to the store following a day of rounds in the countryside to find a wagon tied up to the hitching post. Bright pink letters declared, 'Doctor Phineas J. McCarthy.' Below that was 'Feel younger, stronger, get more done.' Under that was, 'McCarthy's Copaiba.'

15. Copaiba Oil, 1834

Wisdom comes with age, but sometimes age comes alone.

Abiatha and the man I presumed to be Phineas J. McCarthy were in high spirits as I entered the store. He was just over five feet tall, stocky with a reddish beard framing a full grin. A generous handshake launched a salesman's lilt.

"Dr. Allen, it is an immense pleasure to meet you. As I have crossed the great state of New York the news is spreading of a new doctor, a Castleton graduate, who has brought the power of his wisdom and cures to the fine people of Aurora. I am honored to take your hand in friendship. Abiatha here has been telling me of your hard work, your dedication, and the kind ways in which you have treated her. Obviously, the belle of Aurora, Abiatha would give one to believe I am in the presence of a saint."

McCarthy was over the top but having great fun, and Abiatha was beaming. Phineas concentrated on me as if he would soon control every twitch of my face, captivating me enough to ask, "What can I do for you Mr. McCarthy?"

"Dr. Allen, I can do much for you, and I will ask for little. Your sign says, 'No cure, No pay,' and Abiatha confirms the importance you place on helping people, so I will not emphasize the financial benefit of our partnership. After completing my medical studies at the Medical College of Cork, I spent some years with a merchant vessel that imported rubber and cotton from Brazil to Dublin. My travels allowed the opportunity to explore the Amazon jungles searching out remedies for the ills of modern society. And, I found the copaiba tree, what science calls *Copaifera reticulate,* growing hundred feet tall, producing a sap used by natives to improve strength, agility and prolong life."

"Copaiba sap is like an oily black pepper, but add one or two drops to a brewed tea or brandy and it boosts the digestion, bolsters respiratory function and calms nervous anxiety. Rub a couple drops over an aching joint and within minutes you suddenly have the suppleness of a teenager. It makes blemishes disappear and keeps your face smooth and clean as the day you were born. The copaiba in McCarthy's Copaiba is so pure that I implore everyone to use no more than that recommended by the Philadelphia chemist who attests to the purity of each shipment."

I leapt on McCarthy first inhalation, "I am well acquainted with copaiba and purchase what I sell from a reputable supply house with offices in New York and London. They provide a certificate of authenticity and I see little need to change my supplier. Now, remove your wagon from the front of my store?"

Phineas was unstoppable, "Yes, Abiatha assures me you are no fool and that you take great care with the drugs you dispense. Let me just say that I can bring a more potent and reasonably priced copaiba to you than New York or London and you will be supporting proud jungle families who tap the Copaifera trees and distill its resin to create the essential oil I offer you. Please, take this vial, fresh from a case on my wagon. Note its healthful aroma. Open it, see for yourself, it is the highest quality copaiba on earth."

The flat bottom brown glass vial was five inches long, sealed with a rubber stopper. The label simulated the pink letters on McCarthy's wagon, 'Doctor Phineas J. McCarthy, feel younger, stronger, get more done, McCarthy's Copaiba.' I removed the rubber stopper and confirmed a slightly yellow oil that smelled of balsam and pepper. A touch of its contents to my tongue left the bitter taste I associate with copaiba.

A force of nature, Phineas continued, "There is no product like copaiba, and no copaiba better than what you hold in your hand. In the Amazon

I found indigenous people at advanced ages hunting and tilling the soil. Their secret was copaiba, the most powerful antiphlogistic agent known to civilization. Dr. Allen, at no charge I leave you with a box of my copaiba. Use it, sell it. You will not be disappointed."

"Phineas, I do not take kindly to the hard sell," but my interruption had little effect on his cadence.

"You have no doubt heard of Maloney's *Giver of Life*. Johnathan Maloney markets his elixir in stores while he purchases advertisements and tours the country promoting its sales. Both he and the store owners make a profit bringing health to many more communities than a man and a wagon can do alone. I sell my copaiba at 50 cents a vial. Each vial contains at least fifty, two drop doses. At a penny a dose, it's a bargain by any measure. I will travel, advertise, and create interest in this astonishing oil while providing you with my copaiba at 25 cents a vial. All I ask is that you also sell it for 50 cents. Dr. Allen, I carry but three books with me, the *Bible*, a bound copy of *Materia Medica*, and Eberle's *Treatise on the Practice of Medicine*. We are partners in mind, together we can serve the hard-working men and women of Aurora and all of America."

Finally, Abiatha joined in, "Dr. Allen, Dr. McCarthy and I have had a very pleasant conversation and he has gained my confidence. Will it do any harm to consider his offer?"

"Abiatha, I trust your judgement, so I'll give the matter some consideration."

Then, turning to Phineas, "For now, I would appreciate you removing your wagon from the front of my store. Its presence suggests that I endorse your product. I will study the issue and provide you with my response tomorrow. Now, I bid you goodbye."

With that I took a vial of McCarthy's Copaiba and retreated to my upstairs quarters to think. I made a meal of head cheese and cider and dug into my books. The *United States Pharmacopeia* has the following listing:

COPAIBA. Copaifera Officinalis. Copaiba. Copaiva, or Capivi Balsam.

Properties: When recent, of the consistence of oil, becoming thick and tenacious by age; transparent; color pale yellow; odor fragrant and peculiar; taste aromatic, bitter, pungent; soluble in alcohol, expressed and essential oils.

Use: Stimulant, diuretic, laxative; acts powerfully on the urinary passages. Dose as an emulsion, or on sugar.

Eberle makes only two brief references to copaiba. Buchan's domestic medicine recommends it to be taken orally for menstrual cramping. Condi recommends oral copaiba for treating bedwetting in children and topically for treating eczema given its anti-inflammatory (antiphlogistic) and analgesic actions.

Essential oils float to the top when a plant is boiled. They can be decanted off and are stored in darkened glass bottles to maintain their original fragrance. For rose oil the petals are boiled, the leaves for peppermint, lemon peels for lemon oil, seeds for fennel, roots for ginger, wood for cedar oil, and pine gum for frankincense and oil of turpentine. Ethanol, mineral oil, and cottonseed oil are often used as extenders.

The next morning Abiatha told me that Colonel Fillmore had rubbed a few drops of McCarthy's Copaiba oil on his knees and awoke feeling twenty years younger. I was cornered, McCarthy won over Abiatha who recruited Colonel Fillmore. So, attempting to put the matter aside, I mailed a vial to the American Pharmacy Association's inspection committee and told Abiatha that it might be six weeks or more before I could make a final determination on Phineas J. McCarthy. Certainly, Phineas would be long gone by then.

The next day posters appeared on every pole in Aurora announcing the 'World Famous Dr. Phineas J. McCarthy' would be giving a demonstration on the miracle cures afforded by McCarthy's Copaiba Oil, 'Straight from the Jungles of Brazil.' Demonstrations were to be held every Monday, Thursday and Saturday evening until all 'Curious and Intelligent citizens' of Aurora had the opportunity to experience the miracle of McCarthy's Copaiba.

Traveling medicine men commonly stage rousing shows, with a little magic, fortune telling, fiddling, juggling, and entertaining stories hyping their special medicine. With little forethought I asked Millicent, William, Rebecca and Hiram to join me for McCarthy's next show. Hiram had already met McCarthy when Phineas somehow talked the Academy into allowing him the use of their front lawn for his demonstration.

Dressed in a silk hat and double-breasted waist coat with tails, McCarthy circulated through the gathering crowd. At 6:00 p.m. sharp he ascended the back of his wagon and after a prayer thanking God for the beautiful evening, his act began. "We are going to have fun this evening! But, before we begin we must thank McCarthy's Copaiba Oil for making it possible. McCarthy's Copaiba oil will put the spark back into your lives. Ladies, mix two drops with your facial cream at night and by morning those hard-earned wrinkles will disappear, and your mirror will prove smooth, healthier skin. You will be so pleased you will beg your husband to use it. Men, apply a couple of drops to that finger you hit with a hammer and it will heal in hours. And every one of us wants to rid ourselves of some unsightly scar. McCarthy's Copaiba infuses the skin with powerful healing agents that eliminate the appearance of blisters, pimples and scars in just a few weeks."

Following this introduction, McCarthy grabbed his fiddle and played a lively version of 'I'll Be with You When the Roses Bloom Again.' To my surprise and disappointment, Abiatha appeared and circulated through the audience seeking volunteers with rheumatism. When finished fiddling, McCarthy asked if 'the beautiful Abiatha' had found 'Volunteers willing to prove Copaiba's power?'

Before each volunteer approached the stage, Abiatha used exaggerated placement of her own hand on her right hip, then her left elbow and finally her neck, corresponding to each volunteer's ailment, while, with fanciful fanfare, McCarthy got the crowd laughing as he 'guessed' the painful area. Then each volunteer was given a little copaiba oil to rub over their pain.

As the laughter settled McCarthy played another tune and Abiatha encouraged the first volunteer to dance with her. Suddenly McCarthy shouted, "Ain't it wonderful! Praise the Lord for McCarthy's Copaiba. You see it for yourself folks. Massage a few drops of McCarthy's Copaiba Oil over that stiff and aching joint and within minutes you too will be dancing."

From this McCarthy broke into a one-man skit acted out on the tiny tailgate of his wagon. He told of a son of the most prominent Chief of a Brazilian jungle tribe who had been mauled by a leopard. McCarthy groaned and winced so convincingly that you could feel the boy's pain. The young man was placed in his hut to die. Before long infection set in and the medicine man was called to relieve his suffering. But the medicine man was prepared. For several days, he had collected the sap of the copaiba tree and massaged the pure oil into the young man's wounds. For good measure, he also had the young man sip a copaiba tea. By the next morning, the boy's fever was gone and he begged his mother to prepare a large breakfast. By that afternoon, he demanded his valet take him for a walk and within two days his wounds were healed.

McCarthy went on, "From that moment I knew that I had to share the miracle of copaiba. I spent months with the natives, and studied all I could about copaiba. I learned how they made the most potent form of copaiba. They taught me how you can place five drops in hot water and inhale the vapors to relieve congestion, cure Pneumonia and arrest Asthma. Those same vapors improve the mood and lighten the spirits. When drank as a tea, Copaiba has a powerful diuretic action that relieves kidney obstruction and prevents bedwetting in children.

Next McCarthy asked if anyone in the audience had a hearing problem. Inviting a middle-aged man to come up to the stage he declared, "I will demonstrate a benefit few people know about copaiba oil. Please tip your head to one side." Then to the audience, "I am placing two drops of McCarthy's Copaiba in our gentleman's right ear. Now tip your head to the right while I drip two drops of copaiba oil in your left ear. Notice how I place my hands over the ears and massage them for just a minute. Tell me Sir, can you hear?"

The man grinned from ear to ear and nearly shouted, "My God, I can hear!" McCarthy hugged him.

At this point, McCarthy lowered his head and appeared close to tears. "I left my Ireland home shortly after my mother's death from consumption. If you ask the next one hundred doctors how consumption starts, ninety-nine of them will say it starts because of a neglected case of catarrh. We have all suffered catarrh with fever, cough, and popping in the ears. Catarrh and asthma can spread throughout your body. My dear departed mother would be alive today if the miracle of copaiba had been revealed to me sooner. This vial I hold contains the miracle that can save the lives of your children, your spouse and your mother. A drop in each nostril, or the vapors of a few drops in hot water will cure catarrh."

McCarthy's pitch resembled a rising gale, "Copaiba oil is rare and so valuable that there are many fakes on the market. But you needn't worry about McCarthy's Copaiba, trust it, it's safe and effective, the original Brazilian tonic. The most powerful weapon for improving health ever discovered. It's available for you, right here, right now, tonight for 50 cents a vial, including my personal instructions for the many ways Doctor McCarthy's Copaiba leads to a better life."

Then McCarthy's gale struck, "And, one of America's best doctors, tonight the good Dr. Allen has joined us. Dr. Allen is proving the purity of McCarthy's Copaiba and will offer it at the same low price long after I continue my journey to bring copaiba to America."

Eager customers rushed the stage as anger boiled. It was bad enough that Abiatha had taken up with this showman, but now he was twisting my curiosity into an endorsement. I barely stopped myself from shouting, "Fraud, charlatan, liar!"

Hiram invited us to see his new living quarters at the Academy and share a brandy. Millicent took my arm, "Jabez, you look as if you want to strangle a cat."

And Hiram teased, "Millicent, can't you see, our good doctor hoped for a monopoly on McCarthy's Copaiba."

Self-control has its limits, "I owe you all an apology. My instinct was to throw the scoundrel out of my store the minute I laid eyes on McCarthy. But, he already had Abiatha bamboozled, and the man has a gift for chatter, confabulation and deception. Many things he said about copaiba are true but certainly not beyond belief. And, that bit about curing deafness, most men who work outside accumulate a buildup of wax that will liquefy with any oil and dislodge with a little massage. Only a first-class hawker like McCarthy makes it out to be a miracle. He has caught me in his web and called it an endorsement. I have not purchased, nor sold a drop of it."

Over brandy I told my friends how I had sent one of the vials to the Inspection Committee for review and analysis. After tonight I was inclined to never sell his product, but for sure I was not going to sell it without analysis.

"The sad thing is, a clever litany will convince people they'll be thinner, healthier, richer or live longer if they'll buy what you're selling. I swear, if you told people they'd be better looking if they ate dirt, they'd eat dirt."

"Jabez, you have more problems than you think," Millicent opined. "Abiatha has surrendered to McCarthy's spell. The man has sold himself to her and she has invested her heart in him."

I did not sleep well that night and rose early looking forward to a stroll with Millicent's mother.

16. Walking and Listening, 1834

Physicians learn by listening to the wisdom of the troubled.

June's early mornings lit our walks. At first, we strolled a block, then two, but Mrs. Johnson held me to thirty minutes as she coaxed her muscles and mind to gain endurance.

I rationalized three goals for muddling our doctor-patient relationship this way. One was clinical. I wanted to learn more about the challenges of aging from the quiet, withdrawn, but reflective, Mrs. Johnson. The second was personal. After my mother's death, turmoil over farm and family overshadowed grieving and Mrs. Johnson posed questions I should have asked myself then. The third is a confession, the walks were a pretext to see the younger Millicent. Dodging rain, wind, and patient calls, we managed about three walks a week, adding a block every few days. When we ran out of blocks, we added some distance into the country. We had been walking a couple weeks when Mrs. Johnson asked me to call her Millicent. "We're to be friends," she said. Soon I was calling her mother Millicent.

At first, we spoke of the things we saw or the people mother Millicent knew in the houses we passed. Gradually we probed each other's opinions, one day hers, another day mine and sometimes ours. Before these walks no one cared to ask either of our opinions about human perseverance.

Two events focused our opinions. Michael Kelly, an Irish immigrant who lived and worked in Buffalo's First Ward was hanged. He had come home drunk and plunged a butcher knife into his wife, killing her. Newspapers reported several hundred spectators came to watch his hanging.

Ralph Waldo Emerson had just published his essays titled *Nature*, and being an acquaintance of Hiram Barney, the Aurora Academy hosted

Emerson's lecture, "On Transcendentalism." Hiram asked William and Millicent Johnson to hold a dinner for Mr. Emerson at the Johnson home and I encouraged Mrs. Johnson to serve as the official hostess. Emerson doted on her, and she performed like a queen. She said, "Emerson put words to my belief that all earthly things are connected to God," and later referred to the evening as her dowager coming out party.

As shocked as we were by the public spectacle of Kelly's execution, it was Emerson who ignited the philosophical element to our walks. Mother Millicent loved how Emerson framed both good and bad events to be divine; therefore they must be accepted and assimilated into our experience. It is forgiveness and understanding that powers personal growth and hard work that delivers the fruit of American freedom.

William and Millicent had described their parent's marriage accurately. Mrs. Johnson loved and respected her husband, but struggled to accept his unpolished curtness in public. Alone he could be very gentle but the occasions when he really listened were rare. His death had raised in her a sense of failure because she never found a way to soften the man. She recalled only one occasion, the death of their first child, when he surrendered to a tender emotion. That day when I sat on her footstool and we both found ourselves crying, she realized that she would have been just as frightened by his tears as she was by his gruffness. Her conclusion, "Men and women are who they are and love is accepting their efforts more than their failures."

The morning after McCarthy's copaiba show, mother Millicent was quick to detect my restlessness. I shared my views about McCarthy and his show and she went right to the point, "Could the real source of your anger be how McCarthy manipulated you? Our instincts and emotions are unconscious evaluations and it seems your instincts were correct. You are not the first to override instinct with intellectual assessment, nor the first to be abused by a skilled manipulator. The first time your good intentions are mistreated, you must blame the manipulator. Blame yourself only if you allow him to do it again. Your resolve will bruise Abiatha's feelings; your kindheartedness will pull her through."

I have learned much from humble and bold patients alike. Such is the privilege of being someone's doctor.

I arrived back at the store to find Abiatha in a cheerful mood. I asked her to sit, "Abiatha, I will concede McCarthy is an accomplished entertainer, but last night's show was a sales pitch of the worse kind. He told half-truths and exaggerated copaiba's potential. It has been my good fortune to have you identified with my business. Your participation in his performance suggests my practice endorses McCarthy's Copaiba, a lie made even worse by my own foolish decision to attend. McCarthy's exaggerations force me to abandon all associations with McCarthy's Copaiba forthwith. In several weeks, we will receive the analysis, only then will I decide if I will sell McCarthy's brand of copaiba."

After a deep breath, I continued, "Be careful. From my first encounter, I have had my suspicions about McCarthy. I know he is ingratiating himself with you. Please, be careful."

As was her habit, Abiatha heard me out in silence, then, "Dr. Allen, you exceed the boundaries of employment and show no appreciation for my situation. Though kind and generous, the Fillmores are anxious for my departure, and I have nowhere to go. I have been in Aurora all my life. You left Vermont to seek adventure. I too feel the need for adventure. Phineas McCarthy promises passage to a new life and I will explore that option. He is kind to me and I believe he enjoys my company."

With an instinct for entrance, McCarthy presented himself to our front door at that very moment. True to my concern, he was carrying a case of McCarthy Copaiba. There were 48 vials in a case that wholesale at 25 cents apiece or $12 a case, but he was happy to accept a one-time price of $10 for my first case.

I ordered the man out of my store. "There will be plenty of time to stock McCarthy's Copaiba should the analysis of its purity be confirmed. That will take several weeks. In the meantime, should you mention my name in any situation whatsoever; I will ask my attorney, William Johnson, to commence a lawsuit against you. And, if you do anything to embarrass or harm Abiatha, I will personally see that you are tarred and feathered on the same grounds from which you hawked your wares last evening. Do not darken my doorway again until the analysis has been returned and do not park your wagon in front of my store, ever! Good day, sir."

That is the longest speech I would deliver to McCarthy. Though Abiatha continued to see Phineas McCarthy, she did not participate in another demonstration.

Aurora's summers boast long, warm days with rare humidity. The coterie of Hiram, William, Millicent, Rebecca and I attended lectures, debates, picnics, and mostly anything that might excite a good argument. Hiram became a close friend, willing to share a brandy and conversation almost anytime. Mother Millicent was much improved, yet our walks continued and her daughter now joined us.

As my new circumstances settled a bit, I realized how much I enjoyed being with Miss Millicent and marveled the difference between mother and daughter. Where mother Millicent would retreat, Miss Millicent would advance. She prided herself in book knowledge and held her opinions with less caution and more intensity. She was lively where her mother was quiet but they both possessed a sensitivity that comes with observation. Miss Millicent retained a classical charm that set her apart from other women. And, when we were seen arm in arm at a church picnic we became fodder for village gossip.

On one morning, without warning, mother Millicent asked what stirred two people to decide that they want to be wife and husband. She fixed her eyes on me for response and I let slip that beauty was an advantage. That sounded terribly shallow, so I quickly added, "but beauty without charm and grace may not hold for long."

Determined to continue the subject, mother Millicent recalled a definition of courtship in an etiquette book once given to her by an aunt. Courtship is the formal prelude to marriage, "but what surprised me was how often it blooms from friendship."

With the hint of a tease, Millicent offered, "If a gentleman, the man should start with a series of quiet attentions in a manner that does not alarm the woman. If interest is returned, the gentleman should warn the lady that the threat of engagement looms. At that point courtship begins and the gentleman neglects all others while he regularly attends church with the lady, gives her occasional presents, and arranges to escort her at all public outings. It is understood that the gentleman will carry the woman's bundles and open doors, as any gentleman does for all ladies. However, the suiter must appear overjoyed to perform these tasks for his lady of interest. Should the gentleman prove unerring in his performance, the lady may determine the affiliation will be mutually beneficial."

Then, for her finale, Millicent added, "Look at you Jabez. You are always careful to avoid careless dress and you keep yourself clean, neat with necktie in place, at all times. Have you considered your prospects?"

"Millicent!" mother Millicent gasped, "Even you must observe formalities expected of courtship. Jabez, I am afraid my daughter has viewed her parents' marriage through a child's eye. I am older and possess the cool blood of experience. God gives men and women more than friendship, he gives them husband and wife, love and life."

"But mother, a wife can be her husband's best friend. Sure, a woman is a female in her body, but in her essence, she is equal to man. Marriage joins the labor of friendship and the commitments of love; the blessing of society and the union of hearts. It is the continuous work of caring and charity that builds the shelter of love. Frankly mother, you were the most charitable friend father could have hoped for." Millicent respectfully added.

I looked at the two women carefully, attempting to divine the full meaning of this exchange. Though I had not known them six months ago, they were both objects of my adoration. We walked silently for a few moments when I realized they had taken each other's arm and had drawn each other close. Now, at the front walk of the Johnson residence, it was time for me to engage my work day.

The transition was gradual but Millicent and I made steady progress towards courtship and I became her regular associate at Sunday church services. We made no formal announcement, yet we became a couple and soon our friends orbited the two of us.

17. Lectures, Sectarians and Quacks, 1834

*The success of a quack lies in his ability to
please his customer's fantasies.*

I was still waiting for the analysis of McCarthy's Copaiba when the botanical healer Samuel Thomson secured the Aurora Academy for his traveling lecture show. Quacks are untrained men playing doctor but sectarians play doctor as steadfast devotees of a particular theory. The McCarthy type of quack entertains while making no secret about his intent to sell. Sectarians seduce by promising serious magic backed by fairy-tale theories. In my opinion, Thomson was a sectarian.

Despite the experience at McCarthy's performance, Millicent, William, and Rebecca convinced me to attend Thomson's lecture. On the carriage ride to the lecture I tried to explain why regular doctors hold such animosity towards the sectarian style of quack by relating a second case of malpractice I had encountered in my first few months of practice. A type of sectarian, this quack claimed centuries of Indian medicine theories.

Lloyd was a lad of twenty with a common summer fever for which a friend consulted a doctor claiming special knowledge of Black Creek Indian medicine. Lloyd faithfully consumed a large pellet of "black mud" and a quart of black liquid as directed. By the next morning, a burning pain in his throat made it impossible for Lloyd to swallow, but the doctor was nowhere to be found. I then became involved and found Lloyd suffering from acute mercury overdose with loose teeth and ulcerations covering his swollen throat and tongue. I swabbed his mouth with an astringent, applied an anodyne plaster to his neck, poured a teaspoon of Laudanum into each ear with a cotton ball to secure it, and had him breath in the vapors of vinegar and alum. Through that night Lloyd passed copious, offensive stool. By morning the oral ulcers were gangrenous and his tongue had essentially decomposed, the slough of which I removed. The lad's need for drink was so severe that I passed a gum elastic tube and introduced half a pint of cold water and a dose of paregoric (camphorated opium). Over the next several hours he struggled through violent episodes of cough producing putrid black sputum. During one of these episodes his respirations arrested. He perished, a victim of mercury poisoning caused by an uneducated practitioner claiming the magic of special knowledge.

During my apprenticeship, Thomson's book was required reading so we might understand the power of sectarian marketing. He paid newspapers to print stories hawking his system and welcomed women to join his ranks. But the real genius was the last page of his $20 book. It was a certificate, suitable for framing. Just print your name, enter the date, and you became a Thomsonian doctor, authorized to use the patented Thomsonian botanical medicines that could be mail ordered from Thomson.

I don't deny the probability that unknown and helpful medicines are yet to be discovered. However, I do condemn all those who would administer to the sick while denying science. Certainly, there is enough suffering without hubris provoking more. Sectarians set themselves apart by declaring that they are scorned apostles of truth, declare regular doctors the enemy of truth, and willingly drain the patient's purse.

―――――

I winced as Hiram Barney gave Samuel Thomson's formal introduction, calling him a medical pioneer. Then, as if to further excite my hostility, Thomson began his lecture by reciting a poem from his book:

> The Priest pretends to save the soul,
> Doctors to make the body whole,
> For money, lawyers make their plea,
> Thomsonians save it and dismiss the three.

> Come freemen all, unveil your eyes,
> If you this slavish yoke despise,
> Now is the time to be set free,
> From Priests' and Doctors' slavery.

The sixty-year-old Samuel Thomson described his childhood as the son of a New Hampshire, Baptist farmer who held a great curiosity about herbs. Thomson was only age four when he also became enthralled with the properties of botanicals, particularly *lobelia inflate*. One day he gave a leaf of lobelia to a hired laborer who commenced a profuse trembling sweat, vomited, and cursed young Samuel out of fear he was dying. But, after a hearty dinner and an afternoon of euphoric, vigorous labor, the man turned to praising Samuel. At age eight Samuel suffered some undefined illness that was cured by a neighbor lady's botanicals and he soon became her apprentice.

Later Thomson's mother died from what her doctors called "galloping consumption." Samuel suffered the same condition but found remedy using herbs. Thomson's final epiphany came when his wife became ill after childbirth and the remedies of several regular doctors failed her. Thomson cured her with herbs and roots, and vowed to never again hold any confidence in regular doctors.

In 1805, the Lord summoned Thomson to give up farming and share his deep understanding of botanical cures. Convinced formal education could only pervert his insights, he took straight to lecturing across New England, New York and Ohio. In 1822, he put all his knowledge together in the first edition of his book, *New Guide to Health; Or, the Botanic Family Physician*. That, and all subsequent editions, begin with a chapter called 'The Narrative,' describing hundreds of cures and declaring all regular doctors to be frauds.

Truth has enemies, according to Thomson. One jealous regular doctor bribed a local Sheriff to accuse Thomson of murder after a patient consulted him too late in her illness for any remedy to work. The jury realized the hateful conspiracy and easily acquitted him. And, everyone knows, the medical profession bribes politicians to thwart petitions requesting equal licensing for Thomsonian practitioners. Fact is, regular doctors claim the false aristocracy of Science and use Latin to keep secrets from their patients.

Thomson did not need science to believe that all illness stems from obstructed perspiration. Cold is death, so heat with perspiration restores the natural state. His 'Number one' treatment, lobelia cleanses the stomach, overpowers cold and promotes a free perspiration. Difficult cases require his 'Number Two' treatment of cayenne pepper to intensify heating and rid the bowels of putrefaction. Numbers three and four are various teas or tonics concocted from roots, leaves, or bark. A steam bath improves outcomes at every step. "Anyone who can cook and follow a recipe can avoid wasting money on regular doctors."

Here Thomson claimed, "Lobelia cures only if the patient is threatened by death. If healthy, lobelia may exert little effect. If taken too late, it will also have little effect. Lobelia faithfully cures when cure is possible."

Thomson assured the audience that agents were waiting outside the lecture hall to answer questions and arrange for the purchase of his book and a subscription to his magazine. They might also secure one of the few remaining openings at an upcoming Thomsonian Society meeting. He closed with a prayer. "God, thank you for blessing me with the wisdom to make your gift of safe medicine available to the wonderful people of Aurora. Thank you for calling out the evils created by those who study Anatomy and Physiology. Just as Jesus cast merchants out of the temple, so too must we declare the evils perpetrated by regular doctors. Grant everyone this evening the courage of their newfound wisdom and direct them to your natural remedies. We thank you God, for revealing a system that allows loving parents to protect their family from death and disease. Amen."

After the lecture William, Rebecca, Millicent and I retired to Hiram's new apartment for a brandy nightcap. I am not certain who first asked my opinion, but with my dander up I broke right into a lecture, "I have little respect for anyone who would take a short cut to knowledge, or dupe those who are sick and fearful. Thomson attracts the naive with the simplicity of Lobelia, then he lightens their wallets with an overpriced book and subscriptions to newsletters peddling testimonials about his scheme. I don't like being called, 'The prevailing medical aristocracy intent on draining the wallet of common men,' when he is the one who obtained a patent so all profit from his self-styled system goes to his wallet. This while graduate doctors freely publish their discoveries in journals."

Millicent interjected, "I have read Thomson's book. His system is appealingly simple. One just looks up a symptom and selects a remedy from a rather short list. In orthodox medicine, it seems every doctor offers a different medicine for the same symptom."

Hiram was also acquainted with Thomson's book, "I tried Lobelia and, like Thomson's farmer, I puked, sweated and then felt nearly euphoric for several hours. Unpleasant start, but sweet ending."

I responded, "That's just it, Thomson counts on that Lobelia euphoria. It's like tobacco, or the cure-all tonics that contain opium and cocaine. Only Thomson adds instructions for sitting on a stool covered in blankets while soaking your feet in hot water."

Millicent pressed on, "Jabez, regular doctors can be quite negative about new ideas. I hesitate to ask what you think about Homeopathy. There are reports that more patients of Homeopaths survived Cholera epidemics."

Millicent was correct, Homeopathy posed an even greater challenge to regular medicine than Thomson, and I took full advantage of her opening, "I have come to believe that people approach illness two ways. Some place their faith in anyone who convincingly promises a cure. Others place their faith in professionals who derive their knowledge from formal training augmented by Science and practice, bedside experience. Homeopaths call regular medicine Allopathic, saying that our treatments are intended to produce symptoms opposite of those produced by disease. They dismiss our traditionally organized medical schools, apprenticeships and exams by organizing their own institutions that focus on their brand of sectarian dogma. I suppose that is somewhat better than Samuel Thomson refusing to allow his followers to organize a college because he feared formal training would corrupt his God inspired system."

Samuel Hahnemann's 'like cures like' (*similia similibus curantur*) theory of Homeopathy reached America in the 1820s. Hahnemann was a graduate German Physician who supported himself by translating English medical books into German. In 1790, while translating Cullen's *Materia Medica* he suffered a fever, which he treated with high doses of quinine according to Cullen's recommendation. The quinine worsened his palpitations, flushing, and thirst before effecting its cure, convincing Hahnemann that curing disease required the symptoms of the illness to be amplified. In other words, a patient with fever should be warmed, not cooled. This is Hahnemann's First Principle of Homeopathy, a German word meaning 'like cures like.'

Hahnemann's Second Revelation was that only minute doses are needed to remedy illness. He diluted various substances to the thirtieth power and they are now sold in numbered bottles and prescribed according to a chart of patient symptoms. The dilutions are mostly water, so, unlike some of our remedies, Homeopathic remedies pose little risk. The Cholera epidemic should teach us to avoid overtreatment. It does not confirm the efficacy of dilutions.

Dr. Hoyt told me that for several years the Erie County Medical Society allowed regular physicians who dabbled in Homeopathy to remain society members. Then, the ever-argumentative homeopath, Dr. Nash Hull Warner, took to charging allopath's with poisoning patients. Warner maintained that failure to understand the mechanism of homeopathic cure does not mean it is ineffective. He asked, "Who in this room can explain why, or how, Epsom salts works? And, as for dilutions, is not strychnine diluted before use?"

Along the way, several American medical journals reviewed the available homeopathic textbooks and reported a lack of Science to support infinitesimal dilutions, recommending that scientific practitioners not accept Hahnemann's doctrines. That has not stopped a few Aurora homes from purchasing the 'Domestic Homeopathic Kit' containing a rack of dilutions with symptom charts. The instructions for these kits state, "Homeopathic medicines are prepared so that the right one will cure, but the wrong one will not injure."

What I did not predict on that 1834 evening was how successfully Homeopathy, and its magazine *Domestic Physician*, would compete with regular medicine. In 1842, Oliver Wendell Holmes would publish an essay titled, "Homeopathy and Its Kindred Delusions." Better than I, Holmes used humor to compare Hahnemann's dilutions to spiritualism and animal magnetism. Holmes concluded that anyone proclaiming, 'Great is Hahnemann!' would be equally accurate proclaiming, 'Quackery is immortal.'

Dr. Nash Hull Warner continued to champion Homeopathy in Erie County. Privately, I knew him as a quiet, dignified man with quick insight and a commanding presence. He was a regular graduate Physician who served as the Director of the Marine Hospital in Buffalo. However, when Dr. Warner damned regular doctors in his essay promoting homeopathic remedies for Asiatic Cholera, the Erie County Medical Society dismissed him. Dr. Warner then joined with fifteen homeopathic colleagues to organize the Erie County Homeopathic Medical Society, open a Buffalo Homeopathic Hospital, and edit the short-lived *Homoeopathist Medical Journal* that gave voice to his opinions. He also played a part in the 1844 founding of the

American Institute of Homeopathy and the opening of several homeopathic medical colleges.

On that evening of Thomson's lecture, I also opined about an Austria modeled Hydrotherapy institute planned for Aurora. Hydro-therapists encourage cold water enemas, cold sitz baths, drinking cold water, taking cold showers and brisk rubbing of the body. Several hydrotherapy spas in New York charge a lucrative $5 to $10 a day, more than even the warm mineral spas in Saratoga and Clifton Springs. Sylvester Graham, the Presbyterian Minister, lecturer, vegetarian calls himself a hydro-therapist while also advocating for the consumption of his coarsely ground wheat flour. Graham believes that sexual activity should be limited to procreation because it depletes the body and leads to early death, adding that self-stimulation caused blindness. Hiram once attended a Graham lecture at the Springville Presbyterian Church titled, "Science of Human Life: Rules governing diet, physical activity, sexuality, and bathing." The lecture was so graphic that several women fainted.

I could not leave my sectarian rant that evening without a mention of the Eclectics who follow the teachings of New Yorker Wooster Beach. Eclectics embrace medical science, but choose many botanical remedies. My medical philosophy can seem eclectic at times, and I do embrace the thoughtful studies of men like Constantine Rafinesque. Rafinesque studied botany and herbalism in his travels from Constantinople to France and then America. He holds a professorship in Botany at Kentucky's Transylvania University and has written extensively about the medical flora of the United States. Rafinesque explains the science behind herbals like goldenseal, echinacea and the purple coneflower. I do not consider myself an eclectic, but I do choose remedies that I believe will work best for my patients.

My real concern is how well marketed delusions pervert reasoning. Homeopathic dilutions, spiritualism, mesmerism, water cures and lobelia highs reveal the human fondness for magic. "I hope for something better, for a medical enlightenment. I fear the sectarians would send us back to the age of philosophical rationalization. I also fear that regular medicine is loath to accept new ideas, like my stethoscope for instance. The very existence of Thomson's system and Homeopathy reveals a lingering mistrust of regular medicine."

Millicent interjected, "Jabez, you give these matters more than a passing thought. And, your frustrations with those who would question your science is unambiguous, but, as you said, many will view the issue purely as a threat to your pocket book." Millicent's tone was one of concern and the challenge she described was a serious one.

Sleep did not come easy that night. I worried my sectarian rant mimicked a school boy showing off his book learning. When I wrestled my mind from that preoccupation I worried that a smug farm boy from Vermont could not rise to the Johnson sophistication. Millicent was inquisitive and intelligent, and even when challenging, her demeanor was polite and proper.

Soon a midwife's messenger disrupted my sleepless consternations. My attendance at the labor of a woman having her first child was needed. By 6:00 a.m. in the morning I resorted to the application of forceps and delivered a healthy girl. Upon returning to the store I attempted a nap in my quarters but sleep still avoided me. The University at Cork had responded. They had no medical college, though plans were underway to start medical lectures in 1837. They also had no record of a Phineas J. McCarthy. Anxious that the analysis on McCarthy's Copaiba would also be disappointing, I now worried about Abiatha.

18. Snake Oil, 1834

The heart must learn to laugh, love and endure betrayal.

I often feel energized after a night where the skills of being a doctor are challenged and the outcome is good. Apprehensions about the previous night's sectarian rant seemed long ago. Back at my quarters, I made a cup of coffee and ate a breakfast of hard crusted barley bread and cheese while I read Eberle's textbook description of the sectarian menace. I also checked every reference Eberle made to lobelia which confirmed its usefulness in asthma, bronchitis and whooping cough. It certainly was not the cure-all advocated by Thomson. Now I faced the problem of Phineas J. McCarthy.

When I descended the stairs, Abiatha simmered with excitement as she handed me an envelope from the inspection committee of the American Pharmaceutical Association. "It arrived just as I was leaving last evening," Abiatha explained. "I was so excited that I asked Phineas to come to the store this morning so we could celebrate together. He should be here any time now."

It was disappointing to hear that Abiatha was still seeing McCarthy but I agreed to wait until he arrived. I had not found the nerve to tell Abiatha that Phineas' was already caught in a lie about the University of Cork.

The morning progressed quite typically. Abiatha waited on store customers, I compounded several prescriptions and administered to four patients in my examination room. The last was a ten-year-old boy who had fallen from a tree and sustained a typical Colles fracture to his right forearm. I needed Abiatha's assistance to provide traction while I realigned the wrist and applied a splint.

Soon it was noon and McCarthy had not shown. Abiatha was inclined to go to the Fillmore Tavern where McCarthy was staying and usually took his dinner. I felt it best we first open the envelop:

September 19, 1834
Dear Dr. Allen:

Thank you for your inquiry regarding the contents of McCarthy's Copaiba Oil. We are pleased to provide these services to our members.

It is our standard to apply several analyzing techniques if preliminary tests suggest that the sample is adulterated. In the case of McCarthy's Copaiba Oil, we have performed two internal analyses and sent the sample for a third outside chemist's opinion. All three analyses confirm very similar contents:

Mineral oil (major component)
Trace fatty oil likely to be tallow
Trace capsaicin or ground chili peppers
Trace oil of turpentine
Camphor
Cedarwood balsam (likely)

Copaiba is a relatively inert essential oil but unlike mineral oil it is not heat tolerant. The oil in this sample demonstrated heat tolerance typical of mineral oil. We cannot rule out the possibility that there are trace amounts of copaiba.

The sample you submitted is consistent with other samples submitted to our offices and typical of products sold by itinerate salesmen or in general stores. Most prove to be spiced mineral oil.

We suggest that you report this fraud to your local authorities and seek indictment. Selling fake medicines through fallacious marketing undermines efforts to protect the public and provide legitimate drugs. Our analysis should withstand challenge by those who imagined relief from the fraudulent substance and refuse to admit they were duped. Any delay and the huckster will leave the jurisdiction where they perpetrated their crime.

   We appreciate your membership in the American Pharmaceutical Association and your use of our services. Please consider this letter as your invoice and remit $2.50 at your earliest convenience. We will appreciate follow-up should you formally accuse the source of this fraudulent sample.

Sincerely,

Frederick Rhomehouse

Chair, Inspection Committee

American Pharmaceutical Association

I looked at Abiatha and saw defiance, "It is not true. They are lying just because Dr. McCarthy doesn't belong to their organization. He is funny and entertaining, but he is no snake oil salesman. He helps people. They're the crooks, their inspection is a sham."

Letting the other shoe drop, I told Abiatha about my letter from the University of Cork and that they have no medical college nor have any record of McCarthy's attendance.

Abiatha was in no composure for work. Millicent had been right, Abiatha's entanglement made the news impossible to digest. I suggested that she take the rest of the day to sort things out but I needed to be unambiguous, "I know this news is not in line with your personal experience. I am sorry for that. I also realize that my response is far easier than yours, but we both need to face the truth. I would not sell McCarthy's Copaiba Oil in my store, nor will I employ anyone who continues to keep his company. My sympathies are for you and you alone. My anger is directed on McCarthy only."

Abiatha immediately left the store juggling anger, fear, confusion, hurt and agitation, unable to decide what to feel. By late-afternoon, as my lack of sleep was claiming its due, Abiatha surprised me by returning to the store with a look of troubled sadness.

Abiatha had spent most of the afternoon searching Aurora for McCarthy. Mrs. Fillmore said he left the tavern that morning in good spirits, issuing his usual compliments for her cooking. He said that McCarthy's Copaiba Oil was flying off the shelves and he had to make almost daily rounds of the general stores to maintain their stock. He was so busy that he would be unable to take his dinner at the tavern.

Abiatha borrowed a horse and visited as many stores as she could, but no one had seen Dr. Phineas J. McCarthy that day.

Her search exhausted, she returned to the Fillmore tavern where she and Mrs. Fillmore inspected McCarthy's room. They found all his possessions gone. His ultimate cruelty was what he left in the room. Abiatha and Jerusha Fillmore found a half case of McCarthy's Copaiba oil and a note that read:

Dearest Jerusha and Abiatha,

    Sorry for my sudden departure. As you mentioned, Dr. Allen has the report confirming the special purity and nature of my vital Copaiba oil and it is essential that I assist another village in their search for health.

    I will send payment for my room and board forth with and leave these vials for the Colonel's relief. Thank you all for your hospitality. Aurora has blessed me and I love you all.

Dr. Phineas J. McCarthy

I doubt any note could have seared a larger wound in Abiatha's soul. It contained no personal goodbye and yet another unfulfilled promise, left by a man who owned her heart.

19. Courtship and the Mansion of Happiness, 1834

Each day infers a promise for tomorrow.

The next few weeks reaffirmed Abiatha's personal strength. She bore the McCarthy wounds as a stoic, returning to her duties with her usual proficiency. My new normal included spending Sunday afternoons after church at the Johnson home playing a board game called *Mansion of Happiness* with Millicent, mother Millicent, William and his fiancé, Rebecca. The game's instructions begin with a poem, two lines of which are:

> At this amusement each will find,
> A moral fit to improve the mind.

It is a pious but very popular game in which one tries to avoid spaces labeled 'Sabbath breaker,' which sends the player back 6 spaces. The player must also draw a card that might sentence the player to a turn at the whipping post for sins of audacity, cruelty, immodesty or ingratitude. Rebecca saw the game as a rehearsal for teaching children the Christian way of life, but the game also encourages players to tell revealing stories. It was during one of these games that William announced he and Rebecca had a firm November wedding date. Mother Millicent was delighted.

When Hiram Barney joined us for the occasional Sunday dinner there were too many people to play a board game and the men retired to the library for cigars and brandy, freeing the ladies to plan the wedding. William loved to argue and Hiram was quick to take his bait. One of their best arguments occurred after the preacher based a sermon on an essay by Thomas Carlyle titled the "Sign of the Times." Originally published in the *Edinburgh Review*,

Carlyle's essay made a sensation in America for condemning the significance modern man places on inventions, machines, science and individual achievement. William defended the value of science while Hiram worried society was ignoring the religious foundations of humanity. I goaded the both of them.

On another Sunday William challenged the Academy's acquisition of the 26th edition of *Aristotle's Masterpiece: The Secrets of Generation*. In print since 1684, the book used detailed diagrams to provide reliable information about procreation and sexuality. It was quite the opposite of the stork narrative written by Hans Cristian Anderson, and in stark contrast to Sylvester Graham's warnings about the evils of sex. Hiram argued that farm children may see animals mate, birth and nurse and still require accurate information about humans.

As the summer entered fall, Millicent and I launched courtship. Families who had tried to interest me in their daughter, niece or neighbor, now invited Millicent and I for tea and pumped us for information that might enrich their gossip tallies. Millicent amazed me with her ability to reveal little while probing the pursuits and pastimes of our hosts.

Rebecca Brigham's family believed their daughter's wedding should express their values as well as their joy. The Brigham's reserved the Congregational Church for 10:00 a.m. in the morning on the first Friday in the November of 1834. On the wedding day, they hung a white horseshoe with dangling bells over the church entrance. The local social column described Rebecca's dress as a "fashionable brown and purple striped gown with an empire waist that produced a flattering columnar silhouette." William had a new suit tailored for the occasion, and placed a gold band on Rebecca's left ring finger to symbolize their union. The invited guests followed the new Mr. and Mrs. Johnson as they walked from the church to the Brigham residence where first the bride, then the groom received us into the Brigham home. Millicent instructed me not to congratulate Rebecca as it would imply that she had been lucky to find a husband. That did not stop me from acknowledging William's good fortune.

The Brigham's served a late morning breakfast washed down with multiple mead toasts. It was my first encounter with mead, a semi-sweet wine fermented from honey, and I found it quite pleasing. By early afternoon the wedding cake, a rich dark fruitcake with white frosting, was cut and each guest received their small box containing a piece to take home. As the newly married couple exited the front door Rebecca's brother threw an old pair of shoes in their path for good luck while the rest of us tossed rice to assure a fertile and happy marriage.

After William and Rebecca left for their secret honeymoon destination, Millicent and I walked her mother home. It was only natural that our conversation revolved around adjustments the new marriage necessitated. Captain Samuel Johnson's Will specified that the residence became William's property upon his marriage, and that mother Millicent was to be welcomed in the home until her death. Millicent and her mother loved Rebecca, but Rebecca's proclivity for pious control made them both a little apprehensive.

I was a struggling doctor with a modest income, and pouring every penny into a developing business, but the intimacy of that afternoon overcame my worries. I knelt before Millicent, in the presence of her mother, and asked if she would honor me by becoming my wife. The two Millicent's teased me with several moments of debate, then the younger honored me with our first witnessed kiss. Before I could rise, mother Millicent took my face in her hands and planted another kiss on my forehead.

Within the hour, we decided to use the same Congregational Church but with a very limited guest list. We would ask Rebecca's approval to host the wedding breakfast in the Johnson home. Mother Millicent suggested since change was overtaking all of us, we might just as well welcome it with God's speed and set the date for Monday, 22 December 1834. Then, we asked mother Millicent to live with us as soon as we could find an appropriate situation. Frugality aside, I declared my intent to buy Millicent a ring to symbolize our engagement. Magazines and catalogs were promoting diamond engagement rings and I wanted a diamond to show my respect for Millicent and the whole Johnson family.

―――――

Upon their return, we politely allowed William and Rebecca to exhaust their Niagara Falls honeymoon stories before we shared our news. In celebration William opened a bottle of his French wine and we drank a toast. Foolishly, I rushed into the question about mother Millicent living with us and should have anticipated William's suggestion that such discussions be postponed. Later I took William aside to apologize, but he changed the subject by suggesting that Millicent and I join Rebecca and him on his upcoming business trip to Buffalo where we could visit the shop of a jeweler he knew.

A cold November rain drenched the next few days, but a week later we boarded the Johnson surrey for Buffalo. Just two miles out of Aurora we came to Pratt's Hill where disembarked passengers were gawking at the morning stage coach sunk in the mud nearly to the axles. William and I were still surveying the possibilities when a farm wagon drawn by a plow horse pulled up behind us. No one could advance unless the stage moved. William and the farmer unhitched their horses and with some innovative rigging and the shoulders of five men the stage was freed. Fortunately, most remaining low stretches of Buffalo Road were planked.

Once at Buffalo's American Hotel a bootblack made quick work of the mud on our boots. Benjamin Rathburn, for whom William had done some legal work, had just opened the American Hotel located next to his famous Eagle Tavern. We took occupancy of three rooms, arranged for dinner at the Eagle tavern, and purchased tickets for a play at the Eagle Street Theater. William teased the ladies that he and I intended a late-night visit to Canal Street to explore its notorious bars and games of faro, roulette and cutthroat.

William left to conduct his business while Millicent, Rebecca and I visited Richard James Shibley, Buffalo Silversmith and Jeweler. After trying on several original designs, Millicent asked Mr. Shibley if he sold vintage rings. Moving on to the case of previously owned rings, Millicent found a unique gold ring with diamond chips arranged around a Mexican red agate that, as if by providence, fit Millicent's finger perfectly. "If you agree Jabez, let's make this our special symbol of commitment." As Mr. Shibley and I completed our transaction, Millicent's respect for our soon to be shared finances filled me with hope for our future.

Next, we visited the offices of George Washington Jonson (GWJ) who was at his desk making an entry into his journals. GWJ seemed genuinely happy for our engagement and wished us good fortune. Millicent updated him on several runaway issues before he rushed off to continue his City Council law suit demanding Negro children attend public schools. I noted with amusement that GWJ called my fiancé Millie, but was quickly informed that he would be the only person who would survive calling her Millie. Still, an idea once planted takes on an energy of its own.

On our way back to the hotel, I purchased a newspaper, the *Commercial Advertiser*, then indulged in a nap before William returned. The Eagle Tavern's prime beef lived up to expectations as did the play, a comedy, *Julia: or the Wanderer*, by John Howard Payne whose song *Home Sweet Home* was already very popular. It was a lavish evening filled with laughter and excitement that left no enthusiasm for Canal Street explorations.

Wedding arrangements now consumed every available moment. We booked the Congregational Society Church for the morning of December 22. Millicent arranged a special, but unpretentious celebration and mother Millicent helped with the fitting of a beautiful cream-colored wedding dress. William served as her escort and Hiram as my best man. The Fillmores, the Warrens, Abiatha and Hiram wished us a wonderful life as we departed our breakfast reception for our honeymoon.

Our honeymoon was a spectacular gift from mother Millicent. She had William book us on the season's last steamboat out of Buffalo to Lake St. Clair, just north of Detroit. It took nearly a week to reach Harsens Island and the Lodge on St. Clair where we stayed two nights before returning. Framed by wonderfully white winter landscapes, Millicent and I spent hours making plans and evaluating our prospects. We became husband, wife, and friends for life on that trip.

Upon our return, normal duties resumed. Dr. Hoyt had covered both my practice and pharmacy during our absence but Abiatha saved what work could wait and the backlog kept me quite busy. Millicent did what she could to make the small upstairs apartment brighter with curtains and wallpaper but nothing could make it bigger.

Before marriage entered my plans, I had purchased a small vacant lot on Cemetery Street. It was too small for our growing needs, so I sold it to the widow Elizabeth Judd for a dress shop, but holding the mortgage kept us cash poor. Fortunately, Nathan Waldo, the painter's brother, offered to rent us his home at 738 Big Tree Road. The house was just a block from my office, east of Water Street, and next door to Joseph Howard's hardware store. Like so many homes on the east end of town, it was a fine post, beam and plank home in the Greek Revival style built by Lemuel Spooner in the 1820s. Its 2,600 square feet generously accommodated our hopes for a family and would easily accommodate mother Millicent. The small yard was half taken up by a family graveyard. On the side opposite the hardware store lived the blacksmith, Ephraim Woodruff. Before thawing of the last snow, we had not only moved our few possessions, but welcomed mother Millicent to occupy the front upstairs bedroom overlooking Big Tree Road.

William blessed the move, though we never did have further conversation on the topic.

That first home proved to be our forever home. A few years after our move Howard Hardware fell on hard times. That property had originally been gifted by Jabez Warren to School District No. 1 of Aurora in 1816. The building on the site, also constructed by Mr. Spooner, was where Millard Fillmore and General Warren both taught. Joseph Howard converted the school building into a hardware store in 1827. Howard was a hard worker, friendly and generous with credit. His business faced financial challenges from the beginning. In 1832, he sold the property to raise urgently needed cash, which Howard used to improve his stock. Unfortunately, he only converted his overhead to rent payments. The economic downturn of 1836 put a severe strain on the store's customers and Howard's business. Though Howard faithfully paid the rent, the landlord failed to pay the taxes and in 1842 the Sheriff assumed the deed. The property was sold to Grosvenor Willis in 1842.

I began conversations with Mr. Willis to lease the former hardware store, address 728 Big Tree Road, and by early 1843 we were able to come to an equitable arrangement. I moved my drugstore and practice to the larger, more accommodating building immediately next door to our home.

Nathan Waldo was obliged to sell our home before my financial situation allowed us the luxury of its purchase. Fortunately, relatives of Millicent, T.P. & Emily Johnson, were in a position for investment. They purchased the home in 1841 and agreed to our continued habitation. Finally, in 1848, Millicent and I purchased the house from the Johnsons and advanced our situation from longtime renters to home owners.

We still reside in this home. I am writing this memoir from the upstairs front room that was mother Millicent's bedroom until her death in 1864.

The room's two large windows face south allowing sentry of Big Tree Road and all those who enter Aurora as I had in 1834.

20. Making a Home, 1835

A good man finds what he needs at home.

By 1835 the Erie Barge Canal had pushed Buffalo's population to 9,000. At 2,400 lives, Aurora was the second largest township at the western end of New York. A third of both populations were foreign born, attracted by wage paying jobs. The resulting cash economy meant doctors, lawyers, priests and undertakers also got paid, at least sometimes.

As a bachelor, I had been oblivious to chaos. I worked most of the time, ate or slept when I needed to and read when I was not doing anything else. With the suddenness of marriage, Millicent and I were moving into a new home, begging and borrowing a few items of furniture, and dinner was on the table promptly at noon. Shortly after we moved a late-night patient woke me by throwing an oversized pebble through our upstairs window. The next day we had Mr. Howard from the hardware store install a tube from the side door to our bedroom so patients could shout me awake.

Previous occupants of the home had availed themselves of the community latrine, so at the first thaw Millicent had me digging our own private latrine complete with outhouse. The farmer in me lobbied for the purchase of a cow and a few chickens, but Millicent convinced me of the advantages of contracting with a local farmer, suggesting a garden would do me fine.

Food availability was seasonal, making it necessary to pre-plan a nutritious year-round diet. Mrs. Beeton's *Book of Household Management* figures that a healthy, full-grown man, doing a moderate amount of work (eight walking miles a day), requires daily consumption of four ounces of meat, three ounces of fat, fifteen ounces of sugary or starchy food, and one ounce of salt. Women and young boys need about nine-tenths the amount of food men need, and ten-year-old children need about half. Meat and cereals not only satiate the appetite most efficiently, but have the greatest nutritional value.

Millicent had a talent for securing food in sufficient quantity and variety, expanding greatly on my bachelor's diet of hard crusted barley or corn bread and cheese supplemented by regular meals at a tavern. Millicent added inexpensive sugar to many recipes and pickled, smoked and otherwise preserved foods with salt for winter.

Breakfast was coffee or coco made by boiling yesterday's milk, a warm bit of corn bread with a few bites of cured meat. The largest and most varied meal was the noon dinner which consisted of smoked bacon or ham and sauerkraut in the winter and roast lamb, chicken or pork and asparagus or fresh greens in the summer. Beef was for special holidays. In the evening, we had leftovers that might otherwise spoil and capped them off with a little brandy. Garlic, onions, leeks, mustard and pepper were considered staples because they increased the flow of bile.

Potable water was always a challenge. Rivers, creeks and hand dug wells were often muddy and foul smelling. Saratoga Vichy water and other bottled water was available but expensive. I distilled several gallons of water drawn from the community well each day to use in compounding medicines and carried a gallon home every noon. The cistern along the back wall of our cellar stored a fairly reliable amount of clean water for household use. Distilled whiskey and fermented drinks like apple cider or brandy were generally safe and nourishing. A few people drank beer regularly, though I always found brewing palatable beer difficult. Rum and corn whiskey (sometimes called bourbon) were popular and relatively inexpensive.

Farmers could sell all the wheat they could grow to the cities at a good price, so most of the time we ate a brown bread made from a blend of rye, barley, oats or corn. These breads had a stiff crust that could serve as a bowl or a scoop. The crust would then soften and become quite edible.

Cash poor farmers often paid me in eggs, butter, meat, vegetables, and grain. They slaughtered animals in November, December and January as feed ran low and salted or cured much of the meat for storage with roots and hardy vegetables like beans, potatoes, parsnips and turnips.

Keeping a cow freshened, fed and producing milk took constant planning. Millicent wisely left this to the farmers who could keep three or four cows freshened and still allow newborn calves to consume a good share of the milk until weaned. A newly freshened cow produced milk with the highest cream content for making butter and cheese.

Most farmers maintained an orchard so apples were plentiful and stored reasonably well for baking into dumplings and pies. Millicent and I put up two barrels of apple cider and canned three bushels of applesauce to use as a winter condiment.

We purchased salt, sugar, molasses, spices, tea, coffee, chocolate, flour, rice, and the occasional salted cod, shad, mackerel, and herring at the general store. The stores also carried mustard, cinnamon, ginger, raisins, rum, brandy, and gin.

German Badger Day, February 2, marks the time when you better have half your wood pile remaining or you are going to be cold during the lingering snows of April. It's also when stored vegetables run out or spoil and families subsist on cured and salted meat. Condie's textbook recommends children get regular doses of cod-liver oil, eggs and milk, and sun exposure in late winter to avoid muscle aches, widened wrists, and bowing legs common to Rickets. Scurvy, also common in late winter, is characterized by general lassitude, bleeding gums and brittle hair and can be avoided by eating Sauerkraut. The dry-stone cellar of our home was perfect for the fermentation and curing of ample amounts of Sauerkraut.

Through the winter, Millicent and I treated ourselves to a can of oysters once a month to break up the monotony of winter meals. Most general stores sold canned foods put up by the American Canning Company, but they were expensive, so much so that some wealthy families showed off by serving canned food to guests. Millicent and I share a brandy toast before ceremoniously using a hammer and chisel to open our can of oysters, a treat that seemed more civilized with the ingenious invention of a can opener in 1850.

Though a devote Presbyterian, Millicent endorsed John Wesley's Methodist conviction that 'Cleanliness is next to godliness.' To Millicent cleanliness indicated control, spiritual refinement, and breeding. Magazines picked up on Wesley's message, suggesting the body should be rinsed frequently with water then briskly rubbed with a towel to clean the skin. Once a week we hauled several buckets of water for emersion baths and toweling.

A magazine called the *Moral Reformer and Teacher on the Human Constitution* published by William A. Alcott promoted cleanliness, purity of moral character and started advertising soap in the 1830s. Like many women, Millicent liked the smell of store bought soap and if I washed my hands before coming home she figured I embraced her cleanliness and godliness association. At Castleton our surgery professor, Dr. Woodward, insisted that students wash their hands before and after surgeries and autopsies, offering no rationale beyond linking godliness to cleanliness. Still, the idea of soap would not really take off until 1868 when the unwashed bootblack in Horatio Alger's *Raggedy Dick* proved unrecognizable to his friends after bathing.

Millicent supported the demands of my work but did not take naturally to Physic. As a result, I lived in two worlds, doctoring and the perfect home life she maintained. The stark partition was tested when a Physician in Alden died after performing an autopsy. Millicent was aware that I considered autopsies part of my responsibility and important to my own continuing experience, but she had not considered that there were risks to doctoring.

Our first argument occurred after a spring Debating Society meeting pitting Congressman Millard Fillmore against Ralph Waldo Emerson. Emerson championed individualism within his philosophy of transcendentalism outlined in his *Nature* essay. Fillmore defended the importance of a community view. I took the community view and Millicent the individualist view. The process taught me formal debates are much easier than domestic debates.

As Millicent and I adjusted to our married life I was again impressed with Abiatha's ability to recover from tragedy and disappointment. Following McCarthy's cruel abandonment, she returned to her work as my assistant with her usual dedication. One day I commented that she appeared breathless. She attributed it to a minor weight gain I had not noticed.

But a crisis loomed on the horizon.

21. Consequences of Impulse, 1835

Find a place to invest your humanity.

Abiatha was pregnant. She was forced to reveal her condition to me the morning that Jerusha Fillmore had guessed the obvious. The encounter with Jerusha did not go well. The two women argued, and Abiatha promised to leave the Fillmore residence forthwith. I vacillated between harsh condemnation and empathy between her immediate discharge and my obvious dependency on her work. All I managed was a stunned stutter that brought Abiatha to tears and did nothing to organize my thoughts.

Abiatha refused to identify the child's father, but her ruse was silly. It was a terrible situation and I sent for Millicent to help Abiatha sort out her options. Millicent was convinced that finding McCarthy would be impossible. He was likely using a different name and it was only a guess as to how many towns he had moved onto. Together the women decided the scoundrel's presence was undesirable under any circumstance.

Pregnancy casts a hard truth. Based on her last menstrual period in September we subtracted the customary three months and added a week to calculate that Abiatha's expected date of confinement would be 14 June 1835. With the experience of one previous successful pregnancy and one miscarriage, it's clear that Abiatha had denied the signs of pregnancy until her confrontation with Jerusha. For Abiatha, a week of uterine contractions in late December reinforced her denial even as the threat of miscarriage passed.

Millicent and I were both thunderstruck. The Abiatha we knew was a moral, headstrong woman capable of managing her affairs. That she could suffer such an extreme lapse was astonishing. Quoting John Wesley's admonition that Christians should be guided by a regard for the welfare of others, Millicent convinced me that we must sustain Abiatha through her ordeal. She had nowhere else to turn.

Millicent and Abiatha dismissed the most common option for pregnant single women that of boarding with a midwife who would arrange for adoption. The second most popular option was abortion, which New York State made a felony after quickening. It was estimated that one in five pregnancies ended in abortion and married women, wary of the financial burdens of another child, accounted for the majority. There were at least ten abortifacients available commercially. At least two were perfectly inert. Three others were mild laxatives and likely both harmless and ineffective. The remainder could be quite dangerous, containing active ingredients such as cotton root, black hellebore, ergot, oil of tansy, and oil of savin. Oil of savin is made from the berries of the common juniper and, though reliable as an abortifacient, it can damage the kidneys. This late in pregnancy, surgical abortion was illegal.

Millicent arranged to move Abiatha into the apartment above the drugstore until the delivery. This option would allow Abiatha to continue to support herself working in the store. She would work every day while paying close attention to her nutrition. I would not do the delivery, but Abiatha would engage a midwife and if needed, ask Dr. Hoyt to assist. Millicent's empathy for Abiatha's situation was measured and pragmatic. Her work supporting fugitive slaves had liberated her mind about society's rules, but our support for Abiatha was not born of wisdom, self-preservation or personal enlightenment. The societal norm called for an abrupt dismissal as Jerusha Fillmore had done. Appearing to endorse an unwed pregnancy risked adverse impact on any business, and likely we should have harbored greater concern about our medical practice. But, it was time to repay my debt to Abiatha for making my first year in Aurora profitable.

Millicent set a final condition. Abiatha was to attend church every Sunday and accompany Millicent to prayer meetings on Wednesdays. Millicent would show Aurora she would not shun those who sincerely repent their sins.

Abiatha accepted our conditions. With mother Millicent as our witness, the three of us shook hands and promised to support our project through to its conclusion.

22. Comments on Midwifery

Throughout history wise women sought assistance during labor, delivery and the postpartum period.

Within a couple days Abiatha settled into the apartment above the drugstore. Despite their eviction of the pregnant Abiatha, Jerusha helped give the apartment a personal touch and the Colonel lent a wagon and two employees to move Abiatha's few possessions. Hugging and tears contradicted any deep disaffection.

Abiatha bore her shame much as she bore all hardships, with quiet dignity and a dedicated work ethic. As her pregnancy become impossible to conceal, Abiatha answered even the most insensitive questions by village gossips with a simple refrain, "I will love this child with all my heart."

Like most people, Abiatha had little knowledge about procreation beyond what she witnessed on the farm. Abiatha's hallmark curiosity now focused on my textbooks, including Dr. John Roberton's textbook based on outcomes at a London Lying – in Hospital. Roberton notes three differences between humans and other mammals: Humans have monthly or catamenial menses; a second pregnancy is unlikely while nursing; human fecundity lasts only half the natural life span. The latter peculiarity, Roberton claims, is evidence that God intended women to guide younger generations and humanize domestic society. This was the role mother Millicent intended to fulfill for Abiatha.

It is a challenge for doctors to learn midwifery. Twenty years after I graduated medical college, a trial involving Dr. James Platt White of Buffalo Medical College and a woman who volunteered to allow demonstration of her delivery would show how difficult teaching Obstetrics remained.

Following protocols long established in Europe, two weeks before her expected date of confinement White moved the woman into quarters at the medical college under the guardianship of the janitor's wife. When her labor commenced, the graduating class, twenty-two in number, assembled in the surgical theater and one by one, Professor White guided them through vaginal examinations as labor progressed. Once the infant's head was at the external os the students were permitted to witness the passage of the head over the perineum as Dr. White effected a safe delivery. Care was taken to avoid unwarranted exposure of the woman, and mother and child made a rapid convalescence.

The next day Dr. White's demonstration made the front page of several Buffalo newspapers and the story was re-printed in Philadelphia and New York. A few days later a scathing critique signed "L" described the act as immoral. The critique was so bitter that Dr. White brought a suit for libel against a Dr. Horatio N. Loomis, the alleged author. The four-day trial made international headlines with each side releasing daily summations. Counsel for Dr. Loomis affirmed his disapproval of Dr. White's debauched demonstration but claimed that a Rev. John E. Robie, not Loomis, had authored the critique. Judge Mullett's instructions to the jury gained their own headline, "Public opinion has never been a reliable agent in the administration of justice since it cried 'Crucify Him! Crucify Him!'" Confusion about authorship resulted in Dr. Loomis being acquitted, but the process vindicated Dr. White.

At Castleton, we learned the basics of Obstetrics and Midwifery on manikins. I learned that nineteen out of twenty labors, when left solely to the energies of nature, terminate well under the care of an experienced midwife but it is the role of a Physician to evaluate an obstructed labor. Forceps, developed in 1720, may avoid the need for dismembering a fetus with a cephalotribe (forceps with teeth) or a crotchet hook but their application requires experience learned only under the supervision of my preceptor, brother James.

I have purchased every edition of DeWees' textbook of Midwifery because of its excellent science updates and straight forward explanations. DeWees says puberty starts with changes in the female well in advance of the first catamenia. Common symptoms of headache, pelvic pain and lassitude are due to the accumulation of blood, and resolve with the release of menstrual secretions, only to return as faithfully as the moon. DeWees does not believe the catamenia are actually under lunar control or like the tides, all women would menstruate in unison. DeWees' 1843 edition is the first to report on autopsy findings linking the catamenia to changes in the ovary.

My first delivery in Aurora occurred while Abiatha and I were still setting up the office. I was constructing benches to serve waiting patients when a hatless, flustered, perspiring man in shirt sleeves burst in demanding my immediate attendance to his wife's labor. He had tried Dr. Hoyt and Dr. Watson but they were both out on calls. I, also in shirt sleeves, grabbed my medical bag and followed the gentleman to a large brick home at the east end of town.

The attending midwife reported that, despite a prolonged and arduous labor, the child refused to enter the pelvic inlet. She advised dismemberment and extraction of the infant to save the mother. It would not have been the best moment to explain that neither my forceps, cephalotribe or hook had yet been delivered. The contractions remained forceful and my stethoscope revealed a strong infant heart beat at twice the mother's pulse.

My brother taught strict procedures for maintaining decorum during deliveries. So, to eliminate the possibility of eye contact with the mother during exams, I placed the woman on her left side facing away from me and commenced my exam during the next contraction. The infant was in a transverse lie with a shoulder presenting to the pelvic inlet. I felt my insides churning to the edge of panic.

In a calm voice that surprised me, if not my audience, I explained that the child must be repositioned to effect delivery. I had read about repositioning in DeWees, but had only performed the maneuver once when my father had instructed me to reach into a cow's womb and reposition a calf to a deliverable presentation. Our options were limited and explaining my lack of human experience would only increase everyone's anxiety.

Once I was certain the couple understood the procedure, I dosed the mother with Laudanum and bled ten ounces to blunt the anticipated discomfort. Still on her left side, I lubricated the vagina with fresh lard and inserted my left hand through the mostly dilated cervix into the womb. The position was awkward, but my left hand allowed wrist flexion that matched the contours of the birth canal. In response to my intrusion, a forceful contraction nearly paralyzed my hand. Once the uterine muscle returned to a relaxed state, I accomplished repositioning in relatively short order. As this was the woman's fifth term delivery and eighth pregnancy, delivery of a baby boy quickly followed.

The limp, blue infant made no effort to breath. I wiped his face, applied my mouth to his mouth, and with several exhalations the child took on his own breath. Within two minutes he announced his intent to survive with a modest cry. The midwife gave the boy a tablespoon of molasses in warm water to purge the meconium and I returned my attention to the mother, delivering an already separated and complete placenta. There was a brief gush of blood as the uterus relaxed but firm abdominal massage coaxed a decisive contraction and the bleeding ceased. Mother, son, and doctor all survived.

An astute midwife's concern about prolonged labor initiated this mercifully successful encounter with Mr. Harry Persons and his wife Altie. A man of finance, Mr. Persons owned a large farm and was the nephew of Charles

Persons who owned the Globe. I made several calls to check on mother and son over the next few days and credit the opportunity to serve the Persons family, and my tactful regard for the Persons' midwife, for generating a positive reputation among the local midwives. Being seen walking up the long sidewalk in front of the Person's home was also good for business and patients who paid my fees, making it possible to serve those who could only offer barter.

In anticipation of our own family, Millicent and I subscribed to *Mother's Magazine* published in Utica, NY. I also bought *Advice to Mothers* by William Buchan after seeing the book reviewed in the *Boston Journal of Medicine and Surgery*. Buchan offered six rules for raising children: Be fair, be there, don't wobble, don't pretend to be perfect, don't be too serious, and be polite.

Most women become pregnant within the first year of marriage and give birth at two to three year intervals. The first pregnancy establishes a newlywed's ascent from sexual naiveté. But, with seven children being common, motherhood can exhaust a woman leading to early death. The 1830 census found only two percent of women were over the age of sixty-five. Motherhood is an honorable calling, but too often the family's burden is placed on an oldest surviving daughter.

I only heard one lecturer address the labors of motherhood. Dr. Robert Dale Owen advocated for smaller families, pointing out how the improved finances and better food availability would benefit all of society. Owen's vivid instructions for withdrawal as a form of birth control and his open display of French condoms shocked audiences. This same Robert Owen would later be the first to describe microscopic animalcules in semen and advance a theory that they provided essential nourishment by entering the mother's egg.

Millicent insisted Abiatha join us at most public events that spring and Emma Willard's lecture finally provoked Abiatha to plan for a future. A graduate of Middlebury College, Mrs. Willard published a book titled *A System of Fulfilment of a Promise* and ran the Female Seminary in Troy, New York. Her list of subjects essential for raising inquisitive children included: Religion, Literature, Music, Mathematics and Philosophy. Willard's ideas struck a chord with Abiatha, whose Math skills had been her key to self-support. Even now, despite her eviction and working full-time for me, she was keeping account books for Colonel Fillmore's various businesses.

From early on Abiatha took to loving her unborn child, faithfully taking cod liver oil and magnesia daily. She also tracked the baby's development in her womb by copying sketches from an old edition of DeWees' textbook. Her first sketch showed buds for arms and legs. At three months Abiatha sketched a two-inch-long fetus with bones starting to calcify. At four months, her sketch showed a three-and-a-half-inch long fetus with a nose, mouth, and closed eyelids. At five months Abiatha recorded the exact date she felt the baby move, noting DeWees' description of globular brain. At six months, she noted that a boy would have an empty scrotum, and a girl a clitoris that separated the labia. The seventh month sketch showed formed arms and legs and open eyes. By the eighth month the skin was covered with vernix. At nine months Abiatha sketched a head measuring four inches from the forehead to the occiput and three and a half inches from ear to ear, and noted meconium filled the intestines.

Abiatha asked Margaret Fairling, a midwife with whom I had collaborated on several occasions, to attend her confinement. Though doctors seldom attend normal deliveries, she asked Dr. Hoyt if he would attend if needed. In the last weeks of pregnancy, most village women avoid taxing or undesirable activities beyond some light housework. Abiatha's model was the farm wife who worked until the onset of labor and resumed normal responsibilities a day or two later. In her limited free time she made clothes for her baby.

In a society that valued a perfect nineteen-inch waist, corsets posed a dilemma in pregnancy. Wealthy women withdrew as soon as they were forced to abandon the corset. Other women abandoned their corset in stages, first substituting thin whalebone for steel blades, then eliminating all stays before total surrender. In one journal editorial, Dr. Thomas Carter attributed miscarriage, menorrhagia, amenorrhea, uterine prolapse, and the loss of rosy cheeks to the corset. He warned that by restricting blood return to the heart corsets interfered with nursing and weakened the maternal–child bond.

Pregnancy intensifies the complex connections between the uterus and the brain and Abiatha was not exempt from mood changes and irritability. It didn't help when the newspaper republished a medical journal article claiming a pregnant woman frightened by a bear bore a child with excessive body hair and claw hands. Fortunately, a pamphlet by Rachel Gleason, a midwife and self-declared water cure doctor in Cuba, New York, reassured Abiatha that pampering did more harm than good. Gleason went to the extreme, recommending a cold-water stun bath the day after delivery. She also bragged that she resumed practice within one week of delivery.

During Abiatha's pregnancy, a midwife asked me to consult on a prolonged labor now complicated by sharp abdominal pain. DeWees lists four signs of fetal demise: Collapse of the child's cranium, offensive smell, separation of the hair from the scalp, and a cadaverous appearance of the woman. My stethoscope added one more sign: The inability to hear fetal heart tones. In this case, the fetal head was intact, but I was unable to hear fetal heart sounds; the uterus was tender, and the mother had not felt the baby kick in over six hours. Normally I would ask for another physician's opinion but the midwife held the same opinion as me: Premature separation of the placenta had resulted in the baby's demise.

The fetal head was too high for forceps or cephalotribe, so I had to use the hook to disrupt the cranium and accomplish what is always a grisly termination. The body was immediately followed by the placenta and large amounts of old blood confirming premature placental detachment. Together, we soon brought the bleeding under control, the midwife massaging the uterus and I giving the mother three doses of Ergot. The woman recovered without further problems.

The courage of women facing life threatening difficulties humbles me. After they suffer through pain and peril, women submit to pregnancy a second, third or multiple times, each time fully revitalized and confident. One popular magazine, *Godey's Lady's Book,* suggests women prepare a Will prior to their confinement and reassures readers of a bountiful Christian afterlife. With all her reading Abiatha was fully aware that one in twenty pregnant women die, yet she bore on without complaint.

DeWees' textbook states that surgical delivery cannot be justified. The first recorded Caesarian delivery was performed by Jacob Rufer in 1500. After several days in labor and the failed interventions of three midwives, Jacob surrendered to his wife's pleas and consulted a Lithotomist of good reputation. He and this man, more accustomed to removing bladder stones, placed his wife upon a table, prayed for Divine assistance, and opened the womb to extract an uninjured living child. His wife survived and gave birth to several more children. By the time I entered Castleton, a low uterine incision was known to avoid the peritoneum and allow delivery, but the likelihood that post-operative inflammation would claim the woman's life stood at a fifty percent chance. It would be 1870 before anesthesia, antiseptics, an understanding of the uterine blood supply, and advice not to extend sutures into the uterine cavity, made hysterotomy reliable.

In lower mammals, the womb opens to a pelvic inlet that is in nearly the same plane as the outlet. In humans, the pelvis twists from inlet to outlet, requiring the fetal head to rotate on its passage through the birth canal. The human fetal head is relatively soft, still this need for rotation makes the human labor process more difficult. Labor pain, known as the 'Curse of Eve,' is so natural to birthing that Charles Meigs of Philadelphia believes pain is essential to establishing the Mother–Child bond.

Most women, and Benjamin Rush would disagree. I can confirm the utility of releasing ten ounces of blood, as advocated by Rush, for relief of labor pain. It is not only effective, but seldom inhibits contractions. Beyond venesection I have great confidence in a compound of cinnamon, myrrh, and opium in four ounces of wine. I have tried using Joseph Priestley's nitrous oxide, which I can make by heating ammonium nitrate over a Bunsen burner, but being a gas, nitrous oxide has to be transported in ox bladders and explodes if exposed to a candle. Chloroform (made by mixing chlorinated lime with ethanol) and Ether became popular in the late 1840s. Both are a liquid at room temperature, and can be poured onto a cloth for the lady to hold over her nose and mouth. Once a state of light anesthesia is achieved, the woman's hand and cloth fall away and I have about ten minutes to complete any required procedure.

By 1848 the American Medical Association dismissed Meigs' objections to labor analgesia and soon Ether or Chloroform were used in about fifty percent of deliveries. Physicians are loath to ignore requests for pain relief, though fear and individual perceptions of pain are tremendously variable. I remain convinced that bleeding supplemented by small amounts of opium mitigate both fear and pain without suppressing labor excessively. I resort to Chloroform sparingly.

An exception was a twenty-two-year-old healthy woman in labor for nearly twenty-four hours with ruptured waters and strong labor pains. Still the head refused to advance beyond the perineum. I was called to the home at 11:00 p.m., confirmed the midwife's findings, suggested a forceps delivery, and offered pain control. The patient adamantly declined bleeding or opium and instead requested Chloroform because her sister had had a good experience with Chloroform. The Chloroform induced a brief but profound sleep and good relaxation allowing for a careful, deliberate forceps delivery following the natural curvature of the pelvis with no tearing of the perineum. Mom awoke when her large male child produced his first cry and the tranquil state of her nervous system likely enhanced her recovery.

Upon birth families rejoice, but the Physician knows the risk of hemorrhage has just begun. Preventing hemorrhage begins by controlling the baby's descent and avoiding undue pulling on the child. If any force is needed to complete delivery, it is best applied by massaging the fundus of the uterus. A moderate discharge of blood after delivery signals that the placenta is ready for delivery, but flooding after labor is frightening. Firm massage of the empty uterus will often stop the bleeding. If not, Ergot tea must be administered without delay and firm internal and external uterine pressure applied.

The final worry is childbed fever, experienced by one in twenty women on the fifth postpartum day. It poses a terrible threat to the mother's life and can ruin a physician's practice. As early as the 1790s Scottish doctors reported that midwives and doctors were carriers of childbed fever. In the 1840s, Ignaz Semmelweis, a Hungarian doctor found that washing hands prevented fever, but without a theoretical basis for his conclusion he was largely ignored. Dr. Oliver Wendell Holmes published an article in 1843 in the *New England Quarterly Journal of Medicine and Surgery* encouraging physicians to accept that childbed fever, also called puerperal fever, was contagious and could be carried from woman to woman by attendants. At Castleton Dr. Woodward had urged us to wash our hands following procedures, though other professors scoffed at his excesses. The famous Charles

Meigs of Philadelphia published several essays denying both a contagious cause for childbed fever or the possibility that doctors could transmit it. For me, habits taught by Professor Woodward proved hard to break and by good fortune I have seen few occurrences of childbed fever.

Rich and poor woman seem equally susceptible to depression following delivery, but the condition provides further evidence of the interconnection between a woman's mental state and her reproductive organs. Postpartum depression, also called puerperal insanity, may take the form of melancholia or a mania characterized by overexcited, aggressive, and disruptive behavior. Both forms contradict the loving, nurturing, and cheerful decorum expected of a new mother. Benjamin Rush recommended bleeding to relieve the symptoms of postpartum insanity, but while a generous venesection may be tried, it often disappoints. Opium or Laudanum may be helpful and it may be necessary to remove the woman from all irritating influences including her baby and family. The misery is real; one patient said she preferred the pains of labor to the agony of her melancholia.

There is no safe alternative to breast feeding, explaining why wet-nurses can earn between $4.00 and $6.00 a week when the average weekly wage for a female domestic worker is $1.00. In 1834, nursing vessels looking much like Aladdin's lamp with nipples made of pewter, ivory or silver were available. In 1845, Elijah Platt of New York patented a rubber nipple that soon outsold the rigid devises. In 1860, a commercially produced canned formula advertised advantages over evaporated and sweetened cows' milk but no advantage over breast milk. Weaning may expose a child to fever if undertaken during the summer months or when a child is teething. Generally, a child is weaned between 14 and 36 months, though many women find nursing pleasurable and effective for delaying another pregnancy. Textbooks suggest that some women experience a physiologic response to nursing described as 'an exquisite sense of wedded joy' and suffer bereavement with weaning.

Diseases such as whooping cough, croup, scarlet fever, and Measles are common in the first year but *Cholera infantum* is the most dreaded complication. One in four babies die, affecting intense mourning upon the family. Here I join the Clergy in encouraging parents to take comfort in the belief that their child will be in heaven, free of illness, awaiting reunion upon their own death.

I am privileged to share the beginning of life with families and while hoping to start our own family soon, Millicent and I anticipated Abiatha's delivery with excitement.

23. A Delivery to the Family of Allen, 1835

I do hope I wake up alive.

Abiatha and I seldom discussed issues that might be called personal. Though her importance to my practice and drugstore should not be underestimated, I felt it best to view her situation as that of an employee first, a friend second. Her interlude with McCarthy will make for a lifetime of shame and misfortune. Yet, I saw a genuine bond forming between Abiatha, mother Millicent and my wife. Millicent established the theme for their project, "When life gives you a hundred reasons to cry, show that you have a thousand reasons to smile." Musing about Abiatha's possible enrollment in the Troy Female Seminar interjecting a degree of sorely needed optimism.

Abiatha's pregnancy progressed without incident until 24 June 1835, ten days after her due date. Abiatha was not present in the store when I arrived that morning. Hoping that her long-anticipated labor had commenced, I entered the upstairs apartment to find her in bed and in active labor. Her contractions had become firm and regular around 4:00 a.m. I ran home to fetch Millicent and her mother, sent a messenger to notify Abiatha's midwife, Margaret Fairling, and walked to the Fillmore Tavern to inform Jerusha and the Colonel that labor had started. Abiatha's reconciliation with the Fillmores was nearly complete and I was delighted to have the Colonel pacing the floor of the drugstore and securing updates on the progress upstairs while I took care of patients.

Margaret's initial evaluation was quite satisfactory. Though a good size, the child seemed to be presenting normally and active labor pains had opened the cervix to half of its full dilation. When Margaret came down to inform the Colonel and me of her findings she teased that the two of us easily offered twice the anxiety normally expected of a husband.

As the day progressed the fetal head was slow to descend the birth canal and the cervix slow to complete its dilation. In the afternoon, Margaret gave Abiatha a dose of Ergot tea to strengthen her contractions. Still the fetal head seemed stuck at transition. By late afternoon Margaret reported that an anterior rim of cervix persisted but the slow descent was causing a great deal of cranial molding and caput. Margaret wished to obtain the opinion of a Physician and the Colonel was sent to summon Dr. Hoyt.

Dr. Hoyt arrived within the hour. Margaret had conducted three vaginal exams, all with Abiatha laying on her back but Dr. Hoyt asked Abiatha to roll onto her left side. He confirmed Margaret's exam, including his belief that the presentation was a normal occiput anterior and, though a rather large baby, the head was well engaged in the pelvis. Dr. Hoyt, Margaret and I conferred and agreed that delivery with forceps was the best option. Dr. Hoyt then bled Abiatha of ten ounces, which had the desired effect of relaxing the pelvic muscles and providing some pain control. He then smeared lard in the vagina and with great care applied long handle forceps. Margaret provided fundal pressure during contractions while Dr. Hoyt gently tugged on the forceps handles bringing the baby's head out from under the pubis.

To the surprise of all in attendance, the baby's wrinkled face was looking up at Dr. Hoyt. The child was not occiput anterior but occiput posterior. This upside-down position results in the head presenting at a functionally greater diameter and explains the difficult transition through the birth canal. The cranial plates at the back of the head form a triangle called the occiput, which can be obscured when transit through the birth canal is prolonged. Protracted squeezing of the head causes swelling to accumulate in the scalp, called caput succedaneum, and the sutures overlap to conform to the birth canal. The occiput posterior presentation is not rare, but often heralds a difficult delivery.

With another contraction, we all heard Dr. Hoyt shout, "It's a boy!" Just past 7:00 p.m. the child's delivery was complete and except for the surprise presentation all was going well.

The placenta was expelled in short order and a moderate flooding was quickly brought under control with another few ounces of Ergot tea. A dedicated committee of women including Millicent, mother Millicent, Jerusha, and Margaret commenced to assist Abiatha in the boys first sucking, while Dr. Hoyt, Colonel Fillmore and I shared a brandy toast downstairs.

Dr. Hoyt left out the back door and gave Margaret a ride home in his carriage. The Colonel and I ascended the stairs to congratulate the new mother. The Colonel tenderly kissed Abiatha on the forehead and beamed over her newborn as if the child was a long hoped for grandson. My extended and oddly assembled Aurora family had confronted adversity and its bonds had survived due in no small way to the determination of my wife, Millicent and her mother.

Mother Millicent stayed with Abiatha that night and the next morning requested that I evaluate a sharp pain Abiatha reported in her left lower abdomen. The region was exquisitely tender but her pulse was not excited and I dismissed it as a pulled muscle or a minor injury from a difficult delivery.

Another sign that Millicent's open strategy regarding Abiatha's unwed status had achieved its desired affect occurred mid-morning when Charles Persons crossed the street from the Globe with a kettle of stew and a loaf of bread his wife sent over, providing a delicious dinner for the four of us.

When Margaret stopped by in the afternoon, she suggested that we ask Dr. Hoyt to evaluate the left sided pain. That evening Dr. Hoyt confirmed tenderness with a strong non-excited pulse and confidently applied twelve leeches to Abiatha's left lower abdomen to remove the heat and bruising causing her discomfort.

Late that evening I returned to the store and found Abiatha still in pain. Leaving some compounded cinnamon, myrrh, and opium in wine with mother Millicent, I suggested it be offered should Abiatha request something to help her rest. I also asked Abiatha if she had decided on a name for her son.

"My mother once delivered a child who my father christened Lucas. That boy lived only a few short months. I would like to honor my family by giving the name Lucas to my son," Abiatha replied.

The next day the soreness persisted but Abiatha reported normal urination and passage of stool. She ate, nursed and seemed to be making a gradual recovery.

Lucas thrived under the attention of Abiatha and mother Millicent. When Lucas showed distress, Abiatha could pick him up and almost immediately he would quiet, his fresh blue eyes staring at her as if enchanted. I took joy in pacing the floor with him after he nursed and letting him cuddle to my neck awaiting his burp. Abiatha asked if Millicent and I would be god-parents to Lucas.

On the morning of the sixth day of her confinement Abiatha was seized with severe vomiting, and towards evening a sudden and very copious flooding came on followed by the passage of several large clots. By my arrival in the morning the hemorrhage had ceased but her extremities were cold and her pulse thin and weakened, the tenderness in her belly greatly inflamed. She kept down an ounce of the opium/brandy mixture but it did little to revive her.

That night the hemorrhage returned and I felt it best to consult with Dr. Hoyt who came right over and prescribed eight ounces of a tincture of opium infused with oil of roses with instructions that she be kept completely quiet. He also sent for Margaret Fairling, who cooled Abiatha's forehead with a wet cloth and did what she could to make her comfortable.

On the seventh day Abiatha was nearly overcome with fever. I closed the store and declined all but the most urgent requests for my services.

Margaret, mother Millicent and my wife attended to Abiatha and Lucas. A greatly weakened Abiatha insisted on nursing.

On the evening of the seventh day the flooding returned to an alarming degree. Dr. Hoyt employed various means, but Abiatha died shortly after midnight. Jerusha had joined the watch and she, the mother of Abiatha's dead husband, was holding her as Abiatha whispered, "I do hope I wake up alive." Her last two words, "for Lucas."

―――――――

Dr. Hoyt conducted a post-mortem inspection of Abiatha's abdomen. He kindly sent me a report that read, "The peritoneal surface of all the viscera were healthy but very much blanched. The bladder somewhat distended with urine, and the uterus not contracted as is expected. On the left side, and between the folds of the broad ligament, there was extravasation. There an abscess was revealed and when opened released copious amount of bloody pus with foul odor. The abscess communicated with the upper vaginal cuff by a hole capable of admitting a finger." Dr. Hoyt concluded that there had been "a partial rupture or tear at the cervical canal, the aperture communicating with the general cavity of the pelvis resulting in a large area of inflammation."

Dr. Hoyt's words are clinical. They hide the tears shared by the many who knew Abiatha, tears that mark the departure of a beautiful person for whom earthly encounters had proven unjust.

24. Doctor, Employer or Father, 1835

*We error to assume that today we know what
our preferences will be tomorrow.*

By morning Margaret Fairling jarred us out of our daze with a list of tasks Abiatha's death demanded. Millicent and her mother had already taken over the immediate care of Lucas, and Colonel Fillmore and Jerusha were making arrangements for burial. Margaret was well connected to the small network of wet nurses and promised to find a candidate for us to interview. I was to tackle a short-term plan for feeding Lucas.

One of the newer canned products we stocked in the store was evaporated cow's milk. Goat milk and donkey milk formed a small curd similar to human milk and might have been a better match, but given that nothing was considered a perfect match, canned cow's milk would suffice for the moment. Compounding being my specialty I chiseled open a can of evaporated milk, added a tablespoon of sugar and four ounces of boiled water, then placed a couple of ounces in one of the nursing vessels we sold in the store. The small Aladdin's lamp like vessel had three small holes in a spout through which Lucas could suckle. Lucas quickly emptied the first vessel and soon took a mid-morning nap in Mother Millicent arms.

Wet nursing is an ancient and revered profession celebrated by all cultures, often resulting in a lifetime relationship like Rebekah's wet nurse and her Biblical slave Deborah. Upper class women commonly hire a live-in wet nurse who is expected to meet all the essential needs of the infant. Some wet nurses make it a business, feeding three babies at a time, lactating almost indefinitely and earning far more than male laborers. The physical health and moral character of the wet nurse are measured by the health of the children they have borne, the size and texture of her breasts, and the shape of the nipples. To this, Lucas's committee added a love of children tempered by a placid, cheerful and compassionate disposition.

I speak for Lucas's entire parenting group when I report that we were unprepared for the candidate Margaret Fairling brought to us the next morning. Her name was Civia Morgan, a Negro and former slave, now residing with her family on land owned by Dr. John Watson's brother Ira, also a Physician who practiced in South Wales, five miles south of Aurora. Her youngest child was 14 months old and ready to ween. She and her husband had five children and were struggling sharecroppers with few options for any cash income.

I took Margaret aside but she anticipated my question, "You know, Dr. Allen, Negro women make prodigious amounts of milk, which is proven to be more nutritious than the milk of a white woman. In fact, some Southern women demand a Negro wet nurse. You should be pleased with Civia's availability."

"Margaret, I just don't know. Civia seems nice enough. I have no experience with Negros. I don't know what to expect. Won't Civia stand out in Aurora? Can she read? I know she would be quite a curiosity in Vermont."

"Dr. Allen, Civia's family is desperate for income. We can ask her if she reads, but I fail to see what that has to do with nursing. I delivered her last child and spent nearly a whole day with the family. They are loving, God fearing Christians who have proved themselves honest tenants over the past year. In my opinion Civia is exceptionally qualified to meet your needs. Pardon me, but you would be a fool to turn her down."

With that, my personal education about the Negro race began. As a child, Civia had been a house Negro and learned to read, write and figure over the shoulders of her master's children. Also, she was agreeable to live in our home for three months, returning to her family on Sundays, claiming it was time her oldest child, a twelve-year-old girl, learned to care for a household. She would express enough milk to cover Sunday and gladly assist with cooking and cleaning and all other chores that may be desired of her. After three months, she would return to her home evenings but continue to nurse and tend to household chores. She was willing to do all this for $4 a week, paid in advance. With that, Civia tenderly took Lucas from mother Millicent's arms and began to nurse.

He latched onto her breast and nursed heartily as Civia filled in more details. She and her husband Elmas had been third generation slaves on a Virginia tobacco plantation. They had been promised their freedom by their owner upon his death but the promise was not honored when the owner's son took over the plantation. After the family fled north, they ended up in Griffins Mills when three of their children were struck with Measles and came under the care of Dr. John Watson. Dr. Watson mentioned his brother was looking for someone to tend land he owned in South Wales. With Civia pregnant and having no ties in Canada, Elmas jumped at the opportunity to settle his exhausted family and the Morgans settled into a log cabin on Dr. Ira Watson's property.

Done nursing, little Lucas was sound asleep in Civia's arms. Millicent had given a great deal of thought to the plight of the Negro, and the idea of doing some good was appealing to both of us. Abiatha would probably have scolded me for paying more than I needed to pay a Negro woman, but Margaret had said the going rate for a white woman was $6.00 a week. I suggested Civia use my horse Parsley to fetch her things and by late afternoon she returned with a single sack containing a few personal items. To everyone's surprise she also brought fresh vegetables and between nursing she prepared dinner for Lucas's expanding parent committee.

The afternoon of Abiatha's death Jerusha and the Colonel visited the Presbyterian minister, Reverend John Spencer. He dispatched the church women to prepare Abiatha's body for the funeral, which the Fillmores graciously insisted be held in their front parlor. The parlor would serve as the tavern's public room for the last time as the Fillmores never re-opened their tavern business. General Warren had a casket of hard wood made in his sawmill the very hour he heard of Abiatha's death. Jerusha moved some of her finest possessions, including a sterling silver set, into the parlor and hung a couple of landscapes borrowed from Mr. Waldo to show her respect for Abiatha.

Abiatha's body was buried the next day. Reverend Spencer said beautiful words but he did not know Abiatha as Millicent and I knew her. He focused on her hardscrabble life, but she was more than hardships. Abiatha was a bright, ambitious woman who made people feel good about themselves. When the time came to remove the body the pall bearers carefully carried her out the parlor's second door head first while those in attendance departed through the front entrance. The bearers placed her coffin on General Warren's finest wagon for transport to her family's small cemetery near the home in which she was born. There she was lowered in the freshly dug grave and the Reverend Spencer said a final prayer, which I did not hear because in Millicent's arms little Lucas was crying.

"Softly, little Lucas. We both cry today. You have lost the wonderful mother who bore you and I have lost my business partner. We both must go on."

25. Complexities, 1835

You're alive. Do something.

Civia was a curious woman with a predisposition to explore and mend. She once told Millicent, "As a house Negro I was always to blame, and sometimes whipped for mostly nothing. I learned young that a whip'n for fix'n things was never as bad as whip'n for breaking'em." She loved babies of any kind, dog, cat, pig or bird. One morning we found her reading the Ackerley textbook on childhood disease that I left on the dining room table. There were medical terms she wanted to understand and Civia was a joy to teach. She secured each new fact with a chuckle. It always seemed like something fun was about to happen and if you couldn't see it, well, that'll be okay too.

Civia had a constant itch that could only be scratched by motion, and Lucas had every advantage of her energy. Civia took to accompanying Millicent to the stores and soon was generating the shopping list. Within the month, she was taking daily walks and doing the shopping herself with Lucas firmly affixed to her hip. On her second visit to my office she picked up a broom and started sweeping, an activity much neglected since Abiatha's death. One day Civia was sweeping behind the counter as I was compounding a customer's medicine and needed a bottle just out of reach. By habit I called out, "Abiatha, grab me a half pint brown bottle." Next thing I knew a half pint brown bottle was in my hand and Civia returned to sweeping, humming *Nearer my God to Thee*. I should have thanked her, but tears blocked the opportunity.

In just a matter of weeks, Civia's charm rearranged our lives. It was as easy to fall in love with her as it was with Lucas. Civia even offered a few ideas about rearranging the store for customer convenience. Her project took some time as she could not move anything without reading the label, or jotting a note for later questions.

One afternoon a customer came in to pay the balance on his bill just as I was about to stitch a patient's laceration. I checked Abiatha's ledger, but his balance was recorded as paid. He insisted that I had extended him credit for his wife's medication and he wanted to pay what he owed. Feeling an urgency to attend to my patient, I thanked him and told him not to worry. He thanked me but loathed being a debtor and insisted on paying. Civia, who was usually very quiet around strangers, stepped up, apologized for the urgency of the waiting patient, looked through the ledger, found previous charges for his wife's regular medicine, entered the new charge and recorded the man's payment, handed him a receipt, thanked him, all in half the time it took me to place a couple of silk sutures.

Though I care for patients from every walk of life, I plead guilty to underestimating the talents of people different from me. Unbiased research demanded dismissal of Dr. Cartwright's prejudicial Negro studies. Still, my lack of experience, and shameful narrow-mindedness, caused me to hold limited expectations regarding Civia. The ledger incident broke through that prejudice and I asked Civia what she knew about bookkeeping. Her answer was straight forward, "No Dr. Allen, I don't know much. It took me a minute to figure out what Abiatha had done but it seems she did things sensibly. I just took to the figuring the Master's wife demanded of me over the household expenses."

"Civia, I have a stack of charges I have not entered. Are you confident enough about your letters and figures to manage my ledgers? If you have interest, I would be much obliged? I intend to address the entries, but each day passes without it being done. I think Abiatha would approve."

She replied, "Dr. Allen, you sure do make me proud. Little Lucas won't need me forever and Elmas and I could really use an income. Beg'n your indulgence, if I can study those figures for a couple of days, I will tell you honestly if I can do the work. Of course, there'll come the need to discuss the value of such a service, once you're sure I can do it."

Millicent and I made a series of decisions under the urgent shadow of tragedy, but Lucas had long-term needs. William Johnson rendered a lawyer's opinion that adoptions were informal. If no relatives took in an orphan, they were sent to orphanages. From there some were put on west bound trains to be adopted by families needing farm workers. Lucas wholly owned our affections and we committed to raising him as our own.

Summer of 1835 Millicent suffered her first miscarriage. Mother Millicent's advice to keep quiet about the pregnancy, given the family history of miscarriages, proved good advice. Nine weeks after her last menses, Millicent was awoken with cramping and bleeding. By morning the products of conception had been discharged. I had seen this sequence of events many times, but for Millicent it was very personal and she took it quite hard. Hugging and loving Lucas proved effective solace.

When Lucas was nearing a month of age my brother James disembarked from a stagecoach in front of my store. At first I thought he was an apparition as the letter about his visit would not arrive until long after the hugging and introductions. We both know more about doctoring than talking, and soon James was compounding drugs while I took care of a few patients. Millicent opened a bottle of French wine she had been saving and we shared a wonderful dinner at home.

The next evening Millicent suggested James and I might enjoy a couple of whiskeys across the street at the Globe. That's when I learned all was not well in Vermont. Castleton Medical College had expanded its class size and Middlebury College had started its own medical school producing an abundant supply of graduate doctors, made worse by ever aggressive sectarian competition. Tragically, James lost a patient to childbed fever and the rumor mills were quick to blame James for her death. His financial situation was severely strained and, based on my letters, his wife Rebecca urged a fresh start, possibly in Aurora.

For almost twenty years there had been three doctors practicing in Aurora's upper village. A few months before my arrival, Dr. David Hassack, mother Millicent's former doctor, collapsed and died while readying his carriage for a home visit. Many of his former patients were now my patients. Dr. Watson had not announced retirement, but it was clear that his hours were greatly curtailed. It might be an ideal time to welcome James, though James himself had warned against partnerships. My office space was limiting, but I was seeing at least seven patients a day and the store experienced an increasing stream of business. Having one doctor on premise while another made home visits would make a nice practice.

Over the next several days James accompanied me on home visits and proved a welcomed extra pair of hands. I introduced him to the Fillmores and the Warrens. We spent an evening with Hiram Barney, who was now acting principal of the Academy. It was Hiram's enthusiasm that sold James on the idea of moving. By the end of the week James set his plan. He would sell his house, and bring Rebecca and their son to Aurora.

Civia proved quite capable of taking over my practice records. She checked invoices against shipments, compared prices in mail order drug catalogs, sent out bills and provoked smiles out of almost every customer she encountered. Through it all, if you were looking for Lucas, it was a pretty sure bet that he was still on Civia's hip.

Taber, Norton and Wood started a new semi-weekly stage coach route between Aurora and Olean. I already had a loading stoop in front of the store for the Buffalo line, and the new route went through South Wales, so I signed on as the village agent for the new line, provided they would allow Civia passage to and from her farm. It was a surprisingly difficult negotiation because the stage line feared paying customers might object to riding with a Negro, but Civia settled it by volunteering to ride up top with the driver. Before long a stagecoach line to Warsaw and Rochester also stopped at my store. The extra income allowed me to increase Civia's wages to $6 a week.

I watched Lucas confirm textbook descriptions of growth stages. Little progressions like gripping my finger and lifting his head and responding to the voices of his parenting committee became exciting milestones. By ten weeks Lucas weighed thirteen pounds, recognized faces and jabbered a language all on his own. I noted that Civia suffered spells of harsh cough, but her energy and cheerful ways never waned. A couple of nights Lucas wheezed horribly and tugged at his left ear, but in two weeks was back to normal.

Back in Vermont, my brother wrote that a new graduate doctor intended to purchase the house, and they would be coming to Aurora when their affairs settled, likely when the snow melted in 1836.

At three months Civia weaned Lucas to daytime nursing, which allowed her to return to her family most nights, always leaving a fresh cup of breast milk. Lucas reflected Civia's delight in the universe. He would have made Abiatha proud.

Late September of 1835 the heat and humidity of summer returned, and with it miasmic infantile Cholera. Civia had seen infantile Cholera seize infants with fever, vomiting and profuse diarrhea without discriminating between slaves or plantation owners. Panicked parents demanded my immediate attendance. One father carried his son into the office, the child was alive when he left home, dead on arrival. In Philadelphia over two hundred and fifty infants died of infantile Cholera that summer.

Saturday infantile Cholera struck home. Little Lucas awoke fussy from a nap and his diaper was filled with a loose tan colored stool. Civia reported that he nursed poorly and vomited a few minutes later. Millicent sent Civia to call me home from the office. By my arrival, Lucas had commenced an irritable cry pulling his knees up to relieve a tense abdomen. His head and body were feverish, extremities were cold and clammy, and a third diaper overflowed.

Millicent, mother Johnson and Civia took turns sitting with Lucas in the coolest room in our house, that being the deeply shaded storage room at the rear. He was dressed only in a triangular diaper held on by one safety pin. We immersed him in a tepid bath but it did little to relieve his fever. His cry soon weakened to whimpers interrupted by painful moans, vomiting and more loose stool. Civia offered her breast until he seemed too weak to suckle. Mother Johnson prepared a loose tapioca pudding, which Lucas soon vomited.

Millicent urged me to be aggressive. The Eberle and Condi textbooks both blame a firm abdomen on congested bowels and liver. I applied a flaxseed poultice to Lucas' abdomen to counter inflammation and eight leeches to his temples to relieve the cerebral congestion causing his irritation. Both textbooks recommended one-sixth grain of calomel in union with half a grain of ipecacuanha every hour, but after three doses Lucas's pulse became feeble and he was unresponsive to the brisk toweling Eberle recommended. I fed him drops of a wine and milk punch to revitalize his sinking energies. As the sun set that evening, the child's spirit joined that of his mother's.

We elected to bury Lucas in Abiatha's family grave site, next to the mother who had given him life. Our hearts would willingly have given Lucas our last name and a plot in Aurora's Oakwood cemetery. I insisted

Civia take a few days to be with her family while Millicent and I decided to offer Civia full time employment in the store.

26. Welcoming My Brother, 1836-37

Once you assemble the family, the world can take care of itself.

The nation fell into a recession in 1836, though insatiable demand for apples, grain and cheese in Buffalo and by canal to New York City buffered Aurora's economy. Colonel Calvin Fillmore, Joseph Howard Jr, Joseph Riley, Robert Persons, and others formed the Aurora and Buffalo Railroad Company, then acquired and surveyed the seventeen-mile route to Buffalo. Some Auroreans feared that getting to Buffalo in less than an hour would sully their town, but it was the recession that postponed the project.

I worried enough about taking on a partner during a recession, then the *Aurora Standard* published an announcement that George H. Lapham MD was opening a practice and apothecary near the SB Briggs store, two blocks from my office. Suddenly the doctor count was up to four in a township with 3,100 people and my drugstore had a competitor. The ad appeared the same week I received a letter from James confirming his family's departure from Vermont. Traveling by ox drawn covered wagon, they hoped to cover fifteen miles a day and would likely arrive in Aurora in about three weeks.

The day Dr. Lapham hung his shingle I paid a visit. Dr. Lapham impressed me as a gentle soul, personable, educated at Fairfield Medical College, with exceptional surgical experience. I found myself asking his opinion regarding a patient. I had to conclude that Dr. Lapham's practice would likely be a success. In fact, this first meeting was the start of a long friendship.

I greeted James and Rebecca and their son Charles with sincere enthusiasm. Millicent had arranged our home to accommodate their family until they could secure their own arrangements. That evening we heard all about their trip, and the next day Millicent and her mother borrowed the Johnson carriage to show Rebecca around the upper and lower villages. The Colonel and Jerusha Fillmore joined us for a fine dinner of roast chicken, squash and potatoes prepared by Civia.

While enjoying our after-dinner cigars and brandy the Colonel jumped right to the business prospects for doctoring in Aurora. I welcomed the opportunity to return the kindness James and Rebecca had extended during my apprentice years, but respected the Colonel's business acumen and his concern. To the Colonel it was strictly business, business that I had been viewing only from my perspective. It turned out that James, having his living threatened once, was just as concerned. He could not bear the thought of letting his family down a second time.

The next day we visited Dr. Hoyt who was also pessimistic of Aurora supporting five physicians, but he suggested a new possibility. At a medical society meeting, Dr. Theodore Lockwood of Wrights Corners, twelve miles west of Aurora, spoke of plans to curtail his practice and pursue political ambitions. Dr. Hoyt knew Dr. Lockwood to be a regular doctor of good standing and sound character. The village of Wrights Corners was situated at the junction of three main roads and growing fast. Dr. Hoyt prepared a letter of introduction for James, and we made a trip to Wrights Corners the next day.

Jacob Wright's tavern dominated Wright's Corners and was the site of Hamburg town meetings since the town of Hamburg was carved out of the originally vast Town of Willink in 1812. Hamburg's rich soil made the area popular to a growing base of German immigrant farmers who named their township after Hamburg, Germany. Dr. Lockwood was an engaging, enthusiastic and energetic man married to a woman of equal charm. He did not want to abandon his patients but his interests were changing and his wife wished to live closer to her family in Buffalo. There was another Dr. Allen in Hamburg, a Daniel Allen, who was older and had been one of the twenty-four founding members of the Erie County Medical Society. By midafternoon Dr. Lockwood and my brother shook hands on James renting Lockwood's office and taking over practice responsibilities.

The next day James and Rebecca took the stage to Wrights Corners and purchased a cabin much more modest than the one they left in Vermont. Within the week, they had moved in and James was seeing his first patients. Dr. Lockwood moved to Buffalo, returning intermittently to keep his hand in medicine and give James a few days off.

Fortunately, my practice continued to grow. Civia worked full-time in the store and used the upstairs apartment when weather or fatigue prevented returning to her family in South Wales. Soon we both had a reputation for being in a hurry. One day, just a short distance from my office, a former patient purposefully obstructed my path. Obviously intoxicated, he wanted to complain about my previous suggestion that intemperance lie at the source of his various ailments. Standing his ground, the ill-tempered gentleman announced, "I will not step aside for a fool." My recollection is that I stepped around him with little fanfare and to this day I deny the rumor that I said, "I sir hold no such reserve."

As deep as my roots were growing in Aurora, my application for licensure was not even discussed at either the January or June 1836 meetings of the Erie County Medical Society, so I engaged my brother-in-law, William C. Johnson, of the Fillmore, Hall and Haven law firm. After several letters of inquiry, William shamed the Board of Censors into convening in the Fall of 1837. I presented my original Castleton diploma and answered their questions satisfactorily. There was one final insult, I was charged 62.5 cents for a copy of the licensing certificate that hangs in my office, right next to my Castleton diploma. In June of 1838 I attended my first Medical Society Meeting.

I came to enjoy meeting my peers at the Erie County Medical Society each January and June for daylong sessions. Snow sometimes limited travel by stagecoach or horse to the January meeting, so I paid my $1 fine and made almost all the June meetings. Millicent generally joined me to meet with GWJ and lunch with her friends. We traveled to Buffalo the day before so I could attend both the morning business meeting and the afternoon lectures given by prominent physicians from across America. In 1857 and again in 1872 I served as Vice President and in 1873 I was elected President of the Erie County Medical Society.

Engaging my brother-in-law in the battle for my license added another bond to our status as family and friends. William was also intelligent about finances. Knowing how difficult it was for a doctor to establish a financial estate, he successfully managed a few diversified investments for me, including the $1,000 speculation I would later make in the resurgence of the Buffalo-Aurora railroad. I owe William my gratitude for both his wisdom and his friendship.

27. Allen Family Grows, 1836

Pleasant is the home where each spouse grants the other may be right.

My brother and his family settled into their Wright's Corners cabin in Hamburg and James was busy from the first day, making a better living than he had ever managed in Vermont. Our families visited the last Sunday of every month alternating between Wright's Corners and Aurora.

The man who printed my stationary, Almon Clapp, had commenced weekly publication of the *Aurora Standard* from his print shop in Aurora's Upper Village in September of 1835. I liked the idea of a local paper so, besides the annual $2 subscription, every week I paid 25 cents for a one by one and a half inch, advertisement:

Doct. J. Allen

Physician and surgeon,

Office at corner of Main St and Church Square

Aurora East Village.

Besides local news, Clapp reprinted articles from other newspapers when they were of general interest or supported his abolitionist and temperance politics. Then, in January of 1838 Clapp became famous when he learned that forty ardent Americans were about to invade and liberate Canada from England. His informant said the invading party was camped on frozen Lake Erie preparing for an imminent assault. Clapp recruited volunteers to reinforce a handful of U.S. Army regulars from Buffalo who arrested the invasion force. Clapp was hailed a hero, and taking advantage of the notoriety, moved his presses to Buffalo, renaming his paper the *Buffalo Morning Express*. To no one's surprise, the insuppressible Dr. Cyrenius Chapin was among the invasion force. Sadly, Dr. Chapin caught Pneumonia and died the next week.

When Millicent passed the fourth month of her second pregnancy in 1836 we joyfully announced an expected date of confinement of mid-October. Millicent's approach to pregnancy was different from Abiatha's. Any description of the growing fetus did more to fret than comfort Millicent. She was excited about quickening and loved to have me listen to the baby's heartbeat, but Millicent's energies focused on preparations for receiving our child. Mother Johnson gifted us baby furniture she had stored since Millicent's birth and together they wall-papered the baby room. I predicted a boy because the baby's heartbeat was slightly more than twice Millicent's own heartbeat, and bragged that I was correct half the time.

Pondering my own fatherhood, I started observing families more intently while alternating between an overwhelming urge to protect Millicent to a senseless envy over her central role in pregnancy. Finally, I decided I was simply in awe of Millicent's pluck and determination. Whatever it was, the anticipation was magnificent and I felt grown up in a personal way that the doctor in me had not experienced.

During this, my third Aurora summer, I campaigned for a cleaner village. The discharges of horses, pigs and the stench of public latrines raised a miasmic pall certain to be dangerous to the health and well-being of Auroreans. Foolishly, my initial focus was the many pigs that roam the village each summer. Families purchase a piglet for 50 cents in the spring, brand it or notch an ear to make it identifiable, then release it to live off the discarded garbage, manure and compost of civilization. By October a two-pound piglet could grow to two-hundred-fifty- pounds, providing nearly free pork, ham and lard for the winter. If a family could afford a second piglet, that pig could be sold for three dollars a hundred weight. My first public health efforts were stymied by the economy of free ranging pigs.

With Civia now full time in the store, I became more aware of the shortness of breath that accompanied her severe coughing spells. By force of will she endured them, but I was worried. When asked, Civia admitted to night sweats and spells of tension in her chest. She chuckled recalling how much less she coughed when she was pregnant or nursing, adding, "I've had as much of that as a soul could want. Please don't worry none about me Dr. Allen. I'll be fine. I had the cough my whole life. My father had the consumption and your books say I likely inherited my cough from Papa. Some days I see a little blood but that seems to clear me and make me stronger for it, like you bleed an ailing patient."

Civia's symptoms were common to pulmonary consumption characterized by inheriting tubercles that Rene' Laennec first described in autopsied lungs. Initially the tubercles are just granules, which slowly increase in size until their center softens. Coughing periodically ruptures a large tubercle releasing a cream like bloody sputum. Laennec noted three possible outcomes. Tubercles can spread throughout the body like a Cancer, or devastate the lungs in a fatal condition called *phthisis pulmonalis*, or enter a dormant state. Achieving the dormant state is aided by moving to a mild, genial climate where focus can be given to a proper diet, gentle exercise, and healthy intestinal functions. Those who cannot move must avoid miasma while attending to a good diet, exercise, and regular bowel habits. Eberle's text commends wearing flannel next to the skin to protect against temperature variations. With no opportunity to move, Civia hoped for the best.

As Millicent's due date drew closer, I was anxious about leaving her, but one October evening I received an urgent request to see Edwin Conant, a twenty-eight-year-old man who had stepped on a large nail. The day after the injury, despite a sore foot and an early snow fall, he helped a neighbor clear a field. A week later he began experiencing tingling and spasms in the foot. By the time I saw Edwin, he was feverish and the spasms had spread to his neck, chest and jaw. There was no swelling or discoloration in the foot, but the slightest touch caused spasm.

Traumatic tetanus, more often called lockjaw, is a terrible condition that afflicts healthy men following barnyard wounds that damage nerves with ascending damage to the spinal column. I prescribed Laudanum in brandy and immersed his foot in hot vinegar water. To clear the bowels and reduce the circulation, I added five grains of calomel mixed in molasses and warm wine followed by Epsom salts and senna in a strong tea. I released a full twenty ounces of blood from his arm, noting it to be unusually florid with little buffy coat. Thirty minutes later Edwin's pulse rose to 115, his unrelenting spasms causing continued sweating. I stayed the evening, administering Laudanum in wine every two hours. I tried wrapping his entire leg in moist tobacco leaves that I kept basted with a tobacco infusion. His mind showed no disorder, but the spasms seized his entire body and his back arched in painful contortions.

With little else to try, I laid open the original wound with a two-inch incision one half inch into the foot, still Edwin's pulse rose to 135. At 3:00 a.m. the spasms stopped, his pulse weakened as he whispered goodbyes to his family. By 4:00 a.m. in the morning his spirit joined that of his maker.

It is a physician's privilege to attend men and women at their time of need, but the imperfections of our profession can only be recalled with sorrow. I left Edwin feeling drained and beaten. Experience taught me that soon I would be called to attend a patient with a better outcome, and my confidence will be restored. There are times when families request I immediately depart the bedside of one patient for the bedside of their loved one.

They intend no ill will and their urgency is real. I must move from one case to another with a professionalism that appears coldhearted.

Regrettably, it may be months before the family is able to replace their sadness with the vicissitudes of a happy life.

Once home, I managed an hour's sleep when personal joy displaced my anguish over Edwin. Millicent awoke me with the news that her waters broke. I left immediately to fetch Margaret Fairling who arrived at our home as Millicent's contractions became regular and hard. Once her assessment was complete, Margaret declared all to be going smoothly. I am pleased to report that in spite of apprehensions more akin to that of a husband than a doctor, the progress of labor proved uneventful and early that evening, 15 October 1836, Millicent blessed our lives with a son.

He was well formed, heavy with vernix, and gave a robust cry within moments of delivery. Margaret handed him off to me and just a few moments later announced the delivery of an intact placenta and moderate lochia. I dried my son, wrapped him in his first swaddling and presented him to Millicent. Moments later he was suckling. Seeing mother Millicent on one side, Margaret at the other, and our son absorbing their full attention brought forth the happiest tears of my life.

Millicent broke the anxious tension common to birth in our species by asking me to be the first to voice our son's name. Now fully consumed in a joyous weep I nearly shouted, "Welcome to our family little James Allen."

Part Three: Science

28. Life, Smallpox, Typhoid and Miasma, 1836-1850

Medicine is science entangled with patients.

Civia serendipitously attained an education meant for her owner's children, and developed keen insights about people through the beatings of slavery. Such ambitious curiosity now became an asset to my business. One day a customer showed her little wooden toys he whittled and she asked to sell them on consignment at the counter. Purchased or not, they made people smile as did her generous laugh, careful accounting, and straight forward Christian ways. Civia managed the store front, but she still found time to help Millicent and dote on baby James. With a raise in pay, Civia and Elmas bought a horse, then Elmas rented a bull to upgrade his herd of beef cattle. Before long several taverns in town advertised that they served Elmas' beef.

In the March of 1837, Millicent and Civia put up posters announcing the first Annual meeting of the Erie County Antislavery Society held at the Globe Hotel. The honored guest was former slave L.F. Carver who described problems created by the 1820 Compromise that extended slavery into Missouri. Militant anti-slavery activists invaded Missouri to kidnap slaves, then abandoned them in free states without land or employment. Many were so destitute or lonely that they walked back to the Missouri farms and rejoined their families. Carver had been one of the kidnapped slaves. He was grateful for his freedom, but saw too many men, White and Negro, die in the effort. Not a word was said about Civia and Elmas, but that night I realized that it is not the color of our skin that makes us different, it is slavery that makes us different.

With late fall's chill, Smallpox breached our township in 1837. A Seneca Indian, skilled at climbing beams and rafters, was employed for a barn raising on a farm that bordered the Buffalo Creek reservation just north of Aurora. The Indian showed up with fever and pustules in his hairline. In cities accustomed to outbreaks of Smallpox he would have been sent away, but outbreaks are uncommon in rural villages. Besides, there was a barn to raise.

By mid-day the man was so sick he couldn't work. The farm wife prepared a bedroll in the wood shed off the back of their cabin and over the next two weeks the gentle woman dutifully attended to the Indian, sustaining him on days she thought he would not survive. A week after his recovery one of the woman's daughters developed a high fever, intense headache, and vomiting. Three days later the typical eruption appeared at the roots of her scalp. Within the next two days the pustules spread over her body including the mouth, nose and throat. Despite high fever and occasional delirium, the child survived, though badly scarred. Two men attending the barn raising also developed Smallpox, but incredibly no one died.

After first attending to the daughter's illness, Dr. Hoyt alerted Drs. Watson, Lapham and me. His warning allowed me to immediately suspect Smallpox when I was called to attend to the two men. For the next several weeks we quarantined everyone with a fever.

Drs. Hoyt, Lapham and I met regularly and when no new cases appeared for four weeks we published a letter in the *Aurora Standard* on 27 December 1837 announcing that an epidemic had been prevented. We attributed the survival of the three Auroreans to their previous vaccination with Cowpox. Survival of the unvaccinated Indian, who had been exposed at an Iroquois Grand Council, was remarkable as nearly half of unvaccinated patients die. The heroine was the farm wife who prevented an epidemic of Smallpox in both tribe and village by keeping the Indian isolated at her farm and, recalling Biblical stories about blankets transmitting boils, burnt his bed roll.

In America, rural communities and isolated Indian tribes encounter Smallpox only every ten or twenty years by which time many unexposed younger people are susceptible. By the 1830s vaccination was common though not universal. A process called inoculation predated vaccination by centuries. It involved dragging a thread through a Smallpox sore then dragging that thread through a scratch made on a recipient's skin. Inoculation usually led to a mild case of Smallpox, but severe cases were not uncommon. In 1790 Edward Jenner published his account of Cowpox vaccination (vaccinia is French for cow), using the pus from boils on the hands of milk maids to inoculate patients. When Harvard's Benjamin Waterhouse read Jenner's paper he ordered some Cowpox material and vaccinated his five-year-old son and six servants. When they were exposed to Smallpox, none became ill. Waterhouse tried to franchise America's distribution of Cowpox, but physicians bypassed him and ordered less expensive Cowpox material directly from England. Aurora's Smallpox alarm increased demand for vaccination and popularized the Erie County Medical Society's campaign for county-wide vaccination.

At eighteen months of age little James began to suffer intermittent bouts of fever and cough productive of blood streaked purulent sputum. By age three it was clear our little James had inherited tubercular consumption. We kept James dressed in flannel, even in the summer, and did all we could to minimize his exposure to dampness. We insisted he drink lots of milk and get regular moderate exercise, which, when feeling well he was inclined to exceed. Venesection being the most effective antiphlogistic, I bled four ounces weekly. His periodic remissions caused our hopes to soar and each time his symptoms returned, we worried.

In November of 1843 I became involved in the investigation of ten deaths in the small village of North Boston, just thirteen miles west of Aurora. After consulting a Thomsonian whose herbal remedies failed to curb the epidemic, the village consulted my brother James, who sent for my assistance. Our experience in Vermont made it easy to recognize the fever, rose like rash, swollen liver, and muttering delirium as Typhoid, but the epidemic was so pervasive that we sent for Dr. Austin Flint, the newly appointed Public Health Officer for Buffalo.

Dr. Flint, an 1833 Harvard Medical College classmate of Oliver Wendell Holmes, moved to Buffalo where a fast-growing city at the western end of the Barge Canal offered more opportunity than medically crowded New England. Flint had an intimidating presence, but his thoughtful analyses commanded attention at medical society meetings and his prolific writings had made him an internationally recognized expert on fever. Flint arrived in North Boston the next day, commended us for recognizing the epidemic as Typhoid, and conducted an autopsy on a child who died just before his arrival. Flint pointed out inflamed groups of lymph nodes around the intestines called Peyers patches that had been described by William Gerhard as characteristic of Typhoid in both Philadelphia and Paris.

Next, Flint mapped the cases found in a door to door survey of every home in the township. The first case had been a young man from Warwick, Massachusetts who arrived in the village by stagecoach too ill to continue his way west. Two days after his arrival he died at the Fuller Tavern. Over the next few weeks, fever struck seven out of ten families living in North Boston. In the Fuller Tavern, the disease affected five of seven family members between the ages of 3 and 23. Three died. Other families with Typhoid either frequented the Fuller tavern, used the community latrine, or obtained water from the Fuller well.

Two families lived 40 rods away with their own water supply and latrines. They experienced no cases of fever. The Stearns family lived only

4 rods from the Fuller Tavern, but because of a long-standing feud, held no association with the Fullers and experienced no cases of Typhoid. The Fullers were quick to accuse them of poisoning the tavern's well, but Flint had the water tested by a Buffalo firm that declared it clean and uncontaminated. The Stearns sued the Fullers for slander and would later win a $100 settlement.

Correspondence with a clergyman in Warwick revealed that the young traveler had been well when he left Massachusetts, but there had been a number of cases of Typhoid fever in Warwick. Flint tied all cases of fever to primary or secondary contact with an ill person or their emissions. Death was most likely in those who were young, intemperate or consumed a poor diet. Being over age 25 was protective. In his final analysis, Flint concluded that outbreaks of Typhoid occurred as a consequence of morbid miasmas from the discharges of patients with Typhoid.

Flint eventually published three scientific papers about this epidemic and our work was cited in John Snow's 1855 Treatise on Cholera from a well in London. Flint's first paper appeared in the *American Journal of the Medical Sciences* in 1845, the second in *Clinical Reports in Continued Fever* in 1855, and the last as a paper presented to the American Public Health Association in 1873. Each paper made corrections based on expanding knowledge about contagions.

In 1842, the Buffalo Creek Indian Reservation north of Aurora was purchased from the Seneca Indians who were relocated to reservations in Cattaraugus and Allegany Counties. The former reservation was covered with enough virgin timber to support another decade of lumbering and its dependent industry, tanning. A new pail factory paid workers $1.50 a day and teacher pay rose to $250 per year. The price of butter rose to $0.04 a pound and flour to $4.00 a barrel, facilitated by a deeper and wider Erie Canal. Barter was still important, but more of my fees were paid in cash.

Millicent's family faithfully supported the Congregational Church, which adopted the Presbyterian form of governance and became The First Presbyterian Church of Aurora in 1843. By 1845 the church had dedicated a new house of worship and, while I never saw Millicent lift a board or swing a hammer, raising the structure owed a great deal to her personal energy, energy she also used to exact my regular attendance.

On the night of 18 October 1844, a severe storm hit Lake Erie with several days of strong easterly gales that pushed lake water away from Buffalo. Then suddenly the wind stopped and a thirty-foot wave of water rushed back into downtown Buffalo. I responded to the Medical Society's request for doctors and saw for myself the destruction the seiche caused. Seventy-eight people drowned, the Robert Fulton steamboat and over 200 buildings were destroyed. Dead chickens, pigs, cows and horses littered the streets. That week I saw firsthand how difficult life could be for the city dwelling immigrant dock worker.

In 1845, the telegraph connected Aurora to a fast new world of communication. When American forces invaded Mexico to liberate Texas in 1846, the telegraph office posted bulletins on their office windows, bringing the war directly to Big Tree road, more often called Main Street now.

Hiram Barney, my first Aurora acquaintance, made it to Ohio before me. In 1847, after nearly fourteen years as the Aurora Academy School Master, Hiram's success recruiting students from all over Western New York and Ohio attracted an offer to became Commissioner of Schools for the State of Ohio. I missed our many hours of conversation and the literature Hiram convinced me to read.

In 1848, Lucretia Mott, who Millicent knew through their anti-slavery work, organized the first Women's Rights Convention in Seneca Falls. Millicent stayed home to nurse our second son, Deloran, born on 16 September 1847. I teased that the real reason to stay home was to read the newly published *Wuthering Heights,* but Millicent tracked the convention's proceedings reading Amelia Bloomer's newspaper *The Lily*. Fortunately she never took to wearing the pantaloons that Ms. Bloomer popularized, though she practically memorized Elizabeth Cady Stanton's *Declaration of Sentiments*. Stanton was a graduate of Emma Willard's Female Seminary that had inspired Abiatha.

During the 1840s debates over miasma versus contagions began to appear in medical journals. Austin Flint's paper about the North Boston Typhoid epidemic emphasized how each patient suffered a pattern of identical symptoms and how carefully detailed questioning uncovered a common exposure. By re-examining another forty-eight cases of fever from a Buffalo Hospital, Flint realized there were specific characteristics and exposures that could differentiate Typhoid from Typhus. Each had unique symptoms and exposures suggesting two different illnesses caused by two separate external agents. Flint's findings argued against prevailing theories that illness was an imbalance of humors (Blood, phlegm, black bile and yellow bile) overwhelmingly determined by a patient's frailties.

Eberle's 1831 table of contents lists mostly symptoms, newer textbooks list many more diagnoses. Castleton trained me to treat symptoms, like 'fever' or 'lose bowels.' We were taught to recognize Smallpox but treat it the same as any fever. At North Boston, we diagnosed Typhoid by defining a pattern of symptoms, then asked village families if anyone suffered the pattern. Soon medical society speakers were grouping symptoms into patterns and describing new diagnoses. Diagnoses became the doctor's language and practice became seeking patterns and solving human puzzles..

I had been attending medical society meetings for several years when Dr. Samuel Hunt of Buffalo asked me to join a national network of physicians, organized by New York's State University, attempting to find relational patterns between humidity, air chemistry and community illness. Chemists had discovered nitrogen, cyanogen, carbureted hydrogen, and ammonia in air released by marshes, decomposing vegetation, and sewage. Many thought these chemicals explained miasma, and with Aurora's sinking pond marsh area less than one-mile north of the village, I held particular interest.

Journals were also reporting on the new and perplexing concept of germs. Microscopists discovered tiny animalcules in several conditions and wondered if miasmas may contain living organic germs that could enter and reproduce within the human body. Yet, no germs could be found to cause the two most obvious contagious diseases: Smallpox and Measles.

Others thought fungal spores explained miasma. When a new road was built across the sinking ponds, I was struck by the decay of tree stumps exposed to air after decades of being under water. At first, they looked like they had been buried only a few weeks, but after a warm summer the stumps decomposed. Breaking off a piece of the wood then released a cloud of fungal spores. Fungi are known to love heavy, humid, warm summer atmospheres, feed upon dead vegetative matter in tainted soils and, like some mushrooms, can be poisonous.

An 1835 paper by the Italian, Agostino Bassi, found that a white substance associated with the collapse of silkworm colonies was a fungus. He demonstrated that the spores from the fungus transmitted the disease from one worm to another. Bassi observed that there was a delay before an exposed worm became ill and showed that the fungus was replicating in the worm's body.

So, I agreed to join Dr. Hunt in the miasma and humidity project. We used the Daniall hygrometer to measure humidity daily while also recording diseases we saw among our patients. Dr. Daniel Drake pooled the national data to write his *Systematic Treatise* in 1850, proving a relationship between humidity and intermittent malarial fevers. Hunt analyzed the Western New York data reporting that the prevalence of fever rose when the winds were in the northeast and southwest but the data showed no association with digestive, skin, circulatory, eye, or nervous conditions.

29. Medicine and Science Grapple, 1836-1850

Good doctors must read, but cautiously. Some old ideas are better than new ones.

Historically, the great men of medicine, including Benjamin Rush, used their intellectual powers to sculpt what they thought to be rational theories based on their personal observations. Personal experience was paramount, and apprenticeships served to pass experience onto the next generation. Most graduate physicians relied on personal practice experience rather than books to select each patient's remedy. The Principle of Specificity prevailed, resulting in treatments being doctor and community specific and the incongruities were exploited by sectarians. Thomsonians and homeopaths followed unifying theories laid down in a recipe book. The uniformity implies certainty that is easily mistaken for science.

Some physicians hoped rigid licensing laws would marginalize sectarians, but laws don't win the heart and minds of patients. Regular doctors needed to improve their science and standardize treatments. The ills of humanity are too complex to be solved by one man's observations whether they be Benjamin Rush, Samuel Hahnemann, or Samuel Thomson.

In 1843, the New York State Legislature attempted to make licensing more consistent by transferring responsibility from County Society Chapters to the State Medical Society. But when the Albany County Medical Society responded with multistep recommendations for improving medical practice, the legislators repealed all New York's licensing laws.

But the 1840s was seeing a new medical science emerging in European hospitals where large numbers of patients were being segregated in wards according to symptoms. Grouping patients revealed subtle patterns of disease that were not obvious to solo doctors. Physicians working in these hospitals teamed up to start patient registries, analyze symptom patterns, make diagnoses, and evaluate remedies.

Like many communities, Buffalo's leading doctors joined forces to start a medical school dedicated to the new science. In 1846, Doctors Austin Flint, James Platt White, and Frank Hastings Hamilton joined with politicians like Millard Fillmore to start the University of Buffalo medical school. The initial faculty included specialists in Chemistry and Pharmacy, Physiology, Anatomy, Pathology, Obstetrics, Diseases of Children, Principles of Clinical Medicine and Surgery, and Medical Jurisprudence.

Born in Vermont, Dr. Hamilton attended both the Fairfield medical school and the University of Pennsylvania before studying extensively in Europe. A prolific writer, he had acquired an international reputation in reconstructive surgery, amputations and cataract removal. Five of the founding faculty came from Geneva Medical College, which soon merged into Syracuse University. Former Congressman Millard Fillmore accepted appointment as the first Chancellor of the University of Buffalo and served in that capacity even while President of the United States. The first course of medical lectures opened on 24 February 1847 with sixty-six registered students.

I, along with most medical society members, were part owners, having purchased a $40 certificate of support for the medical college. After initially holding classes at the First Baptist Church, a modern school building costing $15,000 was completed at Main and Virginia Streets in 1849.

The Buffalo Medical College faculty regularly published in medical journals, but it was Dr. White's 1853 demonstration in Obstetrics that brought the school international attention. Following Dr. White's trial, Dean Flint convinced the New York Legislature to legalize human demonstrations and make the unclaimed bodies of convicts and paupers available for dissection.

Dr. Flint also convinced the medical society to support the *Buffalo Medical Journal and Monthly Review of Medical and Surgical Science,* first published in June of 1845. Early issues included Dr. Hamilton's European observations, a review of several cases of acute rheumatism treated with saltpeter, autopsy findings in a case of Aortitis, twins at different stages of development, editorials by Dr. Flint, and a section titled medical intelligence containing bibliographical notices and summaries of articles from other journals. A series of witty articles poking fun at controversies in medicine, published under the byline Smelfungus, made the journal a financial success. Smelfungus ended up being none other than Dr. Sanford B. Hunt, who managed the miasma and humidity study. In 1853 Dr. Hunt replaced Dr. Flint as editor.

After the 1844 release of the Albany County Medical Society report on medical licensing, the New York State Medical Society invited all American state medical societies to send delegates to a meeting in Philadelphia. The meeting addressed four key points made by the Albany report. First, a large portion of the public thought that science and education were not essential for medical practice. Second, engaging in controversy with sectarian adversaries was futile. Third, licensing was unpopular and difficult to enforce. And fourth, medicine must improve medical education, science, and increase uniformity of practice.

In Philadelphia, the delegates decided that a medical association was needed to hold disciplinary control over its members and assume responsibility for enforcing training standards. In 1847, the American Medical Association was established on the existing infrastructure of state and county medical societies. Like guilds, the new professional society would have two purposes. First, promote the welfare of the professional by promoting the interests, standards, ethics, and vision of its members. Second, advance knowledge and continually improve the profession.

Medical Society meetings had long provided fellowship, and a safe place to grumble about low pay and sectarians. Formation of the American Medical Association (AMA), under the very personable Dr. Nathan Smith Davis, created standards for society processes and accountability. Society meetings became forums for presentations, discussions and arguments about the latest medical science and journal articles.

The influence of Benjamin Rush and heroic medical remedies was fading. By 1850 physicians were collecting more patient information and using bleeding and purging in more nuanced ways. The prescriptions I filled in the store became more standardized. Instead of simply draining patients of excess humors, doctors began to nourish and sustain patients.

The AMA established a Code of Ethics borrowed from a book published in 1807 by a London physician, Dr. Thomas Percival. The Code was eventually formalized in a uniquely American tome by Cathell who addressed all manner of medical practice, including the right of a doctor to shoot a menacing dog. Cathell specified five fundamentals to be performed at every patient encounter. They are: Feel the pulse, examine the tongue, inquire about appetite, inquire about sleep, and characterize bowel patterns.

The AMA emphasized the better nature of regular allopathic physicians to create a sense of professional pride. It networked county and state medical societies while encouraging structured observation, numerical analysis, and diagnostic pattern recognition. National meetings brought leading American physicians together at the same time as the proliferation of medical journals were facilitating a broader empiricism. Sharing observations made it clear that disease varied little from one community to the next, debunking the principle of geographic specificity.

At the same time American cities were opening hospitals similar to those in France, England and Germany, relieving the burden on almshouses that had served as the *de facto* asylums for the ill. In 1848 Buffalo's first hospital was opened by the Daughters of Charity of St. Vincent de Paul. Sister's hospital organized its wards according the disease type, cataloged autopsies, and soon became a center of medical advancement and discovery. The poor were charged $1.50 a week including meals, washing, medical attendance, nursing and drugs. The wealthy could enjoy a private room for $4 a week.

Religious fundamentalists could be uncompromising about literal interpretations of the Bible, and distrusting of any science that questioned God's power. But many educated ministers joined doctors in viewing the new science as an effort to understand God's miracles.

I had been excited about beginning medical practice. Now, the opportunity to work with Drs. Flint, Hamilton and White reignited my energies. I forgave the shabby treatment I received when I first arrived in Erie County and found Medical Society programs pushed me to read even more.

Still, it was my service to patients that gave my efforts meaning. My years in Aurora now meant that I spent every day helping friends.

30. Measles and Scarlatina, 1836-1850

Mourning is not forgetting.

I was only minutes off the stage coach returning from one January Medical Society Meeting when Millicent told me that the Ablest family needed my urgent attention. We were regular customers of the Ablests who managed a small farm a mile out of the village and kept us supplied with milk, vegetables, apples, cured pork and beef. Mr. Ablest had requested an urgent visit to comfort to his ailing daughter.

It was a crisp, cold, clear winter night in an unusually mild winter and walking would get me to the Ablest home faster than saddling a horse. Mildred Ablest, a six-year-old attending her first year of school, had been feverish for four days with red, tearing eyes, runny nose, and a painful cough. Earlier in the day she developed the Measles rash. Her parents concern had been her constant headache. On my arrival, she was sleeping.

Typical of Measles, the now florid rubeola rash had begun on Mildred's forehead and spread to her neck and chest. Mrs. Ablest said the rash started as distinct, red, round spots that looked like fleabites. The spots became so numerous that they merged into irregular, raised crescent shaped patches that blanched when pressed. Mildred's eyelids were swollen and I found the red spots with white centers inside her cheeks that confirmed Measles. Her pulse was quick and full. I meticulously listened to Mildred's chest, front and back to rule out Measles Pneumonia, but what really concerned me was Mildred showed no reaction to my exam. Then, suddenly the child commenced a prolonged generalized seizure. Convulsions are of little worry if they occur with the first fever spike in Measles, but this far into the illness they predict a catastrophic outcome.

My alarm was poorly concealed. Mrs. Ablest was now holding Mildred with the slow rocking caress common to mother and ill child. She pierced my own apprehension by asking, "Is my little girl going to die?"

My doctor brain raced to find some forgotten comfort to offer Mildred's mother. In Hungary, a Dr. Katona used tears from children with Measles to inoculate other children, much like Smallpox inoculations protect against Smallpox. And, Jacob Henle, professor of Anatomy in Zurich, suggested the latent period before onset of symptoms in diseases like Measles proves the contagion is living matter. And, like Bassi's silkworm fungus, an incubation period means the contagion is replicating itself into a critical mass of particles capable of causing illness. Only living things can replicate themselves. Problem was, Henle could not find microscopic living things in the tears of Measles patients.

Useless racing thoughts take little time, but I had to respond to Mrs. Ablest, "I fear the child's stupor and seizure are signs of inflammation in Mildred's brain and present a grave prognosis. I will do all that can be done and will stay with Mildred. Please get what rest you can, it will be a long night. God will determine the outcome."

I remained with the child throughout the night and into the next day. Except for the occasional cat nap, I continuously dropped small amounts of warm wine upon her lips and applied leeches to the child's neck to relieve the inflammatory overload affecting her brain. Mildred's pulse continuing its tense, quick, and sharp character, but the child remained stuporous. Just before noon her pulse slowed and her respirations became irregular. Within the hour her spirit joined that of her Maker. I stepped aside to allow the family full approach, and hide my own tears. My business here was done and I was desperate to return home. Only Millicent can salvage my spirit when it sags this low.

Measles, Smallpox, and Scarlatina can be hard to tell apart in the first few hours, and I dread all three. The Erie County Medical Society's campaign to vaccinate all willing citizens made our 1837 cases the only Smallpox I would see. However, cities like New York experienced Smallpox epidemics through 1850, and Measles and Scarlatina were a nearly universal childhood menace.

Scarlatina has little of the cough or runny nose typical of Measles. Scarlatina starts with severe sore throat, large weeping tonsils, strawberry tongue, and swollen neck glands, looking more like the early quinsy of diphtheria. The Scarlatina rash appears on the second day and is both sandpaper rough and scarlet bright. Sometimes called scarlet fever, the rash starts in the groin, eventually covering all but the palm and soles. There follows a dramatic peeling of skin five days later. Scarlatina has long thought to be of miasmic origin because of its prevalence during warm, humid weather and low marshy districts. Contagionists, however, argue that the pattern of spread proves Scarlatina belongs in the same contagious category as Smallpox or Measles. A third of children with Scarlatina will develop dropsy, others suffer months of acute rheumatism or experience chronic draining from the ears and loss of hearing.

I was asked to see thirteen-year-old Roisin, a girl who had recently arrived from Ireland's dreadful famine to live with her uncle's family. She spent an afternoon with new friends catching frogs at sinking ponds before becoming ill with a fever and sore throat. The second day she exhibited the Scarlatina rash, confirmed after her uncle consulted Gunn's *Domestic Medicine*. The child appeared in recovery with peeling skin, then developed dropsy like swelling. Roisin's bedroom had been the sick room for two of the family's children who had recovered from Scarlatina a few weeks earlier. Upon their recovery, the room had been scrubbed, whitewashed, and the carpet well beat over a line in the backyard.

Roisin's urine was frothy and, after a few drops of nitric acid, produced a white sediment indicating large amounts of albuminous matter. Following instructions in Condi's textbook, I relieved the fluid overload by releasing four ounces of blood daily and administered nitrate of potash and digitalis to produce a diuresis. I also instructed the Roisin's aunt to immerse her in a warm bath daily and dry her skin by vigorous rubbing using a flannel cloth. It took several months, but the edema eventually cleared and Roisin made a full recovery.

Aurora experienced one outbreak of Scarlatina that I could not trace to miasma. It was the habit of a local farmer who supplied fresh milk to several homes to delegate the daily cleaning of his milk cans to his son. One day the son was ill and inattentive to his task. The next day he developed the Scarlatina rash. Over the next week an outbreak of scarlet fever could be traced to the farm's milk customers. The relationship was so obvious that I was forced to consider a contagious spread of Scarlatina.

Like Smallpox and Measles, there was little a doctor could do to arrest the course of Scarlatina. The possibility of sudden collapse during the acute phase means bleeding must be reserved for highly resistant fevers or complications like dropsy. Sponging with tepid water lessens the dangers of fever and a black mustard sinapism applied to the neck relieves the symptoms of throat inflammation. Some advocate for the use of quinine and once the peeling is complete, a final purge of the bowels should be undertaken.

Other complications include the accumulation of an abscess behind the tonsils. These peritonsillar abscesses must be opened by lance to avoid the formation of a draining sinus under the ear. Acute rheumatism can also present late. One fifteen-year-old girl I attended developed several warm swollen painful joints on the sixth day. I wrapped her joints in subacetate of copper and prescribed oral salicin at doses high enough to cause ringing in her ears. I limited her diet to chicken broth, mutton broth and eggnog. Under this rigid regimen, the child regained the ability to walk at three months and returned to normal activity by six months. Fortunately she developed no detectable dysfunction of her heart.

Controversy continued over the nature of contagions, but quarantine became a universal strategy for isolating illness. It gave communities and doctors something definite to do, and makes sense if contagions are living matter with a limited sphere of infectivity, unlike miasma or chemicals that might waft over great distances. Reports of Smallpox being carried on blankets shipped across the ocean made destruction of nearly any object touched by a fever patient important to the quarantine protocol. What could not be destroyed was washed in the chlorides of lime and soda.

The care of children is a challenging mix of success and failure, but provides a doctor an opportunity to observe the internal workings of families. I have taken the view of Roisin's uncle who compared life to a great river. At our source, parents and siblings make early contributions. Soon our little stream receives the tributaries offered by teachers, friends, and peers. We aren't a true river until joined with our own adult family. As a doctor my river is further enriched by the many tributaries offered by patients. The person I am, and the doctor I wished to be, like the world's greatest rivers, mingle many waters. I will add that it was my marriage to Millicent that make my waters sweet. Doctoring frequently commands my urgent attention, but there is never a moment that Millicent does not rule, for it is she who makes for a truly rewarding life. Taking care of families has proven this.

31. Family Life, 1845-1854

A doctor's life is a series of vignettes woven together by humanity.

Civia's landlord, Dr. Ira Watson died in 1845 and his brother, Dr. John Watson, focused more on managing his brother's farm and progressively less time in practice. Dr. Hoyt, in his later years, enjoyed a political career, so when his son, Dr. Horace Hoyt, came to town in 1848, Dr. Lapham and I were thankful for the help.

Some weeks could be harried, so one beautifully quiet Sunday afternoon I tried hanging a hammock deep in the wood stand behind our house. The plan was that Millicent would inform any inquirer with non-urgent problems that I was 'out.' Slumber had just overwhelmed me when several neighborhood boys voiced great curiosity over seeing a man in the woods on a hammock.

Most of the time I enjoy the busy life. Millicent knows that. When I complain, she grabs my mutton chop sideburns, jiggles my face and provides an encouraging kiss. When my spirits need a boost, she lifts them, and when others grumble about the deficiencies of modern medicine, she defends me. Millicent is an exceptional queen, managing our home and family with devotion and taking advantage of my preoccupation with doctoring to pursue her interests in church and the abolitionist movement. Together we make a whole wonderful team.

The longer I practiced, the more Auroreans I came to know, renewing friendships daily. Albert Fenster illustrates this continuity. As a child, I vaccinated him, stitched up two lacerations, and set a Colles fracture of his left wrist. When I made a house call on his sister with Measles a few months after the fracture, he waved hello from a tree in the front yard.

Albert grew up learning his father's shoemaking business. He invited Millicent and me to his wedding, memorable for a Fenster cousin playing the fiddle with the enthusiasm of a hen house rooster. Albert's secondary skill at hunting and fishing kept his wife and growing family well fed. One early April he was playing a trout in a stream swollen with spring runoff when he slipped and took a thorough wetting. Fever soon followed and by the time I was asked to call on him he was consumed by a cough producing thick brown sputum. Wet crackles over his left lower chest confirmed Pneumonia that I treated with one grain of aconitum every two hours, adding a dose of calomel and castor oil to cleanse his bowels. The next day no breath sounds were heard over the left lung and his pulse remained rapid. I stopped the aconitum and started *veratrum viride* in a dose of six drops every hour to slow his pulse and respirations. The next morning Albert was sweating profusely and his pulse was forty. He admitted to taking extra doses of veratrum to hasten his recovery. I stopped the veratrum, released sixteen ounces of blood, and over the next three days his pneumonia yielded.

With a growing family, Albert's resources were slim. We bartered for a fine pair of shoes made just to my liking, and I purchased another pair for Millicent. Our children had little need for shoes from May through September, but I purchased the boots they wore through the winter from Albert at an exceptionally fair price.

I would go on to care for Albert's wife, deliver his children and care for them into the next generation. At every encounter, Albert and I told exaggerated stories about falling out of outlandishly tall trees with laughter that grew larger than our fabled trees. We were friends, each with his own skill, sharing respect and affection forged through the passages of life.

After the disappointment of two miscarriages, Millicent blessed our home with a second son in 1847, the fine, healthy boy I mentioned who kept Millicent from Seneca Falls. We named him Deloran Johnson Allen in memory of mother Millicent's first-born child who had lived only a few months. Millicent and Mother Millicent agreed in allowing a child's furtive adult to blossom, offering children only the occasional prod to assure proper direction. Millicent's intuition for finding each child's exceptional quality and guiding that child through exploration of that talent is remarkable. Deloran was a wanderer. When he was about two and a half he wandered into the wood stand behind our house and it took three hours to find him. We were nearing despair when General Warren found Deloran playing with a toad in the creek behind his home on Water Street. The adult Deloran would take up farming in Kansas.

James, our first born, suffered multiple bouts of Pneumonia and by age ten suffered the progressive wasting of pulmonary phthisis. Mother Millicent frequently held him, comforted him, mopped his forehead and hid his blood streaked sputum. Dr. Lapham did all he could for James, but we had to accept that the child had been born with a disposition towards tubercular consumption inherited from my father's side. Condie's textbook dismissed any idea that consumption is passed by a contagion, arguing that families hand down an overabundance of venous blood resulting in the accumulation of serous fluid in the lungs.

Sick children exhibit a countenance of peace and acceptance that adults see as courage. They humble all who open their hearts to them and little James was no exception. Pulmonary hemorrhage was the final event, draining little James's life in a matter of minutes. My first born and beloved son, James Obadiah Allen, born in 1836, still small for his age, died in mother Millicent's arms at age twelve. Dr. Lapham's autopsy confirmed pulmonary tubercles. Civia took James's death very hard, upset that God had granted her, but not little James, resilience against the tubercular consumption they shared.

When little James died, Millicent was pregnant with our third son who we named Orange Fargo Allen. Orange means original and popular, but, as much as we liked the name, our Orange became known by my mother's maiden name Fargo. Born in 1849, Fargo always enjoyed helping his mother and doing projects around the house. He took on chores and made lists as soon as he could write. I had purchased ten acres of land a mile from our house on Porterville Road that had been fallow for several years. As a teenager Fargo declared himself a farmer of that land and when he married the pretty and well educated Emma Hanna Griffin in 1875, he built a home on the property, establishing himself as an Aurora activist and community leader.

It would be 1854 before our fourth and last child was born. Millicent insisted we name him Jabez and you might say he took the name seriously, becoming my shadow while still a toddler, pouting when I couldn't take him on house calls, and asking questions about everything medical. Jabez would sneak a medical book to his room and read by the light of a candle he pilfered from the pantry. I had to repress my amusement at these little insurrections, agreeing with Millicent that he could have burned down the house.

Every day after school Jabez showed up in the drugstore, first sweeping the floor, then by age thirteen he helped with compounding medicine. When he was fourteen we made a call to a farmer who dislocated his shoulder while breaking a horse to bridle. As is typical, the farmer's young strong muscles held the humerus out of joint. I tied a sheet around the man's chest, then, with a short length of rope tied the sheet to a tree, thus anchoring his torso. Next, I instructed Jabez to pull the man's arm away from the shoulder in slight downward and forward direction with an even, gentle force. I then put one hand under the hollow of the arm and the other on top of the humerus lying anterior to the shoulder. Once the extension applied by Jabez was sufficient, I eased the humeral head back into joint. As usual, the shoulder reset with a sudden jerk, a clunk, and a painful yelp, followed by near total relief. As a smile overtook our patient, Jabez was leaning on the tree trunk retching. We left instructions for our patient to apply towels soaked in hot vinegar water to his shoulder twice a day for four days so the ligaments would tighten. On the ride home Jabez thought maybe he was more interested in Chemistry than surgery, and true to his word, by his Aurora Academy graduation he was a compounding expert.

Jabez was sensitive with a generally serious countenance and moods that tended towards melancholy. I longed for him to attend medical college and join me in practice. Jabez had a disciplined work ethic, perfect for long demanding hours of the Physic business, but his passion was for the science of drugs.

32. The Spirits Rap, 1850s

Mobs go mad all at once, individuals recover their senses one by one.

On the evening of 31 March 1848, the Fox sisters heard a knocking sound coming from the east bedroom of their parents' Hydesville, New York farmhouse. The next night Maggie Fox, then fourteen, and her sister Kate, then eleven, convinced their mother that the knocking conveyed sophisticated messages. The April 1 date appears to have gone unnoticed.

Mrs. Fox became so excited that she invited several neighbors to hear the strange knockings. When she asked the source to guess the age of a close neighbor, a correct number of raps replied. Mrs. Fox then asked, "If you are an injured spirit manifest it by three raps." The knocking's reply proved that Maggie and Kate were communicating beyond earth's mortal bonds. The neighbors searched the house and found strands of hair and fragments of bone in the cellar, believing they proved rumors that a peddler had once been murdered in the Hydesville farmhouse.

When the story reached Isaac and Amy Post, prominent in Rochester's spiritualist movement, Maggie and Kate were invited to give a demonstration before a group of likeminded activists in their home. It became an emotional reunion with the knocking thumps of the Post's recently deceased daughter. Impressed, the Posts arranged for a public demonstration before 400 attendees. Afterwards the constable's wife took the two girls off stage where they were disrobed for examination. Finding no evidence of trickery, most attendees departed convinced the sisters had communicated with spirits.

At the time Horace Greely, editor of the *Weekly Tribune,* was backing an upstate New York tour of Dr. Franz Mesmer disciples advocating a theory of universal magnetic fluid. They waved their hands over 'mesmerized' volunteers to induce a relaxed hypnotic state often associated with visions of a departed loved one. Greely wrote up the Fox story and publicized their invitation to New York City where they met another aspiring spiritualist calling himself the 'Poughkeepsie Seer,' Andrew Jackson Davis. Davis knew just how to market the prodigies. His pitch, "Communicating with the dead assures salvation by teaching the living about heaven and hell."

After their successful New York debut, Davis organized Fox sister tours from New York to Cincinnati, charging a dollar for admission and offering limited private sessions to those wanting personal attention. In advance of their arrival, Davis paid local newspapers to carry stories of the sisters' special communications, including his favorite, The Conjuring of Benjamin Franklin's Spirit.

Motivated by skeptic curiosity, Millicent and I attended one of the public séances offered by the Fox sisters in Aurora. Each session was limited to twenty-one attendees paying one dollar each. The upstairs meeting room at the Globe Hotel was bathed in blue shaded gaslight as we entered. There was a table of food with small plates and a little sign that read:

> "Please partake of this fare. The spirit you seek is drawn to nourishment and encouraged by your contentment. Like us, the spirits seek sustenance."

Maggie and Kate mingled with each of us, speaking in voices so soft they were difficult to hear. With each approach they hugged us, then held our hands giving the impression of a very private conversation. They asked the reason we came and what message our departed loved one would like to hear. Maggie did most of the talking, but neither girl took notes.

I was surprised at how Maggie's questions provoked an urge within me to speak with our son James, now dead nearly two years. Millicent said she longed to speak with her father who would enjoy hearing that she had a family of her own. Maggie and Kate asked intriguing questions about one pleasant memory, one memory we never had shared with the person, and details about the individual's death.

A chime sounded, directing us to take our seats. The sisters retreated behind a black screen in the corner of the room while Mr. Davis explained that it was critical to maintain a total number of occupants evenly divisible by three. No one could leave the room until the séance was completed. He, the sisters and the twenty-one of us made up twenty-four total. There had been six choices on the food table. There were exactly twenty-one plates, spoons and napkins. There was to be no talking unless specifically addressed by one of the sisters. Finally he warned participants to avoid alcohol until the cock crowed the dawn of a new day.

As Mr. Davis took his seat I studied our collected spirit travelers. The group included farmers, businessmen and laborers who together paid $21 for one of the sister's two shows that day. Even assuming a fifty-percent overhead, these girls were making more in one evening that many attendees made in a month.

Another chime and the sisters emerged from behind the black curtain and sat in straight back chairs completing our circle. In front of them was a small oval table covered with a long black cloth on which sat a loaf of bread and three candles they lit as the lamps in the room dimmed.

Maggie started, "We are deeply saddened by the loss each of you have experienced and are privileged to share with you God's unique gift so generously bestowed on us. Communicating with the dead is serious and frightening business for both the living and the dead. By our silence, we show our respect for those spirits with courage to speak. So too, it is essential that everyone hold hands no matter what transgresses. Tears can be wiped away later. Releasing the circle of belief frightens the spirit and extinguishes the communication."

The sisters then broke the loaf of bread into thirds. Steam rose from the broken loaf and its freshness filled the room. Each sister took a bite of the center piece of the bread, they then closed their eyes and remained silent for several moments. Soon, they began to chant unintelligible words.

Suddenly, Maggie unleashed a forceful voice, "Our beloved Silas Abrams, we bring you gifts for life unto death. Commune with us Silas Abrams, and move among us. Join our bond of good will. Fear not our intentions."

In response, there was a loud rap that seemed to arise from the floor. Maggie said, "You are welcomed among these assembled souls as a friend and messenger. We are all pleased by your presence and respectful of your great exertions. One rap confirms and two raps deny. Please be open to the limitations of the living and accept our attentions."

Over the ensuing hour, the Abrams and several others were provided the opportunity to speak with dead relatives or friends through a code of knocking sounds. Neither Millicent nor I were among those so blessed. The ability of Maggie and Kate to recall stories shared during the conversations before the séance was remarkable. At the end, Maggie thanked the spirits who chose to attend and suggested that those spirits not revealing themselves might be welcomed at another time. Then, following a few more unintelligible chants, we were instructed to release our hands and break the link.

As we were leaving, I took a more critical assessment of our fellow spirit travelers. Some were patients who had offered me barter instead of money for my services. I say this meaning no accusation of being cheated, rather I know the precious value of a dollar to these families. I might simply mark their attendance as the cost of entertainment, except there are many a lecture or evening of music that cost only a nickel. Millicent opined, "People realize they are not in control, but think someone or something must be. Some find assurance of an eternal life in the scriptures, others require more certain evidence." However, I join those who dismiss the sisters as the 'Rochester Knockers and Rappers.'

That same week the *Commercial Advertiser* in Buffalo covered the Fox sisters' spiritualism as a serious religious marvel in a story no doubt written by Mr. Davis. The article infuriated me. Regular medicine was embracing the science of observation, record keeping and experimentation at the same time as the Homeopaths, Thomsonians, Hydropaths and now the Spiritualists were pushing magical thinking.

The Fox sisters opened in Buffalo's Phelps House Hotel, which happened to be the residence of Dr. Charles Coventry, Professor of Physiology and Medical Jurisprudence at Buffalo Medical College. After attending a performance, he wrote a letter to the Buffalo *Commercial Advertiser* concluding that, "Such spectacles must propel all men of science to discourage all further waste of time, money, and credulity on the folly perpetrated by the Fox sisters."

At Dr. Coventry's urging, the Erie County Medical Society appointed a Committee of Investigation consisting of Dr. Coventry, Dr. Austin Flint, Dr. Charles Alfred Lee, two community leaders with credentials in science, and me. Our letter of appointment to the committee attributed the sounds to the agency of the younger sister, most likely produced by manipulation of her joints. Though some physicians worried that exposing the sisters might alienate citizens who embraced Spiritualism, such caution was not entertained in the letter of challenge Dr. Flint published in the *Commercial Advertiser*.

The Fox sisters responded by publishing a letter welcoming such an inquiry. In part the letter claimed that, "The investigation will contribute to an understanding of the important and mysterious manifestations for which we are honored to serve as an exceptional and uncommon agent." Both the Flint and Fox letters were reprinted in several New York newspapers.

Dr. Flint, a man of boundless energy and habitual urgency, managed to schedule the examination by our committee the very same week and in the same Phelps Hotel used for their previous séances. To begin Dr. Flint suggested the sisters assume positions that would best demonstrate their abilities for our committee. The sisters chose to sit side by side on firm, upright chairs, but asked if we might invite another attendee to bring our total to a number divisible by three. Coventry invited a proper lady known to reside at the Phelps.

Maggie and Kate lit three candles on a short table before them and began their incantations much like the Aurora performance. They soon confirmed the presence of a chatty, rapping spirit. At the close of their initial demonstration the sisters expressed their delight with how accommodating the Phelps was to spirits.

Now, Dr. Flint placed the feet of both sisters on cushions to prevent solid contact with the floor. The table with the three candles was carefully arranged but the spirits proved unarousable. Maggie explained that the presence of so many skeptics had likely fatigued the spirits. Flint apologized and removed the cushion under Kate's feet, still no spirits could be awakened. Now Flint removed Maggie's cushions, and in very little time the spirits awoke and the knocking recurred.

In the last phase of the examination the lady Dr. Coventry recruited was instructed to firmly hold the younger Kate's knees. After introductory incantations, the spirits returned. Flint then instructed the woman to firmly hold Maggie's knees, at which time spirit communications could not be produced.

To our surprise, Margaret, the older sister, was the source of the rapping. Kate's role was to reinforce Margaret's memory and add to the sing-song nature of their incantations, but otherwise Kate's collaboration was entirely passive. With the mechanism of the rapping revealed, Dr. Flint ushered in two women known to be capable of producing similar rapping sounds by flexing their knees and ankles. The wooden Phelps Hotel floor produced results every bit as sonorous as Maggie's. Flint explained to those present that the broad articular surfaces of the knee joint allow considerable lateral motion in young women with supple ligaments. With the foot firmly planted, a sudden lateral force can generate a rather loud noise.

Flint rushed publication of our investigation into the March 1851 issue of the *Buffalo Medical Journal*. In the article, Flint expressed sympathy for people who seek remedy from grief in spirit communications. He expressed concern that similar reasoning has caused men of science to believe things that are later proven false. Flint acknowledged that it remained for others to expose the mechanisms used by the many other showmen touring America.

The sisters, of course, protested, complaining that our committee was typical of non-believers and not unlike those who denounced Galileo's theory of the planets. A committee of doctors proved no match for the marketing skills of Andrew Davis who continued to market the Fox sisters' spiritualist movement for twenty more years. As I prepare this memoir Maggie and Kate Fox no longer capture newspaper headlines and rumors suggest intemperance has consumed their resources.

Flint's paper was dismissed by some as a scold, begging the question, is it a doctor's duty to educate and enlighten the community? After all, we are not priests; we are only doctors.

33. The Fugitive Slave Act, 1850-1860

Until you own your soul, you are a slave.

In 1848 Aurora had been all abuzz about Millard Fillmore being elected vice president on the Whig party ticket with Zachary Taylor. Fillmore's father, Nathaniel, had moved from Vermont to a farm just south of Aurora in 1820 at the urging of his brother, Colonel Fillmore. When Millard completed his law studies in 1823 he joined his father and worked as a teacher, surveyor and attorney. By the time he married Abigail Powers in 1826, he was a well-known and gifted speaker. In 1828, at the age of twenty-eight, Millard won election to the New York Assembly. In 1832, he began four terms as a United States Congressman where his skill at negotiating compromise propelled him to Chair of the House Ways and Means Committee. President for only sixteen months, Taylor took ill after a meal of cucumbers, cabbage, corn and an enormous bowl of cherries washed down with a jug of iced milk. Despite the best of modern remedies, including calomel, quinine, and opium, Zachary Taylor died five days later. Suddenly in the July of 1850, Millard Fillmore became President of the United States.

Millard Fillmore's thoughts about slavery were obscure, though shortly after New York outlawed slavery in 1827, he defended, *pro bono*, a man accused of being a runaway slave. In 1850, a recklessly divided nation was threatening war and there was desperate need for middle ground, so Fillmore signed the *Compromise of 1850*, a Bill largely negotiated before Taylor's death. The Bill admitted California as a free state and the territories of Utah and New Mexico would vote on allowing slavery. Zachary Taylor, himself a Louisiana slave owner, believed that slavery would be a non-issue in the new territories where sugarcane and cotton would not grow.

Appended to the Compromise was an updated *Fugitive Slave Law* that made it a crime to not help capture any runaway slave. *Article 1 of the Constitution* had equivocated on slavery by declaring a three-fifths compromise. But the *1850 Fugitive Slave Law* affirmed slaves as property, warranting property right protection for slaveholders. The *Fugitive Slave Law* superseded State laws by making it a Federal crime, punishable by six months in jail, if any Northern state official or citizen did not arrest and return a fugitive slave. Proof of slave ownership required only the testimony of a claimant. Runaways had no avenue for defending themselves against any accusation and anyone returning a slave to the South was eligible for a bounty.

Many in Aurora and Buffalo were outraged by the new law. The First Unitarian Church of Buffalo, where Millard and Abigail worshiped since moving to Buffalo in 1830, saw several of its congregation quit in protest. Millicent's abolitionist friend, George Washington Jonson, knew that Fillmore had to appease the South, but he did not anticipate being declared a Federal criminal. Overnight the Underground Railroad became America's greatest act of civil disobedience since the Revolution, though it now required potentially punishing commitment. Because of the *Compromise* Fillmore lost the Whig nomination in 1852, and the party soon ruptured along North-South divisions.

Agents and bounty hunters infiltrating the Underground Railroad, posted advertisements and combed the northern states looking for runaways. Moderates, abolitionists with families, and those who harbored no real opinion about slavery, faced difficult choices. Others, like Harriet Tubman from Buffalo, known to John Brown as General Tubman, were unceasing in her travels along the Appalachian route in the aid of escaping slaves. North Elba, New York's Gerrit Smith, a philanthropist, Liberty Party's candidate for President in 1848, and cousin of Elizabeth Cady-Stanton paid legal expenses of people accused of violating the *Fugitive Slave Law* and opened his home to fugitives. Many Presbyterians, Quaker activists, and Millicent somehow stayed active in the shadows.

In the winter of 1851 two men entered our drugstore, purchased several items, and struck up a conversation with Civia. Before sunrise the next morning these same men, accompanied by the Sheriff and an arrest warrant, arrived at the South Wales cabin occupied by Civia and Elmas. The warrant spelled out their intention to transport the whole family back to the Virginia plantation from which they had fled sixteen years earlier. Our Sheriff jailed the family, but insisted on following New York's due process to confirm ownership, giving Millicent time to engage Gerrit Smith's attorneys.

Most Auroreans assumed that Negros living in New York were freemen. To bounty hunters, the brands burned into their right shoulders proved they were the property of Virginia's William Green who offered a bounty for their return. As was his custom, Judge Conklin scheduled a hearing on the case two weeks hence, and Millicent initiated a campaign to purchase the Morgan family's freedom. But with Elmas valued at $800, Civia at $700 and their children at $450 each, it was an insurmountable task. She did raise more than the bounty offered for their return.

The morning of the scheduled hearing, the cell holding Civia and Elmas and their children had been jimmied. Just how the family secured their escape was never ascertained and the bounty hunters simply vanished. Over the next week, Millicent and members of the Mission Committee of the Presbyterian Church crated the contents of the family's cabin and shipped them to the Elgin Settlement at Buxton, Ontario, care of Civia and Elmas Morgan.

Civia wrote every few months. Elmas resumed farming in Ontario and Civia's skills at writing and numbering secured her a job as Assistant to the

Bursar for the Elgin Community. She claimed a desire to return to Aurora and the drugstore, but she could not miss us more than I missed her. Civia was both an employee and a friend. We shared laughs, heartaches and memories and found unique ways to meet the needs of patients.

In 1852, Harriet Beecher Stowe published her book about George, Eliza, and Harry Harris, runaways who also fled to Canada at the conclusion of *Uncle Tom's Cabin*. With every page of her novel, I pined for Civia's curiosity and talents. If I held any hope that her decision to flee could be reversed, that hope died with the *Supreme Court's Dred Scott decision* of 1857 that essentially declared slaves, and former slaves, ineligible for citizenship under the *United States Constitution*. Then, in 1863, at the height of the Civil War, we received word that Civia died from tubercular consumption.

Civia would have enjoyed a new service my store offered in the years after her departure. The Italian Physician, Pilipppo Baldini, wrote that eating cinnamon ice cream could relieve aches, chocolate ice cream improves disposition, and lemon ice cream settles upset stomachs. Like Civia, ice cream makes all the drudgeries of life more palatable. I had the name for my new soda fountain etched on the mirror behind the counter. It read, "Civia's Fount."

34. Cholera, 1850s

Every Physician must master the panic that attends impending failure.

With nearly 250,000 people packed onto Manhattan's island marshes, New York City suffered a barrage of Smallpox, Yellow Fever, Measles, and Malarial illnesses despite all arriving ships waiting through a period of quarantine. Still, sailors, traders, shipbuilders, craftsmen, and cart-pullers must interact if commerce is to function. Poor immigrant neighborhoods suffered the most, while the upper classes blamed moral laxity, intemperance, or the seasoning required of a new world.

The Cholera epidemic in 1832 was a disaster of spectacular proportions, according to Castleton professor, Dr. William Tully. Painful cramps, vomiting and profuse diarrhea killed nearly a third of its victims within hours. Cholera, long known in Asia, made its way into Europe in 1831. Then, in 1832, it struck America's back door, traveling down the Saint Lawrence River from Montreal to the Hudson River Valley and the Erie Canal. New York's Governor, Enos Throop, proclaimed that, "An infinitely wise and just God has seen fit to employ pestilence as one means of scourging the human race for its sins."

Cholera first struck the poor, ill fed, and intemperate, but soon the upper classes succumbed often spreading the epidemic as they fled the cities. The New York Medical Society published alerts, but most rural villages considered themselves invincible and had no authority to clean streets, public privies or wells. It was the job of free ranging pigs to consume most of the garbage, horse manure, and dumps of morning pots. In the July of 1832, the State Legislature empowered each municipality to establish a board of health, but few understood what the boards should do.

By 1834 Cholera relinquished its grip on America and the health boards disbanded having endorsed the general idea that water good enough for a horse is good enough for a human.

Then, in 1848, Cholera reemerged in Europe and by the April of 1849 it reappeared in New York City, Boston, Philadelphia, Cincinnati and Buffalo. The new Sisters of Charity Hospital in Buffalo admitted 233 patients, all treated with hourly administrations of calomel and opium. Over half, 128 patients, died. Immigrants laborers, both Irish and German living in marshy areas of Buffalo's first ward, suffered the most.

My first case was Jeremiah Spooner. Jeremiah began experiencing stomach cramps on the stagecoach returning from attending his brother's wedding in Cincinnati. The rice water diarrhea began as he arrived home. By the time I was called, Jeremiah's leg and arm muscles were cramping. I gave him 100 drops of Laudanum orally, and the same quantity as an enema. I repeated the Laudanum in doses of 40 drops every fifteen minutes and applied a warm stimulating sinapism to his abdomen.

Eberle considers Cholera an extreme dysentery that requires calomel to force the release of bile known to accumulate in the liver. But I had read that patients treated with homeopathic dilutions were more likely to survive the 1832 epidemics in New York and Philadelphia. A pamphlet by George Hawthorne provided evidence that Cholera is spread by miasma and recommended patients be given Opium and forced to sweat off the excess fluids otherwise accumulating in the bowels. So, I kept Jeremiah warm and continued hourly doses of Laudanum. Eighteen hours into his ordeal Jeremiah was overcome by sleep while I caught a nap in a chair next to his bed. Two days later he returned to managing his Elm Street cheese making business, though for two weeks Jeremiah was troubled by irregular and urgent intestinal dejections.

Within an hour of Jeremiah's recovery, I was called to attend a fifty-one-year-old man who arrived on the same stagecoach. He came to Aurora to buy hardwood for furniture craftsmen in Cincinnati, and called on several lumber mills before registering for a room at the Globe Hotel. A short while later he became ill. I was equally aggressive in his care, but after lingering for two days the man died alone in his room while I was attending a woman employed by the Globe. She survived but her two-year-old daughter was dead within eight hours of developing symptoms.

I sent a messenger to alert Drs. Lapham and Hoyt the moment I realized that Jeremiah had Cholera, and it is likely my messenger started the rumor that Aurora was facing devastation. George Hawthorne might believe Cholera was not contagious but the common citizen was already convinced of its deadly capacity to spread death.

Three days elapsed without any new cases, then a forty-year-old sawmill employee became ill and died. The next day his wife became ill but recovered. A couple of days later another man died. One day later two new cases emerged and both died. Then once again there was a pause of three days when seven deaths occurred. Over the next forty days Dr. Lapham and I recorded forty-three deaths and thirty-one cases that recovered. That summer the Erie County Medical Society recorded the deaths of five physicians, but by the grace of God, neither Dr. Lapham, Hoyt, I, nor any of our family members became ill.

The actual number of cases of Cholera in Aurora is unknown. Some patients did not consult a Physician, others left Aurora hoping to avoid the epidemic and became ill in their community of refuge. My brother James heard about one family who became ill shortly after arriving at the Wright's Corner home of relatives. Three children died but all the adults survived. A pastor who prayed with the family became ill and died. His wife survived.

Reviewing our cases, Dr. Lapham and I identified all five reported grades of Cholera. Some suffered only abdominal cramping and moderate diarrhea. Others were temporarily incapacitated by copious evacuations. Approximately half progressed to the third grade with rapid pulse, tenting skin and muscle cramps. A fourth phase of sallow uremia very often led to the final phase of death. Dr. Lapham felt we should draft a pamphlet, similar to the one published by the New York City Board of Health, for distribution in the community. Ours read as follows:

Notice

The severest form of dysentery has invaded our community. It is called Cholera and is to be avoided. Dr. Lapham and Dr. Allen recommend that all households with symptoms of diarrhea and vomiting restrict their travels and remain at home to limit the exposure of others to the influences that transmit this condition. To all others, we recommend:

Be temperate in eating and drinking.

Avoid crude, wilted vegetables and fruits.

Abstain from cold water, when you are heated.

Above all abstain from ardent spirits, and if habit has rendered spirits indispensable, take much less than usual.

Sleep and clothe warm.

Avoid labor in the heat of day.

Do not sleep or sit in a draught of air when heated.

Avoid getting wet.

Take no medicines without advice of a graduate doctor.

Dissolve one pound of sulfate of iron in a large pail of water and empty it into the out-house once a week.

Despite our simple instructions, many Auroreans employed specious preventives advertised in magazines or hawked by itinerate salesmen. Most contained alcohol. Others promoted camphor sugar and vapors to neutralize Cholera's miasmic taint. The Village Council burned pitch on Big Tree Road for two weeks. Newspapers and Buffalo's City Council alternated between dismissing the devastation Cholera visited on immigrants as the seasoning required by the tough American continent, or as punishment for moral laxity. In rural villages, where the poor mingle with the wealthy and the temperate with the intemperate, the indiscriminate nature of Cholera was more apparent.

President Taylor declared a national prayer day in August of 1849. The pious in our community attended church but those most in need of prayer spent the day imbibing their favorite preventative. I worried that all the church going reinforced the belief that Cholera was God's punishment for poverty, intemperance or debauchery. Lapham, always a great man for statistics, proved that poor isolated farm families who tended the fields, produced a harvest, but ate well throughout the year, were the least likely to suffer Cholera. Lapham also confirmed that Auroreans who had survived the 1832 Cholera epidemic were unaffected in the 1849 epidemic. Finally, cleanliness and healthy diets did more to limit Cholera's influence than did all our remedies.

Between 1849 and 1854 no twelve-month period passed without Cholera attacking somewhere in New York. Pulmonary Tubercular disease killed more people, but the sudden death of Cholera terrorized everyone. In Chicago, a Dr. Byrd declared an ozone deficiency caused Cholera and soon his Sulphur pill remedies were being sold by the millions. Then the whiskered Old Jacob Townsend's smile appeared in every magazine advertising a Sarsaparilla guaranteed to prevent Cholera. The Director of one New York cholera hospital claimed regular consumption of beef tea prevented Cholera, though his own statistics refuted the claim. The *Buffalo Homeopathic Medical Journal* bragged that science had proven one of their dilutions, taken regularly, prevented Cholera. My family remained well, bothered only by occasional common diarrhea. We took no preventatives, yet I was accused of protecting my family with a secret tonic while letting others suffer. I distilled large quantities of water for compounding medicines and each day I carried a couple of gallons' home for Millicent and the boys to drink. Perhaps it was unsoiled water, or perhaps we had all survived Lapham's first stage without realizing it was Cholera.

In England, a Dr. Farr noted that communities located in the higher elevations experienced fewer Cholera cases, and one-third fewer deaths, than communities along the coast or near river banks. To Farr this proved that miasmic vapors accumulating in valleys and low lying areas spread Cholera in a manner similar to Yellow and Malarial Fevers. To Hawthorne the cholera miasma was, "Forced from the bowels of the earth by subterranean commotion, released through fissures in multiple locations." The American Medical Association (AMA) formed a Committee on Practical Medicine and Epidemics that concluded Cholera was the direct result of debauchery and intemperance and was not contagious. Lapham and I were both disappointed when Austin Flint echoed the AMA in a commentary for the *Buffalo Medical Journal*. Any observant community physician already knew that with only a few questions we found contact with a person or place previously visited by Cholera, similar to North Boston's Typhoid epidemic.

In the September of 1852 the eastbound stagecoach driver handed me a message from Rebecca, my brother's wife. James was ill and she hoped I might attend to him. Having never received such a request in the sixteen years since James and his family settled in Wright's Corners, I ran out the side door of the store and into the side door of our home to show the message to Millicent who agreed that I should depart immediately. The Globe's stable saddled my horse for a hard, fast ten-mile ride to James's cabin.

James was prostrate on his cot soiled by near constant rice water evacuations and Rebecca was doing her best to keep him clean. His eyes were sunken, his energies consumed by abdomen pain and muscle cramping. With the breath of a weakened sparrow, he pleaded for relief, by death if necessary.

Rebecca filled in the details. Two days earlier James had been called to attend to a Mitchell Morgan, a sometimes laborer and full-time drunkard, who lived in the basement of Batlow's Tavern along with two women who suffered their own intemperance. These three ne'er-do-wells got by with some honest work, occasional pickpocketing and a regular trade in sexual favors. When Morgan did not attend to sweeping the tavern floor that morning, Mr. Batlow entered the tavern's basement intent on evicting all three reprobates only to be repelled by an appalling stench. Morgan and the two women were sprawled on the dirt floor in their own filth. Without further investigation Batlow summoned my brother. In the basement's dim light James confirmed one male and two females laying on a wet dirt floor each with but a few rags of cover. One woman was already dead and the other woman joined her before the hour was out. Morgan lasted until mid-afternoon. James could do little except provide Morgan with a few doses of Laudanum. Certain he was dealing with Cholera, James spread carbonic acid powder over the bodies and around the basement, then summoned the Constable. When no one would help, James carried the bodies out and loaded them onto a wagon that the Constable drove to a field and burned.

No one thanked James, nor paid his fee. Fearing the intensity of his exposure, he dosed himself and Rebecca with a drachm of camphor sugar every hour. Still, the next morning James awoke with vomiting and diarrhea flecked with rice like mucous and the fishy smell of Cholera. He dosed himself with one hundred drops of Laudanum, and terrified Rebecca with instructions to abandon him, burn his clothes and bedding after his death, and scrub the room with carbolic acid. Rebecca firmly rejected his directive, instead sending for their son Charles who delivered that message to the stagecoach driver.

Feigning invincibility, I commanded Rebecca and Charles to leave the room, clean themselves, and allow me the full burden of care. They both refused. Employing the newest remedies, I mixed thirty grains of bicarbonate soda with water and did my best to get James to drink. He was so near stupor that I interspersed stimulant sips of brandy. My confidence was in tumult, and my insides were near panic. I grabbed for anything that might possibly help, including a standard hospital dose of calomel, which I had shunned when treating Jeremiah. I feared being wrong to do it, and I feared being wrong not to.

All deaths leave a wound. Doctors carry on, suppress gloom, and deny fallibility. The intense intimacy of being with a person at the moment of death propels us to attend the next. Being a good shepherd at the boundaries of life is a personal honor whether it be for a patient I just met, one I've known for years, or my brother. The effort is not without delusions of success; they are essential to engage the battle. The good physician balances efforts to conquer with the need to comfort, always mystified by the nobility patients discover in their season of death.

James lapsed into a coma and died six hours after my arrival, his body producing mucous flecked stools until an hour before an agonal death. Rebecca was at his side nearly continuously. Charles faithfully assisted, lifting and supporting his father so Rebecca could maintain a modicum of cleanliness and respectability. It was a dreadful ordeal.

Millicent arrived the following day intending to help Rebecca while I cleaned up the loose ends of James' medical practice. By mid-day both Charles and Rebecca were showing the first symptoms of Cholera. I feared for Millicent's safety as she provided comfort to Rebecca in ways I could not. Within two days, Cholera extinguished my brother's entire family.

Millicent and I bathed in chlorinated lime. We took nothing from the home, burned the cabin with all its contents and the clothes we had been wearing. It was extreme, but neighbors demanded their village be rid of Cholera. Millicent said a prayer as it collapsed. James was only forty-eight years old, Rebecca was forty-two and Charles was twenty-one. We were allowed to bury them in the community gravesite a short distance from their home, but only after Millicent and I prepared their bodies with chlorinated lime.

For two more years, Cholera lingered among the immigrants who flocked to work on Buffalo's docks. Ruthless pestilence, poverty and overcrowding were hazards of a new life and the government did little more than distribute pamphlets that encouraged bathing in several languages.

Mary Abigail "Abbie" Powers Fillmore wanted to do more. In 1854, the daughter of Millard and Abigail Fillmore was twenty-two and arguably more popular than her father. Abbie attended private school in Lenox, Massachusetts before graduating from New York State Normal School. She was conversant in French, Spanish, German, and Italian and taught in Buffalo city schools until Zachary Taylor's death in 1850. Her mother's chronic infirmity forced Abbie to join her parents in the White House where she charmed dignitaries with impromptu performances on the piano, harp, and guitar and became the darling of newspapers around the world.

When antipathy for the *Fugitive Slave Act* denied Fillmore the Whig nomination in 1852, the family returned to Buffalo. Twenty-four days later, Mrs. Fillmore died and Abbie continued managing her father's post-presidential affairs. Hoping to lift her father's spirits, Abbie accepted a heavily publicized trip for a newly completed railroad from Chicago to Rock Island. The former President gave rousing speeches at every stop, but Abbie's sociability captured the headlines. If you read a newspaper, you knew Abbie.

Abbie brought attention to the needs of immigrant children by touring schools, including those operated by the Sisters of the Sacred Heart in Buffalo's first ward. Every summer between 1849 to 1854, Cholera tormented those living where ships, canal barges, and the city mingled to transfer grain in one of America's busiest ports. Buffalo's *Commercial Advertiser* lauded the energy with which Abbie Fillmore embraced students and charmed teachers. At the end of one such day, Abbie boarded the afternoon stagecoach to Aurora with plans to help her grandfather, Nathaniel Fillmore and his second wife Eunice, settle in as our new neighbors on Big Tree Road. Upon arrival Abbie purchased a few peppermints at my drugstore to settle an upset stomach. I am told she retired at 10:00 p.m., but awoke an hour later with diarrhea and vomiting. She alerted no one until after midnight when her grandfather sought my urgent attendance. Millicent, a close friend of Eunice, accompanied me crossing the few feet of lawn separating our side doors.

Abbie's suffering was acute. Retching, rice water diarrhea and painful muscle cramps left little doubt she was in the grasp of Cholera. My treatment over the next several hours would be bicarbonate of soda and Laudanum every hour. I withheld calomel and applied a sinapism of powdered black mustard over the liver area. Fearing the worse, I advised Nathaniel that a messenger be dispatched immediately to summon the President from Buffalo.

Former President Fillmore arrived just before Abbie breathed her last at 11:00 a.m. the next morning, Wednesday, 26 July 1854. She was buried in the family plot in Buffalo's Forest Lawn Cemetery in a grave marked only with her initials. I sent no bill, but Eunice gave Millicent a cameo brooch and the Former President presented us with a silver teapot. Some say tragedy reawakened the warrior within Mr. Fillmore, but I believe the harried life was his only comfort from a frightful loneliness.

In 1855 Dr. John Snow of London published his second pamphlet titled, *On the Mode of Communication of Cholera*. In it Snow pointed out that one of the two water companies serving London drew its water from the upper Thames and the other from the Thames after it received London's discharges. Customers of the latter were far more likely to suffer Cholera than customers of the former. Referencing Dr. Flint's paper about our Typhoid epidemic in North Boston, NY, Snow mapped Cholera around several London wells proving that water exposed to human discharges carried Cholera. His maps also showed Cholera traveled from city to city along the path of human trade, never spreading faster than people travel.

By the mid-1850s Cholera once again vanished, reappearing in Europe in 1865 and in North American in 1866. This time, all informed persons recognized that Cholera was spread by contagion. New York City's Council on Hygiene proved that sanitary measures limited Cholera's impact and that survivors were not vulnerable to a second attack. The City of Buffalo, and nearly every village in the State, adopted sanitation programs and the free ranging of pigs was greatly curtailed. Most villages formed health boards charged with the task of separating water supplies from human discharges.

Snow's treatise shifted blame from lifestyle to an external agent. He remained unsure if the contagion was a chemical poison or a living germ, but recommended destruction of bedding, clothing, and excreta of those suffering from Cholera. Burning my brother's home has always troubled me, but according to Snow, it was expedient.

35. Breakthroughs, Cancer and an Ovarian Cyst, 1851-1860

Surgery is a heroic form of battle waged to save the patient's life.

For three months I have been making weekly visits to Sheldon Hendrick's farm to assure he has an adequate supply of the medication I compound from opium, brandy, Chloroform, and cherry syrup. Sheldon's life is being consumed by Cancer. Lectures at Castleton warned that if cancerous tumors are not accessible to the knife when discovered, there was little to do other than manage pain, calm the nerves and strengthen the body's resources. When Sheldon first consulted me, tumors were already palpable in his abdomen, neck, groin, and axillae.

Journals regularly publish cases hawking cures using nitric acid or sulfuric acid mixed with saffron, lead, mercury, arsenic, copper sulfate mixed with borax, quicklime, or potassium permanganate, botanicals and homeopathic dilutions. Yellow dock root, borrowed from local Indians, is very popular. When I asked the opinion of a Seneca medicine man who helps me collect plants and herbs, he shrugged, "We use yellow dock as a tonic and laxative; the white man hopes for more. That's okay, hope can cure." He helps me collect yellow dock root to sell in the store, but when asked, I quote my Seneca friend's statement of hope.

One of Aurora's mill owners developed multiple tumors in his mouth and neck, which he believed to be Cancer. A Seneca woman he employed collected and boiled yellow dock root for him. He took four ounces four times a day, holding the decoction in his mouth before swallowing. In four weeks, the tumors disappeared. Then there was a farmer, this one a patient of mine, with a Cancer on his scalp which I removed with great care. Some roots of the Cancer escaped my scalpel and the cancer returned. I offered to burn out the roots with hot iron picks. He felt this too severe and purchased yellow dock root to apply as a sinapism. The man returned in two months to prove my error and demonstrate complete healing of his scalp.

I struggle to make sense out of such reports. Incredible recoveries and remissions populate folklore and medical journals alike, but for the most part, Cancer patients do not fare well. Dr. Leroy d'Etoilles at the French Academy of Science searched for a Cancer cure in 1844 by collecting hundreds of cases from 170 practitioners in France. He compared the survival of those who accepted treatments to those who had refused all treatment. In the end d'Etoilles was forced to conclude that none of the therapies consistently prolonged life. In 1854 reports from the Cancer Hospital in London counted only 146 patients out of 650 cases were still alive one year later.

Besides the stethoscope, my class was one of the first at Castleton to receive instruction on the use of the compound microscope, which at the time produced distracting refraction rainbows at higher magnification. By the 1860s, optics improved and reports began to follow Professor Rudolph Virchow's lead in describing cells in tumors as irregular, immature cells with large nuclei.

Dr. James Paget put forth a theory that there was both a constitutional element and a local element required for Cancer to start. The constitutional element, often inherited, flows through the blood exerting its influence in tissues susceptible to Cancer under conditions of mental stress or poor nutrition. A second element is produced in an organ or tissue that has been damaged by trauma or inflammation. Cancer caused by a constitutional element is not curable, if due to a local element, removal of the growth may cure it.

Fibroid tumors of the uterus, one of the first tumors to be examined under the microscope, contain chaotically arranged cells but do not metastasize. I followed journal reports and injected the fibroids of three women with Ergot to little advantage. I also tried running electrical current through needles piercing the abdomen into a fibroid without success. At one medical society meeting I listened with enthusiasm as Dr. Edward Jenks of Detroit described surgical removal of fifteen large fibroids through abdominal incisions in women with pain or heavy bleeding. When asked he revealed only two women survived post-operative inflammation.

I am committed to keeping abreast, but ricocheting from one new remedy to the next is unlikely to help my patients. A cautious habit exposes me to five possibilities: Sometimes I stick with tradition too long; at other times I attempt treatments that fail; sometimes I appear incompetent; at other times I have nothing to offer; at times great responses occur for which I get more credit than I deserve. Oh, there is a sixth, occasionally I am right. I have fallen into a pattern of trying a promising remedy three times and it either becomes my standard, or it is rejected. It is not exceedingly scientific, but it generally avoids undue harm.

Chloroform and Ether were breakthroughs that inspired surgical approaches to Cancer my Castleton professors could never have foretold. In 1846 Dr. Oliver Wendell Holmes coined the word 'anesthesia' in an essay praising how a Boston dentist, William Morton, used Ether to render a woman entirely insensible to pain while Dr. J.C. Warren removed a tumor from her arm. Then, in 1847 Scottish physicians reported similar effects using Chloroform. Chloroform is fast and reliable but causes occasional irregularities in the pulse. Ether is somewhat less predictable, and may cause nausea and giddiness.

By 1850 Drs. James Platt White and Frank Hamilton of Buffalo regularly reported surgical advances at Erie County Medical Society meetings. Like surgeons around the world, new procedures developed on dogs and soon applied to patients creating a new breed of specialized doctors.

———

One winter day in the early 1850s a young boy burst into my office hollering, "My mamma's baby's stuck. Ya gotta come quick, please!" The boy said his mother had been trying to have her baby for weeks and the midwife wanted my consultation. I followed the lad on horseback to a cabin off the main road past Griffins Mills. A low mid-winter sun gave sparkle to crystals floating in the air. By the time we approached the modest cabin, I was driven as much by its promised warmth as I was by the intriguing story.

Before even introducing me to Mrs. Sally Crossline and her husband David, the midwife dismissed the delay in consultation on the husband's refusal to allow a man to exam his wife and anxiously demanded that I hurry the delivery with Ergot and Laudanum. I sensed a combination of anger and fear in the cabin's mood. Silently at first I applied my stethoscope, but could find neither fetal heart sounds nor detect contractions. Then, continuing my most professional comportment, I engaged a litany of words and actions, approaching Sally expectantly. I kept asking questions while I washed the trail dirt off my hands, applied lard to my right hand, and gently rolled Sally onto her left side. Then, allowing no opportunity for protest, I commenced an exam.

Sally's abdomen gave the impression of a term gravid condition, but on exam the mass was clearly not a fetus. In fact, a normal sized uterus was displaced to a deep posterior position. I motioned David to approach and softly explained that there was no baby. Rather, Sally had a watermelon size tumor arising from her left ovary. The Crosslines needed to confront a new reality. "We must seek yet another consultation. I wish to call in Dr. James Platt White of Buffalo Medical College. Dr. White describes an operation, under ether, that he has applied to women suffering from tumors like the one afflicting Sally. He is the only man in the country I would trust with such a delicate operation. Dr. White, I believe, can return Sally to a productive and happy life. Failing that her health will deteriorate."

It appeared that David was considering my proposition when the midwife offered an untimely reminder that the same Dr. White had committed, "The immoral act of allowing medical students to not only exam a woman in labor but also to attend the delivery of that same woman in a class room." I resisted challenging the midwife's protestations. Her errors in the case had already dealt me the upper hand.

I took the hands of both husband and wife and continued. "Yes, the Dr. White I recommend is that same exceptional professor, surgeon and teacher. He concentrates his attentions on the diseases of women and has more experience than anyone in the field. There is no baby to concern us and you have some time to make a decision, but that time is limited. Without intervention Sally is unlikely to survive this growth and we must trust that God will provide the support she needs to survive surgery. Your choices are difficult but they are not complicated."

I returned to my office to attend my afternoon patients. That evening Presbyterian Pastor Coure from Griffins Mills paid a visit in the agency of the Crosslines. He opposed the intervention for two reasons. First, he knew such operations to be dangerous. Second, heroic interventions challenge God's will.

His intrusion might have seemed an annoyance except that I shared his concerns. His well-chosen words suggested an educated background common to Presbyterian Ministry. As we spoke it became clear that Pastor Coure was a fully informed participant in the choices facing the Crosslines. Confident of his agency, I indulged the Pastor with my review of the woman's condition while Millicent, ever the faithful Presbyterian, served us tea.

At some point I asked, "Pastor, if on my return from the Crossline cabin this morning, I had come across a man yelling for help from a hole in the river ice I would have grabbed the longest branch I could find and, laying across the ice, would have offered it so the man could pull himself from that hole. I trust you would do the same?"

Pastor Coure responded, "Of course I would, anything necessary to save one of God's children." He now revealed a third concern, "However, the branch would not possess the moral shadow under which Dr. White has chosen to practice his trade. I am acquainted with the sensation Dr. White created with his desecration of that poor trusting woman who sought his attention during her confinement. Exposure to a horde of students defied all proper decorum. I am also informed that Dr. White freely uses Ether in the process of confinement and labor. I know this to be contrary to the opinions of Philadelphia's Dr. Meigs. Does White not know, or does he not care, that pain is essential to establishing the mother–child bond?"

Relieved that all concerns were exposed, I continued. "Pastor, I have known Dr. White for almost ten years and I find him to be a man of the highest principles. I am a graduate of a respected medical school but I assure you that my education would have benefited had I the opportunity to study under as learned a gentleman as Dr. White. He suffers only in the self-confidence that comes with the summative skill he has acquired in using the knife to cure patients. Newspapers sensationalize events to boost their sales. I assure you that Dr. White provided the woman with the best care, and that he charged her no fee. The bargain struck was mutually agreeable. His skills are above reproach and I trust him. I am acquainted with the writings of Dr. Charles Meigs, and assure you that Dr. White's reputation will one day eclipse that of Dr. Meigs."

It was time for Pastor Coure to go but in parting he generously concluded, "Dr. Allen, I see that you are well read and no quack. You are acquainted with the conditions that afflict my parishioner. I appreciate your time as well as your concern for her welfare. Thank you, and thank your wife for the tea."

He left me with no clue as to his inclination, though it seemed the pastor's mission was not to obstruct. Given the grim situation, I held great respect for the role Pastor Coure was playing.

The next morning, I received a telegram from the pastor. It simply stated, "Proceed with arrangements." In turn I sent a telegram to Dr. White in which I briefly described Sally's condition and asked for his consultation. His response showed more enthusiasm than the legs of Aurora's telegraph operator who handed me a return telegram minutes before Dr. White arrived by stagecoach. White was eager to confirm Sally's situation and add her to his case series of ovarian tumors. So, I hitched my carriage and we departed for the Crossline cabin.

Absent much of the formality he displayed at Society meetings, it was a charming and personable Dr. White who approached the Crossline cabin. David was just making his way from the barn carrying a shot gun. I was still hitching the horse when Dr. White inquired about the morning's hunt and introduced himself. Inside, and in obvious discomfort, Sally was cleaning a freshly shot rabbit.

After conducting his exam, he told David and Sally that he agreed, "Surgery is the only remedy. Ether now allows for meticulous and careful operations and we have greatly reduced the occurrence of post-operative inflammation following protocols using dilute carbolic acid recently described by an Edinburgh surgeon. The surgery will leave you unable to have more children, but I am afraid the tumor has already made pregnancy impossible. I have performed this operation repeatedly, and I am confident in my ability to remove the tumor. The operation will be painless and I will provide you with injections of a new form of opium called morphine to relieve pain after surgery. I will do all in my power to assure that you return to the warmth of this cabin. It is my recommendation that we proceed."

At this point, Pastor Coure arrived. As if greeting an old friend, Dr. White stood to shake the Pastor's hand adding, "Reverend, if everyone had the clarity of understanding you demonstrated in your discussion with Dr. Allen, American medicine would be much the better for it." He then repeated all he had just told Sally and David to assure that the pastor, and by repetition the Crosslines, grasped the details. Within the hour arrangements were outlined and tasks assigned to all those present.

The next day Sally, and her neighbor, Jane Arnold, left my drugstore on the afternoon stagecoach. Jane was to provide support and assure propriety during the ordeal while David tended to the farm and the children. The two women were lodged at a rooming house near the college where for one week both ate the special diet Dr. White had arranged.

One afternoon Sally was visited by Dr. Frank Hastings Hamilton, Professor of Surgery at Buffalo Medical College who was to assist Dr. White. On another day, Sally and Jane were escorted to a room unlike any they had seen. She, Jane, and Dr. White were in a deep well with a large window on one wall. The well was surrounded on three sides by benches mounted on a steep incline on which several dozen medical students sat. With careful attention to modest draping, Dr. White repeated Sally's exam for the benefit of the medical students. He then responded to their questions, and asked them questions about pelvic anatomy and surgical techniques. To Sally Dr. White acted like two different people. He was gentle and kind addressing her, switching instantly to a formal task master when addressing the students. Sally was more exposed than she had ever been in public or private, but Dr. White's management of the situation never made her feel ill-treated.

Later Sally shared what she learned during the demonstration. She learned the ovaries produce eggs and that every month one ovary or the other forms a pea sized cyst that discharges an egg into the Fallopian tube for transport to the uterus. Dr. White said the rupture of the egg cyst causes the cramping and hysteria common to women prior to the catamenia. Ovarian tumors result from the corruption of this process. Professor

Meigs of Philadelphia reports some tumors contain a gallon of fluid and debris and that a Dr. Ephraim McDowell had performed the first operation to remove a cyst nearly forty years ago in Danville, Kentucky. Ether now allows improved surgical technique, but peritoneal fever and inflammation were serious risks after surgery.

Finally, on Tuesday evening both Dr. White and Dr. Hamilton came by the boarding house to announce that surgery would be the next morning. They told Sally she was to eat nothing more until after the surgery and that she must bathe prior to their summons in the morning. They left Sally with woolen underwear, drawers, stockings, and a nightgown she was to wear after her bath.

The next morning Sally was removed to the operating theater where I surprised her. Dr. White had honored me with a request to administer the Ether. Following a protocol established by Dr. Hamilton I tightly packed cotton wadding in a glass container, which I then soaked with Ether. I sat with my back to the students and Sally's feet to the light from the large south-facing window above us. I assured Sally the Ether would keep her asleep and pain free through the procedure. After a few twitches, she was asleep and two mirrors were positioned, one to focus the light and another to allow the students to see the procedure.

In the corner of the well the two surgeons had already rolled up their sleeves and washed in dilute carbolic acid. Their surgical instruments were spread out on a clean linen cloth wet with carbolic acid according to Dr. Hamilton's protocol. After exposing and washing the abdomen with carbolic acid, Dr. White handed the knife to Dr. Hamilton who made an incision down the midline from the umbilicus to the pubis. Then Dr. White separated the linea alba so perfectly that very little bleeding occurred. With hands moving in a well-rehearsed dance, the two men exposed the tumor, identified the uterus, lifted the cyst, tied off blood vessels with carbolic soaked catgut and in twenty minutes the ordeal was over and the incision closed.

As the fog of Ether lifted, Sally asked me if she was alive or dead. I gladly informed her that the procedure was done, it was a success, and that she was very much alive. The applause she heard was not that of angels, but three dozen medical students.

After Sally was removed from the theater, the cyst was placed on the operating table. Dr. White was pleased, even boastful, in reporting that the cyst had not ruptured during surgery. Next, Dr. White cut open the cyst and immediately a foul odor infused the room. The cyst was multilobulated and contained fragments of hair, teeth, and skin mixed in a sebaceous, sticky fluid. Dr. White informed the students that more than half of the cysts reported by Dr. Meigs were of similar character.

Sally remained in the rooming house for another week before returning to her family. No signs of fever or inflammation developed. In late May while making calls in Griffins Mills I stopped at the Crossline cabin to see how she was doing. With great delight, I report that I found her helping with the spring planting.

36. The War, 1860-1870

*We are intent on killing our fellow Christians
and creating a scar of hatred.*

For Congress, and the sixteen doctors serving in Congress, compromise between the North and the South had run its course by 1861. Millicent's anti-slavery certitude armed her with passionate convictions and I preoccupied myself with doctoring hoping we could avoid killing each other. The 1860 census showed that immigrants invigorated the North's wage based economy making up thirty percent of western New York's population now at ninety people per square mile. Our counties were more densely populated than any area in the South. Aurora's fertile soil grew surpluses of wheat, corn, apples and dairy products while supporting cheese production, canning and craftsmen of all types. As an economic model slavery would fail on its own.

With an income of $2,000 a year, half of it coming from the drugstore, I was doing well. Some of my colleagues struggled to make a living competing with an estimated 6,200 doctors in New York State. New York was also producing more medical graduates than any other state from new medical colleges opening in burgeoning canal towns. None-the-less, I continued my $40 annual support to our Medical College in Buffalo and appreciated the new ideas its faculty brought to the *Buffalo Medical Journal* and medical society meetings. They kept me abreast of new procedures in anesthesia, antiseptics, surgery, fracture care and improving instruments like stethoscopes, speculums, laryngoscopes, otoscopes, ophthalmoscopes, bedside thermometers, sphygmomanometers, hypodermic syringes, and microscopes.

Though politically passive, I worried when a marginal Illinois lawyer was elected President. My doubts did not restrain Millicent and 75,000 others from cheering Republican Abraham Lincoln's speech from the balcony of Buffalo's American Hotel on his way to the inauguration. The next month, on 15 April 1861, the Confederates captured Fort Sumter and immediately Millard Fillmore and other prominent men encouraged military enlistment with fiery speeches that predicted the South would be humbled in just a few months. Congress authorized the Secretary of Treasury to issue one-hundred-fifty million dollars' worth of Treasury notes and a National Bank was reconstituted to establish a standard currency as legal tender for all debts, public or private.

The Civil War was about to transform my family, my profession, my country, and my neighbors. So much of what was, was never again.

By June 750 new enlistees of the Erie County Regiment under Colonel Edward Chapin set out for Elmira to join the other nine New York regiments and form the New York Volunteer Infantry. Only fourteen, Deloran, burned with his mother's ardor for punishing the South, but was not eligible for service until he was sixteen. Orange, age twelve, was still absorbed by the diversions of boyhood and joined our six-year-old Jabez in taking little notice of the national calamity. Needing cash as desperately as it needed soldiers, the Union offered families the opportunity to exempt their sons from service by paying a six-hundred-dollar fee. Millicent and I would show our patriotism by paying the fee as each boy turned sixteen.

One morning, just before the start of the school semester, Millicent found a note from Deloran on the dining room table, its words lifted from those fiery speeches remain emblazoned in my mind.

"Dear Mother and Father,

Circumstances compel Stephan Pratt and I to fulfill our duty to God and Country. We are to take up arms in support of the right and just cause of freeing slaves from their irons, and castigating the South for its treachery. Please do not seek us out. We will return heroes to the freedom of all men. I will ever be faithful to you and write when I can.

Love, Deloran"

I telegraphed the Buffalo recruitment office without response. I telegraphed Colonel Chapin who responded a week later. Most of the regiment had already joined the Federal Army assembling in Washington and a search of enrollment lists did not reveal a Deloran Allen or a Stephan Pratt, but Chapin admitted the army accepted the name and age declared by any healthy-looking young man. His only encouragement was that an error in the enlistment papers resulted in the entire New York State regiment signing papers requiring only three months' service.

It would be two months before we heard from Deloran. He joined the Army in Elmira using the alias John Allen and lied about his age. Almost immediately he was transported to Washington and two weeks later his skills in writing and arithmetic got him assigned to a unit shipping off to Kansas assisting an Army Major in tracking supplies for the western front. Before leaving Washington, he witnessed the first beaten and demoralized Union troops return from the Battle of Bull Run. At three months Deloran re-enlisted and for the next four years we celebrated every Deloran letter just as we had his first.

Deloran's participation made the war personal and explains my rage when Townline, a village just north of Aurora, voted to secede from the Union in the fall. The town had voted for Lincoln, but railed against the taxes necessary to support a war. Before long rumors spread that Townline citizens were colluding with Jefferson Davis and Confederate General Jacob Thompson stationed in Canada to burn the City of Buffalo. Enrollment at the Aurora Academy soared as parents sheltered their sons and daughters from the anticipated attack. But little transpired, taxes got paid and mail got delivered in Townline.

Most Civil War soldiers could read and write letters home. Those reprinted in local newspapers followed our troops now under the command of General James S. Wadsworth of Geneseo. Their first assignment was building a fort near Arlington to guard Washington D.C. It became known as Fort Buffalo. They would go on to fight in the second battle of Bull Run, then at Antietam under McClellan, and later under Burnside at Fredericksburg. By the end of the war, Aurora boys fought in Yorktown, Chancellorsville, Gettysburg, Rappahannock, and made it all the way into Alabama where General Wadsworth was killed after being shot off his horse in battle.

All told, nearly ten percent of Union soldiers and twenty-five percent of Confederate soldiers died. For every soldier who died in battle, two died from disease. Cowpox vaccination became required, effectively eliminating the threat of Smallpox and making Measles the most serious problem for new recruits. The Army kept records on everything, showing that daily quinine rations dramatically reduced Malarial Fevers. Also, clean water, good food and sewage management kept more soldiers battle ready. Caring for the thousands of wounded and sick forced physicians to work in teams, exposing stark differences in competencies. To cope, the Army defined education requirements and made physicians pass a competency exam. They also wrote a job description for nurses.

In winter of 1863-64 I joined the Erie County Medical Society team of doctors sent to help at the Camp Rathburn Prisoner facility in Elmira. The camp's original purpose was to process new army recruits from New York.

By 1863 the harsh life in the Confederate army led to soldiers collapsing from hunger, unable to fight or flee. The surge of captives led to the transition of Camp Rathburn from a capacity of 2,000 troops to a prison anticipating 6,000 confederate soldiers. Before long more than 12,000 Confederate prisoners were calling Camp Rathburn Hellmira, half of them in tents and suffering from malnutrition, exposure and disease.

Though proven capable in battle, Commander Major Henry V. Colt of the 104th New York Volunteers could not overcome the impossible conditions, nor tame a staff of former Union combat soldiers who felt the rebels deserved harsh retribution. With no assigned Army physician at the prison, Colt relied on the volunteer efforts of one local physician. Ironically, the camp grave digger was an ex-slave named John W. Jones who read a Bible verse at the gravesite of every Confederate he buried.

Major Colt demanded an inspection and the Army sent the capable Military Surgeon Charles T. Alexander who recommended an onsite hospital and increased sanitary facilities. The response was a sign to designate one tent a hospital and the digging of a few more outhouses next to Foster's pond, which soon spilled sewage into the Chemung River.

An exasperated Major Colt allowed, some say invited, a reporter from the New York Herald to visit the camp. The reporter took a pro-Union view, claiming the Confederate prisoners were treated better than the Union soldiers imprisoned at Georgia's Andersonville prison. He witnessed Hellmira prisoners eating rodents to supplement their rations and saw the new graves of four hundred prisoners who died the week he visited, but did not report either.

Finally, the Army assigned Dr. Eugene F. Sanger to the camp who within days documented 793 cases of Scurvy. Realizing he was overwhelmed, Sanger requested the New York State Medical Society send teams of physicians for two-week spells of duty at the camp. As part of the Erie County team I treated mostly chronic unhealed wounds and dysentery. Outside assistance meant more attention, and soon the army increased the workforce, constructed new outhouses, improved drinking water, increased rations, and added daily servings of sauerkraut.

The Camp Rathburn experience helped me appreciate the challenges Deloran faced providing for large armies on the move. Deloran wrote of his frustration about not seeing combat, but he also told of sleeping in cat naps by his desk to keep up with the urgencies of his job. Returning from Hellmira I wrote Deloran to tell him how proud I was of his work and how it was men like him who transformed the war to one of attrition, giving Lincoln the confidence to emancipate the slaves.

Union soldiers returning to Aurora also needed my attention. One veteran suffered deep burns from an exploding canon. After three months in an Army hospital he returned home where I visited him three times a week to debride and redress his wounds. We spoke of many things, including the embarrassment he felt when female nurses changed his bedding and dressed his wounds, but at least the nurses made conversation. The doctors threw off his covers and talked as if he were not even present. Once, when European physicians observing military medicine visited, he made a joke about wanting a nickel for the demonstration and no one seemed to notice.

Returning soldiers brought Cholera, dysentery and Typhoid home. This time Aurora implemented sanitation measures developed by the Army and greatly limited outbreaks, making 1866 the last time I cared for a Cholera patient. Typhus also disappeared after a few weeks of good food, clean-living and a new set of clothes.

Before the war any physician who read a medical journal or attended a society meeting knew washing hands before surgery or after autopsies lowered the incidence of inflammation and fever. The Army mandated surgeons wash their hands and use antiseptics, proving these measures reduced morbidity and mortality, and that wounds healed faster if pus and dead tissue were removed by frequent dressing changes. Army records also proved that after a leg or arm was shattered by a mini-ball, the death rate is cut from thirty-eight percent to twenty-seven percent if amputation under anesthesia is performed early.

Jerad Michaels, a nine-year-old boy fell out of a tree, sustaining an open compound fracture of his femur, an injury that is uniformly fatal after weeks of gangrene. Jared, however, fell out of the tree after the war, so I followed Army procedures and irrigated the wound with dilute carbolic acid to remove all debris then realigned Jared's femur with traction and redressed the wound daily with a carbolic acid-soaked muslin for ten weeks. A year later, Jared was again climbing trees.

The Army also proved that many fevers respond well to the stimulatory effects of quinine and alcohol, further limiting the indications for bloodletting and calomel. At one point the Surgeon General of the Union Army, Dr. William Hammond, issued an order eliminating calomel from Army medical supplies, but a Chicago medical journal responded with a review of calomel's importance and the American Medical Association pressured the Army to relieve Hammond of his commission. Dr. William Gail, a former apprentice in my practice who served as a Union Army surgeon, rarely saw bleeding or calomel used during the war. Gail said his team of doctors challenged each other and shared new ideas, including those of Dr. Andrew Still, an Army surgeon from Kansas whose theory of spinal manipulation and muscle massage he called Osteopathy.

As the Union Armies penetrated deep into the south, supplying fresh food became difficult. Soldiers scavenged for anything beyond the salted meat in their rations. Many came home with slow healing wounds typical of Scurvy that closed after a few weeks of home cooking, fresh vegetables, and sauerkraut. Bloody flux was common and even the Army agreed it could only be remedied by calomel. Soldiers attempted to cure the repeated bouts of bloody diarrhea with 'Rats-Dung' made of ground deer antlers, but eventually most required calomel to purge the intestines of poisons. Soldiers also brought home a severe form of bronchitis called Influenza, named by ancients who attributed the attacks to the influence of planets. It spread through our village in waves causing high fevers, cough, and pain in head, back, and limbs. Young adults and feeble persons suffered profound pulmonary complications and several died.

The war produced many widows, some so destitute that they followed armies from battle to battle laboring in prostitution. The Union army documented over 200,000 cases of Gonorrhea and Syphilis and a number of men gifted their disease to their wives. Two to four days after intercourse with a prostitute the men experience intense itching and bloody discharge typical of acute Gonorrhea that evolved into a chronic milky discharge called gleet. Arriving home their wives experienced a disagreeable itching and aching pain in the pelvis, and occasional debilitating Arthritis. The Army's recommended remedy for Gonorrhea was bleeding and antimony in flaxseed tea to lessen scalding urinary symptoms.

The presence of a painless chancre meant the soldier had also contracted Syphilis, for which mercury was the only remedy. My approach is to prepare one hundred and twenty pills of mercury sublimate to be taken in increasing increments every other day until all are consumed. My greatest conundrum was the adulterous veteran who demanded my discretion regarding their illness, yet desired that I provide a preventive for their wife. I never perfected such delicate negotiations.

Generally returning veterans leaned on each other and got by. Eben Thurston was one combat veteran who found the transition to civilian life particularly difficult. A successful young farmer before the war, Eben returned a reclusive angry man, subject to violent episodes and nightmares.

He got in his mind that a neighbor had paid excessive attention to his wife during his absence. One Sunday after dinner, Eben noticed the neighbor walking his fence line, grabbed a loaded shotgun, approached to within a few feet and discharged the gun into the man's abdomen. Eben then walked to the barn and directed his hired man to fetch a doctor.

During his trial Eben's attorney revealed that Eben had been unable to sleep, feeling compelled to walk his property with a loaded rifle. The attorney reminded the jury of the 1859 acquittal of Daniel Sickles, a New York Congressman who shot a U.S. Attorney after the man had seduced his wife. He also called Army physicians who testified that guarding the perimeter is the act of a noble soldier and essential for survival during war.

Eben was acquitted, but even his deep remorse could not stop his unpredictable episodes of rage, which he described as the fury he summoned to kill and survive in battle. I prescribed regular doses of *Veratrum viride* (Indian poke) to achieve an arterial sedation, slow his pulse and induce a soothing delirium. If he felt an episode coming on, I instructed him to apply cold cloths to his head while soaking his feet in a warm Epson salt bath. For the next year, I visited him regularly. He occasionally talked about the war, but never about combat. The nightmares became less frequent, his farm did well, and he and his wife attended church regularly. One Sunday he was late returning from the barn after morning chores and his wife found Eben hanging from a rafter, a pail of fresh milk left for his family.

Horror eats at a man. Medical journals published accounts of men like Eben who experienced frightfully vivid, chaotic, nightmares. Dr. Jacob Mendes da Costa, a military surgeon, amassed records of three hundred soldiers suffering what he called Soldier's Heart. Typically, the men served in active combat for several months before experiencing episodes of short breath, palpitations, sweating, chest pain, sudden awakenings, and unrelenting fatigue. Mendes da Costa found that even those who could talk about their combat experience still faced an uncertain resolution and sometimes find their symptoms worsen with recall.

Millicent joined the Aurora Women's Society Chapter of Elizabeth Blackwell's U.S. Sanitary Commission. Dr. Elizabeth Blackwell was the first woman graduate of the Medical College in Geneva, NY in 1849. Her graduate thesis on Typhus gained international acclaim as did her lectures on the physical and mental development of girls. As the war began, Blackwell called a meeting of women at the Cooper Union Hall in New York City forming what became the U.S. Sanitary Commission. Despite her pioneering work, Blackwell was demoted and replaced by a man when the Union formally recognized the Commission. Still, it was Blackwell who unified women of every hamlet and village into the major supplier of bandages, socks, pillow cases, quilts and soap for the Union Army. A personal friend of Dr. Blackwell, Florence Nightingale, defined nursing as a profession, dramatically improving the survival of wounded soldiers and creating employment opportunities for widows.

One of the Sanitary Commission's pamphlets specified, "Water suitable for drinking should be free from any considerable quantity of organic or mineral constituents and consequently colorless and without any peculiar odor or taste." Murky water was to be boiled or treated with permanganate of potassium to render it potable. The pamphlet did not suggest that a horse could adequately discriminate good water from bad.

After that first disaster of Bull Run, Clara Barton organized a relief agency for soldiers and their families. When the war ended she painstakingly recording the names and graves of the thirty thousand Union troops buried at Andersonville. Seeking a more permanent platform for her efforts, Barton visited Europe's International Red Cross and founded the American Red Cross out of her home in Dansville, NY.

And there was the eccentric but brave, Dr. Mary Edwards Walker. Walker was a Syracuse Medical College graduate who applied to work at a military hospital but was assigned to nursing. She completed a second medical degree at a hydropathic medical college but when she again was refused appointment as an Army physician, Dr. Walker followed the Union Army from battle to battle and inserted herself into treating wounded soldiers. Forced to camp outside the Army's perimeter, she was captured and confined to Confederate prison where her skills saved the lives of many fellow Union prisoners and she became the only woman to receive the Congressional Medal of Honor. After the war, Dr. Walker found lecturing more lucrative than doctoring, touring the United States and Europe in her iconic attire of a long black knee length tunic over dark trousers tucked into boots and accessorized by white kid gloves and a wreath on her head. She so challenged masculine society that one newspaper recommended her lecture be retitled, "Clitoridectomy and its Uses."

The higher standards and expectations established in the Union Army became the backdrop for a malpractice case in which I was asked to testify. The woman bringing the lawsuit suffered urinary irritation for which Dr. Clark of Lockport, NY prescribed fluid extract of uva ursi. After the second dose, the lady suffered nausea, vomiting, cold sweats, palpitations and vertigo. When she complained to Dr. Clark, it was noticed that the Lockport apothecary had filled the prescription with veratrum viride instead of uva ursi. The woman won an $800 settlement.

Of the original 750 men enlisted from Erie County, 490 survived. Good schooling kept Deloran in Kansas managing the mechanics of war for which the Army deeded him land in Kansas. There he married Sylvia Mary Etta Parker, the daughter of a successful Kansas farmer from the town of Six

Miles. After his father-in-law's death, Deloran merged the farms and, like his grandfather Allen, took up a mercantile farmer's life, turning his war experience into buying and selling farming and manufacturing equipment. Millicent and I yearned for more time with our three grandsons and four granddaughters in Kansas, but the distance and war had stolen them.

Deloran's friend, Stephan Pratt was less fortunate. Stephan remained with the New York regimen and acquitted himself bravely in battle. His family received no further letters from Stephan after Chancellorsville where a Union defeat left two thousand Union soldiers on the battlefield and another six thousand in a Confederate prison camp. His fate was never confirmed.

The centralization, record keeping, and forced travel of war changed American society. Lincoln was the first to call this a Civil war, but civil it was not. It was a war, like most, instigated by those with an economic stake in the outcome and fought by brave young men. President Lincoln's assassination proves the killing did not end at Appomattox. However, the term 'United States' became a singular noun. Newspapers no longer referred to America as "The United States are," now they wrote, "The United States is."

War changes families. Deloran was in Kansas, Orange was fifteen and convinced he wanted to be a farmer, and Jabez, our youngest, shadowed me in the drugstore. Mother Millicent's health declined and on 21 October 1864, Millicent Townsend Johnson, maiden name Crisfield, died. As per her wishes, only immediate family attended her burial in Oakwood Cemetery.

37. Post War Health in the Home and School, 1866-1876

All families have virtues, and all are frightened by some hidden thing.

The Aurora Debate Society resolved that in his Gettysburg speech, Abraham Lincoln elevated the principles of the Declaration of Independence over the mistakes of the Constitution. Over the next few years the country formally expanded citizenship by passing the Thirteenth, Fourteenth and Fifteenth Amendments and the American economy grew to equal England's. Postwar vitality finally saw completion of the Aurora to Buffalo railroad on 22 December 1867. Within five years the line extended to South Wales, Olean and then to Emporium, Pennsylvania, connecting with the New York Central system in Buffalo and over nine-thousand miles of American railways. My $1,000 railroad investment provided handsome returns and easier access to Buffalo and Erie County Medical Society meetings resulted in my becoming President in 1873.

Then, in the mid-70s the country plunged into recession and railroad profits dropped. Our Buffalo/Aurora railroad had no competition, but many routes were overbuilt and lines were often redundant. Many railroads merged and the larger companies laid off workers or cut their pay. Rail workers struck in 1877 and blocked all rail traffic through Buffalo. After four days, militia units called in from neighboring counties so outnumbered the pickets that the strike was abandoned, the ringleaders arrested, and nothing gained.

I had always identified with workers and farmers, but being a stock holder forced my reflection. Capitalism depends on both investors and workers; each being entitled to a fair return. Though capitalism might have a dazzling capacity for development, the recession and wage cut revealed its troubling weaknesses. In a village, I care for both the wealthy and the poor. They face remarkably similar challenges of life and family, and employ remarkably similar solutions.

Capitalism thrived in Aurora. Harvey W. Richardson began buying and storing cheese from twenty-four cheese makers in surrounding towns and erected a large building next to the railroad on Elm Street. His *Cloverfield* brand became the largest selling cheese in the United States, employed several dozen workers, and generated cash for farmers. Another Aurorean, Cicero Hamlin, used the railroad to transport and trade horses. Hamlin was a successful farmer who built a huge barn north of the village for his Standardbred harness race horses. Fame found him after his purchase of Mambrino King, a descendant of the famous Mambrino. Hundreds of tourists arrived by railroad to picnic at his farm, watch his handsome trotters exercise, and see Mambrino King, "The world's most beautiful horse." Horse breeding, training, trading and racing became big business in Aurora.

Aurora's expanding economy kept me fairly compensated and allowed me the luxury of treating the poor, which I have never considered charity. Rather, I find the wisdom of those who labor under the inequities of social order enriching.

Homes and businesses gradually filled in the mile between the lower village of Willink and the upper Aurora village where once the Aurora Academy stood in isolation. In 1869 Jabez Warren's two valley settlements merged and incorporated as East Aurora. A short while later Willink's landmark Eagle Tavern and its adjoining block burned to the ground. With no lower village meeting place several organizations reorganized, including the Aurora Academy Lyceum that offered expanded programs of music, poems, essays, recitations, and discussions.

The larger village attracted the circus for a week every summer. In the first show of the Great Central Park Menagerie and Circus in June of 1872, a circus worker, George C. Gordon, collapsed and died. Ever the promoter, circus owner Henry Barnum, paraded his ninety wagons through town to bury Mr. Gordon in our Oakwood cemetery in a plot very near that of our son James.

It was the steam engine that powered capitalism, and like many innovations added new medical challenges. Steam engines blow up unless excess pressures are vented, but those releases can produce serious scalding. The most horrific burns occur to children drawn to play near locomotives and railroad tracks. Also, on warm days when passenger car windows are open I commonly see a passenger or two with a coal cinder in their eye. Removal was deceptively easy. I simply instilled a drop of cocaine, flipped the upper lid, and removed the offending cinder with tweezers. Then there was railroad-spine caused by the jostling and bouncing of long train journeys that required several days of traction to relieve bruised spinal nerves. Lastly, horses frightened by an approaching train occasionally stop before their teamster and his wagon are off the tracks, teamster and wagon taking the full measure of a cow-catcher's impact.

The Odd Fellows also changed medicine by introducing programs they called health and life insurance as extensions to their fraternal mission to: "Visit the sick, relieve the distressed, bury the dead and educate the orphan." Their insurance proved so popular that, together with the Daughters of Rebekah, the Odd Fellows became the largest fraternal order in the United States, exceeding even the Free Masons.

Premiums were initially calculated using English actuarial records, but losses forced the Odd Fellows to concede that life expectancy in the United

States was shorter than in England. The marvelously rugged American was a myth. In response, the Odd Fellows and the American Medical Association joined forces to advance public health, sanitation, population registration systems, and the licensing of doctors.

When commercial insurance companies entered the market, the Atlantic Mutual Life Insurance Company offered lower premiums to patients who consulted homeopaths and was boycotted by the American Medical Association. Another, the Mutual Life Insurance Company of New York, bragged that they had amassed more data than anyone about life and death in America.

Before insurance, patients only sought doctoring when they were sick, but insurance companies paid for exams on applicants claiming to be well. I was asked to find disease that had no symptoms, disclose intemperate habits, report dangerous employment and render a prediction about future health. The company paid my fee, not the patient, and the exams became a small but important source of income. Though many of those I examined became my patients, I struggled with the question of who I represented, the patient or the company,

---

Central heating and coal furnaces emerged as the new status symbol. Men were relieved of spending hours cutting trees, splitting wood, hauling it, stacking it, and carrying out the ashes. A coal furnace required only a couple shovels of coal twice a day from a bin of coal delivered down a shoot into the basement. Heat from our newly installed coal furnace rose through a large vent cut in the centrally located dining room floor and penetrated the whole house through more vents cut in the floors of the upstairs bedrooms.

Coal lightened the workload for men, yet somehow it was women who bought and read magazines. Prices fell as more magazines were purchased, fueled by curiosity created by the intermingling of Americans in the Civil

War. Advertisements included pictures of young women with happy children and were often tied to stories promoting the advertised product.

Newspapers cover current events, but magazines deliver themes. *Mother's Magazine,* published in Utica, invented the word 'parenthood' while advising women about fostering Christian values in their children. Children had always become adults simply by mimicking their parents, gradually taking responsibility for doing chores on the farm. *Mother's Magazine* characterized children as empty vessels with the potential to grow into perfect human beings if mothered correctly. Fathers being marginally irrelevant. But Millicent's parenting never changed. Her jocular child rearing philosophy was, "At the end of the day I ask myself, did I feed the children, did I like at least one thing they did, and are they still alive? All three in any one day means I did my job." Millicent's self-confidence avoided much drama.

Much more than that, Millicent encouraged learning, including our favorite magazine for children called *Our Young Folks,* which enticed our boys with illustrations while exposing them to celebrated writers like Henry Longfellow, Harriet Beecher Stowe and Charles Dickens. Magazines also took on diapers and corsets. After generations of wearing Bloomingdale Brothers steel or whale bone reinforced corsets for a perfect nineteen-inch waist, *Mother's Assistant* magazine told of a woman with delicate health who threw her corset into the ocean on her way to America. Now seventy-one, she was the mother of eight children, walked eight miles a day, and taught Sunday school. Another woman wrote that her father happened onto her first fitting for a whalebone buckram and immediately chased the corset-fitter out of the house. Now grown, she never had a headache and credited her father for her good health. Soon magazines carried ads for Bloomingdale's new stylish girdles, absent the whalebone. Magazines also took on the tight swaddling of babies in favor of clean loose clothing and encouraging diapers be washed between each use instead of simply hung to dry. This made babies smell better, but I was surprised how little it did to prevent diaper rash.

Equally influential were home medical books, peddled door to door by traveling salesmen. Some families called me only after they exhausted every recommendation in their book, or demanded that I do exactly what their book recommended. I learned to ask a litany of questions and conduct a thorough patient examination before offering any opposition to the family's book. Once I gained the family's confidence, I merged my remedy with what I could accept from the book's remedy yielding to a belief that healing is more likely in families that work together.

Advertisement made some patent medicines, like Pe-Ru-Na, a national brand. Nearly one-third alcohol, Pe-Ru-Na suggests a tablespoon before every meal to prevent lassitude. Another, Mrs. Winslow's Soothing Syrup for teething is a sugar solution fortified with morphine. At one-fifth alcohol, Lydia Pinkham's Vegetable Compound is "good for the kidneys" and "female weaknesses." Pinkham's ads ask, "Do you want a strange man to hear your problems?" Writing to Mrs. Pinkham, one woman with a prolapsed uterus wrote, "Doctor tells me I can have the trouble removed but thought I would write and ask you if the Compound would cure it." The company replied, "By all means avoid instrumental treatment for your trouble. Use the Compound as you have been, faithfully and patiently. It will eventually work a cure." Other nostrums, more popular with men, guaranteed a cure for genital debility and seminal weakness.

The American Medical Association appointed a committee to evaluate patent medicines but little came of it. At the risk of defaming myself, I carried some patent medicines in my store as they made a significant contribution to my income. When asked, I tried to guide patient selection, but ingredients were often secret. I did post a sign prohibiting consuming Pe-Ru-Na in the store or on the plank sidewalk out front.

At some expense, I purchased many of the home medical books and recommended a few. Edinburgh's William Buchan first published his *Domestic Medicine* in 1769. It inspired over 100 editions, including several that plagiarized the title. Most popular in Aurora was John Gunn's version of *Domestic Medicine*, which he distinguished by the subtitle, *Poor Man's Friend in the Hours of Affliction, Pain, and Sickness.* Gunn's one-thousand pages included advice and remedies derived from respected medical writings on everything from a wife's proper behavior to coping with a child who indulges in the 'solitary vice.' Even the most modest cabins owned three books, a Bible, a hymnbook and Gunn's *Domestic Medicine*. Another popular book was edited by the British physician James Parkinson, famous for his 1817 Treatise on Shaking Palsy, titled *The Town and Country Friend and Physician.* Many books sold a mail order medicine chest to complement their recommendations.

A community Pastor with a draining tumor in his cheek consulted Gunn's book and concluded the draining was essential to healing and a sinapism would encourage continued drainage. The tumor first appeared in January. I became aware of it in April when his wife purchased sinapism plasters from my store. In November, he sought my advice and I judged the tumor to be an eroding Cancer, but the Pastor engaged me in a debate with his medical book. It took three more visits before he consented to excision, which by that time was an extensive process, left a sizable scar, but had little impact on the fire and brimstone he generated from his pulpit.

In the 1840s William A. Alcott published a personal hygiene textbook for secondary schools titled, *The House I Live In.* Accurately grounded in Anatomy and Physiology, the book attributed the wondrous human body to God's construction, and disease to moral and physical transgressions. He made no reference to reproduction, human sexuality, birth control, or sexually transmitted diseases, leaving children to the mercy of misinformation. And, misinformation was plentiful, making for unique understandings and unique rules of decorum, leaving a doctor to stumble into many unrealized indiscretions.

Magazines, on the other hand, seemed purposefully intent on disrupting all notions of decorum. Advertisements for diaphragms, condoms, spermicidal douches, and a vaginal syringe like implement for inducing abortions were common. Aphrodisiacs, cures for venereal disease, and abortion services seem to be the economic mainstay of some publications. Wedding announcements attracted mail offering devises for sex and birth control. Some magazines feigned sophistication with code words like "French" for contraceptive, and "Portuguese" for abortion.

Soap soon emerged as the advertised defense against the germs scientists were finding everywhere. Sir Alfred Power described the skin as a dangerous point of entry for contagions in his book called *Sanitary Rhymes*, starting with:

> The outside skin is a marvelous plan,
> For exuding the dregs of the flesh of man.

Soap companies, like the Larkin Company of Buffalo, paid for stories touting the virtues of regular washing and bathing. Extensive advertising, pyramid sale schemes, and mail order sales convinced women that cleaner and better smelling people were happier people. Once the family was clean it was natural to promote laundry soap to replace the drudgery of boiling clothes clean. Then it became downright patriotic to use toothpaste. Portraits of well-dressed men and women exhibiting bright smiles exploited rumors that Europeans once ridiculed the poor condition of American teeth.

Millicent's favorite magazine was the *Atlantic Monthly*, founded by Ralph Waldo Emerson, Oliver Wendell Holmes, Henry Wadsworth Longfellow, Harriet Beecher Stowe and John Greenfield Wittier. Many evenings Millicent interrupted my journal study by reading an *Atlantic* poem as if she were an actress on my private stage. I liked the *Atlantic's* commentaries on political issues and it was the first place we read the words to Julia Ward Howe's *Battle Hymn of the Republic*. After the war a series titled *The Freedman's Story* gave voice to former slaves suddenly liberated in an uninviting land.

I become friends with Aurora's two booksellers, each generously allowing me to loiter among their shelves. I had eclectic tastes, reading and re-reading *Don Quixote*, countless biographies, and John Heckelwelder's two volumes titled *Account of the History, Manners and Customs of the Indian Nations*. Thoreau put words to pleasant forest walks and Emerson inspired me to seek a personal truth in life's daily chores. According to Millicent, I do not read books, I make battle with them. The many ear-marks, underscored lines and notes make my revisits quick and satisfying but leave my books unattractive to a bookseller. Millicent teased that our house will collapse under the accumulated weight of books.

Millicent and I took two trips to Long Lake in the Adirondacks where we experienced forests much like the Vermont of my youth. On both trips, we hired guides who impressed us with their knowledge of the flora and fauna. We canoed several lakes with Indian names, observing bear, moose and elk in near silence. Lunches were a cold bite and a cup of tea near a trailside spring. Breakfast and evening meals were substantial repasts followed by fireside coffee. One evening around the campfire an Algonquin guide joined us telling tales of his ancestors punctuated by the beat of a hand fashioned drum, each followed by a song with a guttural native timbre and rhythm. His mood was transcending, and his dignified, courteous manner opened our hearts to aboriginal pride.

In winter months William, Millicent's brother, hosted string quartet recitals every forth Sunday afternoon. The first violinist and concert master was the music instructor at the Aurora Academy. He was obliged to satisfy the Johnson's love of Bach concertos, but eclectic in his other choices. The cellist was a physician from Wales who immigrated from Hungary where he had pursued music before finding his calling in Physic. The viola was played by another enthusiastic semi-professional who was widely known in our community for his Saturday night fiddling. The second violin was selected from among the talented young students at the Academy. During summer months, the organists Hermann Hanns-Wetzler and William Macfarlane escaped New York City's heat by touring upstate villages and performing on local church organs. They made the new Presbyterian Church organ sound like God himself was rejoicing.

The idea of etching has frequented my ambition and every few months I optimistically purchased some new etching tool. I splurged on an etcher's press and a special table called a "jigger" to store my accumulating supplies. But slow business hours have never sufficiently accrued for me to gain the competence my many tools would suggest. The only product I have ever saved is an etching of that Algonquin Indian. Though I sense Millicent finds my representation lacking, it is as I remember him, and the memory pleases me.

Parsley developed arthritis in the right foreleg and had to be put down several years after my arrival in Aurora. After that I contracted with a stable rather than keep my own horse. This arrangement guaranteed a fresh horse when, after a day of house calls, another urgent visit was requested. Most commonly I was assigned a Missouri Gelding named Boaz. Unlike his name, he was not swift but he had a soft mouth and a comfortable disposition around excited children. When I felt the need to make a good impression I used a carriage, but horse drawn carriages only covered only three to four miles per hour as opposed to the fifteen miles an hour an athletic horse might do. Boaz was well-trained and on truly exhausting days we could cover as much as thirty-five to forty miles by varying gaits between a walk, a trot and a cantor.

Magazines and medical journals recorded, reacted and shaped changes in American society and medicine. They also lessened the isolation of solo village practice. I always carried reading material with me and used every opportunity to learn. I exercised what control I could over my working hours, but had little control over urgent demands. Fortunately, having an adjacent office and home allowed the luxury of dinner with my family most days. Millicent is a skilled organizer and accommodated a hectic schedule.

38. Tonsillitis, Diphtheria and Emerging Contagions, 1870-1876

Turning chaos into order is but a momentary delusion.

By 1870 the impeachment of Andrew Johnson was over, Ulysses Grant was President, and Dr. Samuel Mudd was still in jail for setting John Wilkes Booth's broken leg. Through it all, two oblong glandular bodies in the back of the throat made continuous work for doctors. Tonsils are the site of repeated inflammation and can remain swollen for years. I was taught that the best remedy for acute Tonsillitis was the application of leeches just under the ears. I got better results using warm vinegar water gargles with honey. Of course, as in all inflammations, the bowels must be kept open.

I am inclined to revisit Tonsillitis patients two days after the initial treatment. Abscesses may form that must be pierced with a lancet to release pus, relieve the pain, and prevent a fistula opening into the neck. After an abscess resolves, the tonsils must be removed. I am inclined to use the tonsillar guillotine because it allows adequate removal of the tonsil and is much less painful than pulling the tonsil away from its bed using a wire noose. Tannogallic acid gargles are required to arrest bleeding after a Tonsillectomy.

Some sore throats do not primarily affect the tonsils. Such was the case of Mary Saggar, a three-year-old girl I was called to see. Upon entering her sick room, I found an anxious little girl leaning forward at the edge of her bed, holding herself up on outstretched arms and drooling. Her rapid respirations emitted a shrill whistling noise interrupted by short episodes of violent coughing, classic signs of acute Epiglottal Edema.

Her pulse was rapid, small and sharp. I administered two grains of antimony in two ounces of water and positioned Mary on her mother's lap to release four ounces of blood from her arm that revealed a thick buffy coat. To open her bowels, I gave her two grains of calomel with senna followed by a mixture of warm milk, water and molasses which, within the hour produced an adequate movement.

Epiglottal Edema narrows the airway making it so hard to breath that sudden collapse is a dreaded complication. Through the night, I administered several more doses of antimony but by morning the child was clearly losing strength. I asked the parents to allow me to perform a Tracheotomy. They refused, confident of God's will. I begged they consider that God had placed me in their home with the skills necessary to save Mary's life. By noon Mary was overcome with exhaustion, her extremities lost their warmth, and her lips turned purple. Within the hour Mary's respirations became intermittent, and her frightened eyes turned peaceful as death claimed her soul.

During my nearly twenty-four hours at the Saggar home I noticed the family owned an unspoiled copy of John Gunn's *Domestic Medicine*. It would have alerted them to the signs of acute Epiglottal Edema and given them greater confidence in a surgical approach, but neither parent was schooled and neither could read. I sent no bill and expressed gratitude for the cured ham her father delivered to the office that winter. I see about one child a year with Epiglottitis. Most are more fortunate than Mary Saggar.

Diphtheria mounts the most malicious of all direct attacks on the tonsils. Caley Walsh was a six-year-old girl with sore throat and earache starting just a few days after attending Christian summer school with eight other children in the small hamlet of Jamison, two miles north of Aurora. The child was feverish with an accelerated pulse, fetid breath, tender neck glands and tonsils covered with a thick fibrinous, almost leather like secretion.

Her voice was weak and hoarse and coughing produced painful spasms of choking.

I administered several doses of antimony, calomel and senna. Yet, over the next few hours Caley's respirations became more labored and any attempt to swallow was agonizing. Caley's parents were bold, pragmatic people, who allowed me to cut a slit into the child's windpipe into which I placed a cannula. The cannula comforted her breathing and allowed me to suck out the deadly secretions, a process I repeated several times an hour for six hours and as needed after that. Before each suction, I applied several drops of Sulphur in limewater to Caley's throat with a quill to loosen the tonsillar membrane. After suctioning I had the child take one ounce of diluted alcohol spirits with quinine and inhale steam over a bowl of hot camphor water. It was an intense twenty-four hours before the tonsillar membrane stopped accumulating. I sutured the opening in her windpipe, leaving Caley with a small scar marking her successful battle with Diphtheria. I prevented the inflammation from affecting my own throat by chewing a plug of tobacco after each suction.

While attending to Caley I learned that several of the children from the Jamison Congregational Church school were similarly ill and sent word to Dr. Lapham and Dr. Gail. As was his nature, Dr. Lapham suggested that we secure the assistance of the Minister and canvas school attendees to isolate all possible cases of Diphtheria. We found that all but two homes reported cases of membranous Diphtheria, some rather mild. One disease–free home had withdrawn their child from the class for unrelated reasons. The other disease–free family had recently moved from Geneva where two of their children had been afflicted by Diphtheria earlier that summer.

Dr. Gail visited every home in the Jamison hamlet and found that eighty-five percent of the children and thirteen percent of the adults in the church families experienced a case of Tonsillitis. One adult and seven children died, or about one in five. There were three nursing babies, none of whom became ill. The homes met all accepted standards for cleanliness. Some homes had hand-dug wells and others took their water from a community well. The water had a perfectly clear appearance and both microscopic and chemical analysis revealed no contamination. Four months later, one last case occurred in a hired man working for the Geneva family. He survived.

When Dr. Lapham presented our findings to the Erie County Medical Society he made four observations: Every patient had contact with someone attending the Christian summer school; the disease affected mostly children though it spared three nursing babies; the family previously exposed in Geneva did not succumb to this epidemic; cleanliness did not ward off Diphtheria. Several at the Society meeting affirmed our observations with stories of their own Diphtheria epidemics while others recalled several corroborating journal reports. Society attendees passed a resolution stating that it would be prudent to isolate any person suspected of Diphtheria for at least three weeks, clothes should be boiled in water after recovery, and physicians might wash their hands to limit their own agency in spreading the contagion.

Our community survey made us feel rather scientific. Not long after, Dr. Edwin Klebs reported finding a vegetative organism in the secretions of Diphtheria patients that he thought might be the cause. Our friend, Austin Flint, warned that just because an organism is found in the presence of Diphtheria, it might not be the cause of Diphtheria.

A common skin inflammation also raised contagion questions. Erysipelas, also called Impetigo, is a red, warm, raised, shiny area that can be very tender. Some patients complain of general lassitude, headache, and loss of appetite. As the inflammation matures small blisters of various size form and fill with a cloudy yellowish serum. By my own microscope, I have confirmed the animalcules reported by Microscopists in serum from the blisters. However, another form of itchy Impetigo is related to contact with the leaves of the *rhus toxicodendron* vine and commonly called poison ivy. Microscopists have not found animalcules in the blisters of itchy Impetigo. In both situations, blisters form, rupture and become crusty. The painful form of Impetigo often spreads to other children, starting in an area of a minor injury or after a violent fit of anger. The poison ivy form occurs only after exposure to the *rhus* vine. Both are treated by cupping to draw out the offending inflammation followed by warm bathing and the application of linens soaked in a mineral salt solution called Calamine. The bowels must be kept open and it is wise to boil clothes and bedding once the lesions have resolved.

Another skin condition, Ringworm, was convincingly associated with a fungus in the 1840s. In extreme cases, it forms a kerion that looks like a patch of Impetigo. One autumn the Aurora Academy matron requested I examine several children she saw scratching their heads. The children had circular bald spots from which I scraped a few scales, applied a few drops of potassium hydroxide, and examined under my microscope. The hyphae of the fungus *trichophyton tonsurans* were quite obvious. All thirty children were affected and several had the more advanced form of pustular blisters called a kerion. I instructed all classrooms be aired, cleaned, and that Sulphur be burned for six hours in each classroom. Parents were instructed to bathe and scrub the children twice a week with castile soap, after which they were to be sponged with vinegar. They were then to apply a compound I made from precipitated Sulphur, ammonia-chloride of mercury and carbolic acid in a zinc oxide ointment. Skin scales can spread Ringworm, so bed linens were to be separated and boiled twice a week. Sharing of hats, combs, brushes, towels, and everything that contacted and infected children was strictly prohibited. The students were to consume a serving of meat, milk, cracked wheat, and eggs once a day. Baked apples and mashed potatoes were to be consumed at least every other day. After two weeks, all except two of the children with kerion pustules were cured. I lanced the pustules and after another four weeks of treatment, they too were cured.

Ringworm's association with a fungus and Bassi's description of the silkworm fungus, convinced many Microscopists that all human contagions might be fungi. Still, those who remained committed to the logic of miasma mounted a vigorous protest.

In 1863, Britain's Dr. Jeffery Allen Marston, stationed in Malta during the Crimean War, undertook an intensive search for the offending fungus in Undulant fever, a condition he discovered passed from animal to man. A few years later I recognized my first case of Undulant fever in Jeremiah Stone, a particularly successful sixty-one-year-old farmer who complained of intermittent lassitude, sweating spells, and body odor much like wet hay. Over several weeks of symptoms, a poor appetite led to significant weight loss. He blamed worry about failure of an expensive English bull he purchased off a farm in Vermont to improve his herd. Numerous breading attempts had failed and the bull had to be put down when it developed crippling joint swelling. He sent for me because he had developed a pain in his back and left leg.

Jeremiah had a fever of 102 degrees and was breathless. His throat and tonsils were mildly inflamed and his pulse was weakened. Using my new bi-aural stethoscope, I found moist crackles in his lungs, a soft systolic murmur and an enlarged heart. He had multiple tender glands in his groin and axillae, an enlarged spleen, and his testicles were sore and tender. He winced when I tapped on his lower spine.

The pattern brought to mind what I had read about Marston's Undulant fever, also called Malta or Mediterranean fever. Out of blind curiosity I asked about his animals and was surprised to hear the story about his bull. A story very consistent with reports of Undulant fever in Vermont cattle exposed to bulls imported from England. Jeremiah went on to say, "Every damn heifer that bull impregnated aborted and, if the cow did not die from retained placenta, she developed hot swollen joints or inflamed udders and had to be destroyed. Worse idea I ever had."

Like Jeremiah, Marston described symptoms of Undulant fever to be intermittent but could find no cases of Undulant fever being passed from human to human. Marston determined that it passed from animal to man during butchering or drinking milk from an infected cow or goat. Some animals appeared sick, others well. Stillborn fetus and retained placenta were the most consistent signs that the herd carried the disease. It was now infecting one in five herds in England.

For Jeremiah, I compounded salicylate powder and digitalis to be taken three times a day. Over the next several months his symptoms improved and his episodes of fever gradually ceased. The swelling in his glands persisted for nearly a year and he continued to require occasional doses of Laudanum for his back pain. No other family members developed symptoms.

The more that was revealed about the microscopic world the more mysterious the tiny world became. Microscopists found germs everywhere, but Bassi's silkworm, ringworm, and the discovery that yeast was the agent of fermentation sustained interest in fungi. Microscopists were also finding animalcules, now calling them bacteria, Latin for small rod. Still, no bacteria or fungus could be associated with obviously contagious diseases like Smallpox and Measles and not all bacteria caused disease, even when injected into animals. It seemed impossible that something as small as bacteria could exist in different forms, some dangerous and some not. Then bacteria of different shapes were reported, some round cocci and others with funny helical forms.

Some very smart colleagues remained convinced that all disease was the result of unique characteristics within the individual. Individual differences caused symptom variations, not contagions. Others rationalized more complex processes. Individual behavior certainly influenced illness, but unique contagions might explain why epidemics spread through a community producing similar symptoms in many people. If the agent of disease was external to the patient, it would explain why some epidemics are stopped by isolating those who are sick. A physician who recognized a pattern and diagnosed a specific disease might stop further illness.

39. What Meaning Has Death, 1876

All worthy physicians can be forced to their knees.

I never intended to bequeath my name to a child, but Millicent encouraged me to christen our fourth son Jabez Allen, Jr. The name defined the child. While still a toddler and in command of only a few words, Jabez would pout when I could not take him on house calls. Even his mischief revealed a precocious bent as we had to scold him for reading medical textbooks in bed by candlelight. He was always asking questions, and by age seven he swept the store in exchange for a lesson about measuring, mixing and compounding drugs. By age thirteen he was helping me prepare stock compounds and by his graduation from the Aurora Academy he was an expert druggist.

Like his grandmother, Jabez had a predisposition to despondency. Despite my encouragement, it postponed his decision to enter medical college until 1874 when New York reinstituted physician licensing. Jabez was twenty when he attended his first semester of lectures at Buffalo Medical College. Another difficult episode of melancholia delayed his second semester, he continued his apprenticeship with me and attended his second course of medical lectures in 1876. Kochan Reclaw is the last patient my son and I cared for.

Kochan Reclaw, an industrious twenty-eight-year-old Polish immigrant, supported his wife and two children on a small farm south of the village. The farm provided food, but like many farmers, the family's need for cash obliged Kochan to take day jobs at the Spooner Tannery. In the spring of 1876, the tannery received a shipment of Argentinean sheep hides that needed to be transferred from railcar, to ox cart, to the tannery a half mile away. It was hard work paying $1.25 a day.

Kochan separated, lifted and carried over a thousand dried hides. By the third day repeated hoisting of the grimy hides wore a sore on the right side of his neck. That evening his wife gently washed and dressed the wound with muslin. Four days later the wound bubbled and turned black. That's when Mrs. Reclaw sent for me.

Jabez and I arrived at the Reclaw cabin to find Kochan with a rapid pulse and feverish. On his neck the sore was three inches across, covered with coal black eschar and surrounded by vividly red swollen skin. Kochan was my fourth case of malignant pustular Anthrax in a tannery worker, but Jabez's first.

I supervised Jabez's methodical debridement of the black eschar followed by swabbing of the wound base with dilute carbolic acid, and covering it with a black mustard poultice and a muslin dressing. We attached twelve leeches to Kochan's neck, shoulder and chest to reduce swelling and dosed him with quinine and senna in brandy to open Kochan's bowels and reduce his fever. Jabez elected to stay the night to make detailed notes about his first case of Anthrax. Proud of Jabez's interest, I promised to return in the morning.

The next day, despite Jabez's night long efforts to reapply leeches and administer multiple doses of quinine, the sore on the right side of Kochan's neck was again covered with black eschar and draining copious amounts of serous fluid at the margins. New pustules had formed over the upper chest. Several large glands could be felt under his left arm and neck.

Dr. Frank Hastings Hamilton, Professor of Surgery at Buffalo Medical College, was considered a national expert on the management of Anthrax. His work corroborated that of Dr. A.N. Bell of Brooklyn City Hospital, who had reported on Anthrax since 1862. Bell attributed Anthrax to the influence of a poison that could be transmitted to humans by the blood, tissues, and milk of affected animals. Bell postulated that earlier papers by Pierson from Massachusetts, by Pennock in Philadelphia, Carpenter in Louisiana and Wells in New York all described cases of Anthrax, concluding that Anthrax, murrain, malignant pustules, Siberian plague, splenic fever, malignant edema, and wool sorters' disease were one in the same. In his final treatise on the subject, Bell endorsed Dr. Hamilton's management of Anthrax, but warned that one in four patients die despite proper management.

Tanning had gotten an early start in Aurora where lumber mills guaranteed a steady supply of bark used to soften leather. In the 1860s, just as most of the virgin forests had been cleared, chromium (long used to prepare cat gut for suturing) replaced bark and made for a suppler leather. Modern society uses leather for clothes, shoes, harnesses, bags, vessels, hinges, and so much else that tanneries operate wherever creeks can carry away large quantities of waste. The Spooner tannery, one of two in the upper village, was owned by Dorr Spooner, son of the man who built many of Aurora's houses. Its effluent is released into Tannery Brook, which empties into the Cazenove Creek.

Preparing leather is a multistep process of soaking, liming, de-hairing, fleshing, de-liming and softening hides. The demand is so high that tanneries import raw, dried hides from China, Africa and South America. These hides arrive stiff, hard, and covered with blood and filth from the slaughter process of their home country. The hides must be rehydrated and softened in water, producing such a foul-smelling broth that in 1860 New York State required chlorinated lime to be added before discharge. Argentinean hides now threatened Kochan Reclaw's life.

Upon my return that morning I reviewed the work of Dr. Hamilton and Dr. Bell with Jabez and we continued to follow their recommendations. Once again, we cut the eschar from the enlarging ulcer on Kochan's neck and shoulder, then used a stronger solution of carbolic acid to cauterize the wound's base. We followed this with another black mustard poultice and muslin dressing. Our supply of fresh leeches was exhausted so we initiated dry cupping and continued doses of senna and quinine in brandy. Jabez stayed another night.

The next day Kochan remained ashen, feverish and his neck, upper chest and arm were deformed by the massive swelling. New pustules appeared and drained copious amounts of serous fluid. In some areas muscle was now exposed. We added doses of opium and Jabez elected to spend a third night at the Reclaw cabin.

Jabez was maturing as a doctor and shedding the self-absorption of youth that I thought had made him susceptible to melancholia. I felt growing excitement for our future practice together. Supervising Jabez was like living a continuous symposium of ideas, questions, and mutual interrogations. Jabez's natural disposition was to tackle one problem at a time, wrestling with it until it was solved and he amazed me with his depth of Chemistry knowledge and his attention to the details of college lectures. We bonded at the interface of science and humanity.

The next day Kochan Reclaw's neck and chest were completely involved in gangrenous cellulitis covered with zones of collapsed black leather like eschar and his endurance was fading. Of the four cases of malignant pustular Anthrax I had attended, only one had spent the patient's vitality this rapidly. By noon he was in a state of near collapse, his temperature was below normal and pulse weakened. He perked up after injection of six minims of strychnine hydrochloride. But, two hours later his urine turned black and Kochan showed no response to a second dose of strychnine. Farmer, husband, father, part-time tannery worker, and Anthrax victim, Kochan Reclaw died on the afternoon of the fourth day of Jabez's continuous attention.

In her grief, Mrs. Reclaw insisted on a full accounting of his death and asked that we perform an autopsy. She needed to understand why such tragedy had befallen her family.

Autopsies demystify death for both the family and the physician. To see and hold the exact cause of a patient's death opens the mind and advances comprehension of the disease process. It is a privilege that requires skill and should be practiced with deference. It is the last step in caring for a patient and the first step in caring for the next patient.

My son, Jabez, did not take as naturally to the knife as he did to pharmacy, but he was willing and capable of performing Kochan's autopsy. I kept notes as he described the dissection. Jabez made an incision from each shoulder to the xiphoid then down the midline to the pubis. This released large amounts of serous fluid from the areas of the neck, shoulder, upper arm and chest. The lungs were covered with petechiae and the heart was bathed in a non-hemorrhagic effusion. The intestines and liver showed hemorrhage, the mesentery contained enlarged lymph glands, and ascitic fluid flooded the abdominal cavity.

We decided to remove some of fluid from the grossly enlarged spleen for microscopic examination but as Jabez touched the scalpel to spleen it burst. In the momentary commotion, he sustained a deep cut on the palm of his left hand and was sprayed with splenic contents. He completed the autopsy by carefully replacing all examined organs and suturing the original incision. When finished, we both washed our hands in carbolic acid.

I was anxious to demonstrate the filamentous bacillus Bell had described in the spleen of his Anthrax patients. Jabez showed me a technique he learned at college that involved using crystal violet to stain a smear of the splenic fluid dried on a glass slide. Under the microscope, we observed the now purple bacillus described by Bell. I made a call on Mrs. Reclaw and Jabez made arrangements for the transfer of Kochan's body to the undertaker.

Three days later a vesicle formed where Jabez had stabbed his left palm. Within hours the little blister became the size of a bean and filled with a bloody, serous fluid and itched such that he thought it might drive him insane. Fearing the vesicle to be the Anthrax, I opened and cauterized its base with phenol as recommended by Dr. Hamilton.

Over the next two days the wound became a half inch ulcer covered with black eschar, and pain replaced the itching. Soon several small vesicles formed on the back of Jabez's hand and a red streak spread up his arm to painfully enlarged glands at his elbow and left axilla. Jabez had Anthrax.

The very first, and all subsequent editions of the American Medical Association's Code of Ethics insists that physicians not treat family members. We prevailed upon Dr. William Gail, who during his apprenticeship in my office had befriended a younger Jabez. William's first recommendation shocked us out of any vestige of complacency. Based on the Anthrax he had seen while in the cavalry, "An immediate amputation of Jabez's left arm above the elbow will give Jabez a three in four chance of survival."

Jabez refused. Despite plaintive begging by Millicent and me, he refused.

Over the next few hours William applied eighteen leeches to Jabez's hand and arm to relieve the edema, draw off the poisons and limit extension of the disease. He also prescribed jalap and senna to keep Jabez's bowels active and facilitate the actions of the liver. Doses of quinine and salicylate powder were dissolved in brandy and administered every two hours. By the next day, the back of Jabez's left hand developed a dark purple depression that was devoid of sensation and was soon surrounded by new vesicles causing William to acknowledge that Jabez bore a particularly violent occurrence of Anthrax. Jabez assumed a resigned melancholy, resolute in his decision to endure, unwilling to live with one arm, and accepting of God's will. William declared an unqualified crisis and demanded that Jabez allow amputation of the arm.

Millicent prayed that God would open Jabez's mind. I threatened forceful restraints to save my son's life. Still, Jabez remained steadfast, his intellect unimpaired. William reminded me of our own discussions during his apprenticeship and my firm admonition that conducting surgery against the patient's wishes was not just a break with the AMA Code of Ethics, it was an immoral presumption of God's intentions. As the day passed, the entire forearm became severely swollen, rose colored and painful. Glands in the axillae swelled to the size of pigeon's eggs and his hand demonstrated the first signs of gangrene. We applied fresh rye flour poultices every two hours and continued the application of leeches to the arm.

Mentoring young physicians is a great responsibility. I accepted only a very few apprentices in my years of practice. It is not the traditions of Physic that I find difficult to teach. Traditions are little more than a manual, and all learners are too eager to place their confidence in a manual. The challenge is ingraining a vision of science, values, and compassion to guide the selection of treatment. Patients are in crisis and expect more than an expedient textbook recitation. We are their partner against illness and a harbinger of hope, obliged to exert all effort to secure the most appropriate and effective remedy with honest appraisal of our potential.

Before Jabez, William Gail had been my favorite apprentice. In the two years he spent living with our family he was not only enthusiastic about medicine and science, but he encouraged six-year-old Jabez. William is the son of Reverend Samuel Gail from the village of Wales, a few miles south of Aurora. After graduating the Aurora Academy, William took his lectures at Buffalo Medical College. He then volunteered as a Medical cadet in Stanton General Hospital in Washington DC and joined a cavalry division. In 1866 William returned to Aurora to practice medicine and had been the first to suggest we invite Jabez to join us at Erie County Medical Society meetings.

William possessed the gravitas and the dedication we needed, if Jabez were to survive.

Skin on Jabez's forearm collapsed, exposing vessels, nerves, and muscle. His pulse became irregular, small and rapid. He had difficulty swallowing. Small sips of brandy and morphine provided only temporary relief. Nothing we did had the slightest influence over the fatal tendency of Anthrax. Jabez sunk into delirium. Just before noon on 25 June 1876 my son and namesake was delivered to our maker.

A son, my best friend and business partner, died just as his life had taken direction.

Surges of sorrow, need and grief always drew Millicent and I closer in a complicated balance that allowed private torments their expression. Jabez had invigorated me. His death aged me. I was obsessed with the worry that I had apportioned my attentions conditional to his achievements. I yearned to believe in a spiritual life so I could tell him how important he was to me.

As physicians, we witness survivors who are consumed by death of a loved one. We see others appear to simply move on, reserving their grief for cloistered times. I cannot detect any consistent difference in their capacities, just in their way of surviving. After Jabez's death I trudged ahead and forced myself to focus, but my reflections were consumed by death.

Little James' death from Tubercular disease followed a long illness and much suffering. At age twelve he was but a young lad, a human vessel only partly filled. My brother James died administering to those who needed him, still yearning for our native Vermont. The sudden loss of his entire family left the impression they had simply moved away. When my mother died, I was immediately preoccupied with the forces of change. The death of my father had been distant and the death of mother Millicent came after several years of decline. Always, the preoccupations of my busy, self-centered life obscured the heartbreak.

Jabez was in the bloom of his life. Full of plans, excitement and learning. He was a human vessel modestly filled and eager to define himself. I was sixty-eight, well past the time for a man to arrive at a personal understanding about survival and loss, but it was an effort I owed to Jabez.

Millicent took great comfort in God and we held hands more than at any time of our marriage. So many friends, patients and people we hardly knew said it is such a terribly sad thing for a young person to die; and it is. But if memories are the measure of a person, can dying young be so much worse that dying old when memories are overflowing. There is very little in our mind when we are born, and so much more when we are old. Given the choice, would we not prefer to lose an empty purse rather than one we had filled. Perhaps that explains a parent's private pain of losing a child. It is parents who fill the child with labors of love, hope, devotions and time.

Many might have considered it quite proper if I, an old man, had pricked my finger and died. I would join them in that assessment. I have lived a good life. Yet, I am preserved, and Jabez is dead.

I allowed the waves of grief their ebb and flow, losing Jabez in shards over several months as the memories of our hours together replaced the gloom of his death. Pain never abandoned my thoughts, but I chose to treasure his precious contributions to my life's purse.

Millicent had now been my wife for forty-two years. She is a wonderful companion who, in the urgencies of my career, had not received the gratitude she so faithfully earned. As I took stock, I gave up house calls, focusing on the drugstore and those patients who came to the office. I did not have the resources to cease work, but I could curtail the time it consumed and spend more time in the company of the woman I loved and who so generously loved me.

In the year following Jabez's death, I became absorbed with the work of Germany's Robert Koch. Koch used the unique animal/human interplay of *Bacillus anthracis* to prove that the bacterium we saw in our microscope caused Anthrax. The journals all carried summaries of how Koch grew the Anthrax bacteria in culture and showed that the cultured bacteria formed spores that when injected into animals once again produced Anthrax. He did not need humans to prove that a bacterium can cause disease. Still, there were those who refused to believe that Koch's germs held more than a loose association with the true poison.

It is a physician's privilege to accompany so many individuals in their search for personal truth. I believe my son was on that path. Men like Koch achieve great fame by an obsession with a truth that others missed. There is also great truth to be discovered in family, and in befriending the everyday man.

40. Comforting the Mind, 1850 to 1884

A disordered mind consumes both the intellect and the body.

The episodes of depression and melancholy visited upon Mother Millicent Johnson and later my son Jabez generated within me a deep-seated curiosity about the mind. In my first year of practice twenty-six-year-old Eunice Turner's eight-year-old son Joseph came down with Measles that progressed to delirium and death. Soon the three younger Turner children suffered their own serious cases of Measles. They survived, but the terror haunted Eunice. Her complexion turned sallow, her bowels became agitated and she wept daily. Her husband was a glass importer who traveled often, leaving Eunice in the care of his mother. It was Eunice's mother-in-law who asked that I visit after Eunice suffered an episode of generalized twitching, unintelligible speech and collapse.

By my arrival, Eunice had returned to her usual self and my exam revealed no injury or abnormality. Then as I mounted my horse to depart I was summoned to witness a second attack. Eunice lay on the floor in a rigid quiver, partially aware of her surroundings. Her utterances were forced belching that I would not describe as speech and she had no loss of urine or feces.

The symptoms of spasmodic hysteria are both fascinating and difficult to distinguish from epilepsy, mania, or catalepsy. Like my Castleton professors, I attributed hysteria to the uterus until encountering a number of men with spasmodic hysteria in my first few years of practice. All that seems required is an irritable nervous system that encounters a situation exceeding the mind's capacity for reason. Applying leeches to the scalp will reduce blood and inflammation causing brain dysfunction and cathartics will rid the body of inflammatory byproducts from the liver. Long term recovery requires commitment to moderate exercise and conversation. The subject of conversation is unimportant, but husbands and mothers seldom show a natural propensity for healing talk. I encouraged Eunice Turner's family to engage Margaret Farling, the midwife who assisted the births of Abiatha and Millicent. Margaret's aptitude for talking cures produced complete resolution of Eunice's symptoms in a matter of weeks.

Dorothea Dix awakened America to the needs of those with mental afflictions. Miss Dix's parents both suffered intemperance forcing her father, a Methodist minister, to relocate frequently. At age twelve, Miss Dix's grandparents, Dr. Elijah and Dorothea Dix, took her into their Boston home and provided her a liberal Unitarian education. By age eighteen Miss Dix was teaching. In 1824, at the age of twenty-two she published *Conversations on Common Things*. A book formatted as a conversation between mother and daughter that became a very popular source of facts and values for woman.

Suffering her own nervous irritability, Miss Dix took a cure with a community of English Quakers. Upon returning to America, she advocated for the establishment of asylums with a labor force trained in the care of the insane. At the time, New York State law required families to restrain relatives considered a threat to themselves or others, but violent or suicidal behavior, hallucinations, and delusions often forced removal of the individual. Patients were then placed in an almshouse or with any household willing to provide shelter for a fee.

Dix's campaign led to the opening of the New York State Lunatic Asylum in Utica, New York in 1843. Within a year, it housed over a thousand patients. The first Medical Director, Amariah Brigham, received a salary of $1200 and a home on the asylum campus. Brigham founded the *American Journal of Insanity*, and encouraged Utica's patients to publish a widely distributed weekly newsletter they called *The Opal*. As other states opened similar asylums they joined with Brigham to form the Association of Medical Superintendents of American Institutions for the Insane whose first campaign replaced the term 'alienist' with the European designation of 'psychiatrist.'

Dr. Brigham, and his successor Dr. John P. Gray, also trained professionals interested in treating the insane. At an Erie County Medical Society meeting, Dr. Gray bragged that talk sessions organized around farming, gardening, carpentry and needlework resulted in forty percent of Utica patients being discharged in less than a year. No patient was ever chained, instead patients at risk of harm were placed in the Utica Crib, a bed with a thick mattress, slats on the sides and a hinged top that created a safe space eighteen inches deep, six feet long and three feet wide.

Buffalo got its own asylum in 1861 when the Providence Retreat opened near the Sisters of Charity Hospital on thirty acres of beautiful, well-kept lawns owned by Dr. Austin Flint. The first Director, Dr. William Ring, employed many of the programs developed at the Utica Asylum.

Years of practicing in one community has taught me that afflictions of the mind are generally transient, often recurring, and not under the devil's influence. Hippocrates, Benjamin Rush in his 1812 book on mental illness, and Austin Flint all rationalized that the highly-innervated uterus made women more susceptible to nervous disorders. Common medical remedies included bleeding, leeches applied to the scalp, and purging of the bowels. Priests advocated exorcism and protestants promoted the power of prayer and fasting, but I bear no witness to the success of any remedy beyond that of regular exercise and conversation.

In 1851, Professor Edward Jarvis studied the records of 32,214 patients admitted to 358 hospitals across Europe and America, including those from the Utica Asylum. He found 181 different causes of insanity, many patients having more than one. Jarvis calculated that eighteen percent of insanity results from bodily disorders such as epilepsy and head injury. Intemperate use of alcohol, opium and tobacco caused thirteen percent. Abuse of the genital system and sexual indulgence caused about five percent. Childbirth, pregnancy and difficulties associated with female reproduction caused between five and nine percent. Twenty-two percent of patients had an insane parent. Admissions were precipitated by intense excitement including, sudden elation, jealousy, remorse, envy, infatuations, religious anxieties, undue parental severity, and passions such as hate, revenge and ambition. Jarvis observed that, "Insanity is the price which we pay for civilization."

While interesting, such data do little to help when the village doctor is asked to aid individuals who do not quite fit into society and may suffer a degree of insanity. There are many unique, wayward, and eccentric characters whose manners and habits are considered unusual and bothersome. Within a circumscribed life their function can be satisfactory, their productivity adequate, and there may be little reason to force conformity or remedy.

Each person seems to possess a fixed amount of nerve energy. Insanities and nervous exhaustion occur when work or worry are excessive, exercise inadequate, rest unfulfilling, diet poor or alcohol overindulged. Like Jarvis, I impugn the hurried life and expectations sparked by newspapers, magazines, steam power, and telegraphy.

Dr. George M. Beard described a form of nervous exhaustion seen in the upper class in 1869 that he called neurasthenia. Such a label implies that the doctor has made sense of the patient's troubles. Still, like all forms of insanity, the patient must first be removed from all sources of tension, consume a bland diet, rest and submit all decisions to others. I make frequent visits looking for the first sign of improvement at which point I prescribe a structured regimen of walking and conversation. Opium, morphine or spirits, if started to initiate rest, should be used sparingly and may prolong disability.

Hypochondriasis is a special form of relapsing nervous exhaustion. The hypochondriac suffers a strong sense of physical illness, which borders on delirium yet judgment in other matters remains intact. They use vivid terms such as crawling, bursting, piercing, boiling, dead, or torn to pieces to describe symptoms of excessive mucous, abdominal gas, palpitations, anal pain, headaches, and disturbed sleep. They often quote, with selected accuracy, whole sections of medical books and though improbable, their concern often lies within the limits of the possible. One patient, Aretus Wiley, a sprightly, good-natured thirty-year-old store owner with an excitable temperament suffered a severe episode of Hepatitis that left him apprehensive long after recovery. Any indigestion or abdominal discomfort convinced him of fatal Cancer fanned by a biased reading of Gunn's *Domestic Medicine.* He lost weight loss by experimenting with food limitations causing both of us to worry. Once I remedied burning on urination by prescribing carefully measured quantities of spring water bottled in Maine and sold in his store. If his wife or I dismissed his complaint, he accused me of not caring and her of not loving him. Eventually he visited every physician in Aurora and several in Buffalo. Aretus' final delusion was a bladder stone. He purchased a microscope, examined his urine daily for several weeks, then sought treatment from a lithotritist in New York City. I do not know the training of the lithotritist who opened Aretus's bladder nor what was found, however inflammation set in and he was relieved of all earthly sufferings.

The compulsivity that torments the hypochondriac is known to advantage their labors in other fields. Aretus Wiley left a well-run and highly organized general store to his wife and children that sustained the family for many years.

Except in rare cases of tumor or gross brain anomaly, autopsies offer little understanding about the causes of insanity. Bucknill's 1858 *Manual of Psychological Medicine* categorized mental afflictions according to three overriding behaviors: *Emotional* insanities (melancholia, monomania and mania); *intellectual* insanities (idiocy, delirium, delusions and hallucinations); *volitional* insanities (phobias and anti-social behaviors).

Mother Millicent Johnson and my son Jabez were predisposed to the emotional insanity of melancholia, characterized by a temporary delusion fixated on sadness. More than a depressed mood, melancholia has the tendency to cycle. The rare patient may experience episodic mania. Proper sleep, diet, talk, fresh air and moderate exercise are essential to recovery. Dr. Flint's text recommends hypophosphite of lime, and the phosphide of zinc, but in my experience, drugs do little to quicken recovery.

Hallucinations and delusions characterize the intellectual insanities. Bucknill defines hallucinations as false auditory or visual perceptions, delusions as discerning something untrue as real, and illusions as simple as miss-interpretations, like a shadow on a wall. Disordered thinking generates repetitive, usually unproductive, and occasionally violent actions. Mania is an active perversion of intellect in which ideas and emotions cycle rapidly without order or connection. Defense attorneys argue that extreme anger is a form temporary insanity. It can make a rational person lose all powers of self-control. Assisting an agitated insane person must start with arranging for quiet seclusion. Early in my career I relied on opium, but since the 1870s I have used bromides and chloral hydrate to sedate, occasionally resorting to Chloroform. I have found cold compresses and soaking the feet in cold water is surprisingly helpful.

On her wedding day, moments after leaving their wedding luncheon, one young woman I cared for confessed to her husband that she was pregnant with the child of a prominent community gentleman. Straightaway she sequestered herself for several months with a midwife awaiting her confinement. Near term the astute midwife requested I examine the woman where upon I confirmed minimal abdominal distension and unequivocal proof of virginity. After many gentle and leading questions, she revealed that she had never met the accused gentleman. Oddly, the next day the young woman acquired a cough leading to Pneumonia with high fever and delirium. She nearly died. Upon recovering, her delusion had passed and she was reunited with her husband, raised a family, and suffered no further insanity.

But many afflictions of the mind are cluttered by setbacks. One family sent their well-educated twenty-two-year-old son to a southern retreat for treatment of persistent sullen moods. When an episode of agitation required restraint in a strait jacket he was sent home where continued mania required two weeks of regular bleeding and multiple daily doses of a compound I prepared from hyoscyamus, camphor and opium. The mania resolved and he improved, but over the next twenty years he cycled between episodes of mania and melancholia. One day he was found dead of a gunshot sustained while hunting alone.

Suicides confirm mental affliction and are themselves acts of insanity. Despite assurances from his wife, Ernest, a thirty-two-year-old farmer, feared he had not stored adequate food for his family. His melancholia became intense and one day he cut two deep wounds on each side of his neck with his razor. When his wife discovered him, he fled across several fields and jumped into a former salt pit filled with icy snow melt where he madly tore at his cuts. Neighbors bravely secured his rescue and still agitated, he was brought to my office for surgery. I convinced Ernest to drink several drams of opium and commenced a nearly two-hour, difficult surgical repair after which I arranged for his wife and a brother to board the train to Buffalo where Ernest was hospitalized at the Providence Asylum until spring planting. I attended to the medical needs of the family for many years and while he returned to a productive family life, recurrent bouts of melancholia complicated many winter months.

Monomaniacal delusions can drive patients to over work, murder, burn (pyromania), perform sexually perverse acts (erotomania) and steal (kleptomania). Monomania is a fixation on an idea that disrupts normal behavior, such as Captain Ahab's monomaniacal quest to kill the whale in Herman Melville's 1851 novel *Moby Dick*. Other monomanias include: Staying thin, exaggerated affections for people or things, and narcissism. The patient is driven to perform a behavior which is often perceived as a duty, or directed by a superior being. To be considered an act of insanity the act must have no motive except to satisfy a delusion. Bucknill considers craving alcohol (dipsomania) or opiates to be variants of monomaniacal behavior.

Temporary insanity can lead to irreconcilable acts. I became involved in a case one Sunday afternoon when a daughter surprised her parents by bringing to dinner a much older man known in the community as an intemperate laggard. During dinner, the daughter announced that the couple was engaged and would marry within the week. Overwhelmed, her mother shouted ominous vindictive insults at her husband for allowing such a man in their daughter's life. She then retreated to the kitchen, reappearing moments later to offer apologies for her outburst and distributing servings of apple cobbler. Within the hour, the husband and the fiancé became nauseous and soon both men were delirious with profuse diarrhea. Both had a distinct garlic odor, an irregular pulse and two hours later both men died.

The symptoms and the mother's detached reaction were unsettling. I suspected poisoning and the mother freely admitted I would find a container of arsenic in the kitchen that she used to keep beetles off her roses. I alerted the coroner who ordered me to perform autopsies. I used sulfuric acid under the protocol of the Marsh Test to examine the stomach contents of both men. Both revealed arsenic.

The woman confessed her crime to her attorney who pleaded that the woman's actions were driven by a justified insane impulse. At trial, a jury found the woman not guilty and recommended confinement to the New York State Lunatic Asylum at Utica where she remained for one year. She has lived a quiet existence in her home under the care of her never wed daughter.

When normal memory becomes enfeebled we say the patient has developed an intellectual insanity called dementia. Words are echoed, the patient's interests diminish to personal wants, their attentions are preoccupied by trifles and eventually immediate situations make only a transient impression. They may be alternately placid or irritable, but occasionally demonstrate flashes of their former selves. The majority of dementia is incidental to old age and referred to as senile dementia. Bucknill asserts that the senile form of dementia may be prevented, postponed, or slowed by judicious exercise of the mental faculties, suggesting the brain deteriorates if not used.

Idiocy is a congenital dementia, often with cranial abnormalities. The first sign is an inattentive infant but there are wide gradations from minor incapacities to a profound, almost unconscious presence. Our messenger, Charles, is an imbecile, but demonstrates how the right environment can support a productive life. Though palsy gives Charles' walk a perpetual stagger, walking is his favorite activity. He can't read, but counts and has a remarkable memory for addresses. He shivers with joy when given a package to deliver and many Aurora businesses have become his informal guardians. He conducts daily rounds with astounding punctuality and shares a joyful enthusiasm that cheers us all. For a penny, preferably shiny, he will deliver a letter or a package anywhere in town.

Bucknill uses the term imbecile to denote a deficiency of the mental powers less severe than idiocy. Theophilus Letty is another case who lived productively in the shelter of his family until age forty-two when his parents died without leaving a will. The Court appointed a judge to consider placing Theo's share of the rather large estate in the hands of a trustee. Theo opposed this arrangement and marched into my brother-in-law's law office with an inelegant demand for representation. William asked Dr. Gail and myself to render an opinion regarding Theo's capacity. Theo answered our questions with considerable understanding and shared a private journal he kept. His writing contained errors in grammar, spelling and word choice, but demonstrated reasonably insightful observations and our exams revealed no profound disability. The judge ruled Theo competent and he was allowed to take possession of his parents' property. Aside from being gullible to many salesmen and at least one woman who exploited his naivety, Theo managed to operate a modestly productive farm for many years.

Grovemont, an isolated valley village not far from Aurora, embraced, even encouraged, marriages between cousins for several generations. Progeny of these families include one dwarf, one child born deaf and several children I would classify as imbeciles or idiots. An 1848 Massachusetts study found forty-six percent of children born of consanguineous marriages to be idiots, compared to the statewide rate of one percent. As I became familiar with Grovemont families, I found their children possessed tender affections for their mothers, contributed hours of demanding work in the fields, and were accepted as productive members within their community. Grovemont supported a compassionate diversity that in some ways was admirable, but woefully preventable.

Epilepsy, long classified as an intellectual insanity, was the topic presented by Professor William H. Thompson from the New York Academy of Medicine at an Erie County Medical Society meeting. Thompson theorized that epilepsy is a physical disorder of the brain, more like the sudden spasms of the lungs characteristic of asthma than insanity. In epilepsy, the brain triggers sudden general spasms of muscles resulting in distorted facial features, dilated pupils, and suspended respirations. Attacks even occur during sleep, leaving only a bleeding tongue as evidence. By contrast, the insanities build slowly and do not resolve so quickly.

Thompson found no evidence of a predisposing epileptoid personality, finding most patients to be no more self-willed, obstinate, erratic, or argumentative than the general population. He reminded us that Julius Caesar and Napoleon Bonaparte experienced epileptic paroxysms and in some cultures seizures signal a special relationship with God.

Though enlightening, Dr. Thompson's studies provided no new remedy. Daily doses of cod-liver oil improve nerve nutrition and a drachm of capsicum in a pint of hot water taken each night will excite peripheral nerves, creating a reciprocal decrease in brain excitations. Large doses of the bromide of potassium can cause bloated facial features but may help difficult cases. Once a patient has gone two years without a seizure they should be considered cured and treatment should be stopped.

At Castleton I was schooled in trephination. The ancients believed that drilling holes in the skull relieved cranial pressure and released morbid brain substances. Occasional medical journal reports advocate for trephination but when a physical treatment is demanded by families I encourage a weekly application of leeches or venesection. A rare colleague has suggested that I lack the courage to drill a hole in a patient's skull. They may be right.

I am not infallible in my judgements of insanity. My tragic recommendation for placement of Alvin Forsyth is a matter of public record. Alvin, a twenty-seven-year-old epileptic and known imbecile, brutally assaulted an elderly Marilla couple who had sheltered and befriended him. It had been over two years since Alvin's last seizure when, in the winter of 1862, both his parents passed. Because of his placid personality and good work habits, I recommended placement in the home of Mr. and Mrs. Mason.

Several months later Mr. Mason and Alvin celebrated the end of the fall harvest by sharing a jug of corn whiskey. According to Alvin, Mr. Mason began mimicking Alvin's curious mannerisms causing an angered Alvin to strike Mr. Mason with a large stick. Wounded, Mason crawled to safety under a heavy dinette, but with unspent rage Alvin entered the bedroom and beat Mrs. Mason ferociously. Frightened by the terrible things he had done, Alvin set the house on fire and ran away.

At the trial, lawyers introduced my records to confirm Alvin's history of epilepsy and entered a plea of insanity, pointing out the lack of any discernible motive for his crime. The superintendent of a reputable asylum described the act as an unconscious and uncontrollable impulse of epileptic alienation and mania. The jury ruled Alvin insane and he was remanded to the Utica asylum rather than a penal institution.

I remain distressed by this verdict. It is my firmly held opinion that the tragedy resulted from intemperance, not epilepsy, and Alvin's crime was one of manslaughter, not insanity. Such misplaced justice fosters the stigma and fear Dr. Thompson hoped to dispel.

Medical reports about sexual inversion in Civil War armies helped me understand my patients with similar urges. Another study of twenty-seven civilians revealed no unique personality trait attributable to homosexuality. Most are men of perfectly natural appearance and only a few demonstrate cross-gender mannerisms. Many had found heterosexual relationships unsatisfying, often spending years being unaware that there were others like them. All feared disclosure due in large part to an 1828 New York State law mandating ten years' imprisonment for sodomy.

I have learned to follow the patient's lead regarding personal issues of sexuality. One does not have to be homosexual to have unique sexual impulses. Rather than defining their personality, these urges are generally described as 'interests.' Though human passion can be quite diverse, many people find someone with similar passions.

Irwin Michaels was a young man in his thirties and the progeny of a family with high social stature in our community. His muscular development was normal but he was short and possessed long eyelashes with thick dark hair. As a child, he showed little interest in boyhood pastimes while developing a talent for writing and remarkable skills at the piano. Irwin dressed with a stylishness rarely found in men and nibbled at food in a manner more typical of women.

After graduation from the Aurora Academy, Irwin studied law but found success writing for national magazines about issues of poverty and social programs. To stabilize his income, he opened a book store and made regular buying excursions to New York City. I had been a regular customer for several years when one day Irwin told me about being approached by men of homosexual desire and finding himself overcome with similar attractions. He wanted the joys of family and asked if I could prescribe medication to reverse his inclinations.

Classified as an emotional insanity, I assured Irwin that all my reading indicated sexual inclination was a behavioral preference that might be reversed. The best I could offer him was advice to enter courtship with a female acquaintance of pleasing character and with time the association would render normal inclinations.

I continued to frequent Irwin's business and we became good friends. Occasionally I would see him in the company of a woman at a lecture or concert, but he never married. His trips to New York continued and over the years I had occasion to meet his friend from New York who visited Aurora frequently. I suppose he provided some fodder for gossip, but he was successful in his business affairs and contributed to the community in meaningful ways.

Dipsomania, or the morbid craving for alcohol, is a tendency that one may be born with or may acquire. Either way the intemperate person suffers a monomania that injures one's self-respect and leads to periods of remorse. Despite calamitous consequences, neither discouragement nor despair stops their drinking.

Every newspaper and magazine posts advertisements for the pleasures of alcohol. This one for the Globe Hotel states:

> "*Our Temperance House is open!* The premises have undergone a thorough repair and are fitted up in a style of neatness, which will render it worthy of patronage. The Bar is constantly supplied with the choices of wines, liquors and the table will at all times be furnished with the varieties of the season. Nothing shall be wanting to render the stay of guests agreeable. The barns and outhouses are commodious. The hotel is confident it will render itself as a place of comfort to the citizen or traveler."

Our local weekly paper carried many stories that should awaken any reader to the hazards of drink. One titled *Deplorable Accident* described several friends who after a successful hunt had their game cooked at a public house and amused themselves with a sham fight that included discharging their guns loaded with only powder. One participant, a Mr. James Wilson, suddenly exclaimed that he was shot, causing great laughter from his companions, until it was found that a ramrod discharged from the gun of Mr. Clough had struck him and passed entirely through his body. He died later that evening with physician in attendance.

And if that did not sober the inebriant, there was another story titled *Death by Intemperance*. Isaac Button, better known as Billy Button, died the previous Sunday morning from the pernicious influence of 'ardent spirits.' On the previous afternoon Billy took a liking to the jug of rum provided at a house raising and was soon drunk. He remained so until morning when, despite the exertions of a physician, he was pronounced dead.

Dipsomania is curable, provided one can secure the patient's cooperation. Punishments and legal penalties are ineffective. Just as contagions must be avoided to preserve health, so too must the intemperate make a solemn pledge to abstain from alcohol. Pledges will be broken but they add resolve to self-control. Cravings, and the incidence of delirium tremens, are lessened if the body is well nourished and the patient is engaged in consuming work with moderate exercise. Stomach tonics without alcohol may help.

I finish my discussion of the mind with a comment on tobacco. In 1839 Harvard surgeon John Collins Warren Jr. reported that tobacco is a common cause of Cancer of the tongue and lip. We often hear that sugar will rot the teeth and handling of toads will produce warts, but we are seldom told that tobacco is perilous. Once a habit, tobacco can be difficult to abandon. The good news is that the more irregular one's use of tobacco, the more disgusting one finds each encounter.

41. Germs, 1878

Science is the unearthing of mistakes.

After my son's death I arose many mornings feeling worn-out. I devoured news about Dr. Koch's experiments proving a bacterium caused Anthrax, including the extensive review of his work that appeared in the *Atlantic Monthly*. The debate was joined by Dr. Satterthwaite who believed that all bacteria were variations of one vegetative organism; Dr. Hurd's assertion that bacteria shared properties with both algae and fungi; and those who denied Koch's work had disproven a role for chemicals and miasma. When the 1878 American Medical Association's annual meeting was scheduled for Buffalo, Millicent prevailed on me to attend. She thought hearing and debating the men writing for medical journals might not only provide a better understanding of Jabez's death, but reignite my spark for medicine.

More than germs stirred medicine in the 1870s. For one thing, our physical exams gathered more information and we looked for patterns of signs and symptoms to which we could apply a diagnostic label. We didn't just treat symptoms any longer, we treated a diagnosis, and diagnoses were the way we communicated.

By 1878 the skills of physical examination differentiated the well trained, capable physician from the quack. When Austin Flint was appointed Dean of Buffalo Medical College he instituted a curriculum based on his Harvard training and that of the best French colleges. Flint, who bragged that he had notes on over ten-thousand patients, required students to observe and keep notes on large numbers of patients they examined at the almshouse or hospital, honing their skills at differentiating abnormal patterns from normal. These intense afternoon experiences forced a structured group clinical experience, much improved over the happenstance experiences during my unstructured apprenticeship.

Flint and I became friends in a formal professional sense. We were fascinated by new things and shared a love of work, enjoyed patient care, liked to read, loved to argue, and fancied ourselves as New England castaways. My energies focused on service to the people of Aurora. Flint's energies drove him to theorize, write, and teach. His passion was to improve our profession, mine to help patients.

The bi-aural stethoscope, otoscope, ophthalmoscope, sphygmomanometer, and thermometer were in common use and providing doctors with information the patient could not know. Flint understood the stethoscope's potential before most doctors owned one. Building on the work of Corrigan and Laennec, he discovered the meaning of the sounds generated by the heart and challenged me to listen to every patient, regardless of symptoms. My first stethoscope was one piece of hollowed cedar wood with a concave bell at one end and a convex end that fit my ear. When Flint embraced the bi-aural stethoscope in the 1870s he wrote a brief note to suggest I make the change. My cedar stethoscope was fine for distinguishing wet from dry breath sounds, but with the bi-aural I could distinguish pleural effusions from pneumonia or pleurisy using vocal fremitus and egophony. At nearly the same time the hypodermic needle became available. With it I could drain those pleural effusions and provide relief to many of my tubercular patients.

My skills with the stethoscope also improved my income. The insurance industry paid a bonus to physicians who could render an opinion about an applicant's lungs. Deaths from lung disease, particularly Tubercular consumption, were a major loss for insurance companies. I became a preferred examiner, rendering reports that lowered premiums for those who I found well and providing an opportunity to counsel those with early signs of consumption. Some of the latter group became grateful, steadfast patients.

Medicine became much like connecting puzzle pieces to reveal a diagnosis. Austin Flint's 1879 textbook lists dozens of diagnoses that did not even exist when Eberle's 1831 textbook was published. I found seeking patterns, solving puzzles, and making diagnoses intellectually gratifying activities that improved my ability to prognosticate and to select a treatment. Diagnostic labels made me think more about external factors causing disease, rather than blaming the patient's weakness, intemperance, ungodliness, or impropriety.

The relationship between the stethoscope and the hypodermic needle demonstrates how advances merge and build on each other. By 1878 the stethoscope had replaced the mortar and pestle as the iconic symbol of the Physic profession.

Way back in 1673, van Leeuwenhoek wrote the Royal Society about microscopic creatures he called animalcules. Leeuwenhoek found them almost everywhere he looked, in pond water, infusions of pepper and ginger, in scrapings from his teeth and between his toes, and in his feces. The next big step for microscopic animalcules came with Bassi's 1835 indictment of the silkworm fungi. Bassi's discovery fit with what we know about mushrooms, some of which cause fever, gastro-intestinal irritation and nervous dysfunction. Fungi culpability was further advanced in 1836 when Cagniard de la Tour discovered fermentation depended on the replication and reproduction of yeast. The next year Schwann reported a process much like fermentation occurred during the putrefaction of meat, only it was caused by the replication and reproduction of bacteria.

Since receiving Leeuwenhoek's letters, the Royal Society commissioned endless experiments designed to prove or disprove Aristotle's theory that yeast generated spontaneously in wine, or that animalcules and maggots spontaneously generated in wounds. Finally, in 1859 Pasteur found yeast spores on the skin of grapes and proved these spores reproduced and multiplied within hours of exposure to the juice of crushed grapes. If the spores were washed off, wine did not happen. Two years later, Francis Porcher of Charleston proposed that a fermentation like process in the body explained Scarlet fever, Measles, and Smallpox.

Then came Koch's 1875 discovery that Anthrax bacteria form spores that float like dust and were every bit as infectious as the Anthrax bacillus itself. Koch's experiments were as elegant as they were painstaking. He transferred a drop of blood from the spleen of an Anthrax infected mouse into an eye from a recently butchered ox, then repeatedly studied minute quantities of the eye's contents under his microscope for serval days. The initial few rod-like bacteria grew into great long filaments of bacteria that later grew little buds. Eventually, the filaments fell to pieces and only the buds remained. Assuming these might be Anthrax seeds, he injected these spores into healthy mice who soon died of Anthrax fever. To be certain, Koch repeated the cycle through another generation of bacteria, spores and mice.

The next year, 1876, Scotland's Joseph Lister toured America lecturing about his improved antiseptic techniques. Lister noted that inflamed wounds smelled like putrefied meat and that dilute carbolic acid (phenol) prevented both putrefaction of meat and inflammation in surgical wounds. Following his protocols, deaths after amputation in Edinburgh's hospitals dropped from forty-five percent to fifteen percent.

Equally energizing was the 1877 report by John Tyndall, a student of Pasteur proving that living matter floated in the air. His pamphlet starts by describing how he collected and burned the dust illuminated by a beam of sunshine, proving dust was organic. Tyndall next invented a U- tube apparatus, which he cleaned with carbolic acid, then layered with boiled hay juice. He exposed his apparatus, with and without his U-tube, in his study, bedroom, kitchen, library, the roof of his house and on a mountain slope. When exposed to the air the hay juice media grew organisms. But, if shielded from settling dust by the U-tube, no contamination occurred.

Some thought animalcules were tiny insects, too small to be seen with the eye but capable of laying even tinier eggs. Alternatively, if animalcules were more like plants, they might produce a tiny seed. Koch and Tyndall unlocked a new microscopic universe of floating spores more like the latter. By the 1878 AMA meeting, medical journals were flooded with microscopic breakthroughs.

Naysayers were not about to give in. Besides bacteria, journals published reports claiming to prove that fever was caused by ozone, electricity, chemical compounds, decaying vegetable effluents, heat, moisture, and miasma. Practice changed little. We bled patients a little less, and used quinine and salicylate salts a little more. We stimulated body functions with brandy and nourishing foods, and purged the bowels of accumulated bile. Experiments on dogs published in 1869 had proven that calomel did not increase the release of bile from the liver, so we began using less toxic non-mercury containing cathartics to open the bowels. But even good doctors are slow to abandon basic concepts.

By the start of the 1878 AMA meeting, arguments about external factors causing disease dominated the centuries held belief that disease was due to weakness and imbalance of humors. But, the fragmentation of new information often produced misleading diversions stoking quarrels between contagionists and non-contagionists, microscopists and chemists, statisticians and clinicians. It made for exciting conventions.

From my vantage as a village doctor, I hoped that attending the meeting would allow me to see over the scientific horizon. I understood how doctors in large hospitals caring for many patients with similar conditions might discover patterns, but I took care of individuals with unique personalities and behaviors. Determining if my patient's problems fit a diagnostic pattern added the intellectual challenge.

The meeting in Buffalo was opened by AMA President Dr. T.G. Richardson of Louisiana who honored me with permanent membership in the AMA. The award recognized my two terms as Vice President and one term as President of the Erie County Medical Society and I suppose it rewarded all those dues I had paid.

Erie County's Dr. Thomas F. Rochester welcomed the 475 attendees and recommended tours of Buffalo's City Hall, the Special Department for the Insane at our Almshouse, the Niagara Grain Elevator, General Hospital, Sisters of Charity Hospital, the Providence Asylum, the Widows and Infants Home of St. Vincent de Paul, and the Le Couteulx Deaf Mute Institute. Attendees were advised to stroll along the banks of Fredrick Law Olmsted's Delaware Park Lake and the Medical College Faculty offered use of their halls, museums, preparations, and laboratories.

My former apprentice, William Gail, was an official New York State delegate, joining doctors from all over America and Europe at this, the 29th annual meeting of the AMA. The schedule was tightly packed with committee meetings and lectures spread across several downtown hotels.

Right after the gavel closed the opening ceremonies, the members of the AMA Committee on State Medicine and Public Hygiene took up debate over the impact of germs on community health, which quickly devolved into arguments over the very nature of epidemics. Anti-contagionists reasserted their contention that there could not be multiple different species of something as tiny as bacteria. They claimed a recent Royal Society report that animals injected with bacteria from dirt did not all get sick proved bacteria can't be a primary cause of disease. Chemists argued that such studies prove contagions must be chemicals. Besides, everyone knows Lister's carbolic acid denatures most chemicals as effectively as it kills bacteria. Germ believers said Koch proved the *Bacillus antracis* exists in two forms, one which is readily destroyed and the other a hardy spore that can survive extremes and drift like dust.

Shouting overruled listening until a germ advocate rose to the podium to describe experiments in which pus, filtered to remove bacteria, causes only transient illness when injected into animals, whereas unfiltered pus causes two phases of illness, one immediate and a second phase that is more intense. The delay can only be explained as the time a living thing needs to replicate itself into critically dangerous numbers. Perhaps chemicals cause the immediate illness and replicating bacteria caused the delayed illness. Only living things replicate, so a delay proves that contagions are living things, but bacteria might release chemicals that cause illness.

A physician visiting from Berlin described recent work by Otto Obermeier who found minute organisms in the blood of patients hospitalized with relapsing malarial fever. Obermeier died after injecting himself with these organisms. Other German scientists have since confirmed that the blood of malarial patients contains infectious organisms during episodes of fever and after a delay the organism causes malaria when injected in others. They called the delay an 'incubation' period. Malarial fever, ague, intermittent, and relapsing fever had never been clearly distinguished, one from another, but their relationship to miasma had seemed obvious. Finding a germ in malaria patients sent tremors through the committee.

Others rose to remind delegates that no bacteria, vegetative matter or minute organisms have been found in Smallpox, Measles, Rubella, or Chicken Pox, all of which have long been considered contagious diseases. Each can be transmitted by pus, mucus, blood, excrements, or expectorations and each disease becomes evident in secondary cases only after a delay. If no bacteria are present, the germ theory for contagious disease doesn't work. Even the great Edward Jenner believed his Cowpox vaccination prevented Smallpox by transferring a chemical agent.

The germ theorists countered that spores answered every miasma challenge. They postulated that fungi and bacteria might all form spores under certain conditions. These spores might survive both time and extremes to float like dust and cause a disease specific to their nature. Some spores might be so tiny that they can't be seen under the normal microscope. They called these really tiny spores viruses from the Latin for poison, and assured the committee that more powerful microscopes will find them. Germ skeptics said such a tiny world falls apart under the scrutiny of logic and the chemists argued that it is preposterous to assume a living thing could be smaller than bacteria.

The official minutes simply stated that some members believed germs might eventually explain the occasional epidemic and some inflammations. The committee's output was a resolution much like the previous year's. It recommended streets and homes be kept clean and all households should have access to clean water and nutritious food.

At noon the next day, William Gail and I joined Austin Flint at a table for ten. Before the wine was poured, Dr. George DeSlava recalled that the 1860 National Quarantine and Sanitary Convention had declared miasma the one true threat to public health. He worried that germ advocates were dismissing Benjamin Rush's observations about the dangers of vapors arising from slaughterhouses, swamps, cesspools and sewers. DeSlava also reminded our dinner table, John Snow himself concluded that the Cholera contagion, given its rapid onset, had to be a water based chemical.

Austin Flint admitted he was conflicted. Koch and Obermeier may have proven microscopic organisms cause Anthrax and relapsing fever, but the role of bacteria in other diseases was unclear. Flint urged continued discussion as he was struggling with how to frame the debate for the second edition of his textbook.

Several table companions echoed concern that the existence of unique types of bacteria each capable of only one disease was just too complex. Only miasma could explain an illness spreading suddenly over a large area striking only the weakened and intemperate. One doctor condemned germ advocates for denying God's anger at modern society's turpitudes.

Flint's guest, Dr. Henry Bowditch, described an epidemic of diphtheria he investigated at Ferrisburg, on the shore of Lake Champlain. After the initial case, several days passed before three more cases appeared. These were followed by a smattering of cases before the disease broke out in several dozen people. Then another week passed before the largest wave of citizens became ill. In Bowditch's opinion, if the Ferrisburg contagion were carried by a chemical or miasma, the onset of disease should have been simultaneous in all exposed. Bowditch opined, "The only way to explain the epidemic spreading in waves is to assume that between waves the causative agent is replicating and expanding its numbers, what Germans scientists are calling an incubation period."

As our roast turkey and mashed potatoes arrived, Dr. Moore of Rochester, NY said he recently started spraying carbolic acid on surgical wounds. "I'm seeing fewer febrile excitements, fewer destructive inflammations and under the microscope I seldom find bacteria. I repeated Lister's experiment and heated garden dirt in an oven to a high temperature and sprinkled it on wounds made on a dogs' back. The wounds healed without the inflammation, pus and bacteria of wounds sprinkled with fresh dirt. It isn't dirt, it's bacteria that cause wound putrefaction."

Another table mate challenged Dr. Moore, "The cornerstone of medical management has been, and always will be, the elimination of poisons from the body by bleeding and intestinal excretion. Even if vegetative critters contribute to disease, they still must be driven out of the patient. It is downright malpractice not to."

Discussion continued well past the queen cake desert. As was his nature, Austin Flint summarized, "The novelty of these findings should fire our imagination, but I agree, we must not ignore what is already familiar to us. Much of what we are seeing comes from the mathematic analysis of records from a large numbers of hospital patients. I worry that we are turning doctors into statisticians and ignoring special characteristics of the individual. We are told that large numbers neutralize individual peculiarities, but we do not treat our patients as if they were one homogenous mass. No, we conduct careful examinations, become fully aware of each individual's peculiar circumstances, and we tailor remedies accordingly. Mathematicians may calculate an average life span, but they cannot tell us what day our patient will die. Take bloodletting as an example, studies by Dr. Pierre Louis find that bloodletting does not shorten the average course of Pneumonia for a thousand hospital patients, but admits it benefits some patients if performed early. It strikes me as unlikely every disease has a specific cause, or that the universal cause is a germ. We must not suspend clinical experience."

The first afternoon lecture was given by B.A. Watson of New Jersey who posed three questions to be addressed before concluding that an illness is caused by bacteria. First: Do the symptoms of the disease in question depend on the propagation within the body of minute living organisms that are otherwise foreign to the body? Second: Do these organisms arise spontaneously or are they derived from a universe of germs? And, third: How would such organisms find their way into the body?

The audience muttered audibly when Watson pronounced spontaneous generation dead. In the decade since John Tyndall first exposed his broth to the atmosphere, no one has proved him wrong. Watson added, "None of us would view a thistle growing in a field without assuming that a thistle seed must have settled there. It does not take the intellectual effort of Aristotle to assume that, like the thistle, minute vegetative things arise only from their own seed, just as no one would think it was thistle juice, or an acorn, that gave rise to the thistle."

Next Dr. Watson reviewed an 1873 paper by Edwin Klebs. Klebs thought he had discovered a fungus in the throats of Diphtheria patients, then realized that he was looking at a club-shape bacterium. He next showed that his bacterium was capable of causing Diphtheria in a volunteer. However, if bacteria were filtered out of the tonsillar exudate it produced a few hours of illness, proving to Kleb's satisfaction that a bacterium caused Diphtheria and produced a chemical that adds to the symptoms.

According to Dr. Watson, Koch's grand Anthrax experiments challenge all germ advocates to follow Koch's postulates: 1. The bacteria must be present in every case of the disease; 2. The bacteria must be isolated from the host with the disease and grown in pure culture; 3. The specific disease must be reproduced when a pure culture of the bacteria is inoculated into a healthy host; 4. The bacteria must be re-cultured and found to be identical to the first culture.

Watson echoed the concerns of others, Smallpox is the classic contagious disease. It is transmitted by a victim's pus, demonstrates an incubation period, yet no one has found Smallpox bacteria or spores. Watson challenged chemists and germ theorists to work together to explore this contradiction.

The next afternoon, Dr. A.L. Loomis of New York addressed the Committee on the Practice of Medicine, Materia Medica and Physiology. He dismissed Koch's observations as those of a self-proclaimed, solo scientist and braggart, and ridiculed Koch's newest claim that bacteria caused Tubercular Pneumonia. According to Loomis, "the famous Dr. Rudolf Virchow established scrofula of the lymph system causes tubercles decades ago."

One man shouted, "Don't you think dust like germs can be drawn into the lungs?"

Loomis responded, "Of course they can, but like any dust, they are just an irritant. It is entirely the individual's weakness and susceptibility that defines illness. No one of clear conscious can deny that Pneumonia is most likely in damp, unhealthy miasmic environments. There is no reason to assume that germs are the cause."

Continuing to shout above the din in the room, Loomis argued that Tyndall's U-tube flasks placed at dozens of altitudes in the Alps said more about ozone than bacteria. Above 7000 feet, where ozone levels are highest, Tyndall's broth always remained clear. It explains why the best tubercular hospitals, like Ashville, North Carolina and the New York's Adirondack region, are in mountainous areas with high ozone. Loomis concluded, "The influence of ozone has been given too little regarded. Abandoned simply because a few bacteria can be found in the lungs of tubercular patients."

The 1878 AMA meeting mirrored the trickle of new science. Single case reports still caught my interest, but analysis of many accumulated cases and experiments comparing treatments provoked the greatest adjustments to my medical care. The problem was that new information arrives in fragments. Some fragments support germ theories, others ignite new arguments, as if germs might be quarreled into fact or fiction.

Readers of *Popular Science Monthly* and *Scientific American* might have been better informed than most doctors. These popular magazines carried concise summaries written in collaboration with scientists, including Pasteur. Even literary magazines like the *Atlantic Monthly*, *Harper's Magazine*, *The Nation*, and the *North American Review* dedicated print space to germ theories. Darwin's 1859 *Origin of the Species* was better reviewed in lay magazines than in medical journals. Some journals even suggested that Darwin's assumptions about the beginning of life supported a role for spontaneously generation.

Cholera produced the worse epidemics of my lifetime and it confounded germ advocates. It appears suddenly in one place, spreads around the world in just months, kills within hours, and disappears rapidly only to re-emerge some years later. Cholera epidemics required a contagion to regress, lie dormant, then re-acquire dangerous habits. Miasmas more logically recede and re-emerge according to the whims of weather and climate. And, ever improving microscopic techniques failed to reveal what must be a very, very tiny smallpox bacterium.

In 1882, four years after the AMA convention in Buffalo, Koch confirmed a tuberculosis bacillus that met all of his postulates; postulates that have proven to be a powerful, but difficult, set of rules for germ theorists.

I enjoy my association with men like Austin Flint who are driven to discover, question and share opinions. Buffalo medical college professors speak at every medical society meeting and Flint is a regular at every American Medical Association annual meeting, serving as its President one year. After moving to Louisville, New Orleans and finally Bellevue Hospital in New York, Flint visits Buffalo frequently and publishes often. His 1879 textbook is the most popular medical textbook in America. In it I recognize snippets of our most heated arguments.

Still, untrained sectarians who base remedies on folklore and misconstrued science remain.

Part Four:
Apoplexy

42. Apoplexy at the Ebb of Life, 1884-1885

Heaven should be our happiest memory.

I started assembling these memoirs in the fall of 1884, several months after being struck by apoplexy. My memory of that morning is vaporous, but I have been reminded that I shaved and joined Millicent at breakfast. Moments later coffee drooled out of my mouth and I tilted leftward onto the floor. Some hours later William Gail, our son Orange, and Millicent were hovered around me. I was in bed. Through a haze, Millicent was speaking in soft gentle tones I couldn't understand. She leaned over to kiss me and a tear dripped onto my cheek; her gloom so intense that I started to weep.

William spoke in somber tones that began to pierce my muddled haze. He said I had suffered a stroke, the extent of which was unclear. I speculated silently, "Orange is away from his farm, Millicent is crying, William is concentrating on me, I must be dying."

William's words gradually penetrated my brain's corrupted machinery, but it took an absurd effort to orient my mind and understand. Even when awoken from deep sleep my brain had always worked well. Now thoughts jammed together as if traveling too narrow a path, like the time I carelessly inhaled Ether. I ordered my brain to attention; then figured that if I stood I could better achieve clarity.

I gave my body the command to stand, only to find my muscles had joined my brain in its revolt. My left arm and leg were tied down or too heavy or something. Commands were ineffectual and movements lopsided. William and Millicent held me down, gently at first, their faces bearing alarm. I mounted a greater effort that also proved inept and feeble and garbled sounds escaped my throat. Tears now flooded Millicent's eyes.

Certain my brain could force its command, my third effort caused my right side to lurch against my inattentive, heavy, immobile, unresponsive left side in a graceless gesture that caused it to nearly slap Millicent who pleaded with me to be calm and lie still. Orange took Millicent's position and delivered a forceful shove back into the pillow.

The doctor objectivity in me began its assessment, but when I sought William's confirmation that I had suffered a cerebral affection with hemiplegia, all I generated was spit, garble, and vowels without consonants. I also noticed that when William moved on my left side he seemed to disappear while Millicent and Orange stayed in view on my right. I panicked. My body denied my authority for the first time in 75 years. Death I had never feared, paralysis was crushing.

William took control, "Dr. Allen, you have suffered a fit of apoplexy. Millicent sent for Orange and me early this morning after you had fallen from your chair. You are now in your bed, and you are safe. It is almost noon, and we are delighted that you have finally decided to acknowledge our attention, but you must rest. Millicent has promised us a fine dinner and I am going to stay with you until you recover, or Millicent tires of feeding me."

William's kindness was always coiled within a mischievous nature. In his clever way, he was comforting Millicent and drawing a smile out of me to see if both corners of my mouth drew up. My face delivered what William hoped for as my full smile indicated a slightly less profound stroke. Both Millicent and Orange mirrored my smile.

Explaining the good news to Millicent, William suggested the stroke may not be as serious as he feared. Should no further calamity present itself, recovery was possible. He cited Flint's textbook to describe two conditions that could explain my apoplexy. Given my age, William thought it most likely I suffered cerebral ischemia caused by a clot in the middle cerebral artery on the right side of my brain. The other possibility was cerebral exhaustion given the general pace at which I worked and lived. Whether cerebral exhaustion or thrombus, I would need support for both hygiene and nourishment while waiting out the necessary time for recovery, an interval determined more by providence than intervention.

I wished William had stopped there. Millicent is as kind and attentive as any woman, but she is not one to seek a deep understanding of medical matters. William attempted to reassure her by explaining that Flint describes autopsies showing thrombi in the brain may adhere to the vessel wall and retract, allowing the flow of blood to resume in a matter of hours or days. It is also possible that a clot could break apart and shower other areas of the brain, or the clot may organize and permanently occlude the artery. The latter two scenarios carry a poor prognosis. Aware that Millicent was crying again, William assured her that the next three days would determine which course my stroke would take.

I spat my own garbled reassurance to Millicent, but it was William who took her hand and reassured her that my awakening was good news. He had done much to support my recovery in those first few hours. He and Orange had carried me to bed noting that my left cheek, arm and leg offered no tone and I had only moaned when rubbing my sternum to inflict pain. William followed Flint's recommendations. He placed a small amount of jalap on my tongue to stimulate my bowels and applied a sinapism of hot mustard to my neck to draw inflammation from my brain. To counter the arterial tension, he abstracted sixteen ounces of blood. As the hours passed with little change William administered strychnine as a general stimulant. It was after a second dose of strychnine that I began to arouse.

Over the next few hours my vaporous cloud began to lift. Millicent propped me up in bed and spooned small amounts of a most delicious broth into my mouth. She had to hold a cloth at my chin to catch what my lips refused to contain. Like my speech, my swallowing also refused my usual authority, but her effort sparked my determination.

Through the afternoon my left arm, then my hand and finally my leg began a deep stinging sensation associated with occasionally twitching that so excited William he began to massage both arm and leg. Over the next several hours repeated massaging slowly awakened my left side. By evening I was able to sit up but I could not stand.

Sleep was fitful that night. Whenever I awoke poor William was seated in a chair dozing with his neck at a tortuous angle. I feared he might awake to great discomfort so I grunted out what warning I could, but it did not wake him.

Morning found my thinking back to normal and my left side half-heartedly surrendering to my authority. Still, words would not form. Over the next month, I forced myself to walk several times a day, each day a little farther. Millicent massaged my legs and arms three times a day and spent hours helping me make intelligible words. I knew what I wanted to say but my mouth remained indifferent to my command. With time Millicent was able to construe my meaning and discern my needs, but flowing speech eluded me. Visitors quickly tired of sorting through consonant deficient speech.

I could write. My hands responded to my brain with reasonable accuracy so I returned to my drugstore using notes to communicate anything complicated to employees and patients. Not only was this awkward, but just thirty minutes of standing brought an overwhelming fatigue. I saw apprehension in even my most cherished patients.

I walked every day but the deliberate nature of my steps limited my distance. One morning I was walking to the store when I heard the season's first robin. As I have thousands of times, I looked up to find spring's harbinger. Suddenly up was down and I could do nothing to break my fall. I suffered little more than a bruised hip, but I learned to stop and steady myself before looking for robins. It was advice I had given to a dozen patients who had survived cerebral afflictions.

Riding a horse was difficult. The upper and lower body coordination to mount took concentration, and my legs no longer automatically steadied me in the saddle. Though it was embarrassing to use a carriage for everything, the most crushing realization was my loss of enthusiasm. Every day for fifty years I awoke excited about seeing patients and thinking medicine. Now I was exhausted. Millicent grasped my predicament and, as Abiatha had done so many years ago, sat me at the kitchen table to review our finances. Only this time we had reasonable financial stability, provided I could find a buyer for the drugstore.

We were still considering our options when Erie County enacted legislation to license pharmacists and pharmacies in 1884. Applying for a license was one hurdle too many, and after years of supporting physician licensing, it would be hypocritical to not support similar standards in pharmacy. I approached William Gail about taking over the store and found that he was rejoining the Army as a surgeon. Horace Hoyt M.D., Johnathan's son, was also practicing in East Aurora and was also not interested in the store. Dr. Lapham had a small drugstore in his practice and was comfortable in his situation.

I sent letters to many physicians I knew and posted a notice with the Medical Society of the State of New York. One day a Mr. Frederick W. Gardner announced himself in my store. Mr. Gardner sought to own a drugstore after years of working as an assistant to a doctor in Nunda, New York. I took an immediate liking to the man and offered to make him a partner, but Mr. Gardner was determined to own the business. Soon we came to an amicable agreement on a price. The next day my brother-in-law William Johnson drew up a contract agreeable to all parties, and as holders of Mr. Gardner's loan, Millicent and I were retired.

I ceased work in July of 1884 at age seventy-six. I had no plans for retirement. Millicent always thought me a little naive, but I anticipated being a doctor until the day I was called to heaven. At first I found it a luxury to allow tasks, and their diversions, to consume whatever time they needed. I enjoyed spending more time with Millicent over casual meals, morning walks and watching robins. Still, the chimes of mother Millicent's old grandfather clock made ever slower progress and I found myself pondering silly things, like how wrinkles of the human neck reveal our age.

I took greater notice of how Millicent made our house inviting and comfortable, like the lace curtains she made herself. Being of plank construction our ceilings were not high and Millicent's choice of Victorian furniture styles made for a cozy retreat. The second-floor rooms had the bare essentials: Bureaus, beds and chamber pots. After my retirement, we had my roll top desk, most of my books and years of notes from my medical office moved to the upstairs front room that had been mother Millicent's private chamber. The room has two south facing six over four pane windows with a view of Big Tree Road's east entrance. Since riding into Aurora on Parsley in 1834, every building at the intersection is new and the Globe Hotel is expanded. I can observe the comings and goings of a new generation of Auroreans and the view provides context for many stories. Each evening Millicent and I sit in our matching upholstered rockers in the front parlor reading and sharing interesting bits of news.

On morning walks the slow pace of an old man with a cane encourages former patients to pause and tell Millicent about some moment we shared. The stories brought Millicent closer to the people I had enjoyed for so many years, prompting her to suggest we employ her grandniece, Allie Johnson, to assist me in creating a record of my life. Allie teaches at the Academy, writes occasional articles for magazines, and took to our proposal with unexpected enthusiasm. Millicent also recruited her nephew and William's son, Crisfield Johnson, to join our team. Crisfield teaches at Cornell University and provides a wealth of facts from his recently published history of Erie County.

Within a few short weeks, we established a routine. After our morning walk, I retreat to my study to sort through memories, diaries, office notes and books. Allie, alive for less than half of my career, rides her new safety bicycle from the Aurora Academy, now called the Union Free School, to our home where we spend a couple of late afternoon hours clarifying details. Each evening Allie refines our notes into a narrative for review the next day. Every few weeks Crisfield colors our draft with historic details. They talk as I pirate their youthful talents.

In medical college, I spent hours memorizing medical truths, many of which time has trampled. Benjamin Rush simplified the centuries old legacy of Galen's Four Humors by proposing that all disease results from accumulated bile and inflammatory byproducts. Rush based his theory entirely on his personal experience, logic and rationalizations. Forty years later, Rush's theory was slowly replaced by new ideas developed after experimentation and large numbers of observations carefully noted by teams of doctors and scientists working in hospitals. The 1878 AMA meeting demonstrated how theories, no matter how scientific, cycle rapidly and place a great burden on the physician to keep abreast. It is the physician's responsibility to match science to patient. The art is identifying the potentials and limits of both patient and science. A doctor can be good at the art only if he reads, consults, and knows the science.

Allie and I settled on five themes to organize medicine's progress through my career. First, the theory of geographic specificity was abandoned. No longer is disease considered uniquely local nor the local physician above reproach. Second, discoveries in Physiology, Biology, Chemistry, Epidemiology, and Microscopic Pathology were made possible by the co-location of patients and scientists in large urban hospitals and universities. Third, physicians started measuring patient specific parameters that were well beyond the patient's self-awareness or ability to describe. Fourth, specificity of diagnosis has taken us from remedies based solely on symptoms to remedies based on diagnosis. The fifth theme is the return to licensing regular graduate doctors. No law will banish quackery, but the quack cannot call himself a medical doctor.

Occasionally a grateful family has likened my labor to the workings of God. While I appreciate the attribution, I decline the appraisal. These families are responding to a spirituality that transcends religion and is inseparable from the human condition. The Illinois attorney, abolitionist and orator, Robert Ingersoll, writes that every culture creates a God. These Gods incorporate the culture's ideals of leadership and values and are represented by priests who exact some degree of sacrifice in exchange for peace and happiness. I find Ingersoll's writing liberating. He allows me to respect the beliefs of all patients and each family's personal God. Their beliefs are amazingly similar but seldom identical.

As a child, I was taught that failing God invites infirmity. I say categorically that I do not support this premise. I have known the pious and the non-believer to suffer equally. Neither the sick nor the insane are possessed by evil spirits. Nature knows no distinction between mercy and cruelty and neither do any of the Gods I have encountered.

I have always admired Millicent's faith. She finds comfort in following the traditions of the Presbyterian Church, yet she holds great respect for those of other traditions. Her faith is a power for her, but not a barrier. She does not demand that her Church explain everything, nor that everything that it cannot explain be relegated to magic.

Fortunately, most patients are rich in gratitude, love, and friendship allowing me, a humble village doctor, to know my neighbors well. The pleasures of the medical life far exceed the inconveniences, and the broad science required to be a family's doctor excites interest in a wide range of subjects. The phenomenon of health is exceedingly diverse, the variations of disease are never ending, and the mysterious connection of mind and body awakens intense curiosity. Each encounter becomes an effort of discovery and an exercise in unraveling perplexities. The thrill of human healing is incomparable.

These past few weeks I have suffered a number of minor cerebral afflictions, most lasting only a few minutes or hours. They are not severe, except by their ominous prophecy. My legs grow weaker but the daily routine with Millicent and Allie gets me through the tribulations. Recently we purchased several kerosene lamps. Their intense brightness has made it possible to continue my evening reading at Millicent's side. Much like a lamp exhausting its last drop of kerosene, I am dwindling. I do not fear death. It will be like fading into a faint.

If a man is valued according to his memories, I am well-off. Though ready to accept death, I would postpone the occasion to spend more hours with Millicent and rummage through the memories gifted by patients. My wife, my children, my community and the respect of my patients and colleagues bring me peace.

It is the fragility of life that gives life its beauty. It has been my honor and duty to prolong life. It has never been my duty to prolong the labor of dying.

Postscript

For some life is a series of theories in need of testing.

Dr. Jabez Allen died in the early morning hours of 14 July 1885. The *East Aurora Advertiser* described Dr. Allen as an "old resident and prominent physician of our village" with a large practice "seldom exceeded by a country physician." He "possessed in a very marked degree the confidence of his numerous patients. His devotion to the welfare of those under his care could scarcely have been surpassed and his generosity in other matters was well known to all his friends." Dr. Allen "was highly respected by his medical brethren in both city and country."

His wife, Millicent S. Allen, survived Dr. Allen by fourteen years, dying on 17 December 1899 in the same home she and Jabez occupied throughout their marriage. Millicent continued to be active in the Presbyterian Church and in various women's groups in East Aurora. As is typical of secret enterprises, few records exist to confirm her participation in the Underground Railroad but she is credited with an abiding sympathy for the plight of slaves and activism in their behalf. President Millard Fillmore's gift of a silver teapot and the cameo brooch remain with the family.

Their son Orange Fargo Allen, who died in 1915, and his wife Emma moved in with Millicent and continued to reside in the Allen home. Emma, who died in 1945, passed the property onto their daughter Inez, who continued residence in the home until her death on 23 February 1997. Inez, granddaughter to Dr. Allen, married late in life and taught many an East Aurora child to play the piano. Today, the home at 738 Main Street (Big Tree Road) serves as a small progressive school and is being returned to its original design.

Dr. George H. Lapham died on 14 December 1885 of 'nervous prostration after an operation to remove a mechanical obstruction of the bowels.' A road just south of the village carries his family's name. Dr. William H. Gail, son of Western New York pioneer Rev. Samuel Gail, was born in the town of Wales on 31 October 1840, attended Buffalo Medical College, apprenticed with Dr. Allen and practiced in East Aurora for nineteen years. During the Civil War, Dr. Gail served as a Medical Cadet in Stanton General Hospital in Washington DC, and served as President of the Erie County Medical Society.

In 1890 Frederick Gardner, who purchased Dr. Allen's drugstore in 1884, moved the business to a new building on Main Street where he displayed globes of colored water and sported a bright new soda fountain. Mr. Gardner died in June of 1905 at the age of forty-six. Two graduates of the Pharmacy School at the University of Buffalo purchased the store and renamed it the Cummings Pharmacy. In 1946 Lorren E. Larwood, also a graduate of University of Buffalo School of Pharmacy, purchased the business, renamed it Larwood Prescription Pharmacy, and relocated on Oakwood Avenue in East Aurora in 1988. Larwood Pharmacy is presently owned by two pharmacists, Drs. Rebecca Almond and Linda Andrews, and remains an independent, multiservice and compounding pharmacy.

Harvard expanded requirements from two four-month semesters of lectures to three nine-month semesters in 1869. After Abraham Flexner's survey of American medical education in 1910, medical schools became university based, faculty were expected to engage in research, the curriculum expanded to four years, and students were required to participate in patient care. By the 1930s all states had licensing laws that included passing a standardized exam.

As medical training became dependent on large, mostly urban, hospitals with adequate numbers and concentrations of patients, small rural medical colleges closed. Educational migration to urban centers has resulted in fewer students of a rural persuasion becoming physicians and today fewer generalist physicians practice in East Aurora than in 1840.

By 1893 the New York City Board of Health made bacterial culture and bacteriologic examination available to all physicians. However sterile techniques were not widely understood and three out of four samples were contaminated. By 1896 a commercially available Diphtheria antitoxin came on the market.

The last major American epidemic of Smallpox occurred in Boston in 1901. It caused death in seventeen percent of those stricken. City government and leading medical journals blamed the homeless, unemployed and 'degenerates' for the epidemic. Policemen were sent into the slums to forcibly vaccinate everyone they encountered. In an attempt to prove that a clean, well-nourished, healthy man could not succumb to Smallpox, Dr. Immanuel Pfeiffer toured a Boston hospital for Smallpox victims. Within two weeks he too was dead from Smallpox.

Louis Pasteur speculated that the Smallpox contagion might be too small to be detected with a microscope. In 1892, the Russian Dmitri Ivanovsky described a tobacco pathogen that passed through a filter but still infected plants. He concluded that it must be a chemical. In 1898, the Dutch microbiologist Martinus Beijerinck repeated the experiments and theorized that the filtered solution contained a tiny infectious agent he could grow in eggs. He called the contagion *vivum fluidum*. Finally, in 1931, German engineers photographed a virus with an electron microscope and in 1955 the protein wrapped RNA/DNA structure of a virus was recognized.

Twenty-first century knowledge of bacteria and viruses relegated use of the word germ to something that is dirty, but in the nineteenth century the word encompassed the mystery of microscopic seeds suspected of causing disease. Discovery continues; in 2020, a novel coronavirus (COVID 19) proved the search for remedies against germs continues.

Dr. Jabez Allen served his community with the intent to do good, and advanced his practice of medicine when the mails were slow, books were expensive, and a medical society meeting was three hours away by stagecoach. Physicians of today are flooded with new information fragments. We all are a product of our time.

The Author

Photos and Illustrations

Handwritten diploma from Castleton Medical College as presented to the Erie County Medical Society in 1834 by Jabez Allen M.D.
(*Courtesy Robert Lowell Goller, Aurora Town Historian*)

Jabez Allen M.D. as a young man. (Courtesy Michalann Hobson, great-great granddaughter of Jabez Allen M.D.)

Millicent Allen (Johnson) as a young woman. (Courtesy Michalann Hobson, great-great granddaughter of Jabez Allen M.D.)

Brooch given to Millicent Allen by Mrs. Nathanial Fillmore. (Courtesy Michalann Hobson, great-great granddaughter of Jabez Allen M.D.)

Teapot given Millicent Allen by President Millard Fillmore. (Courtesy Michalann Hobson, great-great granddaughter of Jabez Allen M.D.)

Drugstore on the corner and Home at 738 Main Street (Big Tree Road). Circa 1880. (Courtesy Robert Lowell Goller, Aurora Town Historian)

Gravesite of Jabez Allen M.D. and Millicent Allen in Oakwood Cemetery, East Aurora, NY. (Author)

Selected Sources

Ackerley, G. (1836). On the Management of Children in Sickness and in Health. New York, Bancroft and Holley.

Ancell, H. (1852). Treatise on Tuberculosis, the Constitutional Origin of Consumption and Scrofula. London, Longman, Brown, Green and Longmans.

Barre, W. L. (1856). The Life and Public Services of Millard Fillmore. Buffalo, NY, Wanzer, McKim and Co.

Beach, W. and Bone (1831). The Reformed Practice of Medicine. Boston.

Beard, G (1869). "Neurasthenia, or nervous exhaustion." The Boston Medical and Surgical Journal: 217–221.

Beeton, I. (1907). Mrs. Beeton's Book of Household Management. London, Ward, Lock and Co. (First Edition 1861)

Bell, A. N. (1862). Malignant Pustule in the United States. Albany, NY, Van Benthuysen.

Bennett, J. H. (1869). "Report of the Edinburgh Committee on the Action of Mercury, Podophylline, and Taraxacum on the Biliary Secretion. pt. 2." British Medical Journal 1: 418-420.

Bigelow, J. (1835). "Self-Limited Diseases." Medical Communications of the Massachusetts Medical Society 5: 322.

Billings, J. S. (1876). "A Century of American Medicine, 1776-1876: Literature and Institutions." Am J Med Sci 72 (144): 439-480.

Bogue, D. (1852). The Etiquette of Courtship and Matrimony: with a Complete Guide to the Forms of a Wedding. London, Savill and Edwards.

Boyle, H. E. G. (1934). "Nitrous Oxide: History and Development," British Medical Journal 1: 153-155.

Broussais, F. J. V. (1831). History of Phlegmasiae, or Chronic Inflammations, Founded on Clinical Experience and Pathological Anatomy, Exhibiting a Few of the Different Varieties of and Complications of These Diseases, with Their Various Methods of Treatment. Philadelphia, Carey and Lea.

Buchan, W. (1826). Domestic Medicine: A Treatise on the Prevention and Cure of Diseases by Regimen and Simple Medicines. London, A. R. Spottiswoode.

Bucknill, J. C. and D. H. Tuke (1858). A Manual of Psychological Medicine. London, Churchill.

Burton, R. (1857). The Anatomy of Melancholy. London, Chatto and Windus.

Carter, T. W. (1846). "The Morbid Effects of Tight-Lacing." The Western Journal of Medicine and Surgery 6(2): 166.

Cartwright, S. (1851). "Report on the diseases and physical peculiarities of the Negro race." The New Orleans Medical and Surgical Journal 8: 691-715.

Cathell, D. W. (1882). The Physician Himself and What He Should Add to the Strictly Scientific. Baltimore, Cushing & Bailey.

Clark, A. (1866). "On the best Method of Detecting small quantities of Albumen in the Urine." Proceedings of the Buffalo Medical Association 5(10) 5(10): 391.

Colles, A. (1814). "On the Fracture of the Carpal Extremity of the Radius." N Engl J Med Surg 3: 368-372.

Condie, D. F. (1858). A Practical Treatise on the Diseases of Children, Fifth Edition. Philadelphia, Blanchard and Lea.

Cooke, J. E. (1828). Treatise on Pathology and Therapeutics. Lexington, Kentucky.

Coventry, C. B. (1845). "History of Medical Legislation in the State of New York." New York Journal of Medicine 4: 151-161.

Crawford, J. (1808). "Crawford's Animalcular Hypothesis of Epidemics." The Medical Repository 11: 86-88.

Cutter, E. (1857). "Veratrum Viride as an Arterial Sedative." Boston Medical and Surgical Journal 56: 509.

Da Costa, J. M (1871). "On irritable heart: a clinical study of a form of functional cardiac disorder and its consequences". The American Journal of the Medical Sciences (61): 18-52.

Davenport, R.B. (1888). The Death-Blow to Spiritualism: Being the true story of the Fox Sisters, as revealed by authority of Margaret Fox Dane and Catherine Fox Jencken. New York, C.W. Dillinham.

Derby, G. (1867). "Carbolic Acid in Surgery." The Boston Medical and Surgical Journal. October: 271

Dewees, W. P. (1843). A Compendious System of Midwifery, Chiefly Designed to Facilitate the Inquiries of those who may be Pursuing the Branch of Study. Philadelphia, Lea and Blanchard.

Dix, D. L. (1828). Conversations on Common Things; Or Guide to Knowledge (3rd ed.). Boston, Munroe and Francis.

Domett, H. W. (1884). A History of the Bank of New York, 1784-1884. New York, NY, G. P. Putnam's Sons.

Drake, D. (1850). A Systematic Treatise, Historical, Etiological, and Practical, on the Principal Diseases of the Interior Valley of North America. Cincinnati, Smith.

Dunglison, R. (1841). New Remedies: The Method of Preparing and Administrating them; Their Effects on the Healthy and Diseased Economy, Third Edition. Philadelphia, Lea & Blanchard.

Dunham, C. (1866). Cholera. New York, John T. S. Smith & Sons.

Eberle, J. (1831, 1849). A Treatise on the Practice of Medicine. G. M'Clellan. Philadelphia, Grigg, Elliot & Co.

Fillmore, M. (1852). "Mr. Fillmore's Views Relating to Slavery: The suppressed portion of the third annual message to congress," 6 December 1852.

Flint, A. (1841). "Remarks on the numerical system of Louis." N.Y. Med. Surg. 4: 283-303.

Flint, A. (1850). "Report on the epidemic of cholera in Buffalo in 1849." Buffalo Medical Journal 5(6): 313-333.

Flint, A. (1851). "Symptoms distinctive of typhoid and typhus fever." Buffalo Medical Journal, 7: 449-75.

Flint, A. (1851). "Discovery of the Sources of the Rochester Knockings." Buffalo Medical Journal 6(10): 628-642.

Flint, A. (1852). "On the variations of pitch in percussion and respiratory sounds, and their application to physical diagnosis." American Medical Association, Trans S: 75-123.

Flint, A. (1855). Clinical Reports: Continued Fever, Analysis of One Hundred and Sixty-Four Cases. Philadelphia, Lindsay and Blakiston.

Flint, A. (ed.) (1858). "Anesthesia and Anesthetics." Buffalo Medical Journal 4: 497-502, 583-585.

Flint, A. (1862). "On cardiac murmurs." Am J Med Sci 44: 29-54.

Flint, A. (1874). Essays on Conservative Medicine and Kindred Topics. Philadelphia, Henry C. Lea.

Flint, A. (1879). Clinical Medicine: A Systematic Treatise on the Diagnosis and Treatment of Diseases. Philadelphia, Henry O. Lea.

Flint, A. (1882). "A memoir of Professor James Platt White, MD Buffalo, NY." Commercial Advertiser Press.

Goller, R. L. (2019). Historian's Corner: Unique Gravestone Honors Fallen Circus Man from 1872. East Aurora Advertiser. East Aurora, NY.

Griesinger, W. (1867). Mental Pathology and Therapeutics. London, The New Sydenham Society.

Gunn, J. (1839). Gunn's Domestic Medicine. Pittsburgh, J. Edwards and J.J. Newman.

Hale, E. M. (1866). A Systematic Treatise on Abortion. Chicago, C.S. Halsey.

Haller, J. S. (1982). "The United States Pharmacopoeia: Its origin and revision in the 19th century." Bulletin of the New York Academy of Medicine 58(480-492).

Hamilton, F. H. (1886). The Principles and Practice of Surgery. New York, William Wood and Co. (This is the third edition; the second edition was published in 1872 and the first in the 1850s.)

Hansen, B. (1989). "American Physicians' Earliest Writings about Homosexuals, 1880-1900." The Milbank Quarterly 67(Supplement 1): 92-108.

Hardy, A. V. (1929). "Undulant Fever: A Clinical Analysis of One Hundred and Twenty-five Cases." Journal of the American Medical Association 92(11): 853-860.

Harris, E. (1863). Hints on the Control and Prevention of Infectious Diseases, in Camps, Transports, and Hospitals. New York, Wm. C. Brant & Co., Printers.

Hawthorne, G. S. (1848). The True Pathological Nature of Cholera, and an Infallible Method of Treating It. Liverpool, John Churchill.

Henle, J. (1840). On Miasmata and Contagia, Johns Hopkins Press (Reprinted 1938).

Holmes, O. W. (1843). The Contagiousness of Puerperal Fever. New England Quarterly Journal of Medicine and Surgery. Boston.

Holmes, O. W. (1860). Currents and Counter Currents in Medical Science, an Address Delivered before the Massachusetts Medical Society at the Annual Meeting. Boston.

Howe, S. G. (1848). Report made to the Legislature of Massachusetts upon idiocy. Boston, Coolidge and Wiley.

Hunt, S. B. (1854). "Hygrometric Conditions of the Atmosphere." Buffalo Medical Journal 10(6): 77-81.

Hurd, E.P. (1874). "On the Germ Theory of Disease." Boston Med and Surg J. 101:97-110.

Ingersoll, R. G. (1876). The Gods, and other lectures. New York, D. M. Bennett.

Jarvis, E. (1851). "Causes of insanity." Boston Medical and Surgical Journal 45(15): 289-305.

Jarvis, W. C. (1883). "Tonsillectomy without Hemorrhage." JAMA: 17-18.

Johnson, C. (1876). History of Erie County, New York; Being its annals from the Earliest Recorded Events to the Hundredth Year of American Independence. Buffalo, NY, Matthews & Warren.

Jones, O. P. (1980). "Medical apprenticeships in the early nineteenth century." Buffalo Physician 14(32-50).

King, L. S. (1982). "III. Medical Sects and Their Influence." JAMA 248(10): 1221-1224.

King, L. S. (1982). "IV. The Founding of the American Medical Association." JAMA 248(14): 1749-1752.

King, L. S. (1983). "VIII. germ theory and its influence." JAMA 249(6): 794-798. (Bassi's work with silkworms)

King, L. S. (1984). "XXII. Medical practice: Making a living." JAMA 251(14): 1887-1892.

King, W. H. (1905). History of Homeopathy and Its Institutions in America New York, Lewis Publishing Company.

Koch, R. (1875). "Untersuchungen über Bakterien: V. Die Ätiologie der Milzbrand-Krankheit, begründet auf die Entwicklungsgeschichte des Bacillus anthracis." Beitrage zur Biologie der Pflanzen 2(2): 277-310.

Kohler, C. D. (2010). "Colonel Cyrenius Chapin: The Brave Soldier, The Good Citizen, The Honest Man." Western New York Heritage 12(4): 28-36.

Lee, M. R. (2009). "The history of ergot of rye (Claviceps purpurea): From antiquity to 1900." J R Coll Physicians Edinb 39: 179-184.

Lewis, A. F. (1896). "First appearance, in 1832, of the cholera in Buffalo." Transactions of the Buffalo Historical Society 4: 245-256.

Lewis, D. (1851). "The Pathies Defined." Homoeopathist 2(4).

Lister, J. (1867). "On the antiseptic principle in the practice of surgery." Br Med J 2: 246-248.

Lockie, L. D. (1968). Pharmacy on the Niagara Frontier: The Past and Present. East Aurora, NY, Henry Stewart Incorporated.

Louis, P. C. A. (1836). Researches on the Effects of Bloodletting in some Inflammatory Diseases and on the Influence of Tartarized Antimony and Vesication in Pneumonitis. Boston, Hilliard, Gray, & Company.

Meigs, C. D. (1848). Females and Their Diseases; A Series of Letters to his Class. Philadelphia, Lea and Blanchard.

Miner, J. (1865). "Reasons for fearing the appearance of cholera in other epidemics." Buffalo Medical and Surgical Journal 5: 119.

Mohr, F., et al. (1849). Practical Pharmacy: The Arrangements, Apparatus, and Manipulations of the Pharmaceutical Shop and Laboratory. London, Taylor, Walton and Maberly.

Mohr, J. C. (1978). Abortion in America: The origins and evolution of national policy, 1800-1900. New York, Oxford University Press.

Mory, R. N., et al. (2000). "The Leech and the Physician: Biology, Etymology, and Medical Practice with Hirudinea medicinalis." World Journal of Surgery 24: 878-883.

Mott, F. L. (1930). A History of American Magazines, 1741-1850. New York, Appleton.

O'Donnell, T. C. (1953). Tip of the Hill: An informal history of the Fairfield academy and the Fairfield medical college. Boonville, NY, Black River Books.

Owen, R. D. (1831). The moral physiology: a brief and plain treatise on the population question. New York, Wright and Owen.

Paget, J. (1865). Lectures on Surgical Pathology. Philadelphia, Lindsay and Blakiston.

Parkin, J. (1866). The Antidotal Treatment of the Epidemic Cholera. London, John Churchill & Sons. (Third and last of three editions, 1836, 1854 and 1866)

Parshall, J. A. (2018). "Centennial History of Delaware County, New York: 1797-1897: Delhi." Centennial History of Delaware County, New York: 1797-1897. Retrieved 30 April 2018.

Pattison, J. (1855). Cancer: Its Nature, Treatment, and Cure. London, Charles Westerton. (p. 16 references the work of d'Etoilles.)

Pierson, A. L. (1852). "Malignant Tubercle." Boston Medical and Surgical Journal: 75-78.

Potter, W. W. (1895). "Fifty Years of Medical Journalism in Buffalo." Buffalo Medical Journal 25.

Potter, W. W. (1898, 1899). "A Century of Medical History in the County of Erie, 1800-1900." Buffalo Medical Journal. 37(9, 10, 11), 38(1, 3, 4, 6, 7, 10).

Power, A. (1871). Sanitary Rhymes, Personal Precautions Against Cholera. London, T. Richards.

Ravenel, M. P. (1897). Anthrax-The effect of Tanneries in Spreading the Disease. Harrisburg, Pa., State Livestock Sanitary Board of Pennsylvania.

Riddell, J. (1835). "Memoir on the nature of miasm and contagion." Western Journal of Medical and Physical Sciences 9: 401-412, 526-432.

Ridenbaugh, M. Y. (1890). The Biography of Ephraim McDowell, M.D. The Father of Ovariotomy. New York, Charles L. Webster and Company.

Roberton, J. (1851). Essays and Notes on the Physiology and Diseases of Women, and on Practical Midwifery. London, John Churchill.

Robinson, D. (2011). "Upstate town touts role as 'last holdout of the Confederacy.'" Retrieved 21 August 2018, from http://www.tinyurl.com/yb3x92fb.

Rochester, T. F., et al. (1866). "Action taken by Physicians in Buffalo in view of the probable appearance of Cholera." Proceedings of the Buffalo Medical Association 5(10): 388-390.

Rosen, G. (1946). Fees and Fee Bills: Some Economic Aspects of Medical Practice in Nineteenth Century America. Baltimore, Johns Hopkins University Press.

Rosen, G. (1955). "Problems in the Application of statistical analysis to questions of health: 1770-1880." Bulletin of the History of Medicine 29: 27-45.

Rosenberg, C. E. (1987). The Cholera Years: The United States in 1832, 1849, and 1866. Chicago, The University of Chicago Press.

Rush, B. (1805). Observations on the Duties of a Physician, and the Methods of Improving Medicine: Accommodated to the Present State of Society and Manners in the United States. Medical Inquiries and Observations. Philadelphia, J. Conrad.

Rush, B. (1815). "A Defense of Blood-letting, as a Remedy for Certain Diseases." Rush's Medical Inquiries and Observations. Vol. 4. Philadelphia, PA. Available online at http://bobarnebeck.com/defence.html.

Satterthwaite, T. E. (1875). "Bacteria: Their Relation to Disease." Medical Record 10: 883-836, 849-854.

Savitt, T. L. (1982). "The Use of Blacks for Medical Experimentation and Demonstration in the Old South." The Journal of Southern History 48(3): 331-348.

Semmelweis, I. (1861). Etiology, Concept, and Prophylaxis of Childbed Fever. Madison, Wisconsin, University of Wisconsin Press.

Shryock (1967). Medical Licensing in America, 1650-1965. Baltimore.

Siebert, W. H. (1898). The Underground Railroad: From Slavery to Freedom. New York, The Macmillan Company.
Smith, H. P. (1884). History of the City of Buffalo and Erie County. Syracuse, NY, D. Mason & Co.
Smith, S. (1878). "Some practical tests of the claims of the antiseptic system." Trans. Medical Society of the State of New York.
Snow, J. (1855). On the Mode of Communication of Cholera, John Churchill.
Stewart, E. M. (1934). History of Wages in the United States from Colonial Times to 1928. Washington, D.C., United States Department of Labor.
Stone, J. O. (1869). "The Influence of Emanations Upon the Health of Cities." Bull. New York Adad. Med. 3: 396-404.
Thomson, S. (1835). New Guide to Health; Or, Botanic Family Physician. Boston, J. Howe.
Thomson, W. H. (1887). "The Pathology and Treatment of Epilepsy." JAMA 8(12): 321.
Toner, J. M. (1878). Transactions of the American Medical Association Annual Meeting. AMA Annual Meeting, Buffalo, NY
Traweek, W. B. (1864). "Recollections of Washington B. Traweek: Escaping Elmira." Accessed on 18 July 2016. Available online at http://www.angelfire.com/ny5/elmiraprison/traweek.html.
Tyndall, J. (1882). Essays on the Floating Matter of the Air in Relation to Putrefaction and Infection. New York, D. Appleton and Company.
Virchow, R. (1863). Cellular pathology as based upon physiological and pathological histology. Philadelphia, J.B. Lippincott.
Waite, F. C. (1949). The History of the First Medical College in Vermont-Castleton 1818-1862. Montpelier, Vermont, Vermont Historical Society.
Wallace, W. C. (1854). "Practical and theoretical reasons for the necessity of cleanliness." New York M. Gaz. and J. Health 5(389).
Walshe, W. H. (1844). The Anatomy, Physiology, Pathology, and Treatment of Cancer. Boston, MA, W. D. Ticknor.
Warren, J. C. (1846). "Inhalation of ethereal vapor for the prevention of pain in surgical operations." Boston Med Surg J 35: 375-379.
Wharton, F. and M. Stille (1855). Treatise on Medical Jurisprudence. Philadelphia, Kay and Brother.
White, J.P. (1849). Remarks on the construction of obstetrical forceps with a description of an instrument. Buffalo Med. J. 4:715-721.
Willard, E. (1819). An Address to the Public; Particularly to the Members of the Legislature of New York Proposing a Plan for Improving Female Education. Middlebury, F.W. Copeland.
Wood, H. C. (1875). "Medical Education in the United States." Lippincott's Magazine of Popular Literature and Science 16(96): 703-711.

Acknowledgements

Robert Goller, historian for the Town of Aurora, enthusiastically searched the archives for newspapers, books, and letters pertaining to nineteenth century medicine. Linda Lohr, Medical History Librarian, University at Buffalo, provided access to textbooks and original documents and searched far and wide for references to Dr. Jabez Allen from the assets of The Robert L. Brown History of Medicine Collection. The Buffalo Historical Museum research librarian Cynthia Van Ness provided records of the Medical Society of Erie County. Andrew Danzo, medical editor and journalist reviewed drafts and encouraged me every step of the way. Dr. Gerald Daigler, Pat Daigler RN, and Dr. Andrew Symons provided valuable comments regarding medical issues and content. My daughter, Stephanie Cooper, the Collection Development Librarian for the Public Library of Cincinnati and Hamilton County provided expert review and comments on later drafts. Michalann Hobson, Jabez Allen's great, great granddaughter, provided family records from her great grandmother Emma Allen, wife of Orange, and her great-aunt Inez Marshall (Allen). John Newton PhD operates the Mandala School in the house once owned by Dr. and Mrs. Jabez Allen and allowed access to the house and deed. Dr. Rebecca Almond of Larwood Pharmacy provided valuable snippets of verbal history. Heather and Kody Sprague granted access to their deed on the building now on site of Jabez Allen's second office. Research was greatly facilitated by Google (http://books.google.com/), JSTOR, HaithiTrust Digital Library and the NIH archives.

Most importantly, my wife, Georgia Rosenthal provided daily critiques, was the first one to read most chapters, and whenever my spirit lagged she pushed me on to get the details right. Her nursing experience provided insights a physician sometimes just does not see. Thank you.

Consider visiting my website at: www.thomasrosenthalmd.com